"Great story! This is one of the best science fiction novels I've read in a long time...great job with the characters and the action."

—Writer's Digest

"Petteway is a veteran Air Force Officer and uses his knowledge to bring a very believable description of battle techniques and strategies..."

—Barry Hunter, Baryon Magazine

"The reader is pulled into the story head first, and must fight alongside the Osguards in all of their endeavors. It is a fun and exciting read, and like a good play, it captivates its audience!"

—Tom Johnson, Editor
Fading Shadows Magazine

OSGUARDS: GUARDIANS OF THE UNIVERSE

By

Malcolm D. Petteway

Homecoming
Revelations
Armageddon
Revenge

HOMECOMING

BOOK ONE
OF
OSGUARDS: GUARDIANS OF THE UNIVERSE

MALCOLM DYLAN PETTEWAY

Rage Books LLC
www.ragebooks.net

Osguards: Homecoming

All Rights Reserved © 2001 by Malcolm Dylan Petteway
Second Edition Published by Rage Books LLC October 2009

Edited by:
Karen M. Petteway
James Barnes
Harvetta Colvin
Michael Colvin

ISBN: 0984364501
EAN-13: 9780984364503

Printed in the United States
Rage Books LLC
www.ragebooks.net

"To every man there comes in his lifetime that special moment when he is figuratively tapped on the shoulder and offered that chance to do a very special thing, unique to him and his talents. What a tragedy if that moment finds him unprepared, or unqualified for that work."

—*Winston Churchill*

Prologue—Set Up

The blue majestic beauty of Earth hovered below them, suspended by the invisible hand of God. Its path around the sun, predetermined eons ago by physics, also lay unseen to the naked eye. For Colonel Samuel Patterson, it was the most beautiful thing in the world. He floated, awestruck, studying the scene from the side port, almost mesmerized in an inner trance. He was meditating, reaching for his soul to connect with his mind in order to find the bliss of heaven in a world of hate. Colonel Patterson was the commander for the secret International Joint Space Station called Icarus, orbiting one hundred miles above Earth.

Sam was on the fast track, destined to be a four-star general. He was thirty-seven years old and already nominated for his first star. He was an Academy graduate, and a command pilot with over forty-five hundred hours in the F-4, F-15 and F-16, and over eight missions in the space shuttle. He had commanded at the squadron, group and wing level, with several tours of duty at the Pentagon. This was his second tour with Air Force Space Command out of Colorado Springs, Colorado.

Gray temples started to frame his face and wrinkles began to overrun his boyish good looks. He was a tall man, actually wiry and somewhat stiff, a condition from his days of playing football at the Academy. His brown eyes blazed with goals not yet accomplished and areas not yet treaded. He was selected for this job based on his quick wit and uncanny judgment.

The boisterous Russian, Colonel Ivan Prepovnov, was the second in command and the mission specialist. He had science degrees in electrical engineering, computer science and radar theory. He was not a warrior like Sam considered himself, but a scientist and explorer, rising through the old Soviet ranks and the new Russian military based on his intellect and ability to analyze and decipher the smallest details and form near perfect intelligence pictures for his superiors. He spoke with a thick Russian accent to the point where you mistook his tone for one of an illiterate novice. Ivan would disarm you with his stories of his boyhood to win you over and ease the tension. His jet-black hair, sunken deep dark eyes and pale white skin made him look ghostly, especially, under the red lights of the command cabin. This made it a

1

bit easier for Patterson to think of Prepovnov as a spook, the trade name for a spy. Trust didn't go far between the two. Decades of Cold War training could not be flushed, just camouflaged until needed for future battle.

The third and last member rounding out the crew of the Icarus was a young British Flight Officer named Lieutenant Rick Larson. Larson looked fresh out of high school, too young to smoke, let alone pilot the Icarus. He had curly black hair, star quality blue eyes, and a dimpled smile that reminded Patterson of a young Sean Connery—thus the call sign, '007.'

Icarus, the brainchild of the Reagan Administration was on its maiden flight, with its first crew. In the 1980's President Gorbachev and Prime Minister Thatcher reluctantly agreed to help foot the bill for building the station. Gorbachev agreed in hopes of retrieving much needed technical information for his military, and Thatcher agreed to bolster English claim as still one of the most powerful nations in the world. The Reagan Administration played to their fears, wants and needs in a masterful fit of strategy, politics and negotiations. The result: a $450 billion, twenty-five hundred square-foot eye in space, able to photograph a matchbook on Earth with digital clarity, sniff out heat sources fifty feet below the surface, analyze ballistic data from any test launch, collect radar and electronic signals from any source and most of all, follow and track an entire battlefield. Icarus was the best in intelligence, reconnaissance and surveillance; areas President Reagan called the forefront of modern warfare.

But the peacefulness and beauty Colonel Patterson enjoyed detracted from the awesome responsibility he had before him. Below him, coming into view, was Iraq. An air war had been waging for the past thirty days in what was dubbed 'Desert Storm'. Now he and his crew were ordered to move into position to help facilitate the ground force, which he estimated would start any day now.

It took months of negotiation and power plays by all three administrations to even consider using Icarus during the war. Of course Russia objected at first, but when the Bush administration conceded to allowing a Russian observer take part, they quickly agreed. Now three weeks after Icarus' launch, it was about to enter its first conflict, untested.

"Firing stabilizer thrusters now," Larson informed Patterson.

The black missile-looking station with giant rabbit ears fired gaseous white plumes, stopping its forward momentum, in a symphony of rhythmic blasts.

Patterson turned from the port and huffed. Inside, he knew duty called. He floated over to his station, in the middle of Larson and Prepovnov. He steadfastly strapped himself into the gray chair that resembled a dentist's chair. In front of him, his console lights danced like a Christmas tree. He reached over and clicked the communications button.

"Big Daddy...Big Daddy...Icarus on station...going hot. Icarus on station...going hot."

"Roger Icarus, Big Daddy copies...welcome to the war," a female voice crackled from the speakers.

"IR sensors on, radar capture on, signal recorder on," Prepovnov announced in a thick Russian accent, as he switched on the respective equipment.

"IR sensors on, radar capture on, signal recorder on," Patterson echoed as he checked the status of each piece of equipment.

"Moving antennas to coordinates gulf zero-one decimal four-three-eight by uniform zero-five decimal three-zero-nine," Larson announced.

"Feeding telemetry back to USCENTCOM," Patterson pushed as he switched the final button. "Big Daddy...Big Daddy, this is Icarus...we are hot...repeat, we are hot!"

"Big Daddy copies."

Larson rotated his neck and stretched his arms over his head, listening to the crackling of his muscles as he strained them to the limits, preparing his body for the long watch. He thought of himself as a cop on surveillance, watching and waiting, mostly waiting for something...anything to happen. Then out of the corner of his eye, through the side port window, he caught a glimpse of something. He wasn't sure what he saw, but it was certainly something out of the ordinary. He unstrapped from his seat and floated toward the window.

"Where are you going? The fun is about to begin," Prepovnov asked.

"I thought I saw something," he replied back.

"What could you see? We're a hundred miles above Earth. Free from any junk or satellite orbit," he scolded.

"I thought I saw something," he repeated, now searching the heavens through the port window. He looked right, then up, then left and saw nothing but the emptiness of space. Then he looked down. His eyes widened, and a sour feeling reached into the pit of his stomach. His mind began to race and sweat beamed on his brow. A frown now occupied his usually rugged and handsome features. Fright bore into his soul. The kind of fright associated with the feeling of impending doom. Some call it the chill of death; some call it the devil's spark. However, Larson had one word for it, "Kulusks!"

His voice was just a whisper, barely audible to him. But the results were the same. He was staring at a Kulusk shuttlecraft, easily recognized by its turtle shell hull. He instinctively reached into his thigh pocket searching for his weapon. But it wasn't there. He did not bring it with him on this mission. He closed his eyes and silently cursed.

Then he floated toward Patterson, "Kulusks," he repeated. "I need to get a message to Lilly Station."

"What?" Patterson squealed, swinging his chair around. "We are in the middle of a hot run. You're not doing a damned thing, but getting back to your post," he ordered, pushing Larson away from the radio.

"You don't understand," he begged, "it's the Kulusks."

"The who?" Prepovnov questioned with a smile.

"The Kulusks," Larson continued. "They are out there."

"Out where?" Patterson retorted.

"Out there," he screamed, making another lunge toward the radio.

Patterson had unstrapped all but his leg strap, and proceeded to push Larson once more. Larson twisted in the air, shaking Patterson's grasp with a stiff arm to the forehead. Patterson fell back into his chair.

Prepovnov's smile disappeared as he began to realize his two crewmates were actually fighting. He punched the release for his chest straps and started working on his leg straps when Larson reached the radio.

Larson switched the first thumbwheel dial and was about to switch the second when a pain shot from his neck, down his spine and out through his fingers, toes and the top of his head. He lost all bodily functions as he felt his bladder release. His eyes remained open, but his body numb. The blast lasted almost four seconds, but for that brief moment it felt like an eternity.

Patterson grabbed his arm and slung him back into his seat like a rag doll. In his right hand, he held a stun gun. He looked up at Prepovnov, who now was holding his breath. "I thought I would have to use this on you," Patterson quipped toward Prepovnov. "I never thought I would have to use it on Larson."

Ivan Prepovnov swallowed hard, "What just happened, comrade?"

"Shit if I know," Patterson replied as he pocketed the gun. After taking a deep breath, he turned his attentions back to Larson.

Larson still could not control his body. The only thing he could control was his thoughts; everything else was a piercing numbness, a prickly tingling sensation like a thousand bee stings gnawing at him all at once.

Patterson strapped him into his chair and then grabbed a pair of handcuffs from behind his station and slapped them on Larson, pinning his hands behind the chair. Then Patterson reset the radio, never taking his eyes off of Larson or Prepovnov, who was still in shock.

"I guess those were for me as well?" Prepovnov questioned, pointing to the handcuffs.

Patterson looked away, and whispered, "Only if you did something to jeopardize the mission."

"Well, I guess you had the right precautions, but the wrong man," Prepovnov huffed.

"Maybe," Patterson pushed staring back at Prepovnov. "Or maybe I just needed to keep my eye on both of you."

Prepovnov turned his chair back toward the console, "You have nothing to worry about in me, comrade. It seems like it is your old friends you have to worry about." Then he looked up and huffed, "What now?"

"Now, we continue with the mission," Patterson commanded, as he strapped in next to Prepovnov.

The hatch door leading toward the rest of the complex slammed open. Prepovnov and Patterson swung their chairs around, with the expression, 'Now what?' Larson was still too stunned to move, but what he heard and smelled were very familiar.

The distinctive piercing sound of two-particle generator array beams slicing through air and contacting on human flesh vibrated in his ears, followed by the pungent odor of burnt flesh invading his nostrils. Immediately, he knew his partners were dead, and he knew he was next.

Someone swung his chair around, which forced him to stare at the intruder who killed his crewmates. His eyes focused on himself. He was staring into his own eyes, a mirror reflection of himself, sporting a devilish smile. Confusion altered his reality as he tried to grasp the impossible. However, clarity never reached him as the searing fire of death sprang from his doppelganger's hand and punched a hole through his forehead. Pain and darkness attacked his mind and won. Larson's head tilted to the right, not weighed down by gravity but by the straps pulling at his shoulder.

Two hours later, the vacuum of space ripped the original Icarus crews' bodies from a holding hatch and sucked them into darkness. Their bodies would circle the Earth in a decaying orbit for years. Until one day, when Earth's atmosphere would claim them and start their return trip home. However that return trip would be one of fire and hell, leaving just specks of human cells when they finally came to rest on Earth.

"Big Daddy, this is Icarus, starting our survey of gulf zero-four decimal eight–seven-three by uniform zero–nine decimal five–seven–six."

"Roger Icarus," came the female voice over the speakers. "We lost you for a moment during the first scan. Is everything all right?"

"Oh…we had some radio difficulty, but we took care of it."

"Roger…Big Daddy out."

Chapter 1—Welcome Home

Michael David Genesis woke up smelling the fresh air through his bedroom window. He was still in a daze. His eyes attempted to focus on the wall. Slowly he began to remember where he was. He was in the spare room in his parents' retirement house in Osguard Gardens in Virginia. Gradually, he sat up in the bed taking another breath of the fresh summer morning air flowing through his window. The gentle summer breeze cascaded along the ruffled brown curtains, causing the sunlight reflecting through the window to project a golden glow that danced on the bedroom floor. Michael studied the light as it swayed across his floor. He began to feel free, almost alive again, losing his inner-self to the sunlight's dance. He felt a feeling he had long thought had abandoned his spirit.

It had been a long time since he felt this inner peace. Even though the feeling was fleeting, Michael decided he would enjoy it for the moment. He wanted to enjoy the peace of not having someone staring in his face awaiting a decision. A decision he knew he did not have all the facts to make. A decision he knew would affect thousands, if not tens of thousands of lives at a time. How many times had he made these decisions, using nothing but his God-given intuition or just his gut instinct? But lately, a tiny nagging little voice accompanied each of his important decisions. This voice always objected to his decisions, casting doubt where there once was none.

He was so tired—drained was a more appropriate word. Michael was drained from work, drained from fighting the tiny voice and drained from living the way he did. He was tired of always having to be right. The association demanded it, and he no longer knew if he could perform to the association's expectations. But for now, he was on vacation. He was on a much-needed vacation with his parents. Michael pushed the thoughts of the association from his mind and again concentrated on the sunlight dancing on his floor, allowing some peace for once in a long time.

Michael had been away from home for many years. His parents had retired and moved to Osguard Gardens almost five years earlier. This was the first time he actually stayed with them. Of course, this was the first family reunion held at the Gardens. It was a special event and everyone was to attend. That is everyone from the association—Unlimited Associations Incorporated, as the family residents from the Garden knew it to be. Years earlier, Michael and his cousins had established Osguard Gardens as a retirement community for their families. It was an expensive venture, but his work owed them that much. Now their parents, in-laws and grandparents had a place to retire. The association took care of all their needs. The association provided the house of their choice, the food, the clothing and even the car they drove. They did not have to spend a dime of their retirement or social security money. Michael smiled at that thought and began his personal ritual of preparing for the day.

Michael had just finished his shower when he heard a knock at his bedroom door.

"Yeah?" he bellowed drying his hair with a towel.

"It's me, bro," Shawn's voice boomed from the other side of the door.

"It's open. I'll be out in a minute."

Osguards: Homecoming

Shawn opened the door and walked in. He looked around and shook his head at Michael's clothes on the floor. "I see you're still a pig, little brother," he shouted to be heard over the running water.

Michael was brushing his teeth, but he heard his older brother loud and clear. He spit the pasty saliva from his mouth and smiled in the mirror. "You taught me well. I couldn't do it without you," he joked back.

Michael wrapped a towel around his waist and walked out the bathroom. He saw his older brother sitting on his bed paging through the book he was reading last night.

"Damn, you are still as ugly as ever. I'm sure glad mom saved the best for last."

Shawn raised his eyes to see his baby brother and gave him the middle finger.

"Oh is that how you show your love after two years, Shawny?"

Shawn tried to hold in the smile, but he couldn't. He rose to greet Michael. Michael stood one inch taller, but Shawn was always the taller one in his eyes. Shawn Frank Genesis was the better athlete, better musician and better with the ladies when they were growing up. Michael was just book-smart, as Shawn would always tease him. They slapped their right hands and slid them together until they shook at the knuckles, then they pulled close, hugged and patted one another on the back with their left hands, keeping their right hands in the power shake between them at chest level.

"Good to see you Michael."

"Same here Shawn. Where is Patricia?" They broke the hug and Shawn sat back on the bed as Michael went to the dresser to retrieve his undergarments.

"She's downstairs helping mom cook breakfast."

"So when did you two get in?"

"I got in last night about two o'clock. Sis and her family got in about a half hour after me. Mom told us you had gone to bed. So, we decided to let you sleep."

Michael continued to dress. "So where is my nephew?"

"Maji is with his mom at her parents' house. Debrlina and Maji will be back in time for the games. How about my two nieces? Where are Sharyla and Kashara?"

Michael pulled his shirt on. "Same place. Michelle took them to her parents' house for the night. They will be back in time for the games as well. How about Patricia? Where is her little terror, Mitiah?"

"Oh! He is downstairs getting spoiled by mom and dad."

"Did she bring her husband with her?"

"Yeah, Dad is showing Joe his record collection now."

"I guess we better save him before dad bores him to death."

Michael finished dressing and then he and Shawn went downstairs. Halfway down the stairs the brothers could smell the bacon and eggs beckoning them to the kitchen.

"Mom must be feeling good today," Michael whispered. "Smell that food," he continued.

"What do you think? This is the first time in five uni... I mean in six years we have all been together. And little Mitiah has never seen us all together. He is only two years old," Shawn lectured.

"I know that," Michael rebutted.

The brothers went into the kitchen and saw their mother and sister preparing the table.

"Mom, Patricia. You don't have to fuss over us. We are home," Shawn said as he and his brother sat at the table.

"What, no hug for baby sister?" Patricia interrupted.

Michael looked at his sister. He had let his hunger, instead of his emotions, dictate his actions. He looked at her with her shoulder length auburn hair and wide hazel eyes that seemed to be the consistent physical trait in the entire family. But Patricia Anne Genesis-Archer's eyes did not rain endearment. They rained actual disappointment.

"I think you better get up and give baby sis a hug and a kiss, or you won't live to eat this breakfast," Shawn leaned over and whispered into Michael's ear.

"Now Patricia, you know I wouldn't forget you," Michael said as he stood and gave his baby sister a tight hug and a gentle kiss on the lips with an extra emphasis on the smacking of the lips to make a loud cracking sound as they parted.

"Now that's better. I didn't come all this way to be disrespected by my own brother. Understand?"

"—Understood."

"I don't know what all the fuss is about. You all work for Unlimited Associations," their mother murmured. She put the last of the eggs in the bowl in the center of the table. "From the way you tell it, you own that company. I still don't know what you do. Could be selling drugs for all I know," she continued in a huff.

"Now mom, you know better!" Patricia exclaimed. "You and dad raised us better than that. We are partners in a legitimate business. We are diversified. We do a little security, and a little scientific research, but mainly we are in the export and import trade."

"That's what those drug dealers in New York always said."

Michael shook his head. "Mom, did those drug dealers have enough money to set up a gated community like Osguard Gardens, like we did? Did those drug dealers have the respect of the political establishment like we do?

Come on mom, you're making things up that aren't real. We're legit I tell you."

Just then, their father, Parker G. Genesis, and Patricia's husband Joseph Archer walked in the kitchen with Mitiah. All conversation in the kitchen stopped.

Parker looked around and felt the tension in the air. Then he looked at his wife. "What's wrong? What did you do Elizabeth?"

"Nothing, I just asked them about their business."

"Well, how is business?" Parker shot the question to Michael.

"Business is fine. We are going to have our annual meeting in our Richmond branch next Monday. You know we try to do that every so often so the whole gang can make the reunion. It worked out great this year. Don't you think Shawn?"

"Yeah dad, perfect."

"You know I am so proud of my children," Parker beamed as he sat down at the table for breakfast. "All those years working in the factory—me and my brothers—to see the next generation do so well. It makes those long nights and long overtime hours worth it. Don't you think, Elizabeth?"

"Yeah, Parker. I'm proud of them too. But how come we never get to visit them? They always have to come here. I'd like to go see you in Japan, Patricia; or you in India, Shawn; and you in England, Michael. What's wrong with a mother wanting to visit her kids and grandchildren?" Elizabeth Bessie Genesis knew what buttons to push. She played the guilt card like a Vegas card shark. Making her children feel guilty about denying her the right—that was it—the right to see her grandchildren was insufferable. Besides, she knew her kids were keeping a secret from her. They had been keeping the secret of their success from her for over twelve years. She didn't like it. She didn't like it at all. She passed a stern look at Michael with that thought. He was always the weak one of the three, she thought. She just couldn't understand how they could treat her like this. After all, she was their mother, the woman who gave them life. No, she was going to find out this weekend, even if it killed her. How dare they do this to her? She placed her hand on her hip and pushed a more intense stare at her children. "Well?"

Michael, Shawn and Patricia remained quiet. They could not tell their mother the truth. What they were doing was legal. But what they told their parents was a cover. They knew they could trust their dad with the secret, but their mother loved to gossip and this was too important to chance. There were many lives at stake. None of the cousins had told their parents. Osguard Gardens was a bribe that was supposed to keep the parents happy. But it just made matters worse, especially with the mothers. It made them more suspicious. It must be a maternal thing, Michael thought.

Michael had spoken to their cousin Clyde, who said he recently had this very same conversation with his mother when he visited last year. Maybe it was time to tell the folks. Michael looked into Patricia's eyes. He saw the confusion on her face as well. Her eyes appeared to be saying, *Why not? Why can't we tell them?* Michael bent his right index finger into a hook and raised it so his brother and sister would be the only ones to see. The hooked finger was the street sign for a 'thumbs-up'—an approval of sorts—that Michael, Patricia and Shawn had adapted into their private non-verbal communications repertoire of symbols. Shawn nodded his head to say he understood. Patricia's eyes lifted a little as if the pain of keeping the secret eased a little. Michael had just decided they would bring it up today before the games started. By tonight their mother would know everything. Besides whom could she gossip to now? If the entire Osguard Gardens knew their secret, there would be no secret to gossip—at least inside the gated community.

"Well I'm waiting," Elizabeth persisted in a demanding tone.

Something about her tone reached inside Shawn's gut and ripped at him like a nine-inch knife. His emotions started to boil. He was tired of her nagging, of her making him feel like he was not a good son to her. He had traveled countless miles to be here with her and she has lit into him within the first five minutes of breakfast. Nothing he did was ever good enough. When he painted the house, she told him he missed a spot. When he went to the grocery store for her, she told him he forgot the potatoes. He achieved high marks in school, but it wasn't straight 'A's. He won numerous basketball awards and even went to college on an athletic scholarship, but it wasn't Yale University. All his life he tried to get his mother's approval and love. Now he is one of the most powerful people in the...

His right fist pounded the table. "That's it," he yelled, with his head bowed, staring at his breakfast plate.

She smiled because she thought she had broken him into talking.

"I have had it. I quit! All my life I've done everything in my power to get you to accept me—to love me. But I guess no matter what I do, how successful I am, it isn't enough for you." Shawn turned to face his mother. The pain of his thoughts was visible on his face and in his round hazel eyes. "Mom, we provide for you. We gave you this house, got you out of the city—away from drugs, crime and Lord knows what else. You have no wants. You pick up the phone and call and whatever you want is delivered; food, clothes, furniture—whatever you want. You have a car to drive. We provide that to you." He pointed to his siblings and himself. "We, includes me. I provide for you. How dare you treat us like this? I for one refuse to be treated like this anymore."

Elizabeth's smile vanished.

Shawn stood to face his mother closer.

"In all, I think you have it pretty good. We know you are our mother and we are trying to shower you with all the things we think you deserve, but we are grown and I'm grown. We take care of ourselves. I take care of myself. And quite frankly, if we don't live up to your expectations, well that is just too bad." He turned and started going to the back door. "You don't know half the crap we go through day in and day out. And if you keep this up, you'll never know. You don't have to approve of me. Shit, you don't even have to pretend to love me anymore." He shook his head, walked out the door and slammed it shut.

Michael and Patricia looked at each other. Deep down inside Michael was glad Shawn said what he said. A slight smile crossed his lips. His father saw the smile and turned away.

"See what you have done, mother!" Patricia said.

"What I've done? Your brother was totally out of line with me."

"I think it was you who was out of line," Patricia continued, "out of line since day one. He is your son, your first born. And now he thinks you never loved him. You didn't even try to explain. You didn't even try to tell him you loved him." Patricia stopped to catch her breath. The passion flowing through her was now uncontrollable. "When is the last time you told him you loved him? He heard you tell Michael and me almost every day when we were growing up. But when was the last time you told Shawn you loved him?"

"What?" Elizabeth feigned. "Michael did you hear your sister?"

"Yes, I heard her. And I agree with her," Michael said as he stood up and moved to the kitchen door. Come sis, we have some things to accomplish before the picnic."

"Okay." She moved toward the door. She turned to her husband Joseph, "Joe, you and Mitiah go back to the … Well you know and get Mitiah's things. I'll meet you at the park in an hour."

"Okay, honey," Joseph replied taking his son and moving toward the door with Michael and Patricia. All four walked out the door and let the door slam closed behind them.

"Well Elizabeth, you just drove off the first real family reunion we had with our kids and grandkids. How do you feel?" Parker chastised as he started his breakfast.

Elizabeth stood dumbfounded in the middle of the kitchen. Finally, she recognized what just happened and fear gripped her heart. She opened the door and stepped outside. She saw no one. She looked around the yard, and then ran to the front. There was no sign of her kids. A tear formed in her eye. "What have I done?" she asked herself.

She slowly walked back into the house to see her husband polish off the last of his eggs in his plate. "Parker, what did I do wrong?"

Parker stood and shook his head. "You didn't trust our kids," he commented as he walked out to go to the bedroom.

Elizabeth sat at the table and stared at the plates full of food. "What did I do wrong?" she murmured.

***

Michael, Shawn and Patricia arrived at Osguard Park, situated in the middle of the gated community. They walked to the covered bleachers behind home plate on the baseball diamond. People had started to gather there as designated by the plan. Michael looked around. He recognized everyone—all of them his cousins. Roger, Clyde, Paul, Peter, Walter and Sally were there. They were some of his first cousins he grew up with in New Haven Connecticut. Then there were other cousins he did not realize were family until the association brought them together. There was Rose. She was still beautiful. He did not know they were related back when they were growing up. He had developed a slight crush on her, but that all changed once he found out they were related. They were fourth or fifth cousins. He didn't quite know how. It only mattered that they were cousins.

Then there were people from other parts of the country, the Stones from Oklahoma, the Steels from California, and the Blacks from North and South Carolina. There were many others, so far removed from him, legally they could be considered unrelated. But again, Ortho had tracked and categorized them as originating from one family who lived in New Haven over a hundred years ago.

The homecoming was sweet. Michael spoke to all of them. He did not realize how much he had missed seeing them. Soon all fifty-seven of his cousins arrived and they mingled in the bleachers—with him and his siblings there were sixty participants in the Osguard Reunion Olympics. For twelve years, this group had held the fire that ignited the association. Most of them were between thirty-five and forty, with spouses and children. Time had traveled in their lives quickly and without mercy. They were older and a little grayer. The responsibilities of running the association were evident by the tiny winkles around their eyes. It seemed like yesterday when they graduated from college. Now they were approaching middle age. The thought was more than morbid. It was frightening.

Michael stood and stepped in front of the bleachers. "I am glad everyone could make it," he started. "Today we will start the Osguard Reunion Olympics. The teams are made up and posted on the board behind the bleachers. There will be six teams of ten. We will play basketball, softball and flag football. By the time the barbecue starts tonight we will be hungry, sweaty and tired. Then we start the entire thing over again tomorrow. At the end of the third day, the team with the most victories can claim the prize Top Osguard." Michael paused to let his cousins cheer and pump up their adrenalin at what he just said.

Then he thought a moment. *No better time than the present*, he told himself.

"But first, I have some official business I want to broach with you," he continued. "I know we are all acutely aware of our positions and what they entail. And some years ago when we set up Osguard Gardens we all agreed that our families should not know what we do. But that was over eight years ago, and our parents aren't getting any younger. I think we have accomplished much, and maybe…just maybe, it is time to tell our parents. I know it has been difficult on me, Shawn and Patricia. And I know it has been difficult on some of you—

"—Difficult isn't the word!" his distant cousin Alan Black interrupted. "I think it is time too. My parents are in their seventies. I want them to know," he pleaded.

"Okay, then. How many of you feel it is time to let the folks in on the secret?" Michael continued.

"Does that include in-laws?" his second cousin Richard Genesis queried.

"That includes anyone living in Osguard Gardens, including in-laws," Michael concluded. Michael looked at his brother Shawn and saw a look of disgust land on his face. Michael just smiled and bent his right index finger into a hook and pointed it at Shawn. Shawn just dismissively waved him off with his right hand. Patricia put her arm around Shawn's shoulder and hugged him. Shawn looked skywards and rolled his eyes. Then he looked at Michael and mouthed, "Okay."

"All those in favor raise your hand," Michael ordered. He began counting, but stopped when he realized all sixty participants had raised their hands in favor of his proposal. "Then it is settled. Tonight we bring our folks onboard." Michael smiled and looked at Shawn. He saw Shawn smile. "Okay, let's break up into our teams."

The family dispersed to their assigned venues and the games began for the first Osguard Gardens Olympics.

Chapter 2—The Launch

The Russian Nuclear Defense Command Bunker lay one hundred and eighty feet under the Russian Ministry of Defense in Moscow Russia. It was protected by eighteen feet of concrete and steel shielding. The scientists stated it was built to withstand a direct nuclear attack. It had the latest command, control and communications network to supervise a nuclear attack and any subsequent attack. The Nuclear Defense Command Bunker contained the computer, which had access to the Russian nuclear arsenal. It was where the Russian president would sit and authorize a nuclear attack. The president would order a set of instructions and authorize the instructions through an eight-digit code he would type into the computer. The system was set to distribute his instructions through a series of coded messages. The command bunker was the only place the authorization could be typed.

A white light illuminated inside the security room where three guards monitored the computer room with cameras. The guards turned but were blinded by the light. The first guard shielded his eyes with his left arm as he reached for his sidearm. A blue energy light struck the guard in the chest, leaving a burnt hole the size of a penny. The second guard was still disoriented when he saw the first guard hit the floor. He went to push the alarm, but the same blue energy light hit him. It pierced the back of his head, chiseled through, and escaped through his right eye. The third guard spun his chair and faced the blinding white light. He sat paralyzed staring at a man's shadow in the middle of the light. He did not have time to form a thought before a blue energy light smacked him in the nose and punctured through the back of his head, dissipating in the metal communications board behind him. Death was instantaneous for them.

The security was tight as two armed guards stood watch outside the computer room unaware that General Ivan Prepovnov, commander of the Ministry of Defense Twelfth Directorate, was inside. A momentary white flash of light illuminated inside the room, but went unnoticed by the guards. Sweat glistened down his forehead. He peered around the room as if to see if anyone was with him. He raised his left hand. He was holding a small gray box similar to a stereo remote control. He pointed the eye of the box and thumbed the button. A blue light discharged and blew up the camera he aimed at. Then he hopped down the two circular stairs and moved to the center of the room. He turned and found the other two cameras and dispensed with them in the same quick fashion. He pocketed the control and checked his watch. *Thirty minutes,* he thought. *I only have thirty minutes to get this done.*

Prepovnov lifted the briefcase he carried in his right hand and placed it on the tabletop next to the lone computer in the center of the room. He scanned the room. It was circular and control boards and monitors papered the entire wall. Miniature command stations sat underneath each control board. He thought how familiar the room was. It reflected every control room he'd ever seen—either circular or concaved, with the center point being the main focus of attention, in this case, the command computer.

He broke opened the briefcase and pulled some papers out. Three pieces fell to the ground. Prepovnov whispered several curses for being in too much of a rush. He noted he had to be precise or it would all be for naught. He picked up the papers and placed them on the table with the rest, then sat at the main computer and took a deep breath. Frantically, he scanned the papers, and found they were in disarray. Prepovnov began to organize them in the proper order. The Russian general checked his watch again. He had lost five minutes. Panic set in. Prepovnov stopped and took another breath. *Nothing can go wrong,* he said to himself. He finished organizing the papers. Then the general looked at the door. It was six inches of reinforced steel, vacuum-sealed and airtight. The guards outside could not hear him, even if he screamed—at least that is what they told him. He worried about the security room. He had killed the guards, but the next shift change was in— He looked at his watch. The next shift change would be in twenty-three minutes—better hurry.

He turned on the computer. He knew this very action would alert the people above ground that the computer was turned on. He calculated it would take about fifteen minutes before someone would actually have the wherewithal to check the computer room and not assume it was another false alarm. That is if he was lucky. The computer came alive and asked for a password. Ivan looked at his first sheet. In Russian, he typed in the words '*Red Storm.*' The computer hummed as it checked the password. Next the computer offered him a set of menus. He clicked on '*IMMEDIATE ATTACK.*' The computer then went through a series of programs. The system activated the communications suite and sent preparation orders to all Russian nuclear silos.

Inside Russia's three hundred launch control centers and twenty-eight missile bases, a sharp beep came across the radio. It caught the attention of Silo Captain, Vladimir Chenkovsky of the UI Missile Army, Kirov. He commanded a twelve-man garrison controlling one SS-27 Intercontinental Ballistic Missile. The Russian military had succumbed to the capitalistic sludge of criminal activity since the fall of the Soviet Union. It was hard to keep his people motivated with little food or pay. But somehow Chenkovsky managed. He had won the recognition of his superiors for three years straight for the maintenance and readiness of his garrison.

Of course, what his superiors did not know was his garrison supplemented their military rations with black market activity in the local community, along with a protection scheme from the local businesses. This was the best way he could keep his men motivated and alert. If he did not yield to this behavior, his men would have abandoned their post or something worse—sold technology, weapons or state secrets to the highest bidder. Chenkovsky reassured himself by thinking what he did was ultimately for the good of the state and the people.

However, now there was one more test thrust upon him and his garrison. This is why he deluged his garrison in criminal activity—so they could be ready to fight when and if the time came. Deep inside he expected this to be an unannounced drill; besides, Russia and the United States were on good terms now. In fact the Russian president was to speak in Washington in three days. Therefore, this was someone's idea of preparedness. They had done it so many times before. What was one more time?

He ordered his men to their positions as they had trained and practiced so many times before. Chenkovsky's crew opened their codebooks and deciphered the code. Something was not right. The code did not decipher to the "PRACTICE" table. It deciphered to the "ACTUAL" table. Instantaneously Chenkovsky tapped on his computer a message for the Headquarters, Strategic Rocket Forces. His was one of hundreds of "Please Confirm" messages.

"Confirm what?" Marshal Doshkov, the Sixth Directorate at Headquarters, Strategic Rocket Forces, hammered as he was taken aback by the news.

"It appears all silos received an actual prepare to launch order, sir," the young lieutenant monitoring the threat status replied.

"Is there anyone in the command bunker?"

"No sir, but the threat board said the computer was on. I have been running diagnostics to find the glitch."

"Did you ever stop to think, there was no glitch?" Doshkov shouted. "Get me bunker security."

"I tried that first, the lines are down."

"What?"

"The lines are dead, sir."

"Did you call the Ministry of Defense Twelfth Directorate?" Doshkov roared.

"Yes sir, no answer," the lieutenant squawked, knowing he had not followed the established procedures.

Doshkov looked at the lieutenant with disapproving resolve. "Sound the alarm. Get security over to the bunker now." *–you idiot*, the general wanted to add. Doshkov thought awhile as the lieutenant flew into action. "Get me the president on the line."

"Yes sir."

"Send the silos a negative confirmation."

"Yes sir." Then the lieutenant pushed some buttons and continued as directed.

***

In Washington another bright white light illuminated. This time it was in the war room one hundred and seventy five feet underneath the White House. Inside the security chamber, five marine guards lay dead with the same penny size holes in their bodies. Air Force General Samuel Patterson, Vice Chairman of the Joint Chiefs of Staff, was typing away at the command computer in the war room. An identical reaction in the United States Air Force silos occurred. The Intercontinental Ballistic Missiles, better known as

ICBMs, were prepped and ready for launch. As the missiles came up ready, the threat board at Strategic Command at Offutt Air Force Base Nebraska lit up. In response, Colonel Jason Smith, command officer on duty in the threat room, called General Lisa Strommand, Commander in Charge of Strategic Command, CDRSTRATCOM.

CDRSTRATCOM was in charge of the country's nuclear arsenal, called the Triad. The Triad consisted of the country's nuclear missiles, bombers and nuclear submarines. She ensured the military members under her command were competent and trained to handle nuclear weapons. She was also in charge of the physical security and the accountability of those weapons. But only the president of the United States, through the National Command Authority, was authorized to launch the nuclear weapons. CDRSTRATCOM was unaware of any heightened tensions to cause the launch of all the nuclear weapons in the United States missile arsenal.

"What? Who authorized that?" screamed Strommand over the phone.

"Don't know ma'am. It appears the commands are originating from the war room in Washington," Colonel Jason Smith answered.

"The war room can't connect straight to the silos without going through us first. That is ridiculous."

"Apparently, they can ma'am. And they did."

"Stop it and put those birds back to sleep, Colonel."

"Well ma'am, since the direction came straight from Washington, we have to get the president's approval to do that."

"Shit! I said put those birds back to sleep."

"Ma'am, without proper authorization from the president, I can't do it. Besides if I wanted to do it, I don't have access to the proper Emergency Action Message to stop a National Command Authority message. Only the president, the vice president or the Sec Def has that—remember?" the colonel ridiculed.

"Damn you!" shouted Strommand as she slammed the phone down on its hook. Thousands of warheads were about to rain on Russia, and she had no way to stop it. She was not even sure she should attempt to stop the impending doom. But she wanted to know.

Strommand picked up the red phone and clicked the president's office. Mrs. Terri Charles, the president's secretary picked up.

"This is General Lisa Strommand, Commander STRATCOM, is the president in? It is an emergency."

***

Prepovnov spoke to Patterson through a secure satellite linked communications device that was neither Russian nor American made. "I have my birds ready to fire. How about you?"

"They are ready, but we need to hurry, they are on to me and I just have a few seconds."

"Then put the authentication codes in now and order the launches."

"Roger."

Each of them tapped in the proper authentication codes and pushed the launch button. The codes went through a series of electronic checks and balances. Each launch control center in the silos received their instructions ten seconds after the enter button was pushed in their respective command computers.

***

United States Air Force Captain Daniel Tompkins scrutinized his computer monitor from his command silo in the middle of North Dakota. He had been with the 91st Space Wing at Minot Air Force Base in North Dakota for five years and he had never experienced the exhilaration he was experiencing now. Minot was his first operational assignment after completing his missile training at Vandenburg AFB, California. Prior to that, he spent four years soaking in the imaginary sunshine afforded him at the Air Force Academy in Colorado Springs, Colorado.

He wanted to be an F-16 pilot and thought the Academy would be his best course of action to achieve his goal. Unfortunately, his night vision became poor from late night studying at the Academy under florescent light. He was medically disqualified for pilot training at the 47th Flying Training Squadron at Laughlin AFB in Texas, before his first academic class. He tried to move on and become a navigator, but soon found he could not pass the rigorous academic training. So, he reluctantly settled for becoming a missileer after washing out of joint navigator school in Pensacola Naval Air Station in Florida. He hated every minute of it and counted the days until his commitment was complete.

He felt like a failure and that he had wasted his time at the Air Force Academy. He had withstood four years of physical and mental abuse with the promise of becoming a great military leader like General Hoyt S. Vandenburg, an airpower renegade like General Billy Mitchell, or a fighter ace like Major Richard I. Bong. The Academy officials sublimely planted those dreams in his head for four years and he believed in them. But the Air Force crushed his dreams by saying he was not the best of the best, that he was not the cream of the crop. No, the Air Force stuck him in a hole three days out of every ten to baby-sit a Minuteman III missile, stating he was the vanguard of the United States Military defense—a trained, lean mean fighting machine. Sadly, he thought he was nothing but a key turner for the military industrial complex—not good enough to command a jet fighter and not smart enough to navigate a bomber through enemy territory. No, he felt he had hit rock bottom. He was ashamed, tired and mortified at where life had brought him.

That was until now. He now realized he was in the position of power. He commanded a 60-foot, 80,000 pound, 3 stage, and 202,600 pounds of thrust ICBM with the promise of death and destruction, which could reach out and touch another continent in about thirty minutes. Now he was about to exercise that power with reckless abandonment—and it felt good.

The Emergency Action Message, known as EAM, sweeping across his monitor, flashing like a neon sign, caught his attention once more. His heart was already beating fast since he received the preparatory message ten minutes ago. He no longer felt like a key turner. Now he felt like the national vanguard his commanders always said he was. He and his crewmate, Air Force First Lieutenant Wanda Coles had practiced and trained for this moment in hope it would never come. But their president had determined that deterrence was no longer warranted and a direct attack was necessary, and for once he was glad to be a missileer.

"Message is legitimate," Tompkins yelled to his partner.

"Message is reliable," Coles shouted back.

First Lieutenant Wanda Coles' eyes squinted with anticipation as she went through her checklist once more. She stepped through each checklist item, performing the associated action on her console. Occasionally, she looked over her right shoulder to see Tompkins. Watching Tompkins step through his checklist spelled to her, this was not a drill. She acted without hesitation, but her mind was screaming to stop the insanity. *This can't be happening—this was nothing but a test*, she kept telling herself. But reality set in. The EAM decoded as legitimate and reliable from the real decode book, not the practice book used for exercises. *Shit—this is real*, she finally realized.

As soon as the thought struck her, she regretted having the fight with her husband earlier in the morning. The fight seemed so trivial, now that she was about to start nuclear war. Why couldn't the last thought, the last moments with her husband have been tender moments. She said some awful things to him. But she figured everything would cool down in the three days she would be stuck in this hole with her asshole crew commander, Tompkins.

But now those promised three days were no longer promised. There wasn't to be a tomorrow and she couldn't stop it. Even if she didn't perform her duty, there would be others who would. Her part in the mixture was minor, but important. The world would never know if she did or didn't, because everyone would be dead—including her husband.

Coles felt her lungs burn with fear as she started to hyperventilate. She didn't know she signed on for this. She just wanted a combat position to prove a point—women were just as good if not better than men. Well, she proved it all right, she cursed. A woman was about to help in destroying the world. And her mother told her; it would be men who would end the world with all those wars. *Well mom, your daughter just proved you wrong*, she screamed in her head to her deceased mother.

"Checklist complete," Tompkins shouted.

"Checklist complete," Coles responded.

"Hands on keys," Tompkins ordered as he reached for his key in the middle of his console.

Fighting the impulse not to, Coles reached for her key in her console. When she grasped it, the imaginary shock of realism jolted her like an electric current. She convulsed in her chair as if she were about to have a seizure. After several seconds of twitching, Coles calmed down and turned to her crew commander.

"Hand on key," she shrieked.

"We have a go message…I repeat we have a go message," Tompkins said with a sadistic gleam. "Silo Charlie one—five, turn key on my mark——Three…two…one…mark."

With a heavy heart and against her conscience, Coles followed the order and launched the Minuteman III from its silo.

On two separate continents, General Lisa Strommand and Marshal Doshkov said silent prayers. In thirty-five minutes the end of the world would be upon them.

***

In a surveillance station deep under the Atlantic Ocean on a continental shelf once known as Atlantis, the main status board illuminated with thousands of tracks. The board was an electronic map charting the surface of Earth. From the United States, Minuteman III and Peacekeeper missiles displayed as blue streaks that traveled over the North Pole on an elliptical arch toward Russia. From Russia, SS-24, SS-25 and SS-27 missiles emanated as red streaks that traveled over the North Pole on identical elliptical arches toward the United States.

"General we have—"

"I see Sentinel Timons," General Wang Lo the officer in charge noted. "Countermeasure Alpha," General Lo ordered.

The helm operator attempted to initiate the countermeasure; however, the system indicated a fault.

"There appears to be a malfunction with Countermeasure Alpha," Timons reported.

"Then give me Countermeasure Bravo," the General ordered.

"No response sir."

"Manual override?"

"Nothing sir," reported Timons with excitement.

"How much time?"

"Twenty-five minutes until first impact sir," Timons advised.

"General Lo." The voice echoed over the intercom system.

"Report," General Lo commanded.

"This is security. There has been a security breach in the countermeasures grid control room. The program supporting the countermeasure grid was tampered with. It will take forty minutes to correct." The voice trailed off to allow the general time to digest the information. "Sir, Commander Larson, the countermeasure controller, is missing from his post," the voice added.

The words came as a dagger to his heart. Two thousand ICBMs were thundering skyward carrying nuclear death to two different continents and he could not do a thing about it. The one function of his facility—to stop nuclear war—and he could not perform it. The General looked with pain in his face to his communications officer on the upper level to his right.

"Get me the First Osguard," he ordered.

***

The president of the United States was preparing for a state dinner with African representatives. This was a political function to open up commercial trade with African nations similar to North American Free Trade Agreement. His military aide knocked on the door of the president's private quarters.

"Sir, we have a situation," the aide reported.

The president invited the aide in to explain.

"Sir, it appears…well it seems—"

"Spit it out. What is it?" the president demanded.

"Well sir, it appears we have launched a nuclear attack on Russia."

"What did you say? How?" The president's throat tightened and his voice rose as the news sunk into his consciousness.

The aide shrugged his shoulders, "I don't know." He paused then took a deep breath as he watched the president take a seat and his face draw pale.

"Sir, that's not all."

"There's more?"

"Yes sir, it appears the Russians have launched their ICBMs as well. It appears we both launched at the same time. It's hard to tell who may have launched first."

"Does it matter? Shit, the world is about to end." The president paused. "But surely, our launch was a defensive measure, was it not?" the president asked.

"Again sir, we don't know."

"Can't we call them back, blow them up, or terminate our missiles?"

"Yes sir, but is that wise? We have Russian missiles inbound."

"Get me a direct line to the Russian president," the president commanded as he stood.

Chapter 3—Notification

The game clock ticked past the thirty-second mark in the last quarter of play. Michael's team had the ball at half court and they were down by one point. Shawn had been leading the team with thirty points. However, Jarod Stone, the man Michael was guarding, was holding Team two up just as well. Michael stood to the right side of the basket and ran to post up to the foul line. He wondered why he did this. So far, his brother had taken every opportunity to shoot the ball and had not looked once inside to him for a pass. That was okay. His brother was the best player; he had made All-City and All-State teams out of high school. Playing basketball was second nature to him. Michael knew Shawn was going to shoot the ball.

Michael raised his hands. Defense was loose on him. Why not? Michael's only points were from rebounds. No one on his team actually passed him the ball. Well, he had fifteen points. Not bad for second chance shots. Michael started to turn to flash under the basket for a rebound, in case his brother missed. But something caught his eyes. He flipped back around, just in time to jump and catch the ball. His brother had thrown him the ball. Shock trembled through Michael's body. He had the ball with less than fifteen seconds to go. *Shit what now?* He looked left, and then he looked right. No one was open. With his back to the basket, he faked a turned to the right. He felt Jarod move his weight in that direction. Then he snapped left. *Don't put the ball down; do not put the ball down,* he reminded himself. He turned and faced the basket. The lane wasn't clear and Jarod was shifting back to his left. Michael jumped and aimed. Jarod jumped just a split second later. Michael had to adjust the shot to compensate for Jarod's outstretched hands. He released the ball.

Shit, too hard, Michael thought. He wanted to arc the ball higher. Instead he pushed it harder. The ball sailed over Jarod's hands and toward the basket. *Shit too hard*, Michael thought again as he watched the shot take on a life of its own. The basketball sailed in what seemed like slow motion for Michael. He watched as the ball hit the backboard. He expected it to ricochet like a rock. He wanted to close his eyes, but he couldn't. He was mesmerized like a passing driver slowing to see the outcome of an automobile accident on the side of the road. The ball flipped forward and hit the front edge of the rim. There it balanced perilously for what seemed like several seconds. Then the ball decided to fall. It fell backwards into the hoop.

Osguards: Homecoming

Michael jumped like he'd just won the gold medal at the Olympics. He pushed both hands in the air as he ran to the opposite court to play ten seconds of defense. His shot put his team up by one, but Team two still had a chance to win the game. Michael found Jarod racing to his basket. It was a footrace. Jarod had the lead, and Michael could not catch up to him. He knew the ball was sailing over his head toward Jarod. He didn't even have to look. He just knew. *I have to catch him—got to catch him,* Michael thought. *Why did I waste time celebrating, the game is not over. Now Jarod has a clear shot to the basket,* he punished himself.

The ball caught his peripheral vision as it sailed high over his right shoulder. But another figure caught his attention. Clyde had swept across court and got between the ball and Jarod. He jumped and tapped the ball off its trajectory. The ball bounced backwards toward Michael. *Now is my chance,* he thought. Michael lunged for the ball and swooped it up. He saw Richard and passed the ball to him down court. Three—two—one … game over. Michael knelt down at the sound of the whistle. They won, and he had a big part in it. Damn, it felt good.

***

Michael sat on the bench enjoying a well-deserved break from their victory over Team two, fellowshipping with his relatives, when he heard a familiar beep. As soon as he heard the beep, he threw his towel down showing his apparent agitation. He was enjoying the day, nothing could be that important on the job to interrupt him now.

His cousins looked at him and Mitchell Tower from Team two asked, "Can't they let you enjoy the day without bugging you about something trivial?"

"I guess not," Michael replied. Then he looked around to see who was around. He reached and tapped a hidden transmitter in his choke collar— the same choke collar worn by his cousins and siblings. "Osguard zero-one," Michael answered.

"Sir, this is Earth World General Lo. We have a situation," Rang Lo's voice through Michael's wireless subdural receiver, implanted in his ear.

As soon as Michael recognized the general's voice, he switched his communications collar, commonly called the CC to speaker. The General proceeded to detail all he knew. Several of Michael's cousins gathered around him and listened to the general's synopsis of events. General Lo ended with the fact the missiles would detonate in twenty two minutes and that he and the other Osguards should evacuate. Michael drank in the information and took a split second to formulate a plan.

"General, do you have tracks on all the airborne missiles?" Michael asked.

"Yes," the general told him.

"Download the information to all the galaxy protectors," Michael requested. "Recall all Osguards to their galaxy protectors."

Then Michael tapped his CC again to terminate the conversation, reached into his backpack, and pulled out his Personal Gate Portal, also known as a PGP. It was a black rectangular plastic box, which fit in the palm of his hand like a television remote control. He clicked the left button with his thumb and activated it. Approximately five feet from him, an invisible door slid up to open and a bright white light shone from it. The door made a slight hissing sound as it slid up. It was four feet wide and seven feet tall. Michael stepped into the light and clicked the right button on his PGP. The door slid down to shut, and Michael was gone.

"It looks rough," said Mitchell, Osguard 08.

Shawn nodded in agreement. Each of the remaining nineteen Osguards pulled their PGPs and activated their hidden doors. The bright lights sparkled against the grass background. Each Osguard stepped into his or her light and disappeared.

***

Sixty galaxy protectors sailed hidden by their black color in the recess of the solar system. Each galaxy protector was coated with a special black substance called slitanium that absorbed light. They ran with their lights out and porthole windows blackened, in what was known as stealth mode ten. The ships were two miles in length and one and a half miles in width, with twelve decks of intricate passageways that could confuse a pentagon dweller. The engines were concave and ran the entire length of the ship on the port and starboard side. Each engine melded into a sharp edge point at the bow and stern of each ship. The engines were attached by a spar, connected to the main ship at decks five through seven, centered down the length of the main ship. The main ship was elliptical on all sides similar to a submarine, but it flared in the stern where it contained a launch and receiving pad for its space fighters called defenders and its multi-faceted space transports called startrams. The bow was arrowhead shaped, which sat on top of a reverse pear shape bridge.

***

In the portal room of the *USSTAP Galaxy Protector 0101*, the *Neraka*, an invisible door opened. The technician ran several checks on his monitor and Michael stepped out. Centurion of Operations, Eduardo Sanchez awaited Michael with his black command jacket in hand.

"Do you have a plan, sire?" Sanchez asked Michael in Chaktun, the universal language of the organization.

Osguards: Homecoming

"ARIT, calculate points for sixty galaxy protectors to deflect a chromerion barrier approximately ten miles above Earth's surface and push the assigned spots to all galaxy protectors," Michael said turning to the glass display wall. Michael was speaking to the onboard Artificial Intelligence computer, also known as an ARIT. It was a machine comparable to Earth's sophisticated computers. However, an ARIT was self contained and able to do more computations than any computer Earth had developed.

Sanchez's eyes glowed with understanding. He realized since the countermeasure grid was down; the galaxy protectors would be the countermeasure grid. But the chromerion barrier would not stop the penetration of the missiles, and they had twenty minutes left. Michael took the command jacket from Sanchez and nodded his head in appreciation.

The ARIT spoke in a female voice that cracked over the ship's intercom system in the portal room—

"—Calculation completed."

"Open channel to all Osguards," Michael then requested of ARIT.

"Channel opened," reported the ARIT.

"To all Osguards, we have nukes inbound on the planet's surface and the planet's protective countermeasures grid is down. I need your help to save the home planet. I have a plan. I need you to position your ships to the coordinates I am sending on the data link now."

Michael paused to give the Osguards time to object. He knew there would be no objections. Earth was the mother planet to them. They had parents and grandparents on Earth. Then it hit him—his wife and children along with the parents, our family—they were still on Earth. What if his plan failed?

"Osguards, I think we need to evacuate Osguard Gardens. Have all dependents, including parents and residents of the gardens evacuate to their respective galaxy protectors. I'll get back to you when I reach the command bridge." Then he turned to Sanchez, "Sanchez, have my wife gather my parents and hers, and get them onboard the *Neraka*."

"Tiah," Sanchez reported his compliance in Chaktun.

Michael and Sanchez moved through the sliding door, down the corridor and to the coaster. The coaster opened and they stepped in. Once inside, Sanchez bellowed, "Bridge."

***

Michelle Genesis received the recall message two minutes after her husband Michael. She knew the disappearance of all the Osguards was not a coincidence, but she never guessed the magnitude of the situation.

"Sharyla and Kashara, activate your PGPs now. Go to the ship at once," she ordered her teenage daughters.

"Here, in the open?" rebelled Kashara.

"Yes, here!" their mother ordered with a stern look.

Sharyla pulled her PGP from her pocket and clicked the open button. As she did she noticed other family members doing the same. White light doors speckled the landscape of Osguard Gardens Park.

"What about you, mom?" asked Sharyla with deep concern.

"Never mind me. I have to get your grandparents."

The girls stepped in and the door closed behind them. As the door closed, the look of utter terror showed on the girls' faces. Their mother just waved, as the sight of her daughters disappeared.

Michelle called her parents number on her cell phone.

"Mom, get dad and meet me over at Michael's parents' house, now. It is an emergency."

"What's wrong?" came her mother's voice over the cell phone speaker.

"Never mind that! Just meet me at Michael's parents' house—Hurry mom. Please hurry."

Michelle hung up and ran out of the park. She saw other spouses running as well. She understood this was a total evacuation. She knew her job was to get to the house and step their parents to the ship.

The summer sun beat on her as she ran. She passed by other houses as she noticed black uniformed security personnel from the galaxy protectors stepping out of the light. She knew they were sent to evacuate the houses. She prayed everyone would be found. She saw the black clothed men grab and in some cases shove people into the light of the PGP. They stepped anybody they could find. No identification was necessary. If you were in the Gardens, you stepped to one of the galaxy protectors. The commotion reminded her of a bad horror movie.

Her mind flashed to an old World War II movie where German military personnel abducted the Jews in the middle of the day to send them to concentration camps. The scene she witnessed as she ran through the streets was too frightfully similar. However, these people were being evacuated for their own safety. They did not know it now, but hopefully they would live to know it later. All she could do was yell for them to stay calm and don't resist. She hoped her presence would allow a more orderly evacuation. She didn't know, but she couldn't stop either. She had to get to her in-laws.

Michelle reached the door of her in-laws house as her parents drove up in the driveway.

"What the hell is going on?" her father demanded as he stepped out of the car.

"Can't explain now," she shouted back. She turned and saw Elizabeth and Parker Genesis run out of the house.

"Michelle, what's wrong?" Elizabeth asked.

"Everything. You want to know what Michael and the others are doing. Well today is your lucky day."

Michelle's parents ran to her side as Elizabeth and Parker stepped off the front porch. Michelle pulled her PGP and held it up.

"The world is about to end. The Russians and the Americans have just launched their nukes. If you want to live, I suggest you come with me."

She clicked the open button. An invisible door slid up with a hushing whisper. As it slid a white light poured out and captivated the two elderly couples. Michelle pushed her parents inside the light and grabbed Michael's parents by their arms. She pulled them inside the light with her. All four elderly people were still astonished by the light appearing out of nowhere. Michelle clicked the close button. A split second later the light gave way to another door. They stepped out of the door.

"Welcome to Michael's office. Or I should say ship," Michelle poked.

The room was large and people were stepping out of invisible white light doors all around them.

"Where are we?" Elizabeth croaked.

"We are on the *Galaxy Protector Neraka*. This is Michael's…well we are in a space ship."

"What?" Parker screamed.

"Come on, I will explain later. First we have to get you out of the PGP chamber bay. Someone might step right on top of us here."

She guided the parents through the nearest sliding door.

"ARIT, Michelle Genesis reporting with my parents and the Osguard's parents," she spoke in a language the parents did not understand, seemingly to no one.

"Noted," the ARIT replied over the nearest intercom system, again in a language neither parent understood.

***

"President Repustinov, I don't know how it happened. But I assure you it was not our intention to launch our missiles," pleaded the president of the United States of America, President Frederick Walter Peters.

Peters thought it was fortunate Repustinov spoke English. The time it would take interpreters to translate this conversation would be detrimental. *Why didn't I speak Russian?* Peters thought. *Why does the Russian president speak fluent English? Was it a sign of respect or a sign of something else? Did the Russian president think less of him because he was not fluent in his language? No matter.* Right now, they both had to do something to stop the end of the world.

"My dear President Peters, I can sympathize with you," responded Sergay Repustinov from the command bunker where he and the entire

Supreme High Command had gathered. He did not want to let on he had suffered a similar fate. It would be a sign of weakness. Besides, Repustinov was not sure whether his forces acted accordingly or not. There were American missiles in the air, screaming down on Russian soil. "How can we stop the consequences of your unfortunate accident?"

What? This was not an accident; it was sabotage. He wasn't sure Repustinov wasn't behind this. *Time is running out,* Peters thought. *I will have to be straightforward. No time to play politics.*

"Listen Sergay, my forces were penetrated and the launch was an act of sabotage," blurted Peters. "And I'm not sure your hands are completely clean on this. It is amazing how your forces reacted so soon."

Repustinov was shaken. "You too?"

"What do you mean, too?"

"Frederick, we do not have time to play the blame game. I will give the terminate order, if you do."

"I agree. I am typing the order now."

"As am I, Frederick."

Each leader typed their respective codes to send out the appropriate messages to terminate the missiles, a euphemism for giving the self-destruct codes to the missiles. Peters hit enter and waited. The computer screen went blank. Two seconds later the monitor displayed a green screen and reported '*INVALID CODE.*' Peters checked the packet from the football, the briefcase containing the secret codes controlling the nuclear arsenal. Peters pushed the button on the phone to place Repustinov on hold.

"Paul, is this the right code?" Peters asked his Secretary of Defense, Paul Thompson.

Thompson stepped to the briefcase and checked over the papers. He compared his papers with Peter's.

"Yes sir, it is," he replied in a nervous soaked voice.

"Well it didn't work"

"Try it again sir."

Peters nodded and input the code into the computer once more. The screen went blank and then reported '*INVALID CODE. THIS STATION IS LOCKED.*' This time the computer monitor displayed a running clock counting down the time until the first warhead hit its target.

Sergay Repustinov received a similar message on his station in the command bunker. Repustinov, the president of Russia and the Supreme Commander in Chief of the armed forces, sat back thunderstruck.

"What is this?" he screamed. He retyped the code, pushed enter and the screen reported '*INVALID CODE. THIS STATION IS LOCKED.*'

"Reboot the system," Repustinov shouted.

The Russian Minister of Defense, Ivan Isanmov pushed the power button on the main computer. The electronic hum in the room died. Then Isanmov pushed the button again. Nothing happened.

"Well?" Repustinov asked.

Isanmov pushed the button again. The computer remained powered off.

"Sir, the computers are dead."

"What?"

"Sir the computers are dead. It appears the saboteurs have thought of everything."

Repustinov rolled his eyes then looked at the phone receiver.

"Keep working on it," he ordered to no one in particular. He picked up the phone and placed it to his ear.

"Frederick, I am sorry. We have been sabotaged as well. It appears I can't stop my missiles."

Peters had just taken the line off of hold in time to hear Repustinov. "Sergay, I know. We have the same problem. I can't stop our missiles either."

Chapter 4—The Save

Michael jetted off the coaster and into a large corridor. He turned right and rushed down the corridor. He passed several cabin entrances that housed the offices of his senior staff. At the end of the corridor were two steps, which went up, bookended by a pair of five steps, which went down. The overhanging sign said "Command Bridge" over the steps that went up. The overhanging sign over the steps that went down said "Control Bridge." Michael stepped up the two steps and onto the command bridge. He looked around and saw his staff in position.

"Osguard on the bridge," screamed the sentry at the entrance.

The bridge sat over the control bridge like a balcony. His command chair with its multifaceted buttons, sat in the middle of the command bridge. In front of him sat the ship's pilot and navigator. They had a miniature screen that sat between them. On the right side of him sat Sanchez's chair, similar in design but smaller in stature. On the left of him sat Timothy Mann's chair. Timothy was the Centurion for Engineering. Around the outer walls behind Michael were different workstations, the offensive weapons officer was over his right shoulder and defensive systems officer was over his left shoulder. The communications officer was to his right. He was the main conduit between the command bridge and the control bridge below them, as well as inside and outside the ship. Next to that station was the security officer station. To his left were life support and the science stations. They too were manned.

Michael stepped to the railing of the balcony. Below him were seven rows of stations, which controlled the defenders, startrams and long range ARIT scans. They were also manned and ready. In front of them sat the main viewer. It took up the entire wall, a sixty feet tall by eighty feet wide window to space. It was the window of the ship. In the screen, as well as in the miniature screen between his pilot and navigator, sat a view of Earth surrounded by his sister galaxy protectors. He breathed the scenery in; closed his eyes and thought, *Lord be with me.*

He turned and sat in the command chair. He clicked a sensor on the arm of his chair.

"All Osguards, report when your crew and family are on board," Michael ordered over the secured interspace communications link.

"Osguard zero–one, this is Osguard zero–three," boomed Shawn's voice on the link. "Do you have mom and dad?"

Michael looked to his right at the communications officer, Major Teddy Best. The major nodded in the positive.

"Tiah," Michael replied.

"Thank God," Shawn sighed. Then he clicked the sensor to terminate.

"How much time do we have?" Michael asked Sanchez.

"Fifteen minutes, sir."

"We are cutting it close."

"Tiah," Sanchez sighed.

"Sire, all ships report ready," Major Best interrupted.

"About time." Michael clicked the communications link sensor. "To all Osguards, this is Osguard zero–one. By now your intelligence shops have briefed you on the entire situation. Basically the United States and Russia have launched their nukes at each other. I do not know what precipitated this. But General Lo, the Earth World General, reported Commander Larson sabotaged Earth's countermeasures grid. It appears Commander Larson was not who he seemed to be. I am not sure the entire operation wasn't a deliberate act of sabotage. All I know is that we have to stop it. I propose we use the galaxy protectors as a makeshift countermeasures grid. Placing the ships at the coordinates I have transmitted to you, we can cover the affected areas by projecting our chromerion shields. Hopefully, we can cover everything to absorb and dissolve the radiation from the exploding missiles. I suggest we project the shields to ten…no, make it seven miles above Earth's atmosphere." Michael entered the new data into the ARIT keypad. It quickly adjusted the orbit calculations. "I'm sending you new data. Please adjust your positions accordingly." Michael pressed the transmit button on the keypad. "Once the field is in place, we need to use all our weapons to destroy the missiles before they enter Earth's atmosphere. Are there any objections?" Michael waited to see if anyone objected. As he had hoped, no one did. "Thank you. I will get with you in a few minutes."

"All galaxy protectors are in position and ready," Major Best said after a few seconds.

Michael nodded and tapped the intercom sensor on his chair again. "All ships, project the chromerion field in five, four, three, two, one, now..."

Michael gave a hand signal to his defensive systems officer, Commander John White, to push *Neraka*'s chromerion shield to cover her part of Earth. All sixty ships projected a white light from their bow shield plates. Together the entire northern portion of Earth was blanketed with the white chromerion shield. Michael estimated the chromerion would absorb and neutralize any radiation in the atmosphere. All the missiles were above this field starting their downward trajectory.

"Commence firing at will," Michael ordered over the secure communications link. Each galaxy protector, including Michael's, tracked the missiles in their field of view and let loose with their particle generator array, coronet guns and Asher torpedoes.

Michael watched as the particle generator array, known as a pagenay, shot a beam of high energy in the image of blue light. He followed the light as it pierced the darkness of space with the heat of the sun. The beam hit an ICBM that registered on his monitors as 22.7 meters long with a diameter of 1.95 meters weighing 47.2 metric tons. Michael guessed it to be an SS-27 from Russia as he watched it evaporate, as if it were ice in a frying pan. Nothing but a small amount of gas remained.

Then Michael turned to the coronet guns' monitor. He studied the monitor as the guns shot invisible energy pulses at the speed of light to their targets. The kinematics of such a force cut through a missile with the parameters similar to an SS-25, like a hot knife through butter. The pulses destroyed the ICBM on impact, pounding the metal into dust and eventually causing it to explode.

Each weapon had the strength one thousand times its target warhead. The difference was these weapons systems were clean, no lingering radiation, just pure total annihilation of their targets. The Asher Torpedoes were used less. Their energy did not dissipate with distance, as did the particle generator array or cornet guns. If the Asher torpedoes missed their targets, the ultimate damage would be worse than if they let all the warheads hit their targets.

Michael watched Commander Wang Li, his Offensive Weapons Officer manage his console like a concert pianist. He targeted, coordinated and dispensed the weapons fire regime with such calmness Michael imagined Li's heart rate didn't rise above sixty-six beats per minute. Then Michael stepped up against the railing to get a better view of the large main screen.

He observed the majestic beauty of sixty galaxy protectors unleashing all their firepower above the planet's surface with destructive poetry. The resulting explosions reminded Michael of the Fourth of July celebrations he went to on Earth. The entire sky above Russia and the United States lit up like silent thunderstorms. The vacuum of space deafened the explosions occurring over Earth's atmosphere, but the darkness of space framed the exquisiteness of the tremendous explosions. The chromerion field appeared to be working. The white fields engulfed the explosions like floodwaters.

This was the first time these systems were used since the building of these ships, five universal years ago. No weapon had been fired in anger in any of the sixty Galaxies these ships protected. The mission of the Universal Science, Security and Trade Association of Planets (USSTAP) was peaceful. Yes, prior to the introduction of the galaxy protector, when the backbone of the USSTAP was the galaxy cruiser, USSTAP relied on the Security declaration of their mission more than any other portion. Michael and his cousins had seen and participated in many space confrontations and peacekeeping missions in the seven universal years prior to the inception of the galaxy protector. Many deaths in many regions were attributed to him and the search for peace. But the galaxy protector became a godsend deterrent to space pirates and planetary governments bent on revenge or domination. USSTAP had brought peace to sixty Galaxies and the fifty thousand signatory planets in the Virgo Star Cluster.

It was a great arrangement. USSTAP oversaw the peaceful trade amongst the planets. Each planet was its own master, but outside their solar system, USSTAP reigned. Trade was based on one planet's abundant waste as another planet's rare commodity. For instance gold and diamonds were waste products and sand was a rare expensive commodity on Pierone, a planet in the Litaria Galaxy. Therefore, USSTAP accepted diamonds and gold for trade of sand from planets like Asertinea in the Bletherien Galaxy. This type of trade helped retrieve the necessary goods for production and upkeep of the five galaxy protectors, two hundred galaxy cruisers and the thousands of assortments of exploration, science, medical and trade ships of USSTAP assigned to each Galaxy. Since USSTAP owned the technology and operated the Galactic Gate Portal, abbreviated as GGP, which made travel between galaxies and travel from one part of a galaxy to another through inner space possible, they owned the galactic stock market. All signatories were briefed on all transactions, scientific discoveries; and were allowed to have their citizens join the ranks of the USSTAP. In fact the citizens of their own galaxy manned and commanded all ships, except the Osguardian Flag Ship.

Earth, the home world of the Osguards, was the one planet under USSTAP protection, not aware of USSTAP. This nuclear nightmare could not come at a worse moment. All sixty Osguards were not here just for a family reunion. They were here to participate in the Osguard Senate, which convened every five universal years, translated into approximately six earth years. Simultaneously, representatives from the fifty thousand signatory planets were to convene a special session of the Universal Parliament. The Senate's duty was to review all laws and regulations passed in the Parliament in the last five universal years for approval or veto. Michael as Osguard One, the protector of the Millmum Galaxy, known on Earth as the Milky Way Galaxy, was also the First Osguard, the chairman of the senate. Each of the sixty Galactic Congresses sent a representative to watch the Senate proceedings. All this was to take place in three universal days. Now he was fighting for his home planet's survival.

"Could it be a coincidence that this nuclear sparring occurred when all sixty Osguards were home together for the first time in twelve earth years?" Michael wondered out loud.

"Sire, all missiles destroyed," Sanchez reported.

Michael snapped out of his deep thought. He looked up at the main viewer visible to the Command Bridge and the Control Bridge below. "Cease fire," he commanded.

He walked to the edge of the balcony and gazed upon the white blanket overlaying Earth. "How much longer before the radiation is all dissipated?" he asked his defensive systems officer.

"Ten universal minutes."

"When it's safe, coordinate with our sister ships and bring the blanket down."

"Tiah."

***

Prepovnov, Patterson and Larson began their take-off run. Their Kulusk explorer shuttle veered skyward seconds before the last lightening appeared in the sky. They knew their plan had failed, but did not know how.

"I'd sabotaged USSTAP countermeasures grid. There was no way the grid could have stopped the nuclear attacks," Larson assured them.

"Something went wrong," Patterson added.

"Nothing went wrong," Prepovnov responded. "It was all part of the plan."

"What?" Patterson asked. "The plan was to destroy the Osguards," Larson cried.

"No, you idiot," Prepovnov insisted. "You think the Osguards wouldn't step to their ships before the missiles hit?" He paused and punched a couple of sensors on the glass control panel. "This is just the opening volley to our plan. However the planet was to be destroyed. I don't know what happened there."

33

"Then something went wrong," Patterson screamed.

"I wouldn't say it went wrong," Prepovnov said. "I'd say the master plan has suffered a minor setback."

"You mean I infiltrated the United States Air Force and did everything in my power to reach the second to the top position in that country's military just to aid in the opening volley of some mysterious master plan?" bellowed Patterson. I spent twenty-five galactic years of my life on that barbaric planet for this?"

"As Larson and I have done," Prepovnov added to calm Patterson.

"No, you've got to give me more than that. I have given my life to the Kulusk Empire and I don't know for what." Larson interjected. "To me, the plan has failed. We didn't kill the Osguards, and we didn't destroy Earth."

As they passed Earth's atmosphere, the reason became all too apparent. They had not figured the galaxy protectors would react so quickly and establish a makeshift countermeasures grid. Fear entered their hearts for the first time. The firepower of sixty galaxy protectors could wipe out an entire galaxy and they were in their tiny, minimally armed Kulusk explorer shuttle.

The Kulusks, being the sworn enemy of the Osguards since the galactic revolution over one hundred and fifty universal years ago, had plotted the destruction of the Osguard bloodline at every turn. Once they found out the surviving members of the Osguard family migrated to Earth one hundred and twenty four universal years ago, the Kulusks pushed every conceivable plan for their destruction, but failed. Then Ortho of the parliamentary guard found the surviving line on Earth, and reintroduced them to their home planet of Chaktun. Then the fools allowed the Osguard line to come back to power. They didn't rule a government or planet, but they ruled the largest military, political and economic power in the universe. The universe virtually belonged to the Osguards. What irony: the Kulusks invented their own nightmare, and now they had a chance to destroy it, but failed. They were flying into the jaws of their sworn enemy.

"Stealth factor ten," Prepovnov ordered. This was the maximum stealth factor achievable. The shuttle hull blackened. Its special energy absorbing slitanium coating energized, its windows darkened and all lights were extinguished, in an attempt to evade USSTAP's visual, sensor and scanner surveillance. The shuttle maneuvered at hypersonic speed five galactic planes below the mighty galaxy protectors, then sailed unobstructed behind them.

"Good, we are clear!" exclaimed Prepovnov. "Increase speed to MOP sixty and get us the hell away from this planet." Mass object projection sixty was the fastest speed anyone, including the galaxy protector, could obtain without using a GGP.

Osguards: Homecoming

***

"Osguard zero–one, this is Osguard five–nine" called Sheryl Tower-Jones over the communication suite.

Michael answered her from his command chair on the main bridge. Sheryl's image appeared on Michael's view panel. Sheryl, once a contestant for Ms. America some twenty odd years back, still retained her beauty. Michael regarded his cousin, noticing just a hint of age surrounding her bright hazel eyes. What would those pageant judges say now if they knew Sheryl commanded the science, military and economic trade of Galaxy Fifty-Nine, some two million light years away? "Go ahead Osguard five–nine," Michael responded.

"We've intercepted a trace signature of a Kulusk explorer shuttle exiting the solar system at MOP sixty."

"Are you able to pursue?"

"Tiah," Sheryl complied.

"Sheryl, just pursue. Do not engage. I want to know if this is a Kulusk operation or not."

"Tiah."

"Sheryl do you have your parents on board?"

"No, they are with my sister, Osguard five–two, Cynthia. I have my in-laws with me."

"Do you want to step them off first?"

"No, this is a galaxy protector. We'll be okay. I'll call you back with what I find. Osguard five–nine out." She winked and gave a slight smile to her cousin as her face disappeared.

Michael touched the screen where her face had been and closed his eyes. *I don't know what's going on, but God be with you.* Then he shook his head. *She is an Osguard, commanding the largest and deadliest ship known to humans. I have to stop being overly protective.* Then he opened his eyes to watch Sheryl depart the orbital formation.

Sheryl's galaxy protector, the *Kashara,* maneuvered at hypersonic speed away from the other galaxy protectors and disappeared from the visual spectrum as it increased to hyperlight speed. Once it was safely away from the solar system, the Kashara jumped to MOP sixty. At this speed, The Kashara traveled the cosmos at sixty light years per universal hour.

***

Michael adjusted his view panel to reach the communications menu. He selected Earth World General. The screen went blank and then blinked the word "STANDBY." After a few seconds the face of General Lo appeared on the screen.

"Yes Osguard zero–one, this is General Lo."

Malcolm Dylan Petteway

"General Lo send Pandora's box to the presidents of the United States and Russia," Michael said with a somber look.

"As you wish," Lo said as Michael ended the transmission.

***

Peters was sitting in the war room underneath the White House when he digested all the reports. He could not believe the nuclear weapons had self-destructed with no impending radioactive fallout. Peters thought God was with Earth this day. His earlier conversation with Repustinov confirmed this action was not the doing of either one of them. Somehow both of their security systems were compromised. Both presidents ordered an immediate investigation and stand down of their militaries. Peters went to the Oval Office to contemplate the events of the last hour. As he reached his desk, there was a key sitting on top of it. The note attached to the key instructed him to proceed to the bookshelf and use the key in one of the design areas on the wood frame.

Peters called for his security. He questioned each one about who had access to the Oval Office in his absence. They all replied no one had access. Peters instructed his White House Secret Service agent to do as the paper instructed. The security guard obliged and placed the key in the wood frame design. The bookshelf secret compartment opened and an aged 8mm film canister appeared with a letter signed by President Truman attached. The letter read:

> *Dear Mr. President,*
> *If you are reading this letter, I can only assume a nuclear war has been averted and you have no explanation of how or why. All I can say is we are under the protection of an organization, which has the ability to thwart such a disaster from happening. I advise you to view the film in this canister—alone. It may answer some of your questions.*

Peters ordered for someone to retrieve the 8mm projector out of storage. It took almost four hours before the White House staff could retrieve one. Peters placed the reel into its holder and pushed the play button. On the tape was a bald aging man. He appeared to be in his late fifties and he was sitting next to President Truman. Truman began to speak. He stated the person next to him was a gentleman by the name of Ortho. He also stated Ortho was responsible for the creation of the nuclear bomb that ended the last World War. He continued by stating Ortho was a visitor from another planet eight hundred light years away, called Chaktun, and was on Earth looking for the descendants of Chaktun's ruler, the Maxum. "However, let me allow Ortho to explain," stated the thirty-third president of the United States. Next

Peters heard the voice of Ortho, a pale looking man with blue eyes. He looked normal enough, not like he imagined a person from another planet would look.

***

Ortho began, "It was the third generation and the fourth age of mankind. The first generation of humans was liquid breathers who roamed the universe three hundred and fifty million universal years ago and disappeared around two hundred and fifty million universal years ago. The second generation of man was carbon oxide breathers who appeared one hundred and fifty million universal years ago and disappeared approximately fifty million universal years ago. The third generation is we, you and I, the oxygen breathers. We first appeared around twenty five million universal years ago. Since then two other ages of man have existed. The fourth age of man is space travel and the unification of man throughout the universe. The other generations followed the same course. We can only surmise they have traveled outside our purview once the galaxy could no longer sustain their lives. This was the time of the ruling family of Osguard. Vedar Osguard was the Maxum. The ruler of the entire known galaxy you call the Milky Way. Kulusk, a planet around nine hundred and fifty light years from you, is where the previous ruling Maxum hailed from. They lost rule about one thousand universal years ago, but vowed to regain their power. They began a revolution one hundred and twenty universal years ago. The close of that revolution you are about to witness." The next thing Peters saw was amazing, the image turned to bright vibrant colors. Ortho stated, "You are viewing what we call a holovidpic. It uses hologram technology to recreate events. I have formatted it to play on your projection system. The story you are about to see is a recreation of the records of that time. Watch and learn Mr. President."

Chapter 5—The End of the Beginning

"Maxum, Maxum," the parliamentary guard called. "The Kulusk rebels are in the capital. We are retreating. We must get you and your family to safety."

His personal parliamentary guards and his wife the Maxim, Neraka and their fifteen-year-old twin daughters, Laurona and Nausona, surrounded the forty-year-old Maxum of the Chaktun Republic of Planets, Vedar Osguard, in his office chamber. The Maxum's office chamber sat in the middle of a six-story, one hundred-room palace called the Steeple. Kulusk rebels had penetrated the forty-acre perimeter surrounding the Steeple, and were closing in on the palace. Six Kulusk battle ships were in a synchronized orbit above the Steeple on Chaktun, the third planet in the Gen solar system. Chaktun was almost twice as big as Earth. The Kulusk ships somehow had penetrated the special defensive boundaries in sector forty-five while his main force was quartered in sector sixty. The assault came swiftly and without notice, with the Maxum's main army approximately forty light years away.

All in the Steeple were frightened; however, the Maxum kept a strong front.

"We must evacuate to the Maxum flagship—now," he ordered. "We need to move to the main gate portal room."

He stood from behind his desk holding his wife's hand and scurried through the door with his family and guards. As they moved through the palace corridors, a pagenay blast sailed above the Maxum's head. The guard in front pushed the family to the floor and began firing in the direction of the blast.

"Sire, they are in the palace," the guard observed. "Please stay low to the floor."

The guard fired two more times and paused for return fire. There was none. When he thought it was safe, he and the other guards pulled the royal family to their feet. Just then three pagenay blasts whizzed by their right side. A fierce firefight of blue light ensued between the Maxum guards and the Kulusk rebels. Neraka held both daughters tight to her as she ran with two parliamentary guards flanking her on both sides. The Maxum was in the lead with a pagenay in his hand, firing along with his guards. Laurona and Nausona screamed with each blue pagenay beam that passed near them. They could feel the heat from the beams a split second before the beam appeared. It helped them to maneuver away from the fatal shot before it hit.

The guard to the right of the women took a direct hit in the stomach from a rebel pagenay. He crumbled over in pain and dropped his own weapon. The pain was frozen in his face, as he died a split second later. The smell of burning seared flesh permeated the air. The sight of the dead man clutching what was once his stomach caused Nausona to feel ill.

The Kulusk rebel who killed the guard aimed his pagenay at the immobile Nausona. Neraka saw the rebel and what he was about to do. She screamed, which made the Maxum turn toward her. He looked at her and then snapped his head toward the direction she was staring. He raised his pagenay and gave a quick blast just as the rebel released a blast of his own. Neraka stepped in the path between the rebel and Nausona and took a hit to her left shoulder. The heat of the blast seared the flesh and caused her left arm to go limp. She looked up in agony just in time to see her husband's blast hit the rebel in the face. In an instant, his flesh melted into bubbles, leaving the rebel no time to scream. He just fell flaccid to the ground. The Maxum rushed to his wife only to be stopped by a pagenay blast to the back.

The rebel was not alone. His partner had a clean shot of the Maxum's back and took it without remorse. The guard to the left of Laurona raised his weapon at the sight of his Maxum crumbling to the ground. He fired in the direction of the rebel's blast but missed, instead he hit the column the rebel was hiding behind. A chunk of the column dissipated in smoke as it began to crumble.

The rebel tucked and rolled from behind the column and raised his weapon eye level as he shot upright on one knee. The rebel did not miss his mark. He shot a blast from his pagenay and hit the last guard in the chest. The guard screamed in pain as he felt the burning flesh with his hands. He fell to his knees.

"I am sorry for my failure, my Maxim," he choked out. Then he collapsed at her feet and died.

The Maxim gazed upon the guard and her husband lying dead on the floor in front of her and forgot about her own pain. Her heart filled with revenge and a mother's instinct to protect her young. She picked up the dead guard's gun and in a rage fired at the column the Kulusk rebel ran to for cover. Her rage consumed her. She fired and fired and fired, until the column began to crumble. The rebel ran from behind the column and the Maxim took careful aim.

"I will not shoot you in the back. Turn and face me you coward," she yelled.

The rebel stopped in his tracks. He knew he had the advantage. This was the Maxim. She had no awareness of a pagenay; let alone how to fire it with accuracy. He spun around to his left and started to push the trigger, just as the searing hot blue pagenay blast caught him in the face. Death was instant. The Maxim, giving in to the pain, fell to her knees. She turned to see her daughters in tears as they peered at the carnage. She motioned for their assistance in getting to her feet. They rushed to her and helped her up.

As the Maxim stood, they heard a noise from behind them. Before they could turn a pagenay blast hit the Queen in the back. Her daughters screamed as they watched their mother fall next to their dead father. Nausona and Laurona turned in horror as they saw a Kulusk rebel take careful aim at them. They closed their eyes to accept their fate alongside their parents.

They heard two blasts from a pagenay. But they did not feel any pain. Nausona and Laurona both opened their eyes to see the rebel who had murdered their mother lay dead. Two republican guards walked out of the darkness to the relief of the princesses.

"The Maxum's ship has been destroyed," the oldest guard said as they rushed to the princesses. "We must leave by another way."

Both daughters turned and stared at their dead parents. They wanted to drink in the last sight of them they would ever see, their mother laying face down across their father's back. Somehow their parents' hands appeared to be touching. They loved each other in life and now they would love each other in death. Somehow that seemed to comfort the princesses.

The guards pulled the princesses closer to them as they led them off in another direction. They ran the darkened corridors with stealth and grace. The palace was now overrun with Kulusk rebels with orders to kill the Maxum's family. The darkness of the corridors with the echo of the stoned walls made the experience surreal.

Nausona thought the entire experience a nightmare. She tried to close her eyes to wish the nightmare away. Her heart thumped in her chest as the younger guard pulled her hand in tow through the corridor. Then he tugged her hand hard, grabbed her head and forced her body to the floor. He kept his left hand over her mouth and his knee in the back of her neck. The guard kept his pagenay in the ready position. Nausona was confused. Now she didn't know if he was Kulusk or Chaktun. Was he a traitor or a spy? She struggled to scream, but his knee just pressed harder into her neck. She felt the pressure start to choke her. She ceased her struggle.

On the other side of the corridor, the older guard had placed his hand around Laurona's mouth and they both knelt on the floor. He too kept his pagenay in the ready position. Laurona's eyes widened with fear, because she could see her sister's agony.

Laurona thought about biting the older guard's hand. Then she stopped. They did kill the Kulusk who was about to shoot them. They had to be trustworthy, but what were they doing now. Then in her peripheral vision, she saw two Kulusks approaching with pagenay rifles up and ready. She gestured with her hand that she saw them. The older guard released his grip on her mouth, for he knew she knew to be silent.

Just then, Nausona bit the younger guard's hand. The young guard pulled his hand away from her mouth in pain.

"What are…" She started to say but stopped when she saw the two Kulusks turn her way.

Nausona realized what she had done. The guard was just trying to keep her silent while the Kulusks passed. But in her arrogance, she alerted the Kulusks to their position. She took a deep breath as if to scream, but fear kept the urge lodged in her bosom. The young guard sprung up like a frog, lifted his right knee for balance, then kicked out his left leg, and connected his left foot with the first Kulusk's face. The force knocked him back into his partner.

The older guard grabbed his mation, a knife like weapon, from his belt and flung it at the head of the second Kulusk. The mation caught the guard in the throat just before he fell onto the floor. The younger guard grabbed his mation from his belt and pounced onto the first Kulusk, slitting his throat from ear to ear. The blood spouting from the Kulusk soaked the floor and bathed the young guard. With his face smeared in Kulusk blood, he shot a stern look to Nausona.

The guard's brown eyes, peering at her, highlighted by red blood, were more frightening than the Kulusks to Nausona. She knew she had endangered her life as well as his. And even though he was there to protect her, he would not hesitate to take her life if she compromised them again.

"I'm sorry," she mouthed.

The guard just turned away, holstered his knife and retrieved his partner's knife from the dead Kulusk's throat. He tore his blood soaked jacket and shirt off and threw them in the corner. The disgust on his face told Nausona not to push him anymore.

The young guard then pushed an ornament on the wall above him and a passageway door flung open from behind a mirrored wall. They pushed through the passageway door, which closed behind them. It was dark and wet, full of gloomy corners and bends that contained shredants, Chaktun rodents similar to the rats of Earth. Nausona and Laurona bit their lips in order to endure the filth and dampness. They kept quiet and moved as the guards directed. They drudged for two galactic hours in the knee high raw sewage. A waterfall at the far end of the east garden hid the opening of the passageway. Laurona had admired the waterfall for as long as she could remember, but she never knew a passageway lay behind it.

They waited until dusk just inside the waterfall. When the older guard signaled it was time for them to push forward, they rose and moved without question. They snuck through the garden, and into the twenty-five acres of bushes and trees surrounding the compound. The forest-like terrain gave them great camouflage. Laurona deciphered, this must have been an alternate escape built during the construction of the Steeple some three hundred universal years ago. That was why the large unmanicured trees and bushes, which she always thought were ugly, were part of the compound.

The group moved from tree to tree to bush, stopping to hide behind every possible natural camouflage character in the landscape. The duck and move travel through the compound took another ninety universal minutes, but it kept them concealed from the security cams and the hovering Kulusk air ships searching for them. When they reached the Steeple outer wall, the younger guard pushed a series of rocks in a specific sequence, and the nine foot, four inch thick stoned wall moved open about three feet. The opening gave them enough room to slip out of the Steeple's perimeter.

Outside the wall, the city operated as if there was no attack. People were running about doing their normal business. There were no signs of Kulusks. The Kulusks had concentrated all their efforts on the palace and had not touched the capital city yet. The people appeared oblivious that an attack had happened or that their beloved Maxum was dead. The guards pushed through the bustling crowd.

The older guard led them to a house about two marks from the palace. This was his house he shared with his wife and kids. The younger guard changed clothes and left for his residence, two blocks away. Sonjey, the older guard's wife, was thrilled to see her husband. She had sent the kids to bed earlier, hoping they would wake to the sound of their father's voice. After ensuring the princesses were fed and settled down for the night, he went into his children's room and woke them with a hug. This was the last thing Laurona and Nausona remembered on the day their parents were murdered. They slept soundly in the spare room, as soundly as anyone could sleep with a military force looking to murder you.

The next day the princesses awoke to a scuffle in the street below. Nausona went to the window and peered out. She saw Kulusk rebels searching the houses down the street.

"They must be looking for us," she told her sister.

"We must go!" Laurona replied.

Just then the door swung opened. The girls jumped with fright. It was the older guard.

"I hope you rested well, but now we must go. I had new identi-cards made for you. There is a transport awaiting you at the transport yard. It will take you to Millai in the Clox system. There you should be safe with your new identities. Hurry we must go! I have a change of clothes for you. Hurry, you must hurry! My partner, who was with us last night, has volunteered to be your escort. He will meet you at the transport yard, port fifty-six."

The girls changed into their new clothes and left the house through the back way. They strolled, so they would not draw suspicion. It took them two galactic hours to reach the transport yard. So far all had gone well. The younger guard met them at port fifty-six. With a head nod, the threesome moved in tandem toward the transport entry hatch.

The New Chaktun Transport Line Flight 345 was an old triad class transport. It had two cabins for one hundred and sixty passengers and held a sixty cubic meter cargo bay in the tail end. The rectangular shaped transport was about one third filled when they entered through the front door. Its gray outer hull indicated the transport had been in service quite some time. Two calogenic engines were mounted behind and one on top of the cargo bay area. With calogenic engines, the best the ship could travel was two-thirds hyperlight speed. Laurona calculated it would take almost three weeks to reach the Clox system, some twelve light years away.

Laurona and Nausona made a concerted effort to keep their wind scarves around their neck and cheeks to obscure a clear view of their faces as they moved through the narrow aisle. The young guard, who was now wearing a business merchant's clothing was not as veiled in his movements. He bumped and pushed the passengers in the aisle, searching for their seats. Laurona knew business merchants were known to be rude and obnoxious, and she thought the guard was playing his part just a bit over the top. His manners would bring attention to them, and that is what she did not want. The guard found their seats in the middle of the first cabin, row ten, and directed the princesses to sit down. Laurona took the view port seat, Nausona took the middle seat and the young guard took the aisle seat.

Just as they started to relax, a Kulusk guard entered the cabin. He was checking identi-cards. The princesses were visibly shaken.

"Calm down," their escort urged. "Our lives depend on you staying calm…The Chaktun Republic depend on you staying calm."

It was like the medicine they needed. The thought of their father and mother dying for nothing appalled them. They straightened-up and became the younger sisters to Maji the gem trader. At least that is what the corporal's identi-card stated he was. Just then they realized they did not know the names of either guard who had risked their lives to save them. Now was not the time to repay that courage with cowardice.

The Kulusk rebel reached them and requested their identi-cards. They surrendered them without hesitation. The Kulusk placed the cards into his reader, one by one. All the cards checked out and the rebel went on to the next seat. At that moment a sense of revenge and hatred overcame both the princesses. The will to survive and to fight back burned in their souls like a beacon of rage.

"We will have our day," Nausona promised Laurona.

The transport lifted off on time and sailed toward the morning sun. The view through Laurona's view port was magnificent. It glowed with an orange aura around a bright red center. She took in the image for a few minutes while she meditated. As the transport left Chaktun's atmosphere, Laurona pushed the button to darken her view port. She sighed as she whispered goodbye to her world. Nausona stared at her sister throughout the silent ritual.

"Everything will be alright," she whispered to her sister as she laid her head on Laurona's shoulder. "Everything will be alright."

Chapter 6—The Find

Five universal days into the flight, the transport captain came back to talk to Maji. They spoke in whispers for some time. Maji marched over to the princesses.

"A rebel checkpoint is directly in our path; about two light years away," he informed them. "They are requesting to board this transport to check on what they call *'irregularities'* with the passenger manifest. The captain recognized you two earlier and suspects you are the irregularities the

Kulusks mean. He has a gate portal in the cargo area. There is an abandoned planet ten minutes from here. He suggests we step to the planet. He will slow to manual speed and allow us to step."

"We will be stranded," Laurona replied.

"No. No we will not," Maji insisted. "The captain will supply us food and water to last us two universal weeks. That's about how long it will take before he can pick us up on the return leg. He will have new identi-cards for us. Then he will place us with a resistance cell in the Jamari system."

"I guess that is the best offer we have. Consider it a deal." Nausona felt some assurance from Maji's tone.

Maji nodded to the captain. The captain returned the nod and waved them to follow him. They traveled to the rear of the transport into the cargo area. In the right far corner of the area was a gate portal chamber. The metal elevator-looking box stood seven feet tall and five feet wide, with a depth of six feet. The captain settled behind the control console and set in several coordinates through a series of lighted controls. A porter stepped in with four backpacks containing food, water and sleeping bags. The porter handed the backpacks to the travelers. Maji carried two backpacks.

"Ready?" the captain asked.

Maji nodded. The chamber doors opened and a bright white light illuminated from inside the box.

"Remember the spot you step out at. I will be back to retrieve you in exactly two universal weeks. You must be there when I open the gate portal. I will not have it open for long. Do you understand?"

Again Maji nodded.

"Good Luck and Jus be with you," the captain shouted.

The mention of their god felt strange to the princesses. They were not overly religious in the past. But this was truly a test of their faith, ability and resolve. Their father told them, Jus would test them. Oh how they wished they had paid more attention to those religious lessons. With the captain's words lingering in the air, the trio stepped into the chamber and the door closed behind them.

Five seconds later an invisible door opened and the trio stepped out. They were on the surface of a planet they knew nothing about. The desert floor appeared untouched by humans in over a universal century. The sand was molded into still waves, a brown ocean standing still in time. The gate portal closed behind them with a slight whoosh. They scanned the landscape.

"This way," Maji motioned as he began walking toward a rock formation about five marks away.

The girls looked up and agreed. At least it would provide some shelter from the desert heat and sand. Maji used a scanner to record the journey and to annotate the retrieval point. They reached the rock formation in just under three galactic hours. A good pace, Maji noted. These girls were in shape and did not falter or complain once under his protection—*a far cry from yesterday,* he thought.

Once near the rock formation, Nausona noticed a cave. She pointed it out to the others and without a word; all shifted their course for the cave. Nausona entered the cave first. She stopped in her tracks. This was not a natural cave. It was human made. "Stay here," Maji ordered as he moved deeper into the cave.

He searched in the dark as his parliamentary guard training kicked in. After he was satisfied, he retrieved a light stick from the backpack and activated it. The princesses did the same. The cave was human made, but no human had dwelled in it for a long time. Laurona moved to what appeared to be an ARIT. Laurona reviewed the controls.

"This is Kulusk. Somewhat ancient, but still Kulusk," she responded as she ran her fingers over the ARIT. She activated the ARIT and watched it come to life.

"It still has power?" asked Maji.

"Apparently so," Nausona razed.

"What are you doing? This thing could bring the Kulusk rebels on top of us," Maji warned.

"I do not think so. This place was abandoned prior to the Kulusks losing the Maxum rule over the republic. It appears it was abandoned during that civil war one thousand and twelve universal years ago. I do not think this ARIT can contact anything the Kulusks have today." Laurona replied. "By the way, we may learn something about where we are, or at least how to survive on this rock."

"Fine, but remember, we have no weapons. We are dead if the Kulusks find us," Maji stated as he started unpacking his backpack.

Maji wondered why he had volunteered for this mission. Yesterday, the spoiled princesses almost got him killed. He just shook his head in disgust. Just for an instant, he thought they had some warrior spirit, but that was just for an instant. In his opinion, the princesses had reverted back to the pampered royal pains in the neck the other guards warned him about.

"Look here Nausona, this was a port for prisoners prior to their final transfer to a prison planet," Laurona said.

"What is a prison planet and how can you tell?" Nausona persisted.

"The Kulusks used to send their most dangerous prisoners to distant planets through the gate portal. Remember, back then the gate portal only worked one way. You needed two portal gates to travel back and forth. Thus, the Kulusks could effectively get rid of their political prisoners and never worry about them again. They would just send them to distant planets hundreds of light years away. They had no way to get back."

"Yes, but how do you know this was a port for one of those prison planets?" Nausona persisted.

"Look here, sister," Laurona said as she pointed to the directory coming up on the ARIT. This is ancient Kulusk, but these words here are Kulusk for prison planet." She pointed to the words.

"E-A–R-T-H." Nausona sounded out the two words in her best Kulusk "Yes, I guess it is Kulusk for Prison Planet, ea rth. If this was a port for stepping to ea rth, where is the gate portal?"

"You mean this thing over here," Maji said pointing to the far wall of the cave.

Weeds covered it, but the outline of the metal box was still visible. The biggest one the princesses had ever seen.

"Do you think we can still use it?"

"Its technology is obsolete, but the power still works. The data could be corrupt, but I do not see why not. I can't guarantee where you would end up. Remember, you may not have a way back."

"I'm just looking for options," Maji replied as he rolled his sleeping bag out. "Right now, I am just looking for a little shut eye, though."

Chapter 7—The Cave

Maji and Nausona woke to the mechanical grind of the ten feet by ten feet metal doors opening on the old gate portal. The white light illuminated the entire room like a super nova.

"What are you doing?" screamed Maji.

Laurona activated some controls to close the door. The grinding slow mechanical doors seemed to take forever to close. When they closed, Laurona shut the ARIT down.

"I have been trying to put the coordinates of Chaktun in the gate portal. But it either does not understand the coordinates I am inputting or it is stuck on the coordinates of ea rth. I'm unable tell with this antiquated piece of junk. All I know is there is still a slip stream to this ea rth and I can't redirect it to another coordinate."

Nausona looked at her twin with amazement, "How long have you been up? Have you not been to sleep yet?"

"Maji asked for options. Well, I am working an option," Laurona replied. Her eyes were bloodshot from lack of sleep and her voice bitter from failure.

Nausona went and hugged her sister. No more words needed to be spoken between them. Maji just watched as he witnessed the magic of sisterly love render its silent support in a time of need. They hugged for a while. Their eyes wet from tears that were fighting to let go.

Osguards: Homecoming

"Laurona," Nausona said, "you must rest now. We have two universal weeks to fix this machine. It has stayed here this long; one more day will not matter. Now go fix your bag and rest."

***

In two days the sisters had fallen into a set routine. They would wake and prepare for the day. Then they would meditate as part of their religious ritual to Jus. They would get on their knees resting their buttocks on the heels of their feet and fold their hands in their laps. Then with eyes closed they would hum a silent chant to themselves. This would last for about an hour each day. Sometimes Maji would join them, and other times Maji would not. Those days Maji would not join them; he would go outside and patrol the perimeter. He appeared uneasy about their surroundings—it was Kulusk.

After meditation, Laurona would set out to fix the old portal gate. Its dials and switches were foreign to her. She understood the basic concept of stepping. The portal gate made it possible for humans to tap into the energy of inner space. Inner space was a fourth dimension, which was not of the normal plane. Once in this space, time slowed to almost a halt and allowed travel between two aligned points. The problem scientists had just recently solved was how to align those points. From her studies of the mechanics of stepping, she knew that knowledge was not available when the Kulusks built this particular chamber. She knew from her history lessons, the chambers of these days were designed to go to one select point, the point it just happened to lock into the day the chamber opened for the first time. A series of the chambers were set up in those days as public transportation. A person had to map out a travel route to get where they were going. There must be another chamber on this planet to go somewhere else besides ea rth. But with her luck it would lead to the Kulusk home world. Therefore, this chamber was the best option. If only she could manipulate the ARIT's coordinates and make them a variable input. She spent three to four hours on the ARIT each morning. Then she would break for lunch.

After lunch Nausona tried her luck on the ARIT. She understood her sister's obsession. She understood it so well it became hers too. She spent another three to four hours on the ARIT each day. The cave echoed with the constant sound of the mechanical doors screeching open and slamming shut. The old pulley system using metal chains had become white noise in the background. The light illuminating from the chamber, each time it opened, stopped being annoying around the sixth day. However, not much else was ever accomplished during this time. Maji watched and listened, and kept conversations with the princesses to a minimum. Not until the sixth night.

As part of the sisters' routine prior to dinner, they would practice their Sixana, the most modern fighting technique in the Chaktun Republic. They were quite accomplished in the art. In fact, they both had received top

47

honors in galactic competition several years in a row. Maji always thought it was because they were the Maxum's daughters. But he soon found out otherwise. He watched them go through their routines for six nights and was impressed.

"My princesses."

The princesses were shocked. Maji had not offered them the respect of their position since the night of their parents' death, nor did they request the respect afforded them by normal protocol.

"Yes, Maji," Nausona replied.

"I see you two are quite experienced in Sixana. However, out here the niceties of the fighting form will get you killed," Maji said as he stepped into the makeshift ring the sisters had built. "Remember, you are fighting for your lives, not to win a competition. Your thrusts and hits should not just be accurate, they need to be forceful. See, let me show you."

Maji pulled into position next to Nausona and demonstrated the same routine the sisters practiced. His pretend hits and thrusts were done with so much force, the wind whistled with every movement. His eyes were focused at the target at hand and he did not telegraph the next movement in the routine with his eyes. The sisters noticed a marked difference between how Maji performed the technique and how they had performed it. Maji finished the routine with a turnaround maneuver that pushed the palm of his hands up as if to drive the nose of his opponent into his brain. His movement was so vivid the sisters could imagine Maji hitting the opponent, and that person crumbling at Maji's feet.

"Now you try, princess Nausona," Maji requested as he motioned for her to take center ring.

She complied with Maji's instruction. She began her movement to the right.

"Sharper, princess. You need to move sharper and quicker," Maji yelled.

The princess obeyed the best she could.

"No, you must imagine your opponent. Pretend it is the Kulusks. Pretend it is the Kulusks who killed your people, the Kulusk who killed your father." Both Maji and Nausona paused at that statement. Maji then pushed the final button, "My princess, pretend it is the Kulusk who killed your father," he growled to tug at the anger in her heart.

Upon that urging, Nausona swept back into her routine. Her rage now fueled every movement. The hits were sharper and crisper. Laurona joined in, and the two moved in concert with each other.

Maji continued to bark, "Faster, harder, your movements must be swifter."

The girls continued on, attempting to satisfy their new mentor. The session went an extra hour. Yet, the girls did not feel tired. They felt more exhilarated than ever before. They had released some of the pent up aggression that lay dormant in their souls since their parents' death, the aggression, which their upbringing would not allow them to release. Under Maji, it was not just released, but also focused and directed. It was now a form of revenge and a form of survival.

The seventh day the girls awoke and Maji joined them for meditation. However, this day, Laurona did not go to the ARIT for more agonizing hours of futile work. She and her sister went outside. Just before they exited the cave, Laurona looked back at Maji.

"Are you coming, Toam?"

"I am not your Toam. And where are you going?" Maji said in surprise.

"Outside to practice Sixana. And if you do not accept our offer to be our Toam, we are doomed. Only you can teach us to take what we considered to be art for so long and turn it into a survival skill. I can tell from last night, you are not just a republican guard. You are a Sandson Guard, sworn to protect the Maxum and his family with your life. If my memory serves me, the Sandson Guards are trained in several discreet ways of fighting and killing techniques. Come, you must teach us what you can," Nausona stated in a commanding tone.

Maji stood and complied with the princess. They proceeded outside and began the grueling and lengthy training session. They worked through lunch and stopping for two minute breaks between procedures. The girls were quick learners and the Maji was again impressed with their tenacity and skill. They stopped for dinner and fell asleep soon after, all tired from the day's workout. They repeated the program the next day and the next day. The girls were quick studies and picked up on almost every killing technique Maji demonstrated. Their thirst for everything Maji had to teach them was unquenchable. The more Maji demonstrated the more they wanted to perfect. Soon the portal gate was just a memory, an ornament, decorating the cave. The girls were alive and anxious to get to a resistance cell. They wanted to fight.

***

On the twelfth universal day on the planet, Maji awoke to the sound of a flying craft crackling the quiet of the abandoned planet. He sprang to the cave entrance and peered out. What he saw shocked him speechless. He stomped his foot hard to wake the girls. Nausona woke first and saw Maji at the entrance.

"Laurona, Laurona, wake up. Something is wrong," Nausona whispered into her sister's ear.

Laurona woke up and realized they had company by the way Maji was looking outside.

"Who is it?" Laurona asked.

"Three Kulusk air cruisers orbiting above us and three land cruisers heading this way from the south," Maji answered.

"Can we get out of here?" Laurona asked as she picked herself up.

"No. The air cruisers have the cave entrance guarded. They will only follow us and report where we go to the land cruisers."

"Now what?" Laurona pleaded.

"We go to our backup plan." Nausona said as she walked to the gate portal controls.

"And what would that be, sister?" Laurona harangued.

"Your plan to use this portal device, my sister." Nausona shot back. As she did she noticed a blue light illuminated on the control panel.

"Did you notice this before, Laurona?" Nausona inquired as she pointed to the light.

"Notice what?"

"This light right here."

"No. I never noticed any light before," Laurona assured her as she moved over for a better look. She activated two switches and her face turned from confusion to panic.

"No! No! No! The system has an automatic homing beacon to the Kulusk home world. It activated as soon as I applied power the first day," Laurona screamed.

"How could that have happened? I did not see the beacon activated when I worked the system," Nausona stated.

"It was silent. This light is the transponder reacting to those Kulusk ships outside. They must have been tracking us for the last twelve days," Laurona blurted.

"Well, we know how they found us. But do we know what we are going to do?" Maji interrupted.

"Yes, we go to ea rth," blurted Nausona.

"Are you crazy, that planet is a Kulusk prison planet," shouted Maji as he walked to the far corner to look for a weapon.

"It was over eleven hundred universal years ago. I do not know what it is now. It could be abandoned. It could be the Kulusk home world, as far as I know. But whatever it is, it should have another chamber to get us somewhere else other than here," Nausona lectured.

"Fine, but they can follow us, can't they?" Maji inquired.

"We do not know when they will attack. If we leave now we may get a giant head start. It is a chance we have to take," Nausona pleaded.

"I am afraid it is too late for you, you Chaktun pig," a Kulusk rebel said as he and two others stepped into the cave.

The three rebels pointed their pagenays at the princesses, unaware of Maji who was covered by the cave shadow in the corner. Maji did not hesitate; he kicked the largest of the three in the back of the head with his right heel. This distraction caught the other two off guard. Maji swung his right foot to catch the other two, one by one, in the face.

Laurona rushed to the first guard, who had fallen forward toward them and smashed her thumb into the carotid artery in her victim's neck. Her victim froze as the pain shot to his brain. Then she reached for the mation in his belt and stabbed him in the heart.

Nausona rushed to the rebel who fell to the right. However, he had regained his composure by the time she reached him. Nausona stretched her left leg, swung to the left, and planted her foot in the rebel's gut. Air rushed from his lungs as he coughed up blood. She slammed the palm of her hand into the victim's nose and drove the bone into his brain. Her victim's eyes registered the pain, but his voice could not yell. He just crumbled at her feet.

Maji saw his students in action and dangerous pride overwhelmed him. That split second allowed his victim to recover and catch Maji with a right hook. Maji came back to his senses, blocked the rebel's next blow with his left arm, and pushed his knee into the groin of his victim. The rebel bent over in pain. Maji then grabbed the rebel by the head and forced his face down as he raised his knee again. It met the rebel's face and broke his nose. Maji then swung the rebel around into the wall of the cave, took his mation and stabbed him in the liver. The rebel let out a yell that alerted his companions outside. Maji then took the rebel's head and twisted it, breaking his neck and bringing instant death.

"We are out of time. Get that thing on. We have to go, now," Maji yelled as he picked up one of the pagenays from the ground. Nausona picked up the other two pagenays and collected two mations from her and her sister's assailant. Laurona activated the chamber and the noise vibrated throughout the chamber. The white light blinded the cave. The sisters ran to the chamber and stepped in.

"Maji, let us go now." Nausona yelled.

Just then, three rebels rushed through the cave entrance. However, the light of the chamber blinded them. This distraction was all Maji needed. Maji turned and fired his pagenay and hit the tallest man standing in the center, in the stomach. The searing heat caused the man to crumble to his knees then to his face without making a sound. The two on the flanks dove to the sides and missed the connection to their blue beams of death.

"Go. Go. Go," Maji ordered. "I will destroy the panel after you go. The rebels will not follow."

"But Toam, we need you," yelled Nausona.

A blue pagenay beam seared past Maji's face as he dove behind a bolder near the control panel. The light still distracted the rebels. They could not focus on their target. Maji reached the control panel and pushed the close button. The girls watched in horror as the doors began to close. For a split second the girls started to jump out and help their Toam. But the slipstream had begun its effects and they stood paralyzed until the door closed. When the doors closed they felt a jolt. It was the Toam, destroying the control panel. He was true to his oath. He gave his life in the defense of the Maxum and his family.

**

Maji watched the chamber doors close and counted to five as he tumbled away from the control panel. The blast he gave the control panel was still smoking and working its way into an explosive condition. When he jumped to his feet he saw one of the rebels make a dive to the control panel. Maji raised his pagenay and shot a short blast, hitting the rebel in the arm. He screamed with pain as he dropped his pagenay. Maji saw in his peripheral vision the other rebel trying to move to his flank. Maji had a split second. He twisted on his left heel, pulled the mation out of his belt, and flicked it in the direction of the other rebel. The mation sliced into the back of the rebel's neck with the point protruding out of the front of his throat. Then Maji shot a second blast with his pagenay to the wounded rebel. This blast caught the rebel in the face and burnt the skin until it bubbled, raining death to both in an instant. A few moments later the control panel and the chamber exploded in unison from Maji's earlier blast. He prayed to Jus that the princesses made it to the other side alive. But he had to contend with one more land cruiser and three air cruisers before he could breathe easier.

He swapped clothes with one of the dead rebels in the cave. He placed the rebel's helmet on his head and pulled down the sun visor. Just as he pulled down the visor three more rebels from the third land cruiser entered the cave. They had their pagenays drawn. They looked at the carnage, which surrounded them.

"What happened here?" the older one demanded.

"Resistance fighters," Maji said in Kulusk, as he kept his back to them, pretending to tend to the bodies of the dead rebels. "They put up one hell of a fight. Then they escaped in that old gate portal. This one stayed behind to destroy the controls before we could get to them. I had to kill him." Maji blurted as he stood up and started to raise his visor.

This movement put the rebels at ease as they holstered their pagenays. Maji heard the click of three different holsters and swung around with his pagenay pointed to the ground. He looked at the three rebels to see if he had tipped his hand. The rebels did not look into his face. They just looked at the carnage in the cave. They appeared to accept Maji as one of their comrades. The rebels dispersed to check the dead bodies. Maji snuck around to the cave entrance behind the three rebels. He pivoted and fired three quick blasts, hitting each rebel in the back as they leaned over their fallen comrades. Their deaths were quick and instantaneous.

Maji ran outside the cave and jumped on a land cruiser cornet gun turret. He watched as the air cruisers orbited above the cave. He had to destroy them before they notified their mother ship. They ran circular orbits, separated in altitude by five hundred feet. He calculated when all three ships were the closest to each other in their orbits. He continued watching to make sure it was not a random occurrence. When he knew for sure they were flying set orbit patterns, he activated the turret. Then he swung the gun skyward and gave a thirty-second barrage of invisible energy pulses. The ships were caught off guard and did not have the time to offer resistance. The first one-man piloted ship exploded from the cornet pulses that hit him. The second limped skyward and rotated one hundred and eighty degrees and then plunged nose first into the ground. The third ship's wing was a blaze, but it looked like it was going to escape. Maji felt the impending doom close in on him as he imagined this ship contacting the mother ship. He depressed the trigger even tighter as he prayed to Jus for this monster to die. Finally, the ship exploded in mid air. The flame in its wing must have ignited the fuel source. He took a mental note of that. Their air ships carried explosive fuel near or in their wing structure.

Now he had eighteen galactic hours before the tanker transport would pick him up. Or would it pick him up? Was the mother ship in orbit around the planet? Did the mother ship dispatch this crew to investigate an outdated homing signal and continue on? Whatever the answer, Maji needed to hide and evade for eighteen hours. Also, he needed to pray to Jus for the transport to return. But for now he was alive and hopeful that the princesses were alive as well.

Chapter 8—The Processing Station

Nausona and Laurona remained paralyzed trapped in the white abyss of inner-space. They had felt another jolt just several moments earlier. However, neither could move nor talk to comment on the reason for the second jolt. Both girls wondered what was taking so long for the exit door to open. They had stepped countless times before, and the experience was always instantaneous. After the entry door closed, the exit door would open. It seemed they had been in inner-space for hours. How long would the chromerion field, protecting them from the effects of inner-space, work? The chromerion field generated by a gate portal had never been tested for endurance. What about the oxygen? How much oxygen was left inside the chromerion bubble? Just when the panic of the moment began to arise, the exit door opened to blackness.

Was this outer space? Were they going to step out into the cold black void of outer space? There was no turning back. The protective chromerion field dissipated to allow its occupants to exit the white illumination of the slipstream that carried them through inner space. They had one action to take. They had to step into the blackness. If they did not, there would not be a chromerion field protecting them in inner space once the exit doors closed. The effect would be the same, instantaneous cold death. The death imagined by the most wretched of minds. With that thought and the full ability to move, the sisters stepped out the exit door.

They stepped on a solid platform. As their weight shifted onto their feet, the room illuminated. The air was stale, cold and damp. But it was breathable. They had stepped onto a receiving port, activated upon the arrival of someone through the gate portal system. The room was empty. Both girls scanned the room with their eyes, afraid to move. The room was dusty and adorned with multiple cobwebs. It was obvious no one had occupied this room in ages.

"Where are we Nausona?"

"I imagine we are on ea rth."

"Well let's not keep our hosts waiting," Nausona directed as she pulled out the pagenay from her belt.

"I guess not," murmured Laurona as she did the same.

The girls split up and began reconnoitering the facility. The facility was five decks of winding circular corridors. The corridors were small, not large enough for two people to walk abreast. There were no windows or ports. They discovered no working electronic devices, weapons or apparent damage. It appeared the facility was quickly abandoned. No occupants, no food and the taste of sulfur in the air. After two hours the sisters rendezvoused in what appeared to be the command and control room.

The room was on the top deck and it too was circular in shape. Three chairs sat in the middle of the room facing each other. The chairs had an ancient control ARIT attached to each of them. There were two steps up to get to the chairs. On the outer walls were several ARIT ports with chairs situated in front of them. Nausona mouthed out the ancient Kulusk above each station.

"Prisoner Control. Maintenance. Support. Life Support. Medical. Logistics."

The girls walked to the center chairs.

"These must be the command chairs, Nausona."

They both chose chairs opposite one another and Laurona activated the main ARIT and began searching the commander's log. Both girls studied the logs as best they could. They were written in ancient Kulusk. However they discovered they were in an underwater receiving and processing station on the prison planet. Here the prisoners were indoctrinated prior to release in

54

one of the many encampments on the surface. The indoctrination included re-education and other polite names for torture the Kulusks were so infamous for. However, about twelve hundred universal years ago, the Kulusk empire recalled all soldiers from this outpost to help fight the war. That was the last entry about the station.

"It appears the Kulusks left the prisoners to fend for themselves," Nausona said in disgust.

"No, dear sister. The Kulusks never aided the prisoners once they were on the surface. It appears they fended for themselves even when the Kulusks were here to oversee."

Then Laurona switched menus on the ARIT and called up the prison planets history. Again the sisters worked their way interpreting an ancient Kulusk dialect. The planet, known as Terra in the old writings, was discovered six thousand universal years ago during the inception of the third age. A joint expedition formed by the governments on Chaktun landed on Terra around five thousand universal years ago. It took them fifty universal years to travel the distance in sleeper ships. The colony settled on the planet between two rivers in a fertile valley they called Ubaid. It took another fifty universal years for their report signal to reach Chaktun. By then, the inhabitants of Chaktun had all but forgotten about the expedition. A new global government was in place, and more exciting and closer planetary expeditions took center stage. It was the beginning of Chaktun's space age of exploration. However, since the signal the colony sent was omni-directional, it traveled throughout the universe and was intercepted by the Kulusk Empire. Until then, Chaktuns thought they were the sole humans in the universe.

In Kulusk folklore, descendants of a great king would rise from an uncivilized world and destroy them. The report sent by the Chaktun colonists suggested Terra was that world and the Chaktun Maxum was the great king. One thing led to another and soon the Kulusk Empire saw the Chaktuns as the new threat. The Kulusks too, were about to embark on their space age of exploration; except, their age was based on conquest and domination. Terra and Chaktun would be their first objective.

The Kulusks were more advanced than the Chaktuns at the time. They were able to make the space age travel to Terra in ten years and to Chaktun in fifteen years. Kulusk had perfect alignment to triangulate its forces against both planets. The girls realized the records were speaking of the first encounter with the Kulusks called the First Galactic War. There had been seventeen Galactic Wars involving the Kulusks and the Chaktuns since then. In each one, except the one war one thousand two hundred and fifty years ago and this one, the Chaktuns were the victors. For a brief one hundred years the Kulusks wore the crown of Maxum, but the civil war that caused this station's abandonment brought the crown back to Chaktun and to her family line of Osguard. Somehow, during the First Galactic War, the records of Terra were erased from Chaktun's library.

The records continued to explain that the Kulusks conquered Terra during the first war, and used the planet as a prison planet. They imprisoned dissidents from Chaktun and other planets who opposed their philosophy of conquest. However, they also imprisoned the perpetrators of the most heinous crimes here as well. They built observation stations throughout the planet to keep a watchful eye on their prisoners. The Kulusks would transfer prisoners throughout the galaxy here to Terra and let them fend for themselves on the wild planet without the conveniences of the age. They lived barbaric and Spartan lives in camps called Gypt, Umer and Idus. However bitter their life was, they still lived. With the advent of gate portal technology that Kulusks stole from the Chaktuns, this planet became more useful. They no longer needed to expend resources on ten-year sleeper ships to transport prisoners. They aligned gate portals throughout the galaxy to open on this manmade station several fathoms below the ocean. Then they used gate portals to step them to different parts of the planet surface. It was neat, quick, quiet and most of all, inexpensive.

"Do you think they are still on the surface, Laurona? I mean their descendants."

"Hard to tell. This prison operated for thousands of years. It sounds like they imprisoned women, children and the elderly. They practically populated an entire planet full of angry innocent people along with angry guilty murderers, rapist and thieves. Jus only knows what we will find if we go to the surface."

The screen went blank. Then a gauge appeared on the screen. The gauge indicated something was almost empty. Laurona stared at the gauge and mouthed the numbers.

"We have eight hours of breathable air. It states here the air pumps are off line. They are probably corroded from years of non-use and this damp atmosphere. But I will go see what I can do."

"I'll keep looking through the records to see what else I can find while you do that."

Laurona slipped down the stairs and over to the Life Support console. She thumbed the ARIT a few times.

"I will be back. I have to go to the pumps. The ARIT is useless here."

"Be careful, Laurona."

"I will."

Nausona continued to read the history on the ARIT screen. She reviewed the planet's special motion, composition, landmass geography and other celestial data. Then she moved to the Prisoner Control Panel and thumbed the ARIT for details. The information was not as detailed as she wanted. The Kulusks did not record the names or origins of their prisoners. Just how many were sent to what part of the world. Many were sent to the southern continent. A note was attached to all markings.

"Warning, natural indigenous people of this planet inhabit the eastern most part of the landmass at three–one–two decimal four–three–two, mark eight–nine–nine by two–three–eight decimal eight–eight–eight, mark eight–seven–three. Do not re-locate prisoners in this area. Contamination may cause an unfortunate effect on our presence in the area."

Nausona made a mental note. Maybe they could get help in that area. They might be able to achieve space travel or gate portal technology. Either would be a blessing.

Suddenly, a communications speaker came alive, "Laurona to Nausona."

Nausona saw the communications ARIT in front of her. She tapped it once, "Nausona, go ahead sister."

"I can't fix the pump. In fact she's taking in water. We have to evacuate the station."

"Great, can't we stay somewhere long enough for me to wash my hair?"

"What?"

"Nothing," Nausona said in disgust. "Meet me on deck three; section four; room five. That is where they keep the portal gates. Maybe, we can find one back home or at least to the surface to get some food."

"Alright, I am on my way."

The sisters terminated their communications and each traveled the narrow corridors to the gate portal room. Laurona reached the room first, followed by her sister two minutes later. They began inspecting the ten portal chambers in the room. They located one labeled Kulusk. It was similar to the one in the cave. Laurona knew from experience that she could not change the settings. Even if she could, this one was damaged beyond her experience to repair. In fact the damp atmosphere had damaged all but one.

"Laurona, do you think you can get one good one out of the broken ones in time for us to get out of here?"

"I doubt it sister, but I will try. However, I want to leave this one alone. It may be our last chance to get out of here before we run out of air."

"Agreed."

Laurona and Nausona dismantled nine chambers, searching for usable parts. They assembled one chamber from the parts that worked. It took them seven hours to put it together. Then Laurona tried to input the coordinates of Chaktun in the control panel. It rejected them.

"Laurona, if this is a prison planet, especially made for Chaktuns, do you think their equipment would allow Chaktun coordinates?"

"I never thought of that. Do you know of any other coordinates they may not have banned?"

"Try the coordinates for Remer. Remer is a neutral planet."

Laurona did as her sister requested. Still the control panel rejected the input. They had only one more try, or the control panel would set this chamber to pre-designated coordinates that could never be erased. This was the way the chambers were made in the early days. She set the coordinates for a planet in the Kulusk system. A warning flashed this time on the view port of the control panel, "Chamber can only align to Kulusk home world or one of the nine camps on the surface of ea rth."

"No. I will not accept that!" screamed Laurona.

Another message availed itself on the screen, "Escape in progress. Kulusk gate portal will open in ten micks."

The system counted down in seconds, "nine–eight–seven–six"

Nausona raised her pagenay and blasted the chamber they had spent seven hours assembling. The countdown stopped.

"Now what?" asked Laurona?

"Well, there is one continental landmass the soldiers went to on vacation. And it so happens, this chamber is set to it. If the soldiers went there on vacation and they are no longer on the planet; then it should be safe."

"Yes, and there might be another gate portal room for us to manipulate," Laurona interjected.

"On the surface, we will have time to do it right and reconfigure the control console as well."

"We have thirty minutes of air left. Let me see what is on this station we can take with us," Laurona barked as she moved to the exit.

"Alright, but I do not want to have to come looking for you. You have fifteen minutes. Understand?"

"Understood."

Laurona went through the station as fast as she could. She searched, but found nothing useful. She did not find food, weapons or even clothes to take with them. The Kulusks had left this place empty. She returned to the gate portal room.

"I did not find a damn thing."

"Fine sister, it is time for us to go."

Nausona activated the gate portal control. The door opened and the inner space white light illuminated from it. They stepped in and watched the door close. When it closed, the chromerion field generated around them. They froze in place and the door opened again. The door opened to a green field and a bright blue night sky. The fresh air rolled into their faces and they took a deep breath. The air filled their lungs like a warm bath. They stepped out and fell to the ground. The door closed behind them as they lay in the grass just taking deep breaths. They looked up and saw the stars and a bright full yellow moon. For once since their escape, they felt peace. No words were spoken just the silent thoughts of two sisters enjoying freedom.

Chapter 9—Welcome To Ea Rth

"Wake up, nigga."

Laurona opened her eyes at the words, which were foreign to her. She saw a long metal tube with an opening pointed at her face. It must be some type of weapon. She dared not move. The person holding the weapon was a young looking white male, who appeared to be angry. Her sister turned and found she was staring at the same type of weapon. Two men stood over them, angry and shouting. Shouting in a language familiar but foreign. It sounded like a strange dialect of ancient Chaktun and Kulusk mixed, but still they could not translate it.

"I said, get up, nigga!" the man holding the rifle on Laurona repeated.

Laurona understood the motion of the rifle, and leapt to her feet. Her sister did the same.

"Who are you?" Laurona said in Chaktun.

The man answered her with a backhand slap across the face.

"Don't try any of that African shit with me. Speak English, bitch," he commanded.

Laurona reeled from the sting of the slap. Her anger boiled inside of her. In a split second, she recounted the past month and all she had endured. The deaths of their parents, the escape from the one world she had known and the two weeks on a dead planet. It all enraged her to a point that veins bulged in her pretty bronze cream-colored forehead.

The sisters' hazel eyes met each other in a searing glance, passing a single thought between them. They had been through too much to allow this caveman with an archaic weapon to hit them. However, these two were not alone. There was a third man on an animal, an animal similar to a Chaktun horse, but smaller. There were two other horses without riders next to him. This appeared to be their mode of transportation.

"What the hell do you think you are doing?" Nausona snarled.

Her captor answered her with a punch to her stomach. Nausona bent over, more in surprise than in pain. Her anger boiled. *These men must be what are left of the Kulusks. Therefore, they are the enemy.*

With a chilling scream, the Chaktun battle scream of strength, she notified her sister to begin the fight. Nausona rose up and delivered three quick blows to her captor. The first two were a right left knuckle combination to the sternum, then a right two finger to the throat crushing her captor's windpipe. He dropped his rifle and grabbed his neck, gasping for air. Her sister saw the first blow and rendered her own Chaktun battle cry for strength while she grabbed her assailant's rifle with her left hand, did a quarter turn to her left and raised her right leg and let loose with a vicious kick to her captor's nose. She could feel his nose break underneath the power of her foot. She pushed even harder driving the bone fragments into the brain of her captor. He dropped his rifle, giving Laurona complete control. Laurona regained her balance on both feet, used the blunt end of the rifle, and jammed it into the skull of her captor. The force was so great, her captor's skull split open as the rifle butt broke.

The man on the horse was taken by surprise; however, he raised his gun and fired one quick volley, which missed his target. The sisters reacted in unison. They split, rolled, pulled their pagenays, and each came up on one knee. They fired two quick blasts of the blue light of death. Laurona's blasts found its target in the man's face. Nausona's blasts found its target in the man's chest. The man did not know what hit him. He shot up and over the back of his horse. His body burnt and bubbled from the chest up, unrecognizable as a human being.

"What the hell was all that about?" Nausona screamed as she rose up.

"Don't know, sister. But I suggest we don't linger here much longer. We must go."

They jumped on the horses and rode north. They avoided the main roads and populated areas as much as possible. If this was a Kulusk settlement, they did not want to draw any more attention. They rode until the sun was high in the sky. They stopped to rest at a creek. They drank the water and allowed the horses to drink.

"What fine animals these are," Nausona remarked. "They are so similar to our horses. I wonder if they are Chaktun."

"Could be. The first colony did bring livestock with them. I just can't imagine livestock on a sleeper ship for fifty years," replied her sister.

"There is much about that time that has been lost through the years. Things could have been better than we thought, or they could have been worse. One never knows."

"Well, all I know right now is that I am hungry," Nausona replied. "I have not seen anything but birds and land rodents since we got here. What can we eat?"

"Don't know, but we will find something."

"Laurona," her sister called in a more sympathetic voice. Laurona looked up. "Do you think Maji made it out alright?"

"Don't know. But if anyone could have made it, it would be Maji, or whatever his true name was," Laurona replied as she stood and shook the dirt from herself. "Remember, he was a Sandson Guard. They are trained to do the impossible."

"Yes, you are correct. They are trained to do the impossible," Nausona repeated as she got up and shook the dirt off her as well.

The sisters mounted their horses and followed the creek north for several more miles. They were careful in their trek to avoid people, but soon the hunger pains overcame their sense of evasion. They found themselves on the outskirts of a small farm. The smells emanating from the farm told their stomachs there was food cooking inside. Their immaturity and hunger took over and they decided to see what they could steal for a meal. They crept towards the farm with the sun upon their back. This was a trick their father taught them. The sun would blind the enemy to their presence. Always enter a fight from the sun or exit a fight to the sun. The sun was a great ally if used properly, or it could be a deadly foe if taken lightly.

They reached the window where the smell of cooking food was the strongest. They saw an elderly white woman standing near a black metal hearth. She stirred the contents of a pot and then left the room. The girls climbed through the window and worked their way to the stove.

"What manner of cooking is this?" Laurona whispered.

"I do not know, but it sure smells good."

Just then the lady pushed open the door with a rifle in her hand. The girls were startled. However, the elderly woman was more startled.

"Oh, my God, you're just children. Where are your parents?" the elderly woman queried.

The sisters slowly reached for their pagenays. The elderly woman lowered her rifle and placed it on the table. She stepped toward the girls. The girls stepped back.

"Don't be afraid dears," the elderly woman offered. "You are in the right place. But I was not expecting anyone today and certainly not this early. The sun is still up. Were you forced out of the last station?"

The sisters looked at each other while they released their grip on their weapons. Confusion became evident in their faces. The elderly woman rushed to them and gave them the tightest hug she could muster. The girls were suspicious, but as the love traveled through the woman's arms into them, their suspicion melted. It was the first hug they had received since their parents' death. This lady was not an enemy. However, she spoke the same foreign language as those men who tried to kill them. Where were they? Who were these people? Who could they trust?

"Dears, I must get you to safety. I heard there was a trio of slave catchers concentrating on this route. I think they know I am part of the Underground Railroad. Come with me," the lady said as she motioned for them to follow her into the parlor.

The woman moved a table and a throw rug from its place. Underneath was a hidden door in the floor. She opened it and motioned for the girls to go inside. Somewhat reluctant, they obliged their host. They stepped into a small cellar that housed several cots.

The lady followed them and lit a lantern. "You stay here. I will fetch you some food. You must be starved. If you hear any other voice than mine, blow out the lantern and remain perfectly quiet. Do you understand?" Then she climbed the stairs and closed the door.

"Nausona, what have we done? Are we prisoners or what?

"I think she is hiding us from someone."

"From who?" Laurona questioned.

The door opened again and the lady passed down two plates of food and a pitcher of water. The sisters took the food and water and sat to eat it. The plate consisted of green beans and some pork meat with a slice of bread. They quickly ate the meal, not fully knowing what they were eating. All they knew was it was good and it filled their stomach. They washed it down with the clear cool water from the pitcher they shared. Once they finished the lady came down into the cellar with them.

"My name is Mrs. Betty Lou Gentry. What are your names?"

The girls stared in confusion. Mrs. Gentry repeated herself, this time using hand motions to signify she was Mrs. Betty Lou Gentry. Then she pointed to Laurona and asked again what her name was.

"Laurona," she replied.

Her sister understood and pointed to herself and said, "Nausona."

"Well those must be your African names, cause they sure don't sound like slave names. We got to get you slave names so not to attract attention. I'll call you Lou Anne," as she pointed to Laurona.

"And I will call you Nellie Sue," as she pointed to Nausona.

The girls repeated their new names because they understood it to be a translation of their names into this foreign tongue.

"Can't believe you don't know English. All slaves know English. Something is not quite right here. I can't push you along the railroad without you knowing English. It isn't right. Just isn't right," Mrs. Gentry said as she shook her head. "But I can't keep you locked up down here when freedom for you is just four days travel from here. What am I to do?" Then Mrs. Gentry headed up the stairs, "Well you bunk here for the night and let me sleep on it."

The girls understood the body language and prepared their cots for sleep. They both pulled their pagenays and mations from under their shirts and placed them next to the cots for quick access. If they were prisoners, they still had their weapons and still knew how to use them. They slept for the second night on the forgotten Kulusk prison planet called ea rth.

The next morning the girls awoke to the sound of horses in the front of the farmhouse. A knock on the door and then a male voice bellowed above their heads.

"Mrs. Gentry, have you seen any runaway slaves in the area?" asked Phillip Pathgo. He was a middle-aged man with graying hair who owned the plantation to the west of Mrs. Gentry's farm. It was one of the biggest plantations in the state of Virginia. Along with owning a plantation, he owned many slaves to work his tobacco. He was hard on his slaves. Most of the slave traffic, who ran through Mrs. Gentry's station on the Underground Railroad, were runaway slaves from Pathgo's plantation. Pathgo suspected Mrs. Gentry of aiding the runaways. She had publicly denounced slavery as long as he could remember. However, he did not realize how organized her involvement was.

"Mrs. Gentry, I ask you again. Have you seen any runaway slaves in the area?"

"Well no, Mr. Pathgo. I have not seen any slaves, runaway or otherwise," Mrs. Gentry refuted. "Would you like some coffee this morning, Mr. Pathgo?"

"No, Mrs. Gentry. But I hope you don't mind, my men and I having a look around?"

"No, I suppose not, but why on earth for?" The sisters caught the word ea rth in the language. It was the first word they recognized since they stepped onto this wretched land.

"Well Mrs. Gentry, if you must know. I had hired some slave catchers to catch some of my slaves and the other plantation owners' slaves who have run away from here without a trace. But the men I hired turned up dead about fifteen miles back. Two of them were beat to death and one was burnt alive," Pathgo snapped. "And I vow to catch the niggas who did it."

"How do you know slaves did it? Are there any slaves reported missing in the area?"

"No, not since last week. I'm sure those slaves are long gone by now. But, on the slight chance they are still around and the catchers caught up to them, I promise they will pay with their lives," Pathgo stated as he walked to the back of the farmhouse.

He murmured to himself as he inspected every room in the house. He had his two sons and two slave overseers search outside the premises. Pathgo enjoyed invading Mrs. Gentry's privacy. He knew he would find something to accuse Mrs. Gentry of aiding the slave runaways, and maybe even accessory to murder. He pulled the sheets and covers off the beds in each of the bedrooms. He saw nothing to indicate they had been recently used. He checked the kitchen and closets. Still he found nothing. His anger seethed deep inside of him. He stepped out onto the front porch.

"Jim…Sam…did you find anything?" Pathgo yelled to his sons.

Malcolm Dylan Petteway

Jim yelled, "Pa, I found some horse tracks by the stream. It looks like the slave catcher horses." He could tell by the flaw in one of the horseshoes.

"Did the slaves come up here?" Pathgo yelled down.

"Hard to tell daddy. It looks like they avoided the farm altogether and followed the creek further north," bellowed Sam.

The girls had done a great job of covering their tracks as they approached the house. They stepped on hard ground and did not leave any footprints. Another lesson taught to them by their father. However, the girls sensed the men were looking for them. They had their weapons in the ready position and were set to use them. They listened to every word said, even though they could not understand them. They listened for the shift in tones and the emotion behind the words. They understood Mrs. Gentry was protecting them now. But how long could this frail elderly woman hold out against the passion of the angry man destined to find them?

After thirty minutes of searching, the men left on their horses to go further upstream. Mrs. Gentry knocked three times on the floor and whispered, "They're gone, but you need to stay out of sight for awhile. Don't come up just yet."

The girls may not have understood the words, but they were aware of the danger and did not budge from their cellar hideout the rest of the day. Mrs. Gentry provided them buckets for a toilet and handed their meals to them, but she did not come down to the cellar this day. It was too dangerous.

Mrs. Gentry had been part of the Underground Railroad for over ten years. As a little girl growing up in New York City, she did not understand why the southerners allowed slavery. She did not understand why her country allowed slavery. She was a devoted Christian who advocated *'loving thy neighbor'* and *'Do unto others as you would have them do unto you.'*

This was a characteristic developed in her by her late minister father. They came from a strict Irish home. Her family had immigrated to the United States when she was eight in one thousand eight hundred, to get away from the class struggle, which now plagued her native land. Her mother always pushed for her to be a little lady. Her parents saved for her to go to the best schools and move up the social ladder.

She married, much to her parents' dismay, a southern graduate of West Point. Thomas Gentry swept Elizabeth Louise Monahan off her feet on his weekend visits to the city from West Point. He would dazzle her all day with stories of the sweet South and southern tradition. They married on his graduation day and left New York. They moved west to the Kansas territory, on his first assignment. They had two boys, Josh and Jeremiah during their time out west. They spent twenty years taming the territory for the nation. Josh and Jeremiah followed in their father's footsteps and graduated from West Point twenty and twenty-two years ago. Their visits to New York City while going to West Point helped heal the old wounds with her parents prior to their death. All was good for the Gentry family. Thomas retired to his family farm in Virginia and the boys went off to carve their own career in the military. Only when Thomas and Elizabeth Louise, or Betty Lou as he liked to call her, returned to Virginia did the relationship hit hard times. At the center of it was the subject of slavery. Out west Thomas agreed with all she said, about slavery, about the way to convert the Indians. They seemed to be of one mind, but not in Virginia.

Slavery was the root of business in the South. It was cheap manual labor that allowed the southern gentlemen to get rich. Mrs. Gentry was not averse to becoming rich. She was averse to using the poor slaves as animals to get there. Tearing apart families hurt her to her heart. The Gentry family farm owned a handful of slaves when Thomas took it over from his brother who moved on to Tennessee. She wanted them to stay together as a family. However, when the farm did not produce well, Thomas would sell one of his slaves. The mother slave went first. Then when things picked up, he would buy a concubine for the male slaves. The notion of three to five men sharing the bed with one woman was too sinful for Mrs. Gentry to fathom— especially with the children wondering about their birth mothers. This happened several times. Mrs. Gentry kept track of all the slavery transactions. It was appalling to watch and it was even more wretched to be part of. Then, when her own children were killed out west, family values became dearer to her.

The deaths of their children hastened the already ailing Thomas. His health deteriorated fast and he died exactly one year after his sons. Betty Lou had mourned the deaths of her parents, children and her husband. Her life was over, so it seemed. Eventually, she learned about the Underground Railroad and became involved running one of the many covert stations at the farm. Her first order of business was to release the slaves the Gentry plantation owned. She did so and sent them north, with the promise she would find their relatives who had shuffled through the Gentry farm and send them north also. She kept her word. Using her own money, she bought and released nine slaves that her husband had sold to other farms and plantations. She hoped that they found each other in the north.

Chapter 10—The Beating

Five more days had passed since Mr. Pathgo had visited Mrs. Gentry. The girls remained in the cellar during that time—never once seeing daylight. The cellar began to stink of bodily waste and they required a bath. Mrs. Gentry had told them something, but they still did not understand. But she was gone. They were alone in the house. Mrs. Gentry had left them plenty of food and water. But somehow this was not enough. The sisters skulked up the stairs and into the main house. They left their pagenays and mations inside the cellar. When they lifted the door, the table and the throw rug slipped to the side. Luckily the table did not tip over. They replaced the rug and table over the opening. They slipped toward the back door. They just wanted to sit in the light of the day for a while. They cracked the back door open and took a deep breath. At first it was a wonderful experience. But the more they breathed in, the more they smelled themselves.

"Sister, we need a bath!" Laurona expelled.

"Well the creek is just a half a mark that way. Maybe we can wash down there in the shade where no one can see us," Nausona offered.

"I don't know."

"Things have been quiet for five days now. I think the danger has passed."

"All right, but we must be careful," Laurona warned.

The girls proceeded to the creek, covering their tracks as they went. It took them forty minutes to get to the creek using this technique. But as soon as they dove their dirty naked bodies into the creek the pleasure told them it was worth it. They splashed around and played like the fifteen year olds they were. For the first time since their ordeal began, they were kids again.

***

Mrs. Gentry was at the Pathgo's plantation. She was invited to lunch with them. She worried if the girls would be all right alone. But she knew them to be mature ladies and trusted them to do the right thing and stay out of sight. It took her thirty-five minutes in the June heat to reach the Pathgo plantation and she was very hot, tired, and thirsty. The plantation was very large, with a one-fourth mile dirt way leading to the front steps of the house. The grass was trimmed to perfection and the bushes were edged ever so neatly. The house was white with gray trim. The front porch had four eighteen-inch pillars stretching to the roof above the second floor. The big house had fourteen rooms not counting the kitchen. A black houseboy met Mrs. Gentry's carriage and showed her straight to the parlor where Mrs. Jessica Pathgo had a tall cool glass of lemonade waiting on her guest. As soon as Mr. Pathgo saw his guest sitting in the parlor, he signaled his boys. They went outside and mounted their horses then rode off to the Gentry farm.

The girls finished washing their clothes and lay naked underneath the shade of a nearby tree, while their clothes dried in the summer breeze. Nausona chewed on a grass blade as her sister lay next to her with her eyes closed, trying to imagine what their home world was going through. Laurona thought hard and long of the war. How they assumed they would be the victor and bring the rebels to their feet yet once again. She never thought that arrogance could be the downfall of her beloved world and the death of her loving parents. Now they were fighting for their lives in a world that did not even know them. Why were they hiding from people who lived such a Spartan lifestyle—people who would be considered barbarians on Chaktun? On Chaktun, they had everything they ever dreamt. They had the best education, the best food, the best clothes, and the best entertainment. They were fighting a survivalist war, which they were neither enlisted for nor trained for. What was their next step? Step! That was it. The original plan was to look for the gate portal room. But, where should they look? The day began to take its toll on both young ladies. Laurona and her sister drifted off to sleep as the gentle summer breeze massaged their youthful bronze cream-colored skin.

The Pathgo boys rode up to the Gentry farm. They scanned the area and saw no one in sight. They peered in the windows, and saw no movement. The back door was ajar.

"Now, old Mrs. Gentry should know she needs to keep her doors locked around here. With all these murders happening in these parts, she could be inviting a killer," Sam said as he kicked in the door.

The brothers searched the house and found nothing. They peered in the parlor and began to search the room when their horses neighed outside.

"Something is spooking the horses!" Jim yelled as they ran out the front door.

"I don't see anything, do you?" questioned Sam.

"No, I don't see anything either."

"Maybe we should take a ride down to the creek?" Sam queried.

"No little brother, I think we better walk this time."

The brothers lurked towards the creek. They were not as cautious as the girls, but still they were silent. It took them ten minutes to reach the creek. Sam and Jim peered between the bushes and saw the girls sleeping in the nude at the edge of the creek. Jim motioned to his brother to sit still and just watch them for a while. Jim was hoping others would join them. In reality, Jim was enjoying the view of watching two teenage blacks naked.

Laurona awoke first and tugged at her sister, "We better start back."

The Pathgo brothers did not understand what the slave girl said. She must be talking some African language.

"Oh, Laurona, do we have to?"

"Yes, it is getting late, and we don't know when Mrs. Gentry will be back."

The brothers did not understand what they said, but they caught Mrs. Gentry's name in the conversation. That was it. They had the old bitch. Caught her red-handed. The brothers pulled out their pistols and started to move. Sam motioned for them to wait. The girls were putting on their clothes and he wanted to see more of the show. The girls stood up; unaware they were giving the Pathgo boys the sexual show of their lives. Jim Pathgo was eighteen, his brother Sam was seventeen, and they'd never seen a naked woman, not even a slave woman. Their mother was somewhat religious and would not allow such mischief under her domain. However, now they could watch with full awareness the prettiest sight they ever saw, even though they were slave girls. The sisters' private parts were turned toward the boys as the boys took in the full sight of their beauty. Nature was affecting the boys as they felt the hardening of their manhood. They stayed still until the girls were dressed and waited one more moment as the girls turned their back and started toward the Gentry farm.

"Hold it right there," Sam said as he and his brother stepped out of the bushes.

The girls were surprised and a little embarrassed as they realized their new captors must have been lurking there for a while.

The boys marched their new prisoners toward the Gentry farm and up to their horses. During the ten-minute walk, the girls continued to look for an opening to attack. But an opening never presented itself. These boys never got within striking distance and they kept their weapons trained on their heads at all times. Once they reached the horses, the boys pulled out a set of shackles from their saddlebag. Sam kept the gun trained at Laurona's forehead as Jim shackled Nausona's feet and hands. Nausona dared not try anything because her sister would be killed. Then Jim trained the gun at Nausona's head while Sam shackled her.

Laurona thought the boys were either trained right or they were too scared to make a mistake. Either way, they were shackled and could not defeat them. The boys mounted their horses and ordered the girls to walk. They took thirty minutes to reach the Pathgo Plantation. Once inside the plantation, the boys took the girls to the slave shacks and locked them in the courtyard for all to see. Then they went to the big house where Mrs. Pathgo was still entertaining Mrs. Gentry.

"Dad, we found two slaves down by the creek over by Mrs. Gentry's farm," Sam whispered to his father.

"Please excuse me ladies. There is some urgent business that needs my attention," Mr. Pathgo lied to his wife and Betty Lou.

The two men walked out to the front porch.

"You said near her farm. You did not find them on her farm?" the father asked.

"No sir. They were at the creek. Two beautiful teenage high yellow bitches," his son answered.

"Well that's good except for two things," his father hollered.

"What's that dad?"

Osguards: Homecoming

"First, there are no reports of two high yellow bitch runaway slaves. And two, you did not catch them on Gentry's property."

"Well dad, I don't know about the first one, but the second one is not a factor."

"Why is that boy?"

"Well, because we heard them talking and they mentioned Mrs. Gentry by name."

"Are you sure, boy?" the father said with some excitement in his eyes.

"Yes daddy, I'm sure. They mentioned Mrs. Gentry's name as clear as a bell."

"What else did they say?"

"Well sir, we couldn't understand them. They were talking in some African language."

"What?"

"Yes sir, they weren't speaking English. But they did mention Mrs. Gentry."

"All right boy. Set them up at the whipping pole. We are going to teach them a lesson. Have your brother get the sheriff. I want this Gentry bitch in jail," the father ordered.

***

The girls were shackled to the center pole in the middle of the slave compound. Laurona noticed the population. Mostly mahogany colored people, but their features were similar to the nations of Chaktun. The girls were used to different color skin in humanoids. That factor was based on where they hailed from. However, most Chaktuns were her shade of yellow or lighter. For instance Maji and the staff sergeant who saved them could have passed for any of these idiots trying to kill them. The one true discerning feature was the wide lips and broad nose, which was common to Chaktuns. Unlike the Kulusks who came in one tone—pale white. There was no mistaking a Kulusk. At least not up close. The white folks on this planet seemed to be a mixture of Kulusks and the lighter Chaktuns. But these mahogany people who lived in squalor were definitely descendants of Chaktuns. Even though they were generations removed, they were still her people.

"Laurona, what do we do now?" her sister asked.

"Wait, I guess. Jus will present us with an escape. Jus has not failed us yet."

"You call being orphaned and running for our lives not a failure?" questioned Nausona.

"Sister, do not lose your faith in Jus. We are being tested. Remember, we will return to claim our rightful place in the universe," Laurona urged.

Just then a slave man walked up to them. "Did you say Jus?" he asked.

The girls did not understand him, but they keyed in on the name Jus.

"Yes, Jus. Yes, Jus." Nausona repeated in Chaktun.

"You sound just like old woman Lilly. Let me go get her." The young man said as he walked away.

"Don't go. Please don't go," Nausona and Laurona screamed. But the young man vanished behind one of the shacks. The girls sighed in despair as they watched the figure disappear from sight. Then an old lady came from the same direction speaking in an old dialect of Chaktun.

"You girls know of Jus?" the old lady inquired

"Yes we know of Jus. Where we come from, Jus is our god," replied Laurona.

The old lady sat next to the girls and introduced herself, "I am Lilly, the oldest of the slaves here. I am from the Zulu nation. And you are?"

"I am Laurona and this is my sister Nausona. We are... Well, we are the princesses of the Chaktun Republic of Planets," answered Laurona.

"Chaktun Republic of Planets? What lie is this?" Lilly ordered.

"Sister, remember where we are?" warned Nausona.

"Yes, you are a slave in America. They call this the state of Virginia in the United States of America," warned the lady. "I have no time for your foolishness. Who owns you?" Lilly demanded, slipping into broken English.

"Owns?" asked Laurona, imitating the broken English.

"Yes, who owns you?" Lilly demanded in the old Chaktun dialect.

"No one owns us. We are free citizens of Chaktun," Laurona said.

"No child. You are black and you are in Virginia. Someone must own you, or Mr. Pathgo will. You don't want Mr. Pathgo to own you. Shit, I don't want Mr. Pathgo to own me, but he does. For fifty years, I have been on this plantation as a slave. I was brought over from Africa." Lilly paused as if to remember something. "My king was named Shaka. He was a handsome and cunning leader. He expanded the Zulu realm from ocean to ocean in Africa in what the Sotho called *'difaqane,'* the crushing. He confronted many leaders." Lilly shrugged at the thought. "He conquered king Moshesh of the Basotho nation, Mzilikazi of the Ndebele, and Zwangendaba of the Ngoni, Sebetwane who led the Kololo and the Sotho armies and Soshangane of the Ndwandwe." She took a deep breath looking for the strength to continue "I was captured by Soshangane's army when I was ten years old and I became a slave to the Ndwandwe." Lilly's eyes began to tear. "Soshangane sold me to two white men he entrusted on his trek to the north when I turned twelve. They called themselves the Boers. These white men used me for their sexual pleasure. It was horrible. I hated every minute I was with them. They did things to me no woman should have to endure, let alone a twelve year old child." Lilly turned away, as if she was ashamed.

The sisters looked at her with compassion. Somehow, this gave her the strength to continue with her story. She took a deep, but quivering breath, trying to fight back the tears. "They soon became tired of me and used me as a wager in a game of chance. I didn't understand, but I soon was on a boat with many other Africans—speaking in tongues I never heard. The journey was long and hard. They locked us in chains lying side by side—sleeping in our own bodily waste, sores tearing our skin—our flesh. They fed us little and gave us hardly any water to drink. We only saw the sky three times during that horrid trip. Many of us did not survive. They would throw the dead into the ocean. I prayed to Jus many of nights to let me die. I rather have my body eaten by the sea than stay alive on that boat." Lilly looked up into the sky. "But Jus wanted me to live. For what reason, I still do not know. But I live. Mr. Pathgo's father purchased me right off the boat. I have been here ever since. I have lived all my life as someone's slave—most of it as a Pathgo slave." Lilly switched from sorrow to joy in a blink of an eye. "I thought I would never speak to anyone from the Zulu nation again." Lilly lowered her head. "How did you get here? I thought they stopped shipping us from Africa long ago," she whispered. "Old Mr. Pathgo had to sneak me into the country when he bought me. He told me later, Washington passed a law sometime back, stopping people from bring slaves into the country. He said Washington thought there were enough niggas here."

"Who is Washington? Is he the ruler?" Laurona asked as best she could; copying Lilly's Chaktun dialect.

"Washington is a place not a who. You girls aren't from around here are you?" Lilly scorned. She recognized the confusion in their faces. "Washington is where the president lives. He is the ruler of these United States."

"You're right, we are not from around here and we are not from Africa. We came from, well... Well we came from someplace else," Nausona pushed.

"No matter where you came from, you are good as dead. I hear the overseer is setting the whipping post out. And I guess it is for you two," Lilly lectured. "Here comes the overseer now, I must go. Jus be with you my children."

"No wait. We need to know more about..." Laurona stopped and noticed the entire compound steeling away behind the cabins. Some occupants were running into the cabins as if they saw a ghost. "Nausona, what's happening here? I think we..."

"You two! Shut your mouths," shouted a voice from behind the sisters. They did not understand the words, but they understood it was directed toward them.

The girls turned to see a dirty bald white man with black pants, white shirt and a black vest coming toward them. He cradled a rifle in his arms as he approached the girls. The other slaves squirmed as the overseer unlocked the chain connecting their shackles to the center rail and dragged the girls by the shackles on their wrist to the front of the big house. He locked each girl's shackle so they would face the whipping post with the arms above their heads. Then he ripped their shirts to expose the bare flesh of their back

Mr. Pathgo, his wife Jessica and Mrs. Gentry stepped to the porch.

"Mrs. Gentry, before you go, I thought you might be interested in seeing this," Mr. Pathgo said as he pointed to the whipping poles in front of them.

"Sir, you know I strictly abhor such brutality and I find it quite ungentlemanly of you to parade this wretched feat in front of me. If you must punish your slaves, do so without my blessing or my presence."

"No madam, I am sure you will take a particular interest of these two. I order you to stay and watch. Besides, the sheriff is coming through my gate now. I am sure he would want a few words with you," Pathgo stated as he gave the signal to begin the whipping.

Two men stood at the ready and when they received the signal they let loose with the first strike of their whips. Mrs. Gentry flinched at the sound of the leather whips tearing at the backs of the two slaves. But the slaves did not scream.

"Must you do this in front of me?" Mrs. Gentry again begged.

"Yes, Mrs. Gentry, I must. You see these two runaways were caught near the creek around your property. They mentioned you by name. I think you are harboring runaways. That is what I brought the sheriff out her to confront you about."

Her heart sank in her chest. She was caught; or was she? Who were these runaways? The second strike of the whips hit the sisters' backs in unison. The whips struck the sisters again and again. The whips tore their flesh, seven, eight then nine times. Still the sisters did not yell. On the tenth strike of the whips, the pain tore at their souls. The adrenalin flowed to their muscles. Nausona could not stand it anymore. She let out with the Chaktun battle cry of strength and pulled at the shackles holding her arms above her head. Her sister heard and saw what Nausona was doing and joined her in the Chaktun battle cry. She too, pulled at the shackles holding her arms above her head. The shilling cry echoed through the slave compound. It was a cry none of them had heard before. The cry shocked and scared the overseers. Mr. and Mrs. Pathgo took a step back. With a mighty jerk the chain pulled from the rotten wood of the post and the sisters turned around ready for battle. The look in their faces showed they were ready to kill or be killed trying.

Mrs. Gentry saw it was Nausona and Laurona.

"Stop!" she screamed.

The overseers attempted to fling the whip at the sisters, but they caught the tail end of the whips with their hands and pulled the overseers to the ground.

"Stop this at once," Mrs. Gentry again screamed.

Laurona looked up at Mrs. Gentry on the porch and froze in her tracks. She called for Nausona to do the same. The sheriff now made his way to the porch and witnessed the overseers face down in the dirt holding on to whips that two-shackled slave girls had command of.

"What's going on here, Mr. Pathgo?" asked the sheriff.

"I tell you what's going on here, Sheriff." Mrs. Gentry yelled. "It appears Mr. Pathgo stole the only two slaves who I have and decided to whip them on his property."

"What are you talking about Mrs. Gentry? These girls are runaways found on the creek near your property. You don't own any slaves," Pathgo said in disgust.

"Sheriff, as much as it pains me, I must admit I own those two girls. They were a gift from my brother-in-law in Tennessee, as aid and companionship in my old age. They just arrived yesterday," Mrs. Gentry said as she pulled a letter out from her bag and handed it over to the sheriff. Actually, the letter was an offer of two female slave companions written by Mr. Gentry, her brother-in-law in Tennessee, two weeks ago. What the sheriff did not know was that Mrs. Gentry wrote her brother-in-law and told him any slave sent to her she would immediately set free. She had not received an answer yet, but she knew what it would be. The sheriff read the letter and looked at the slaves in shackles with their shirts torn and bloody.

"I suppose these are the two slaves from Tennessee?" the sheriff inquired.

"Why yes they are. I needed the help around the farm in my old age. I also need companionship. They are not slaves like Mr. Pathgo considers slaves to be. They are my friends. But under the letter of the law, they are my property and Mr. Pathgo has stolen them," Mrs. Gentry argued. "He took them from my property while I was here having lunch with his wonderful wife."

"Sheriff, she does not own any slaves. These bitches are runaways," Pathgo countered.

"Well, Mr. Pathgo, I don't have any reports of any runaways matching these two's description. I tend to believe Mrs. Gentry. She has a letter to prove she was given two female slaves to do with, as she wanted.

The letter is valid and signed by Mr. Henry Gentry." The sheriff turned to the girls. "Is Mrs. Gentry your master?"

Laurona did not understand one word, but she knew Mrs. Gentry was fighting for their protection. "Mrs. Gentry own Lou Anne," she said in broken English as she pointed to Mrs. Gentry and herself.

"Mrs. Gentry own Nellie Sue," Nausona said as she mimicked her sister.

"See there, sheriff," Mrs. Gentry said with a smile.

"Mr. Pathgo, I suggest you release those slaves, tend to their wounds and compensate Mrs. Gentry or I will be forced to place you under arrest," the sheriff barked at Pathgo.

"You can't do that Sheriff. I am the most powerful man in the county."

"Yes, Mr. Pathgo, I can do that, because I am the law in this county," the sheriff said as he placed his face two inches from Pathgo's.

Pathgo never realized how muscular and big the sheriff was until that moment. Sheriff Dan Witt stood six feet tall and weighed about two hundred pounds. His sturdy stance suggested he was all muscle—not an ounce of fat anywhere on him. He stood in front of Mr. Pathgo with a wide brim brown hat and a piece of straw sticking out the right side of his mouth. When Mr. Pathgo did not reply, the sheriff drew the straw from his mouth and flicked it onto the porch without disturbing the intense glare he was giving Pathgo.

Pathgo had played poker many times. He usually could tell whether a man was bluffing or not. But for some reason he could not read Sheriff Witt's face. He glanced down at the sheriff's stance. He saw a man ready to pounce. Pathgo was not ready for this, not now anyway. Pathgo backed away, mainly in disgust but partly in fear. No one had ever defied him in such a matter—not in private and certainly not in public. Pathgo turned and told the overseers to do as the sheriff ordered.

Nervous, the overseers rose to their feet and slinked toward the girls. The girls dropped their end of the whips and allowed the overseers to take them back to the slave compound. There, the old woman Lilly cleaned and dressed their wounds. The cuts were deep and wide. It seemed like no part of their backs was untouched.

"Child, I never saw anything like that. You two just pulled the chains off those posts. Look like you were going to kill the overseers," Lilly bragged in her Chaktun dialect. "You know the slaves hated to see you whooped like that, but there was nothing we could do. Then you just jerked the chains out. And the way you caught those whips. Jus was truly with you."

Lilly rubbed an ointment made from the fat of dead pigs into their wounds. The sting of the ointment was worse than the whip. At each touch the girls flinched in pain. But after a while the pain subsided and a slow cooling relief replaced it. Laurona and Nausona lay on their stomachs listening to the old woman talk. She spoke a broken old dialect, but they were able to understand. Her voice too was a comfort. However, the grief of the situation boiled in the pit of their stomachs as their hearts ached for the sounds of their home planet, Chaktun. They had never experienced such a beating before nor had they experienced this much pain. Their frail young bodies had endured more than they were supposed to. Their soft delicate skin had endured the agony that was never promised or hinted at as they grew up in the Maxum palace. Their lives were not what they hoped. They were slaves; slaves on a barbaric and alien planet. They were slaves to the descendants of murderers, thieves, rapists and political exiles. The thought played like a broken record in their heads. They had lost. They had lost everything. A tear formed in Laurona's eye. She tried to fight it back, but she could not. When Nausona saw the tear drop from her sister's eye, she too began to cry. The two sisters wept until their hearts could take no more. Then they cried a loud mournful cry. A cry they had held back since the day their parents died. Their crying was heard throughout the compound. The slaves knew it was different than the chilling scream they heard earlier. They recognized the sobbing crying of sorrow.

Lilly let them cry. Her first instinct was to console these brave young girls, but she hesitated. Her heart said to hug the girls, but in her mind she knew they needed to be alone. Without saying a word, she left the cabin and gave the young women the space they needed.

When the cabin was quiet again, one of the overseers brought the young women two clean shirts to wear and led them to Mrs. Gentry's buckboard. The compound was abuzz of what the brave young women had done. No slave had taken that type of whipping without crying out in pain. These women took ten lashes, then broke free and caught the whips in their bare hands. Not just one of them, but both. They both broke free and caught the whips at the same time. It was magic. These women were sent to them to give the slaves hope. The slaves beamed with pride: men, women and children. As if they had performed the heroic act of defiance. The overseer knew he had to regain control. But he would not attempt it tonight; it would be first thing in the morning. It would be after the spirit of this day wore off and the reality of their position set back in. They were nigger slaves, nothing more. And so were these bitches. They were slaves, nothing more. And someday he would put them in their place also.

The sisters crawled in the back of the buckboard face down. During the thirty-five minute journey to the Gentry farm, the girls fought the pain racking their bodies at every bump the buckboard encountered. Mrs. Gentry got them to the farmhouse and helped the sisters to the guest room. She had no reason to hide them now. This was a painful answer to her prayers, but now she could keep them here, without fear of discovery, to teach them English in order to move them on the Underground Railroad.

***

Mrs. Gentry nursed the sisters as best she could. Their wounds became infected the next day. The sisters were delirious with fever. Several times, Mrs. Gentry thought she would lose them. However, Mrs. Gentry prayed and prayed. She stayed by their side night and day. She cleaned and dressed the wounds daily. As she did this, she noticed the cuts were healing at an enormous rate. By the end of the seventh day, when the sisters' fever broke, the wounds were tiny scars on their backs. They did not become the huge welts she normally saw on slaves after such a beating.

Nausona awoke on the eighth day, to the delight of Mrs. Gentry, who was physically exhausted.

"Welcome back, my dear," Mrs. Gentry smiled at her. "I thought you were gone for good."

Nausona tried to speak, but her voice cracked. The dry soreness she felt in her throat made her thirsty. Mrs. Gentry handed her a glass of cool water. Nausona looked over to the next bed and saw her sister motionless.

"Is she dead?" Nausona whispered.

Mrs. Gentry did not understand the words, but she recognized the concern in Nausona's face. "No my dear, she is alive. She should wake soon. But for now you need your rest. Your body is still recovering."

Nausona did not understand. She rushed to get up, but became dizzy and flopped back down. Mrs. Gentry explained again, "Your sister, I assume she is your sister, well… Your sister is all right." She pointed to Laurona and made a hand and face gesture suggesting Laurona was asleep.

Nausona seemed to understand and closed her eyes to do the same. Several hours later Mrs. Gentry repeated the same thing with Laurona when she woke. Mrs. Gentry then went to her room and knelt on her knees.

"Lord, oh Lord. I thank you for giving me the spirit and the strength to protect these young children. But Lord, I am just one old woman. I can't fight this fight alone. I need your spirit. I need your wisdom. Lord, I need your strength. I know this is merely the beginning. But I won't give up on them, if you don't give up on me. Please, Lord—help your humble servant. I beg of thee Lord. Help me to protect them. I pray in Jesus name. Amen."

She then kissed her Bible and lay in bed for a much-deserved rest.

Chapter 11—The Rape

"Good afternoon, Sheriff. What a pleasant surprise to see you. May I get you some cold lemonade," Nausona said in her best English.

Osguards: Homecoming

"Yes, I can do with a nice cold glass of lemonade. Thank you. Can you please let Mrs. Gentry know I am here?" the sheriff responded with unusual politeness.

"Yes sheriff, I will do that," Nausona said as she showed the sheriff a seat on the front porch. After she was sure the sheriff was comfortable, she went into the house to inform Mrs. Gentry.

Mrs. Gentry appeared at the door, "Sheriff, to what do we owe the pleasure. We just saw you last Sunday for dinner." Mrs. Gentry pulled up a seat next to the sheriff in the shade of the porch.

"I was just in the neighborhood. In fact, I just came from the Pathgo Plantation. You know they are still upset about what happened with your two slaves last year," the sheriff informed her.

"Now Sheriff, you know they aren't my slaves. I own no one."

"I know what you say, but around here they are considered your slaves. And as long as they are considered that way, they are safe. Once they start acting like free niggas... Well, I don't want to imagine how people will take that," he said with a heavy heart. "You know I like your girls. I think it is grand you teaching them to speak proper and all. And I know you are teaching them to read. I just look the other way. But Mrs. Gentry, Mr. Pathgo doesn't like how you treat those girls and... Well I shouldn't be telling you this, but I think he is about to do something about it. I just wanted to stop by and give you warning. I like Nellie Sue and Lou Anne. They are good niggas." The sheriff looked down to the floor and pulled his hat off his head and twirled it in his hand. Then he took a deep breath and stood up, putting his hat back on his head. "I don't want to see them hurt. Besides, I owe it to my sister to keep you out of harm's way."

"Thank you, Sheriff. I appreciate that," Mrs. Gentry whispered as she reached for the sheriff's hand. She covered the back of his hand and gave it a motherly shake. "Thank you. Your sister was a mighty fine daughter-in-law to me. I still can't believe they are gone."

"Neither can I, Mrs. Gentry. Neither can I," he said with his voice beginning to crack. He stepped down from the porch and mounted his horse.

"Sheriff, why were you out at Mr. Pathgo's place?"

"Damn fool whipped old woman Lilly to death last night," he responded as he turned his horse toward the exit.

"Oh my God! Why?"

"He said Lilly spouted off some fool story about Lou Anne and Nellie Sue being powerful princesses sent by her god to save the slaves. She had his whole compound believing your two girls would come and free them any day. Mr. Pathgo just wanted to show them he was the boss. I had to go out there to confirm she died from the whipping and wasn't murdered by another slave. Poor woman, any way you look at it, she was murdered. But the law states she was Pathgo's property and he could do anything he wanted with her. Even kill her!" he ranted.

Nausona walked outside holding a tray with two lemonades on it.

"Are you leaving so soon, Sheriff?" she asked. "I know my sister would love to say hello to you."

"Yes, Nellie Sue, I have to go. Say hey to Lou Anne for me. I'll catch her next Sunday. I wouldn't want to miss her apple pie. Best damn pie I ever ate."

"Yes sir, I will sure tell her you said hello," Nausona said, enjoying the fact the sheriff was trying so hard to impress her on his command of the English language. From her experience dealing with the people in town, she noted white people could not stand to hear blacks speak English better than them. That made her and her sister work even harder to learn to speak the language well. It did not take them much time to grasp the language. It was a strange dialect, but most of the words had roots in Kulusk, Chaktun and other planets known to the sisters. Learning the language was not a challenge but minor task they needed to complete. She and Laurona needed to know the language in order to help Mrs. Gentry, their savior, in moving runaways through the Underground Railway. Also, they needed to stay in the area as they searched for another gate portal. So far an entire year had come and gone and they still had no luck in finding the gate portal room. Maybe it did not exist anymore. Maybe time or Mother Nature destroyed it. Too many possibilities existed. They could not give up hope. Nausona forced a smile as she waved at the sheriff riding off the farm.

Laurona ran from the fields just in time to see the sheriff ride off.

"What did he want, Mrs. Gentry?" she asked as she sat on the porch steps.

"He stopped by to tell us that Mr. Pathgo is not pleased with us. It seems like old woman Lilly got the slaves stirred up about you two. She had them believing you two were some type of modern saviors, come to free all the slaves. Mr. Pathgo whipped her to death for her stories. The sheriff is afraid Pathgo will try something with you two next." She took a sip of the lemonade. "Great lemonade Nellie Sue." She paused and stood up. "I think it best you two stay close to the farm for a while. Let's wait to see this thing die down." Then she walked into the farmhouse. The words lingered in the air for a few seconds.

"Lilly, dead?" Laurona questioned. "Because of us? No, this can't be happening."

"With Pathgo, anything bad can and will happen to a black person. We have to do something." Nausona said as she sat down next to her sister.

"Yes, but what?" her sister wondered out loud.

"I don't know, but we have to do something."

***

"Laurona, I have to go use the outhouse. I'll be back in a minute," Nausona informed her sister as she left their room to go outside.

"Be careful sister. I thought I saw a snake out there earlier. It is dark out there, you might just step on one and it will bite you," Laurona said, attempting to scare her sister.

"Stop it. You are so terrible," her sister ordered as she left the room.

Nausona was wearing just a nightshirt. She stepped barefoot through the parlor to the back kitchen door. She glanced out the kitchen door window and saw no movement in the grass. She was afraid of snakes. Chaktun did not have snakes. In fact she did not know of any of the planets in the republic that had snakes. This slimy creature was definitely indigenous to ea rth, a perfect place for it. They were dangerous and deceitful little creatures, like the Pathgo family.

Nausona opened the door and took a step out into the night air. It was unusually chilly for this time of summer. Her nightshirt afforded her no protection from the elements. Her skin produced goose bumps as the wind blew straight through her nightshirt. She spotted the outhouse, about twenty-five yards away. What if what her sister said was true and there were snakes out here tonight. Nausona's heart dropped. She had half a mind to turn around. But she did not want to give her sister the satisfaction of seeing her fear. She made up her mind. If she had to go, she had to go. With that thought, she took a deep breath and started running the twenty-five yards to the outhouse. She kept her head down, watching her every step. She moaned in a low tone as she ran as if she were stepping on hot coals. Routinely, she would look up and see what her progress was to the outhouse. She reached the outhouse and moved to the front. She began to open the door when everything went black.

Laurona had moved to the kitchen door to see her sister. She knew she had scared her and wanted to see the fruits of her labor. She watched as her sister ran through the grass. She became tickled at her sister's moans as she ran. Laurona could not hold in the laughter any longer. She chuckled so loud that it woke Mrs. Gentry.

Mrs. Gentry came into the kitchen, "What are you doing Lou Anne?"

"Oh, just watching my sister running to the outhouse. I told her there were snakes out there. She got so scared she ran all the way there, moaning and groaning all the way."

"That is not funny young lady. Your sister is probably scared to death in that dark outhouse. Did she bring a lantern?"

"No, I don't think so. But she will be all right. I am watching her."

"Fine! Then I'm going back to bed," Mrs. Gentry huffed as she returned to her room.

**

Nausona lay unconscious in front of the outhouse. Sam Pathgo had clobbered her on the head with a four foot long two by four piece of lumber. Nausona had relieved her bladder when she fell to the ground unconscious and now lay in a pool of her own waste. Jim Pathgo looked at her for a long time. Nausona's nipples were erect and pressing against the sheer cloth of her nightshirt. Her nightshirt had fallen across her body, exposing the flesh of her thighs. Jim's mind flashed back to the day when he first saw her—the day he watched her sunbathe with her sister by the creek. He never saw any one like her, the bronze cream of her skin, the shoulder length wavy auburn hair and the hazel eyes that still haunted him in his wet dreams. Her body was shapely and muscular; it raised urges in him he did not know existed. Now he was standing over that body, fighting a losing battle against the lust filling his mind and soul.

"What do we do with her now, Jim?" asked his younger brother.

"You stay here. If that other nigga bitch comes out here, you give her the same treatment," Jim ordered as he dragged Nausona by her arms toward the barn fence. He dragged Nausona to the fence and propped her waist front first on the middle post. He lifted her nightshirt to expose her bare buttocks. He caressed her buttocks, pinching them ever so often. His own manhood began to swell, and he soon dropped his pants to set it free. With reckless abandon, he mounted Nausona like a dog mounting a bitch. He continued to force his manhood into her virgin territory. He became senseless with lust and moaned with the pleasure his young arrogant body had never known.

***

Laurona started to get worried about her sister. She had been in the outhouse for over fifteen minutes. Maybe there was a snake in the outhouse. She stepped outside and called for her sister. First she called in a normal voice, but with each passing moment of silence her call became louder. As her calls for her sister became frantic, she walked faster toward the outhouse. Then her walk became a gallop, and then it became a sprint. Laurona thought if her sister was not hurt, she was going to hurt her herself. However, by the time she reached the outhouse, the thought of her sister playing a trick on her vanished. She ran toward the front of the outhouse and paused. She heard the groans of a man. She spun around toward the sounds coming from the barnyard another fifteen yards away. She tried to focus on the shadow near the fence. Then everything went black.

Sam had used the same piece of wood to knock Laurona unconscious. She lay in the dirt face first, bleeding from her head. Sam dropped the wood, picked up Laurona's hands, and dragged her to the barnyard. When Sam reached the fence, he saw his brother raping Nausona. Jim did not notice anything around him. He had his eyes closed, letting the lust rule him. His brother watched for a second and then looked at Laurona. The sounds of his brother's ecstasy and the thought of Laurona swelled in his head. He knelt down next to Laurona and rolled her over on her back. He raised her nightshirt above her head, ensuring her hands were entangled in the nightshirt. He exposed her body to nature's elements. He studied her bronze skin and auburn pubic hair. He grabbed both breasts and kissed her on the lips. He snuggled his body on top of her and pressed against her. Finally, he released his manhood from his pants and entered her with such force it made her body jolt. He stayed on top of her, moving in and out of her with violent force.

"That shit is good, hah little brother?" Jim asked from above Sam. Jim had exploded his passion and pulled his pants up just in time to see his brother hop on top of Laurona.

"Hell yeah, this shit is damn good," his brother yelled as his eyes rolled up in his head. His groans were more animated than his brother's, more for effect and showmanship than anything else. However, he soon lost himself in the passion of the lust. He continued to slam himself into Laurona's unconscious body—each stroke more violent than the last. In his mind, Sam was punishing Laurona through sex. His movements simulated the strokes of an overseer's whip. In the background, Sam heard his brother's taunting voice telling him, "Let that nigga bitch have it. Give it to her good." This message played like a broken record in his head, over and over again.

Jim left his brother to his fun, to get the ax they had brought with them. Their father had requested the heads of these bitches brought back in a sack. Mr. Pathgo planned to parade their heads in the slave compound to discourage any more talk of them being their saviors. Jim reached to the ground and picked up the ax. He thought he might as well chop off the bitch's head now. Then he would move to his brother's prize and let him have the honors. He walked over to Nausona, who still lay on the fence post with her nightshirt up, bloody, wet and unconscious. He turned to see the joyous pain of ecstasy on his brother's face as he exploded his last drop of lust into Laurona.

"Damn that was good," Sam repeated as he stood and pulled his pants up.

"I know little brother, but now we gotta finish the job," his brother said as he raised the axe over Nausona's head.

Just then a rifle blast sounded in the air. The brothers turned to see Mrs. Gentry pointing the gun at Sam.

"What are you two doing?" Mrs. Gentry yelled.

Jim dropped the axe, turned and ran toward his horse on the other side of the barnyard. When Sam saw his brother cower away, he turned and ran to follow. The blackness of the night and Mrs. Gentry's poor vision did not allow her to take another shot. But she yelled, "Stop or I will shoot."

This statement fueled the brothers' passion to leave. They ran faster, jumped on their horses and rode down the hill toward the creek. Mrs. Gentry walked in the direction they ran as if she was attempting to follow them. Then she saw the sisters, bloody and half dressed. She knew in an instant what had happened to them and it made her sick to her stomach. It took her the entire night to drag the unconscious sisters back to the house. The strain coupled with the night air pushed her sixty-eight year old body to its limit. However, with each stride, she prayed to God for the strength. She truly loved these girls, and the worst thing imaginable had just happened to them while they were in her charge. She had to help them now, more than ever. Once she got them into their beds, Mrs. Gentry cleaned them and bandaged their wounds. She remembered doing this the same time last year, and that too was at the hands of the Pathgo family.

Chapter 12—The Blackmail

"Mr. Pathgo, the sheriff is here to see you," the tall dark houseboy stated in a deep frog-like voice to Mr. Pathgo who was enjoying his afternoon brandy in the parlor.

"Show him in Julius," Pathgo urged.

Julius walked out and soon returned with the sheriff in trail.

"That will be all, Julius," Pathgo stated as he dismissed Julius with a wave of his hand.

"Now Sheriff, to what do I owe the pleasure of your visit? Oh, will you please have a seat?" Pathgo urged as he pointed to the flowered cloth chair next to the window.

He strategically chose this chair for his guest because of the view it afforded. When Pathgo's guests sat in this chair they could not help but look through the window at the massive land and the many slaves under Pathgo's command. This gave him the advantage of psychological power over anyone who dared challenge him. And he knew the sheriff was here to challenge him. This sheriff had rebuked his authority all too often. He knew now that backing his election was a mistake. He could not control or buy him. Furthermore, this sheriff showed a weakness to the slaves, something unheard of in these parts. Well, it was unheard of until that Abraham Lincoln fellow from Illinois, with his anti-slave rhetoric, became the Republican Party presidential nominee this year. Well, the Republicans had found a real loser in this election. Lincoln would not get any votes from the true southerner. And without southern votes, no one could win the presidency of the United States.

"Mr. Pathgo, I am here to discuss with you the attack on Mrs. Gentry's slaves last week," the sheriff proclaimed as he sat in the chair.

Mr. Pathgo was shocked. How dare this white trash come into his home and challenge his actions on any slaves.

"Why are you talking to me?"

The sheriff knew Mr. Pathgo would deny the incident; but he was so calm it worried the sheriff. He knew it would be difficult to rattle Pathgo, but he came here to try.

"Mr. Pathgo, I believe your sons had something to do with it," the sheriff stated as he looked into Pathgo's face for a sign. The sheriff searched Pathgo's eyes, his forehead and his lips to see if he could catch any sign of admission.

"No sheriff, I believe you are mistaken. My boys were on the plantation that day," Pathgo replied, taking a sip of his brandy to mask any signs of his deception.

Mr. Pathgo seethed inside at the insolence of the sheriff to approach him so boldly. In his mind, Pathgo knew this sheriff was going to keep pressing.

"Sheriff, why are you so worried about an attack on two nigga slaves?" Pathgo asked showing his irritation.

The sheriff knew he was getting nowhere with Pathgo and decided to lay his cards out on the table.

"As usual Mr. Pathgo, you fail to recognize I am the law in this county. I will investigate and prosecute with the fullest power extended to me by the people of this county, any crime committed in this county. Mrs. Gentry's slaves were attacked, hurt or damaged. I really don't care how you put it, but they were attacked. This is an affront to Mrs. Gentry and a crime on Mrs. Gentry. And if your boys had something to do with it, I will follow through. Do you understand?" the sheriff roared while looking onto Mr. Pathgo's land.

The tension in the air lingered for a few moments after the sheriff's statement. Pathgo was taken aback by the statement and searched his mind for a gracious response. Finally, he decided grace was no longer warranted.

"Now listen here, you piece of white trash, you may be the law around here, but I am the people," Pathgo yelled slamming his drink on the coffee table and moving closer and closer to the sheriff. "I am the people who afford you the right to wear that badge. I am the people who extend you the power to put drunks and horse thieves in jail. I am the people who pay your salary. So don't you come in my house and threaten my family about two nigga bitches. Just who the hell do you think you are? Let me tell you who you are. You are a poor white man with no money, no prestige and definitely no brains. Without me, you would be polishing my boots in the local bar. I consider you just one step above a slave, and sometimes not that much. So you pick up your poor educated, nigga-loving self and leave my property. Now do you understand?"

When Pathgo was finished he was bent over with his face two inches from the sheriff. The sheriff coughed from smelling the brandy on Pathgo's breath. The cough sent Pathgo back two steps.

"That may be true, Mr. Pathgo. I may be all that. And you may be all that powerful. But my sons aren't the ones who forced themselves sexually onto two nigga bitch slaves. What's wrong with them? They couldn't wait for a descent white girl to marry them? Or did Ms. Parker's whores down at the saloon turn them down? What's wrong, Mr. Pathgo? Your sons can't get it up with a white woman?" The sheriff stood up and moved closer to Pathgo so their noses almost touched. "Your sons are the pathetic pieces of white trash in this county, not me. And if they persist in acting in this manner, I assure you, every southern belle between here and Georgia will know what they did and how they did it. After that, I don't expect they will ever meet the proper young ladies to spawn the Pathgo line." The sheriff picked up Pathgo's brandy and swallowed the entire contents. He breathed the brandy into Pathgo's face. "So as long as you have lowlife sons like Jim and Sam, I will come into your house and do anything I damn well please. Do you understand?"

Pathgo stepped back as the words sunk into his head. This wretched excuse for a man had just blackmailed him; blackmailed him over his sons lying with two nigga bitches. The sad thing about it was that if it was true, the sheriff had him in a tight spot. Did his sons lay with those bitches? Could they be that stupid? He decided, yes they could be that stupid. His anger switched from the sheriff, who had played his hand well, to his idiot sons.

The sheriff looked into Pathgo's eyes. He knew he had struck a nerve, the right nerve. He slammed the glass onto the same table and picked up his hat.

"Don't worry, I will show myself out."

The sheriff strutted to the door then turned to Pathgo who was still staring at the spot the sheriff just left.

"I suggest you leave the Gentry slaves alone from now on, you hear?" Sheriff Dan Witt warned in his most commanding voice. Then he placed his hat on his head and left.

Pathgo stepped to the window and saw the sheriff mount his horse and gallop down the drive and out the gate. Pathgo poured himself another brandy and devoured it in one gulp. He flopped down in the chair he reserved for visitors and quietly stared out at his empire. The empire he built for his two sons. The empire his two sons might never get to pass on to another generation, all because they could not keep their manhood in their pants. It would be different if they picked a concubine from the Pathgo slave compound. That was almost expected of a white man reaching maturity. But to force themselves on someone else's slaves was unforgivable. It was.... *It was ungentlemanly.*

"Julius," Pathgo screamed.

"Yes sir, master," Julius responded walking back into the parlor.

"Get my sons and bring them to me, now!"

"Yes master, right away," he responded walking back out of the room.

Several moments later, Jim and Sam walked into the parlor. Their father stared at them from the chair. They recognized that stare. It was the stare of doom. The stare meant they screwed something royally. They already received their punishment for not bringing the heads of those two nigga bitches back with them. But their father appeared to accept their explanation of Mrs. Gentry catching them and firing a rifle at them. He accepted that they did not want to harm a white woman so they left without being recognized. Since the sheriff did not come after them the next day for trespassing, they thought they got away with it. Their father assured them, even if the sheriff came out, he would deny it and put the poor white trash back in his place. They knew the sheriff had just left. Things must have worked out like their father planned, except for that stare.

Something was wrong. The boys stood their ground. They did not budge from their spot. Their father poured himself another brandy and guzzled it down. He looked at his sons standing in front of the couch with trepidation. He felt ill to his stomach. He poured another brandy and finished it in one gulp. Then he turned to his children. He strode over to them.

"Did you force yourselves onto the two nigga bitches I asked you to kill?" he slurred.

"Pa, it ain't like..." Jim started to say, but his father's right backhand across his face cut him off.

"I ask you again boy. Did you rape the two nigga bitches I asked you to kill?" Pathgo pushed out with a deep voice.

"Pa, like Jim said, it ain't..." Sam received the same backhand across the face.

"If I have to ask you again, I will have you whipped in front of the slaves outside on the post. Do not... I repeat...do not sass me on this," Pathgo bellowed.

"What do you want to hear, Pa? Do you want to hear we failed you? Well, we told you that last week. We did not kill them. Mrs. Gentry caught us, just as I was going to whack that bitch's head off," Jim wailed, rubbing the sting from his face.

"Boy, I told you I want to hear the truth," Pathgo insisted raising his hand to slap Jim once more.

"Yes Pa, we took them...we did it," screamed Sam trying to save his brother from another hit.

Pathgo stopped in midstream and redirected his force to Sam. Sam caught a right cross to his left jaw. The force sent him back onto the couch.

"What you do that for?" Sam murmured, wiping the blood from his mouth. "They ain't nothing but niggas. You said yourself; we could have any nigga bitch we want when we felt it was time."

"You idiot. I said any slave from our compound. You could have any slave from our compound who we own and who would do anything we say. You can't go having sex with someone else's slave without their permission; especially, if you go and beat on them," Pathgo lectured.

"I don't see why not, Pa. A slave is a slave; they have to do what we say. That is what you always told us," Jim offered, helping his brother stand up. "Plus it was damn good. If a slave can make me feel like that, I can't wait to get my hands on a real woman."

"You two are dumber than I thought." Pathgo shook his head. He paused for a moment and waved toward the window. "The sheriff knows. And he is going to blab it all over the county," Pathgo offered.

"So what?" Jim replied

"So what? So what? Try marrying a decent woman who will have your kids after she finds out you were so desperate for sex you went creeping in the dead of night to rape two teenage slaves from your next door neighbor. Who would want you then? That is—so what."

"We're Pathgos. Every woman in four counties wants us," offered Sam.

"Yeah, maybe. But there are more eligible bachelors in these counties than you. And no self-respecting woman would have the likes of you two after finding out your first sexual encounter was forced onto two teenage slaves. Think about it, dummies." Pathgo replied in disgust. "What you did last week may have cost you a chance to get a real woman and me grandchildren. The Pathgo line may stop with you two idiots. Slaves will be the only piece of ass you will ever get. And I'll be damned if I have nigga grandchildren."

"What will we do, Pa?" Jim pushed.

"Nothing for now. Let's let things die down. But we will stop all actions against those slaves. Don't want the sheriff to come back out here anytime soon." Pathgo stated, moving back to the chair and staring out the window. "But when the time comes, the sheriff will be sorry he even thought about pushing us around."

Chapter 13 — Murder

"Well thank you for the meal, Mrs. Gentry. But, I have to be on my way back to town. It is getting late you see," gleamed Sheriff Witt after another Sunday meal with Mrs. Gentry and the sisters. He rose from the table eying the last piece of Laurona's apple pie.

Laurona understood the look.

"Go on and take it with you, Sheriff. It is not doing any good here with three people eying it." She picked up the pie and wrapped it in a red and white-checkered handkerchief. You can bring the wrapping back next week when you come for dinner."

The sheriff just watched as Laurona wrapped the pie.

"Well Lou Anne, you must've been reading my mind. How'd you know I wanted that piece of pie?" His face turned red with embarrassment.

"Now Sheriff, we go through this every week. I do declare, I think my sister cuts the pie that way so we can go through this every Sunday," interjected Nausona. "Besides, we are happy you can make it out here every Sunday. It gets kind of lonely with just us women."

The sheriff had to smile at that. For as long as he could remember, he had never thought of blacks as anything but slaves. But here he was, coming to Sunday dinner, prepared by blacks. Not only did he eat the dinner, he was eating at the table with them—something two years back he would have spurned. But there was a special grace with these two—something he could not quite identify. It must be something special, because whatever it was, it made him stand up to the most powerful man in the county a short four months ago. He still could not believe he challenged Mr. Pathgo over two slaves. Either they were witches and had cast a spell on him or he had lost his mind. Whichever the case, standing up to Mr. Pathgo made him feel something he never felt. It gave him a special feeling. It made him feel like a man.

The sheriff took the piece of pie from Laurona and looked up at her and her sister. They were standing next to each other near the cutting table. He stared just for a moment, but in that brief glance his mind developed several thoughts.

For the first time he noticed the girls' big round eyes, how the outside corners etched to a sharp point—and how their eyes' hazel coloring seemed to sparkle as they smiled. Their auburn hair, somewhat redder than one would suspect for a slave, even one who was mixed with white, so wavy and shiny, framed the unique coloring of their skin. And finally, their five foot—six inch muscular frame dared to command respect—a respect he gave freely and without hesitation. He had stopped thinking of these girls as slaves. He had begun thinking of them as people. This was dangerous for a lawman in Virginia, and he knew it. But these girls, so pretty, so innocent and somewhat naïve had been through so much since they settled here with Mrs. Gentry. His heart bled for them—but, why? Why should he care for slaves? He was better than the slave; at least that is what he had learned since birth. But when he looked into these girls' eyes, he knew he wasn't better. He even knew he wasn't equal to them. Something about them made them almost royalty. He shook his head at the thought.

"What's the matter Sheriff?" Mrs. Gentry asked.

"Nothing, Mrs. Gentry—nothing at all." He smiled and put on his hat as he made his way to the door.

Nausona flanked him on the right and Laurona on the left. Sheriff Witt felt a little uneasy for the first time during these Sunday dinners.

"Well, goodnight ladies. I'll see you next Sunday."

Mrs. Gentry nodded and the girls moved to the porch banister to sit, as they always did when the sheriff left. Sheriff Dan Witt mounted his horse and gave one more tip of his hat as he galloped away from the house.

"You know, I am starting to like that sheriff," Nausona murmured to her sister in Chaktun. "I mean he and Mrs. Gentry saved us from the whip and he got those Pathgos to leave us alone."

"Yeah, I guess not all the white folks around here are bad. But remember, no matter how well they treat us, we are still just slaves in their eyes—even the sheriff's," her sister countered.

"Now Laurona, how different is the way we are treated than the way we treated our staff back in the palace. Now that I think about it, we weren't always nice to our people. I dare say we treated them like slaves at times ourselves."

"That was different. Our staff was not slaves, they were...they were our staff. They were paid for their time. They had homes and family to go to at the end of their shift. And we did not separate them from their fathers, mothers, sisters or brothers. We weren't barbaric in our dealings with the staff."

"Yes, dear sister. We weren't barbaric in our dealings with the staff, but can you say we were civilized?"

Nausona's comments made her sister freeze in her thoughts.

Once she was satisfied she had made her point, Nausona jumped off the banister and headed for the kitchen to help Mrs. Gentry clean up.

Laurona sat silent watching the sun set as she contemplated her sister's words. Was she that bad? Did she treat people unfairly? She said a silent prayer to Jus. With a heavy heart and painful memories, she asked Jus to get them back home. When she returned home she would ensure her people were free from the tyranny of the Kulusks and she would make certain all people were treated fairly. Being a slave had opened her eyes. There were more things she was ashamed about in her past than proud.

Osguards: Homecoming

Maybe this was Jus' punishment for her childhood actions. She prayed to Jus. She had accepted her punishment, but it was time for her to go home now. With that thought, a tear formed in the corner of her right eye and flowed down her cheek. She wiped it, took a deep breath and joined her sister in the kitchen.

***

The sheriff was deep in thought. He had traveled home this way many Sundays before, and his horse knew the way home by memory. The sheriff continued to wonder why he was so enamored with the sisters. He was not sexually drawn to them, and he sure was not drawn to them as women. But something begged at his soul to see no harm came to them. But what, he could not tell. Finally, he just decided to accept it. He was riding high over his victory over Pathgo, and he felt good about that. Then he heard a rifle volley and moments later a sharp pain tore through his left shoulder. The force blew him off his horse and he fell striking his head on the ground. The sheriff's world turned black as he crashed into unconsciousness.

The sheriff awoke with a splash of water on his face. The cold water stung at first, but he soon forgot it as the pain in his shoulder reminded him of its presence. The sheriff spit water from his mouth.

"What the hell?"

The sheriff attempted to focus on the two figures standing over him but could not make them out in the dark of the evening. Then a torch highlighted his assailants' faces. It was Sam and Jim Pathgo. The sheriff tried to get up off the ground, but found his hands bound behind him and his feet tied together.

"Well looky here, Sam. Our nigga loving sheriff is awake."

"Well Sheriff, did you just come from having you a piece of nigga ass? Or do you get to do both of them at the same time?" Sam giggled.

Jim looked at his brother.

"You know Sam; I think the French call that—ménage a trois." Then he turned to the sheriff with an evil grin, "You know, Sheriff, I believe me and my brother are jealous. We just got to do one nigga bitch. You get to do two at the same time—the same niggas we did. Now why is that? You must be a better man than us. Oh! That's right. You told my daddy real men don't do that sort of stuff with slaves."

The sheriff started to forget the pain in his shoulder and began focusing his fury at the two brothers. The sheriff's mind searched for options—options to escape or at least get at one of his two attackers. His mind was racing, but no answer came to him.

"Sheriff, you know I should be mad at you for telling daddy what we did to those niggas," Sam interjected. "I mean, it was none of your business—now was it?"

The sheriff did not respond.

"Oh Jim, I think he's scared."

Sam then pulled the sheriff to his knees. The sheriff looked up and saw a noose hanging from a tree.

"Oh yeah Sheriff, that's for you. We figure you like niggas so much, you would want to be like a nigga. And what is the best way to be like a nigga than to die like a nigga?"

"Help...someone...help," the sheriff screamed in fear, turning to see if anyone was traveling the road.

"Shit Sheriff, ain't no one out here can hear you. You might as well just shut up and take this like a man," Jim pushed. "Oops, I forgot. You aren't a real man. You're doing two nigga bitches, and real men don't do that."

"Pathgo, you are crazy. You won't get away with this," the sheriff yelled as he struggled to be released. "I haven't touched those girls. I tell you, I haven't touched them. You are the sick bastards who get pleasure from raping little girls—not me."

"Girls? Did you call them girls, sheriff? They're slaves, not girls—they're slaves you poor dumb bastard. No wonder...Mrs. Gentry has just confused the shit out of you. You can't tell the difference between a slave and a girl. You can only rape a girl...you can't rape a slave. Damn it. Are you a white man or not?" Sam berated.

"Sam, he ain't a white man. That's why we are here—to kill this nigga parading around like a white man."

Jim lifted the sheriff to his feet, and pushed him toward his horse. The brothers pulled the noose over his head and pushed the sheriff onto the horse. The sheriff struggled with them, but the pain in his shoulder was too immense. The sheriff had lost too much blood and became faint as the brothers moved him onto the horse. He tried to kick the horse to go, but Sam held the reigns and the horse remained in place. The sheriff tried to jump off the horse but found he could not move without putting stress on the noose. Jim went to the rear of the horse and Sam moved to the front.

Sam pulled out a piece of paper and read from it.

"Sheriff, you have been found guilty by a jury of your peers of cohabitating with the nigga. Your sentence is death by hanging to be carried out immediately. Signed Phillip Pathgo." Sam folded the paper and returned it to his vest pocket. "I think that just about does it—don't you big brother?"

"Yep, I think it does." Jim concluded.

Sheriff Witt realized he was going to die. His heart filled with fear. His mind raced to find options. There were no options. Just a few short minutes ago, he was having dinner at the Gentry farm with Mrs. Gentry and the girls. He thought the world was right. He thought he was on top of it all. Now he was going to die. The Pathgo brothers were going to hang him and he could not do anything about it. At that thought, the sheriff's fear resolved into anger—anger at the brothers, anger at their father, anger he did not see this coming. His mind flashed to the last conversation he had with Nausona and Laurona. It was a pleasant conversation. But he was somewhat harsh with them for trying to teach him their language. Now he wished he wasn't. He glared at Sam holding the horse in front of him, "Loa tra mae ter, Nausona tae Laurona."

Jim looked up at the back of the sheriff's head, "Goodbye you nigga loving bastard." Then he gave the horse a slap on the rear. The horse bolted, leaving its master in place. The sheriff fell, his feet hanging two inches from the ground. His eyes bulged as he attempted to gasp for air. The fall did not snap his neck. That would have been quick and painless. The brothers did not want that. They wanted to see the sheriff's life drain from him. The brothers moved in front of the sheriff to gloat. The sheriff's face turned pink, then red and then to blue in a matter of five minutes. During this time he kicked and flailed to loosen the rope so his feet would touch the ground, which was still a mere two inches from his toes. However, the rope did not budge and the sheriff could not breathe. He gave a valiant effort, but this only made a better show for the brothers. They laughed and made faces at the sheriff, imitating his distortion as he fought for his life. Eventually, the sheriff realized it was a losing battle. He stopped struggling. He did not want to give the brothers any more satisfying moments during his death.

His mind became cloudy, his thoughts incoherent. His last thoughts were of Nausona and Laurona standing in the kitchen with their radiant smile and shimmering hazel eyes. He produced a smile as the image began to fade. The image faded into blackness, then nothing. Sheriff Daniel Stephen Witt was gone.

"What the hell was that?" Sam asked. "Why the hell did he smile like that in the end? And what the hell did he say? Did he put a curse on us?"

"Don't know," Jim shrugged. "Maybe he repented for his sins and God took him." Jim stared at the smile frozen on the sheriff's face. "Maybe we did a good thing today and made this boy's salvation."

"I guess…but it sure was scary."

Chapter 14—Pick-Up

"Oh dear!" Mrs. Gentry exclaimed while looking out the kitchen window toward the creek.

"What's the matter Mrs. Gentry?" Laurona asked.

"There is a light by the creek," Mrs. Gentry replied.

The lantern glowing at a certain bend in the creek was a sign she had freight to pick up—runaway slaves. This was the signal the runaways were instructed to use at the last station. Each station along the route knew only the signal for the pick up for the next station. Mrs. Gentry did not know where the previous station was or where the next station was located. All she knew was there was no conductor between the station before her or between her and the next station.

She would check the creek every night for the signal once she received word there was freight on the railroad. The word would come from the grocer in town when she went for her weekly supplies. Once she saw the signal, Mrs. Gentry would walk down by the creek as if to retrieve some water. While she did this, she would check to ensure it was not a trap. If it were, she would explain she was just going to the creek for water. Fortunately, she never had to use this excuse. Once she was sure it was not a trap, she would hum a song letting the slaves know she was the contact. Then she would gather them and hide them in her secret cellar.

Usually, the slaves would spend one night in the cellar and move on to the next station the following night. Mrs. Gentry would instruct them to follow the creek until they came to an abandoned cabin on top of a hill. They were to stay at the creek until they were sure no one had followed. Then they were to light the lantern. There a conductor would contact them. They would know the conductor because he or she would hum a song. Then she would hum it for them until she was sure they understood the instructions. She would release the slaves at nightfall. Then she would pray all night for their safe journey.

She knew the slaves at the creek were depending on her. She had to go. She shrugged and started to walk to her room to retrieve a shawl. Then she coughed. She started to feel dizzy. She grabbed the back of a wooden kitchen chair to catch her balance. Nausona grabbed her left arm to help steady her.

"Mrs. Gentry, you can't go out there. It is wet and cold this evening," Nausona preached. She turned to her sister for support.

"That's right, Mrs. Gentry, you can't go out there. You will catch your death in this weather," Laurona offered.

"Well someone has to get them," she insisted, taking a seat in the chair.

"We will go get them," prompted Nausona.

Her sister flashed a terrifying look at her. Nausona blazed her most serious look back. Laurona was not pleased. She came forward to speak, but Nausona cut her off with a shake of her index finger. Laurona closed her mouth and stepped back

"Right, dear sister. We can get whoever is out there."

"Yes, I suppose we can."

"No, I won't allow it. The last time you went out at night…" Mrs. Gentry's voice trailed off. "Well, you know what happened. I can't stand to see you get hurt again." She looked down and tears formed in her eyes. "I don't know if it is a trap or not. With the sheriff gone, we have no one to help us against Pathgo."

"Don't worry, Mrs. Gentry. We can handle ourselves," Laurona interjected, patting the pagenay hidden under her vest. "Last time we weren't expecting it. That will never happen again. I promise. It will never happen again."

Mrs. Gentry felt too tired to argue anymore. She coughed again. This time the cough pained her so; she grabbed her chest in agony. She closed her eyes while clutching her chest. She took a long moment before she even attempted to breathe again.

"Perhaps you are right. I do not feel well enough to make it to the door, let alone to the creek."

"Then it's settled," Nausona ordered. "You stay here, watch us if you must, through the window. But you will stay here, no matter what. Do you understand?"

"Now what gives you the right to bark orders young lady," Gentry murmured. "Don't you know who is…"

Laurona knew Mrs. Gentry was going to say *the master*. This would validate her side of the argument with her sister when she said it.

"—the oldest?" Mrs. Gentry finished.

Laurona's jaw dropped. She was so sure Mrs. Gentry would invoke she was the master and the girls were the slaves. But it did not happen. Mrs. Gentry had yet to invoke that sentiment to them. Now, even when she was sick, she didn't do it.

"I am old enough to be your grandmother you know."

Laurona took the line to heart. Mrs. Gentry had always acted accordingly. She started to realize it wasn't Mrs. Gentry who was tainted; it was she who had been tainted by the system they stepped into. Laurona turned to see her sister glare at her with judgmental eyes.

"Mrs. Gentry, we would be proud to have you as our grandmother. But I don't think Pathgo would agree," Laurona stated without realizing she said it out loud.

"Mr. Pathgo can go to hell, for all I care!" Mrs. Gentry said summoning up more strength than she realized she had to shout the words at the top of her frail lungs. "Y'all be careful. Come back to me, my dears."

"We will," promised Laurona.

Nausona nodded in agreement.

***

93

The sisters ensured they had their pagenays. They placed them in the front binding of their skirts and wrapped shawls around their shoulders to conceal their pagenays. They stuck their mations in the cuff of their boot, which was covered by their flower print skirts. They looked at each other and nodded to Mrs. Gentry as they left by the back door.

They did not bother to cover their tracks. This was the land they had lived on for over a year and they had every lawful right to walk to the creek for whatever reason. The futuristic weapons they carried bolstered their feeling of invincibility. In fact, both sisters wanted it to be a trap.

Bitterness and anger had haunted their hearts since they arrived on this god forsaken planet. The white people were not Kulusks, but they had come to resent them as if they were Kulusks—maybe they resented them more than Kulusks. At least the Kulusks would kill you like a human being; unlike the whites on this planet, who'd rather kill you like an animal. Not just an animal, but kill you like an ant. Well, these ants had weapons to kill them and the sisters were more than ready to use them.

With every step, the rage burned like an internal inferno in their souls. The twins thought of their whipping at the Pathgo Plantation, their rapes and the murder of the sheriff. These thoughts consumed them more than any thought of the Kulusks or their own parents' murder. Revenge lurked in their minds—sweet and bitter at the same time. It was the type of revenge, which could only be quenched by the taking of another life—the type of revenge that blinded their sense of morality—the type of revenge that pushed them to the darker side of their personality. The girls smelled it, tasted it, and damn near could touch it.

"You know, Nausona, what I am thinking."

"Hell yes, I know what you are thinking. You want this to be a trap, so we can kill the bastards."

"That's right!"

"Well…you aren't alone…you're not alone," she said allowing the words to settle in the cool night air.

The sisters reached the creek and knelt at the water's edge as if to wash their faces. Then Nausona began to hum the pre-arranged song. Laurona reached into her dress binding and fingered her pagenay. She ensured the safety was off and it was ready to fire. Then she heard a noise in the brush behind them. Laurona swung around to her left with the pagenay in her right hand and aimed at the shadow. Nausona swung to her right and dropped to one knee, aiming her pagenay at the same shadow. The shadow remained still in the night.

"Identify yourself, now!" commanded Laurona.

The shadow remained still. Then a light shone to their left. Laurona trained her pagenay to the left at the light. Her sister stilled her pagenay on the original shadow. The light moved into the lantern and the lantern illuminated the holder. It was a dark skinned black female. She had her hair wrapped in a cloth and she wore a tattered white skirt and yellow blouse.

"Don't hurt us. We told to come here," the female murmured.

The sisters took a moment to assemble their thoughts. Laurona lowered her pagenay and motioned for her sister to do the same. They both concealed their pagenays into their skirt bindings. Nausona rose.

"Yes, you are in the right place," she replied.

"How many do you have with you?" asked Laurona.

The first shadow spoke. It was the deep voice of a man hardened by labor and broken by a whip.

"It is just me, my wife, and my son."

The man stood five foot eight inches tall, with no shirt and cutoff brown pants. Neither he nor the woman wore shoes or sandals. From the right, the bushes shook as a little boy, merely four years old, stepped out. He wore nothing but a pair of cutoff black pants held around his waist with a piece of rope. The boy and the woman moved toward the man as he motioned for them to come closer.

"Great! We need to go now," commanded Nausona, motioning them to follow her.

Nausona took the lead, followed by the man, the child, and then the woman. Laurona took the trail position. Each sister fingered their pagenays as they walked. They knew they were not out of danger yet. In fact, they invited danger for the same reasons they wanted the rendezvous to be a trap.

They did not conceal their movement to the house. They walked straight and tall to the house, hoping—no praying, someone would see them so they could use their weapons and kill. They did not speak to the slaves, and the slaves did not speak to them. When they reached the house, they assumed caution and moved inside.

The slaves were astonished they were entering the house. Up until now, they were hidden in barns, stables and abandoned cabins. But they never entered a home as magnificent as this. In the light of the kitchen, Laurona noticed the large welts on the man's back. They were the mark of a brutal whipping. Then she saw the welts on the boys back. He too had been whipped. She caught the attention of her sister. She motioned for her to look at their backs. The feeling of compassion and pain distorted Nausona's face.

Nausona's mind flashed back to the one whipping her and her sister received. She thought these people must have endured many whippings as slaves. She had not known what it felt like to be a slave. She never did a slave's job. The work she did around the Gentry farm was of her own free will. It was an unspoken agreement to pay Mrs. Gentry for room, board and rations. She understood it almost as a military obligation of sorts. She felt ashamed for letting the feelings of revenge consume her earlier. If anyone deserved revenge, it was this family.

Malcolm Dylan Petteway

The man had taken his punishment as a slave, but the boy…who would be so harsh and devoid of a soul to take a whip to a little child? The reality of it was that Laurona and Nausona were only two people on a barbaric planet. They could not change it. Just last year Laurona was willing to change a universe, now she was scared to change a planet. How ironic. She and her sister would confront an entire planet bent on total universal domination, but they were scared to challenge a Spartan culture bent on enslaving her kind.

Nausona led the family to the parlor and down into the cellar. She then returned to the kitchen to bring their guests some dinner. Mrs. Gentry had gained enough strength to prepare their plates. There, she saw Laurona deep in thought.

"Laurona, are you okay?"

Laurona emerged out of her deep thought and just stared at her sister.

"We do not belong here," she offered. "But Jus has put us here for a reason. Why?"

"I don't know," shrugged her sister. "And I doubt if we will ever know. At least not until we die," she countered. "But I tell you this much. I don't think it is a punishment. Jus put us here to go through this for a reason. I think it is to make us stronger for when we return to our world."

"Do you think we will ever return to our world?"

"I haven't given up hope yet, sister. Not yet." Nausona picked up two plates. "Are you going to help or not?"

Her sister nodded and picked up the third plate and a pitcher of water, and they made their way to the cellar.

After the family ate, Nausona and Laurona stayed in the cellar with them. They asked them about their slave life. The girls listened to the parents as they told their stories. They could not reveal where they came from, but they had no aversion in revealing the painful life they left. The girls learned firsthand of the backbreaking hard labor, poor living conditions, whippings and killings, and the most heartbreaking was the story of how their parents were sold when they were smaller. The mother told how she was responsible for the washing for the master's family, while her husband picked cotton in the fields all day. The most surprising story was about their jealousy between the house niggas—as they called them—and the field niggas.

The fact the family considered the sisters to be house niggas almost became an insult to them. However, they kept everything in perspective. The family talked the evening away with the sisters participating as a captive audience. Finally, the adventures of escaping caught up to them; and they were too weary to continue. The sisters relinquished the evening back to them.

Laurona looked at the sleeping child. He had slept through the entire conversation. He was tired. Then she noticed a drawing the child did in the dirt. It looked strangely familiar. *No. It could not be*, she thought to herself.

"Nausona, look at that." She pointed to the drawing. "What do you make of that?"

"It looks like a Kulusk gate portal." She paused to take a closer look at it. "Do you think?"

"Could be."

Nausona tapped the father on the shoulder, "Did you ever see that before?"

"Yes'm, it was in the cave we stayed at last night."

"Where was this cave?"

"Not suppose to tell. Rules of the Underground Railroad."

"Listen, it is important to us to get this metal box. It…it is a special box," Laurona pleaded.

"No, can't tell. Swore not to tell," he persisted.

"Listen, it is really, really important for us to get to this box," Nausona insisted.

"Why?"

Nausona thought about it. Then she pulled out her pagenay. She chose a rock on the dirt floor.

"Stand back."

She shot a short blast. The blue beam exploded the rock into sand. The boy bolted up, but did not know why. He looked at his parents and the sisters and determined all was still right. He lay down and fell back asleep.

"I think you better sit down. You told us your story, it is about time we told you our story. But first, I have to swear you to secrecy."

The husband and wife nodded. The sisters sat back down and told them their story. The husband and wife hung on every word. When the sisters were finished the husband and wife chuckled.

"You don't believe us?" queried Nausona

"No, that was good story. I will tell my son that story some day," replied the father.

"What about the cave?" urged Nausona.

The father thought awhile then looked at his wife. His wife nodded.

"That such good story," the father said standing to stretch his legs.

He swung around to the sisters. They were looking at him with hunger in their eyes. Not the kind of hunger for food, but the hunger for knowledge. The father still could not explain how their weapons destroyed the rock. Then uncertainty entered his heart. He turned back toward the wall. Could they be telling the truth? Could they really be from another planet? He was just a slave—a runaway slave. He did not pretend to even understand nature or anything in nature. But the gun was scary. That gun was powerful.

Soon fear replaced the uncertainty in his heart. Then slowly jubilation, of the thought they could be telling the truth, replaced the fear. Negroes with that power, even if they weren't from Earth, gave him hope. The thought gave him pride, something he had not felt since the birth of his son. The father looked again at his wife. She again nodded in the affirmative. Obviously, she had reached the same conclusion.

"I will tell you," he blurted. He spun to face the princesses. He lowered his eyes, "Cave on creek, next to big white house on plantation."

"You mean it is on the Pathgo Plantation?"

"No, it's outside the plantation, by bend in road."

"I think that is where they found the sheriff's body. If you take a left you go to the Pathgo Plantation, if you go right, you go to town," pieced Laurona.

"Thank you, you have been very helpful," replied Nausona.

Armed with the new information, the sisters left the slave family to rest. The family would have another long night ahead of them. They needed to rest. The beauty of the situation was the family could sleep during the day, unlike the sisters, who had chores to accomplish. However, the lack of sleep did not bother them. They knew the location of the one piece of equipment, which could get them home, or at least off this planet. They knew where the gate portal was located. This information energized them throughout the day. A joyous smile remained on their faces—a smile, Mrs. Gentry could not explain and was too happy of its existence to try to explain. The girls were happy; therefore, Mrs. Gentry was happy.

The slaves left for the rest of their journey that evening. The mother and father hugged the sisters and they shared a smile amongst themselves. Mrs. Gentry realized the smile indicated a secret between them, a secret they could not or would not share with her.

Mrs. Gentry passed on the instructions to the runaways. Once she was satisfied they understood the instructions, she let the sisters take them back to the creek. Again, the sisters carried their weapons, and again the sisters wished for an ambush. The ambush did not occur and the sisters were somewhat disappointed. They watched as the family disappeared into the night. Then they returned to the house with plans to visit the cave the next day.

Chapter 15—The Discovery

The cave entrance was covered with vines and leaves. It stood on the east side of the creek, about fifty feet from the creek. One could not see it from the road some one hundred yards away on the west side of the creek. One could not even see it standing directly in front of it on the west bank of the creek. The entrance was about five feet tall and three feet wide. It had another rock, about four feet in diameter sitting two feet in front of the entrance. It made a perfect hiding place in plain sight of all the activity in the area.

"I think I see it," motioned Nausona as she waded in the creek to move to the east side. They had been searching for the cave since sunrise. This was dangerous, for they were not on the Gentry farm and if seen, could be considered runaways. They told Mrs. Gentry they would be down by the creek, washing. They left the house three hours ago. But, hopefully the gate portal was operational and they could leave as soon as they found it.

Nausona's heart jumped at the prospect. Especially now that she thought she found the entrance to the cave. She stepped onto the east side of the creek and peered in the direction of the black hole. Her sister rushed to her. The exhilaration of the hunt drove the adrenalin throughout their entire bodies. Nausona's heart throbbed inside her chest. She could feel it beating. She could almost hear it beating as she drifted toward the rocks. She squinted as if this could give her X-ray vision and she would be able to see through the rocks. Laurona moved to her side and grabbed Nausona's left arm with both her hands.

"I hope this is it," Laurona pleaded. "We've been out here all morning. Someone is bound to catch us out here."

"Be quiet or you will give us bad luck," her sister ordered. "Besides, don't you think it is time we start having good luck?"

They stopped at the foot of the smaller rock in front of the cave. Laurona moved to the left of the rock and Nausona moved to the right of the rock. They pressed to the opening. Nausona reached into the entrance with her right hand and pushed the vines to the right. At the same time, Laurona reached into the darkness with her left hand and pushed the vines to the left.

"After you," Laurona directed.

Nausona shot an edgy glare at her sister, "Why thank you…I think."

Nausona bent down and stepped inside the hole, followed by Laurona. Once inside, the sisters stood erect next to each other. It was a big cavern, disguised by the grassy hill, covering the rocks outside. However it was too dark to see anything. Laurona struck a match against the cavern wall. The small light did not illuminate the cavern much, but it allowed the sisters to guide their steps. They again walked side-by-side, moving deeper into the cavern one step at a time. Laurona noticed items of old, tattered clothing sprayed around as they stepped on and over them. She knew they were at the right place. The clothes were remnants from runaway slaves traveling the Underground Railroad.

Malcolm Dylan Petteway

A slight smile emerged on Laurona's face as she thought *if only Mr. Pathgo knew how close the runaways were staying to his plantation. It would kill him.* The irony of the cave's location tickled her imagination.

The match started to burn her finger. She dropped it as the heat scorched her fingertips. She retrieved another and lit it. She noticed what appeared to be steps. She and her sister followed the steps up. They were still unable to see more than a couple of feet in front of them. They groped their way through the darkness. Laurona thought the cave made a perfect hideaway.

A cave! Of course—a cave! This was how the Kulusks operated in those days. For some strange reason, their gate portals were always in natural caverns. The gate portal they used to get here was in a cavern. She should have thought of it earlier. The gate portal would not be in a man-made structure unless it had to be—like the underwater station. Something about the aura of caverns made the Kulusks feel better about using the gate portal. It could be religious, superstitious or they thought it was necessary to build them in caverns. For whatever reason, Laurona felt stupid for not thinking about it earlier.

"There it is," whispered her sister.

Laurona looked up and saw the outline of the chamber control pad in the flickering light of the match. Nausona raced to the pad and pushed some buttons. The pad barely lit up at first. However in three minutes it sprang to life.

"Thank Jus, for Asher power cells. The power generated by Asher jell lasts forever," Laurona commented.

"Yes, that is why these gate portals can still hum, I guess," her sister added, stroking the pad "Let me run a diagnostic on this thing."

She watched the ARIT readout. She shook her head at every line that came across the screen. The ARIT reported to her immense mechanical failures. Nausona knew that all this time on the surface with the hot wet climate and without continued maintenance had caused the mechanics of the gate portal to degrade. But what the ARIT was reporting appeared to be an entire systems failure—one hundred and twenty errors. The Inner to Outer space relay converter was shot; the coordinate slide lifts were inoperable; the signal finder and signal booster were damaged; the ARIT database program was corrupt and the Asher power jell pack in the Asher power cells for the actual gate portal was contaminated. In other words, even if they could fix the errors, there was no power to operate the gate portal itself.

Laurona looked over her sister's shoulder and reviewed the laundry list of repairs required. However, when she read that the Asher power jell pack was contaminated, she cringed. "Just great. How the hell are we supposed to use this thing," she cried stomping her feet on the dirt ground.

"One thing at a time sister. Let's see if we can repair these other things first."

"Why? I mean, what's the use?"

"If we have to, we can convert the particle generators in our pagenays to give us a one time power supply for the gate," Nausona informed her.

"Do you think that would work?"

"Don't know, but we have to try something."

"Nausona, if it does not work, we are stuck on this planet with only our mations for defense," Laurona added. She turned her sister around so their eyes would meet. "Do you understand what that means?"

Nausona nodded and her eyes swelled, "Yes, I know what it means."

"Well, shut her down. We need to get back before Mrs. Gentry gets too upset," shrugged Laurona. "Plus, we have to come up with a plan of attack to fix this system."

"Okay, let's go."

"Fine, but let me get a few things. Maybe we can work on them at the house," smiled Nausona, picking up parts from the chamber's outer hull.

Then she grabbed the portable ARIT (PARIT) still attached to the main ARIT.

"Let me download the diagnostic information. It will help us devise a plan." She pushed two buttons on the main console and watched as the lights danced. A small tone signaled the transfer was complete. "Now I am ready."

The sisters peered out the cave to make sure no one was outside. Once satisfied, they made their way out and proceeded to the Gentry farm.

***

Here they come. Mrs. Gentry thought to herself as she spotted the sisters from the rear kitchen window. Where could they have been all this time? They had been gone for over five hours. They did not do any of their chores this morning. They did not even do their ritual in the barn.

Since the sisters had been living with Mrs. Gentry, they always rose before the sun and went into the barn. They stayed there for two to three hours every day. Even after their two brushes with death, the girls had to go into the barn. At first Mrs. Gentry respected their privacy. But after two months her curiosity got the best of her. She had followed them one morning and watched as they sat on their knees and performed some kind of meditation ritual. They continued the ritual for about an hour.

Then they would get up and perform a poetic motion of kicks and punches. The beauty of their motion reminded her of ballerina dancers. However, there was something different about their motions. The energy of their movements was not to elicit passion, but to elicit pain. The sharp kicks, the deadening punches, and the exuberance in their faces demonstrated the ability to kill or maim without thought or hesitation. No wonder they had no fear gathering up the runaways that night. Were these girls dangerous or just different?

Yes, they were different and dangerous. They weren't regular slaves and Mrs. Gentry suspected as much. Every time Mrs. Gentry questioned the girls about their past, they would evade the question or change the subject. Mrs. Gentry wanted to know why they could not speak English when they first arrived. All slaves knew English. They had to be slaves who were born in America. They could not have been straight from Africa. Congress had abolished the slave trade almost fifty-two years ago, and these girls were much younger than that.

Some unscrupulous native could have smuggled the girls in from Africa in the hopes of selling them. They could have escaped. They could have eluded the authorities until they stumbled onto her farm. There were many things they could have done. But what was the truth? Why wouldn't they confide in her? Was the truth so horrible, so horrific that it could not be told? But when Mrs. Gentry asked, the girls would just admit they weren't from Africa—no other explanation offered.

Furthermore, their language—what was the language they spoke? Was it the language of an African tribe? It could not be anything else. It was not European. It had to be African. They even attempted to teach her and the sheriff a few words after their Sunday meals.

Then her mind drifted to the sheriff. He had been dead for almost two months now—not just dead, murdered. Pathgo, his sons, or all three had murdered her friend. Those dirty bastards murdered the one true friend she had—over what? Was it because he dared challenge them? Was it because he sided with her on some issue concerning slaves in the area? What was it that made Pathgo want to kill the sheriff? And what was it that made the county citizens look the other way? They murdered the sheriff and no one cared. No one questioned it. No one demanded justice. What could make normal decent people accept the murder of a man who just wanted to help them? It had to be hate spawned from bigotry against the girls…those sweet young innocent girls. Now the girls were her only friends in the world. They had both adored the girls. Now she was the only one left—the only one left to protect and nurture two Negro children.

They were so…so…innocent. They knew nothing of the South. They did not understand slavery. They knew nothing of the country or the land. Many nights, she stayed up with them, answering their questions, teaching them about the South, the North, slavery, the white man and the Negro. They drank the information like cool water on a hot summer day. They never grew tired of learning. They fought to understand. But understand what? They were slaves? Or were they? They carried themselves with poise and dignity, an air of sophistication. Something she never noticed in a Negro before. They carried themselves so well she forgot they were Negro.

She felt ashamed at that thought. It should not matter if they were Negro or not. They were human, and as humans, they were her sisters according to the Bible. That was the philosophy she always tried to live by, but it was hard. It was hard not to fall in the trap laid by the southern bureaucracy. The feeling that the Negro was not human, but a wild animal put on Earth to help the true man, the white man, live the life God intended him to, was one of two schools of thought Mrs. Gentry had to contend with.

The other was amply called the *'White Man's Burden,'* the belief that it was the white man's burden, given by God, to save the world's heathens and bring them to Christianity. This included the African slaves and the Indians out west. She tried not to succumb to either thought, but she always leaned to the latter in her actions. Deep down inside she knew she was no better than the Indians she knew in the Kansas territory then or the Negro slave now. Albeit, she was at a better station in life than them, she was not better. But, no matter how hard she thought it, how many times she reminded herself of it, she found herself acting holier than thou amongst them.

Not so, with these girls. She really felt a kinship with them. She felt a sisterhood, a mother-daughter relationship. Yet she did not know if the girls felt the same kinship with her. She was afraid to let them know. She was afraid to ask. She had lost two children before. Losing these girls would make things worse. Therefore, she lived as if it didn't matter how they felt. But it mattered. It really mattered how they felt and what they did. Why else would she wait at the window this long to ensure their safety? Why else indeed?

She watched as the girls went into the barn and retrieved their tools. She watched as they began their chores. She watched as if nothing happened. She watched as if the day had just begun, and the five hours they were away did not matter. Would she ask them about it? She paused at that thought for several minutes. Then she decided, no. They would confide in her when the time is right. Obviously it was not time yet. But when they did, she would be ready.

Chapter 16—Daily Chores

The morning sun shone through the sisters' bedroom window. Their bedroom faced the east and was the first part of the house to greet the daylight. Mrs. Gentry's bedroom was in the northwest corner of the farmhouse; therefore, she slept just a bit longer than her resident guests. Since her first bout with the flu, she had been taking her time rising in the morning. This suited the sisters, just fine. Mrs. Gentry would just get in the way for what they had planned.

The girls dressed and pushed outside to execute their morning chores. It was mid October and the morning air had a nip to it. The girls dressed warmly, each covering herself with a shawl. Laurona moved to the barn to milk Betsy, the one cow on the farm. Nausona headed to the henhouse to gather eggs for the morning breakfast. On her way back to the kitchen, Nausona met her sister carrying two pails of freshly gained milk. Laurona placed the milk in two pitchers, Nausona counted the eggs into a basket. Nausona then turned around and went back to the henhouse. She retrieved the bag of feed and poured the feed in the pen for the chickens to eat. Laurona retrieved the waste from last night's meal and went to feed the family of pigs in the stockyard. Laurona hated this job. She realized she was fattening up the pigs for an eventual meal. She felt as if she was betraying the trust the pigs put in her. She fed them and they liked her. They did not realize that one day she might be eating them over a fine Sunday meal. As cruel as that sounded, she knew it was the order of the nature of humans. *Humans were on top of the food chain*—so at least she comforted herself with the thought. *Therefore, all creatures on the planet...no, the universe, were subject to human will.*

Unfortunately, the white humans on this planet felt that philosophy applied to non-white humans as well. She thought *slaves were just like the pigs, being fed and kept ignorant of a better life and ignorant of their own self-awareness—only to be led to the slaughter later in life.*

The thought of where humans fit in the universe never occurred to her before, at least not before her incarceration on the prison planet. *All humans, even the Kulusks, should be treated with dignity and respect.* She almost gagged at the thought. But after she cleared her throat, she realized, it was true. *No one had the right to dictate another's destiny.* When she returned home, she would make that the first priority of business. She would not reign as the Maxim and she hoped her sister would not either. Instead they would share with the universe the enlightened spirit garnered during their stay on this prison planet. Security for all humans in their daily pursuit of survival must be assured. Humans must be free from tyranny, free to make their own destiny, not held from self-actualization and have their destiny pre-ordained by a despot. No human was a pig and no human would be treated as a pig when she returned home.

*When she returned home...*the notion of home was still foreign to her. But now she was ready. Ready to go home...Ready to take on the fight her and her sister ran away from almost two years ago. Then she realized she must hurry, if they wanted to work in the cave this morning.

***

Osguards: Homecoming

Nausona fed the chickens while her mind wandered also. She thought about their plight, but in a different way. She thought over the long talks they had with Mrs. Gentry in the evenings, listening to her attempt to explain slavery and why it was so. Slaves were an important element to the United States, particularly in the South. Slaves were essential to the economy and society in the South. It was all about greed—greed stemmed from the agricultural south—greed stemmed from trade. *Ah! There was the bad word in all of this—trade.* With an out of control trade practice, greed was allowed to run rampant.

Mrs. Gentry had said the first Africans landed in Jamestown in 1619 and were considered indentured servants with limited servitude. Once their servitude was completed, they enjoyed free status. Then the plantations sprung up in the South. Slaves became cheap labor. The South exported their agricultural goods, such as cotton, to Europe. And inventions like the so-called *'cotton gin'* did not help. The requirement for cheap labor became more demanding. The slaves became more important to the success of the South's agricultural base. Hence the slaves were critical to trade.

The legal status of the slaves was never defined in the early days. Therefore the country incorporated laws defining the slaves' legal, political and social status. They had none—at least very little. Whatever legal status was afforded the slaves; the masters were not compelled to respect them. Soon a person's station in life was dependent on the land they owned and the number of slaves working the land. The great southern tradition was built on the blood, sweat and tears of a people who could not enjoy the fruits of their labor.

Trade! What was trade? Trade could be constructive or destructive, depending on how one community participated in the endeavors. In the long run, humans only need to trade for what they need to survive. But humans weren't satisfied in just surviving, nor should they be. Humans needed growth, they needed evolution, and they needed to advance. *This was Jus' way. But how could a community grow as a society without trade or without economic stimulants? How could a community have trade and economic stimulants without oppressing or repressing a part of the community? There will always be the haves and the have-nots.*

Communal sharing wouldn't work. That experiment had been tried several times in Chaktun history. Human nature had always prevailed. Greed had always been the objective of wealth and wealth had always demanded greed. But the society they were now living in was the epitome of the lowest point on the oppression scale. Even the Kulusks in their greed had not practiced oppression. Unfortunately, the Kulusks murdered and exiled their enemies, such as to this prison planet, but they did not oppress them into submission in order to fulfill their own goals. *Greed in trade was wrong. There must be a better way.* She made a promise to herself as she fed the chickens. She promised that when she returned she would ensure free and open trade in the universe with non-oppressive societies.

She thought, *when oppressive societies saw they were not economically growing, because of their oppression, they would change to fit the universal concept of what society should be.* She would not force a change, but she would not deal with them either. However in order for it to work, she must build a community with which other societies would want to trade. How could she do that? How could she be discriminating with whom she traded and make her Chaktun attractive enough to necessitate other societies trading with her? How indeed?

She finished feeding the chickens. The morning chores took them about an hour. They packed a lunch and gathered their weapons and materials then set foot toward the cave as they had done every morning since they found the cave two weeks ago. The path had become too familiar. Nausona wondered if she could walk to the cave in her sleep.

As the sisters traveled, they shared their thoughts of the morning. Laurona shared her thoughts of a secure universe with her sister. Likewise, her sister shared her thoughts of free and open trading in the universe with Laurona. At first, the two ideas appeared mutually exclusive. But they talked on the long journey and soon discovered their ideas stemmed from the same observation—slavery. After this poignant discovery, the ideas seemed to meld together as mutually supportive. At the end of their conversation, the sisters made a pact to return to the Chaktun Republic of Planets and not pursue political rule, but to pursue a security and trade agreement amongst the planets. They suspected that a strong defensible economy, based on distinctive trade and inclusive participation, would heal the wounds inflicted by the Kulusks. They still had to find a way back home and build a military to expel the Kulusks out of Chaktun space—but one thing at a time; first, the chamber.

Chapter 17—Confrontation

"Well, well, well! What do I have here?" a voice bellowed from behind the girls.

They were so deep in their conversation they had a lapse in their situational awareness. They forgot to keep an eye and ear open for strangers as they usually did. Now, there was a strange voice behind them, or was it?

"Aren't you two off your master's land?" Mr. Pathgo asked.

The sisters turned to see Mr. Pathgo on his horse about ten yards behind them. Laurona shivered at the thought that they allowed him to get that close unnoticed. Nausona looked as if she could kick herself.

"Well, I guess since you are not with Mrs. Gentry and you are not on her property that makes you...let me see... Ah yes, that makes you," Pathgo paused with a slight grin. Then continued with fervor, "runaways."

The girls said nothing. Pathgo pulled out his saber and pointed it toward the girls.

"I ought to kill you right here," he continued. "But I have two sons, who will be real pleased to run you through with a knife—up close and personal. Start walking."

Pathgo motioned for them to cross the creek to the west bank and head toward his plantation. The girls did as they were told, both wondering what to do next.

"You two have been a pimple on my ass for far too long—a pimple itching to be scratched, but I could not do it in public for fear of embarrassment. Now I get to do it in private. God must be with me this morning. He delivered my enemies right to my door step." Pathgo shifted the saber into the other hand. "You know you should be dead by now. I sent my two boys to kill you six months ago. Those idiots! Instead I found out they fucked you," he hollered. "I sent those idiots to chop your damned heads off and bring them back to the compound, but they decided to fuck you—two nigga bitches. Well, now they get another chance."

Laurona rubbed her stomach as her eyes started to water. Nausona just scrunched her eyes at hearing the words flow from Pathgo's mouth with such ease.

He paused to spit. "Then that damned sheriff comes around and has the audacity to threaten me over my sons fucking you two. That idiotic sheriff." Pathgo looks around as if to see if anyone was around to hear him. "Thank God my idiot sons got that one right. I really didn't think they could kill him, but they did." He paused, thinking of how his wife, with her pious attitude had ruined his sons. Men were men, and they needed to release their sexual tension. Lord knew he had to every so often, even if it was not with his wife. "Thank God the sheriff wasn't a bitch too. My sons would have probably fucked him as well."

Laurona's eyes stopped watering and the vein in her neck popped. Anger swelled in her brain. She had imagined the crudeness of this man. But now that she was in his presence and witnessed the crudeness first hand, she was shocked. Pathgo had no remorse in his confession—he had no feeling of guilt. This man was truly evil. He was evil in spirit, thought and action.

Laurona still did not understand why she and her sister were such a threat to this man. What did they do that was so offensive to him? Was it just because they were Negro, or was it something else? Whatever it was, it did not compare to the offenses they had suffered because of him. If anyone deserved revenge, it was she and her sister. Maybe fate had brought this happenstance meeting. Maybe fate decided it was time to complete unfinished business. Maybe fate had a plan for them. Fate's plan was simple—kill Pathgo.

Pathgo drove the girls onto the road that led to his plantation. He wanted revenge. These girls had caused him more embarrassment than any other slave he could remember—embarrassment that was solely in his mind. Paranoid delusions that these girls could be some type of saviors as old woman Lilly stated also fed his fear of them. It was their African magic that somehow turned a good man into a fringed abolitionist. At least in his mind, that is what he thought the sheriff turned into after meeting these bitches. *Well the sheriff died like a nigga, hung from a roadside tree. In any case, he was able to take the dignity of dying like a white man from that fool,* his mind added.

"Funny, my sons said the sheriff said something in African as they hung him," gleamed Pathgo, surprised that he uttered his thoughts. Then he decided, why not. He was curious anyway. Plus, he felt the human need to brag about his involvement in the sheriff's death. "My sons said that he said, *'Loa tra mae ter, Nausona tae Laurona.'* Now what the hell does that mean?"

The sisters understood the words even with the crude southern accent. The words were Chaktun. But the beauty of the words was lost coming from Pathgo's evil spirited mouth. The words were part of the language lessons the sisters were teaching Mrs. Gentry and the sheriff after one of their Sunday meals. Words the sheriff said he would never use, even on his deathbed. But he used them as the Pathgo brothers hung him. Laurona felt touched by the dying gesture of someone she now realized was a friend. Nausona felt more remorse over his death. She knew it was their association with the sheriff that angered Pathgo into killing him.

"Those words," Nausona gulped. "Those words are Chaktun, our native tongue."

"Chaktun!" Pathgo said in surprise. "You mean the sheriff was talking in African. Damn! We should have killed him earlier," Pathgo stated.

The girls stopped in their tracks. Nausona saw her sister thumb for her pagenay. She did the same.

"Chaktun is not African," Laurona added. "It is the language of my people—my people from the planet Chaktun," she said listening for a response.

"What the hell!" Pathgo murmured.

He thought these bitches were surely crazy. His mind shifted through several thoughts in a split second. However all the thoughts completed with one resolution—*these niggas are too crazy to waste any more of my time.* They could not lead a horse to water, let alone lead a revolt. Why was he so obsessed with their demise? For a quick instance, he thought of letting them go. But that was replaced with the human feeling of self-preservation. He had just confessed to them about his involvement in the murder of the sheriff—a white man. If they told Mrs. Gentry, she may have enough pull in the county to get the new sheriff to investigate. He could not let that happen.

"We are not from here," Nausona pushed to get Pathgo's attention back in the conversation. "We are princesses from another world." She paused for a reaction. She did not hear one, so she spun around to see Pathgo grinning. Her sister also turned.

"The words the sheriff spoke before he died, they are Chaktun," Laurona persisted. "'Loa tra mae ter, Nausona tae Laurona' is Chaktun for 'Pleasure to be with you, Nausona and Laurona.' I am Laurona and this is my sister Nausona. In our language, those words are a pleasant and polite way to bid farewell. I thought it proper you knew that."

"Why do I care what your African names are, or what those words mean?" Pathgo argued.

"We told you, we are not African," persisted Nausona.

"Oh, you're African all right. This is some sort of trick. Well I am not falling for it," replied Pathgo, more agitated than angry now.

"This is not a trick. We are Chaktun, just as your grandchildren will be," Nausona shouted.

"My what?" Pathgo asked in shock.

"Your grandchildren," replied Laurona, pulling back her shawl to let Pathgo see she was pregnant. Nausona pulled hers back as well, showing she was also pregnant.

"It seems when your sons fucked us…as you say, they left their seed," Laurona continued.

"I see," Pathgo smiled. "And this is supposed to elicit sympathy from me? Well let me tell you bitches something." Pathgo knew if he had any second thoughts about killing them, those thoughts just disappeared. He could not let them live, carrying his bastard grandchildren. He could not pollute the bloodline with half-breeds. Even though they were yellow enough to have white blood mixed in them already. "You and your bastard kids won't see the light of another day. You die today. Then no one will know of my sons' indiscretion with two nigga whores." Pathgo yelled.

"Tell me something, Pathgo!" Nausona pitched, wrapping her fingers around her pagenay. "Did you ever find out how those slave catchers died— especially that one who was burnt?"

Pathgo gave her a blank look. Then she pulled her pagenay from behind her, followed by her sister a split second later.

"These pagenays burnt them, and you are about to die by Chaktun hands. You remember, that place we just made up—Chaktun?" she mused.

Pathgo laughed. He studied the black sleek five-inch rod in their hands. It had a forty-five degree curve to it, appearing to fit snuggly in their hands. It was similar in cut to a dueling pistol, but smaller. He saw no hammer, no barrel, just two rods joining to a sharp point. "Go ahead, shoot me with your space gun," he goaded.

"Our pleasure," Nausona laughed.

"Before we do, say hi to hell for us!" Laurona exclaimed.

The sisters pushed the thumb trigger and did not release it in the normal prescribed time. Pathgo's eyes widened in that split second he saw the blue energy of death steering toward his face. He had no time to react, no time to scream. The event barely had time to register in his brain, before the searing heat overloaded his sensory nerves with pain. The pain lasted a split second before death overcame his body. The brain instantly shut down. But that was not enough.

The sisters held the trigger for ten seconds. The continuous blue energy beam overheated the pagenays and sent a burning sensation through their hands, but their adrenalin kept them from feeling it. The blue blast hit, burnt, melted and evaporated Pathgo's face, hair and skull. His body stiffened from the pain he no longer felt. It stayed upright on the horse until the end of the blasts. Then his body lunged backwards. His foot tangled in the right saddle strap as his horse turned in fright and ran in the opposite direction toward town. The horse dragged Pathgo's headless body through the dirt and grass as it ran. The pagenay heat seared the blood and the throat had a black coat of skin covering the opening where his head should have been.

The sisters stood still with their pagenays in hand as they watched in sickening delight, the demise of their most dreaded enemy on Earth. Both rubbed their six-month pregnant bellies as if to tell their individual unborn child, *it's all right...your grandfather would never try to hurt you again.* The thought of their children sharing the same blood as the monster they had just vanquished scared them. Both reflected for an instant, *what if my child is like that?* Then the idea faded. Chaktun blood was too strong in them to produce monsters. These children might be hampered by the Pathgo bloodline, but they would not be handicapped.

"We better head back to the farm. This place will have too many people out here looking for him or his killers for us to do any good in the cave," Nausona offered.

"I am glad that bastard's dead," Laurona yelled.

"Come on, we can celebrate later," her sister urged.

"I'm glad that bastard's dead," Laurona repeated.

***

The sisters returned to the farmhouse and found Mrs. Gentry had not awakened yet. Laurona went into Mrs. Gentry's bedroom and saw her in bed, pale and violently coughing. Mrs. Gentry was sick. She had pneumonia, an inflammation of her lungs caused by a bacterial or viral infection. Laurona immediately recognized it. Pneumonia seemed to be the universal sickness. It was the price of being the third generation of mankind, the oxygen breathers. The lungs were susceptible to illness because of their delicate composition. It was the only part of the body constantly exchanging substances from outside the body with substances inside the body—oxygen for carbon dioxide. Every planet had their version of it. But whatever version you had, it could be deadly. It was deadly when not treated correctly or not treated in time. However, it was more deadly in these barbaric conditions, absent the modern medicine and technology to which the sisters were accustomed. Nausona retrieved cool water and cloths for compresses. Laurona attempted to make Mrs. Gentry as comfortable as possible.

Mrs. Gentry's health had been failing ever since she dragged the girls back in the house the night they were attacked. The girls had seen signs, but did not recognize them. She had a dry hacking cough. She regularly was short of breath and she regularly felt dizzy. The sisters were in their own little world and imagined Mrs. Gentry's condition was symptomatic of her age.

However, now they knew. They knew she had given away part of her spirit that night she saved them from their attackers. They had never properly thanked her. Now, the part of her spirit that remained wanted to leave her as well. They could not allow that. Mrs. Gentry had been the first real person they met on this planet. She opened her home to them and had saved their lives at least twice. Now, she depended on them. They had to be there. Nothing else mattered, not even getting the gate portal operational.

Laurona placed the cold wet compress on Mrs. Gentry's feverish head. Mrs. Gentry was soaked in sweat. Her body was burning with fever. Laurona moistened another cloth and wiped the sweat from Mrs. Gentry's body. Then she placed a blanket over Mrs. Gentry. Sweat was good. It was the body's way of regulating its temperature. However, Laurona knew she had to keep Mrs. Gentry dry and warm as well. She had to allow the sweat, but keep the body dry. She had to allow the fever to run nature's course, but she couldn't allow the temperature to rise. Even if they had antibiotics it would not help. Mrs. Gentry's symptoms, coupled with blood stained sputum and cyanosis suggested viral pneumonia. At Mrs. Gentry's age, the mortality was assured. When…and Laurona was being optimistic here…when Mrs. Gentry recovered, it was imperative to watch her for lung damage.

Chapter 18—Confession

Sheriff Leroy Dillard Johnson rode up to the front porch of the Gentry farm. Sheriff Johnson had been the deputy under Sheriff Daniel Stephen Witt. However, when Witt was found murdered outside of town, Johnson assumed the duties of sheriff. And one of those duties was to have dinner every Sunday afternoon with Mrs. Gentry. This was a perfect fit to his schedule. Even though Johnson was not as tall or muscular as Sheriff Witt, Johnson had a quiet strength that commanded respect. He was more of a lady's man. He was more particular about his dress and appearance. He wore the clothes of a southern gentleman, even though he was not one. His suit was beige. The coat had a split tail stopping just below his buttocks. He wore shinny black boots and carried a riding crop under his arm. When the girls first met him, they assumed he was just like Pathgo. But they soon found his demeanor was similar to the former sheriff's.

"Hello Mrs. Gentry," the sheriff bellowed with a smile as he greeted her.

Mrs. Gentry was in her rocking chair on the porch enjoying the fall day. It had been almost four weeks since she first became ill. She now felt well enough to sit out on the porch. She managed to wave at the sheriff as he tied his horse to the hitch below the porch.

"And how are we feeling today, Mrs. Gentry?"

She tried to speak but it still hurt to talk. She mouthed the words, "Just fine...Just fine." Her voice seemed to crack as she attempted to speak again.

"That's fine, Mrs. Gentry. You don't have to speak. I know it still hurts," said the sheriff. "Where are the girls?"

Mrs. Gentry pointed toward the door. Just then Nausona appeared in the doorway. "Oh! I was just asking about you and your sister. Do you need any help?" the sheriff smiled at her.

"No sir, we are just fine. Why don't you sit on the porch a while with Mrs. Gentry? She could use a visitor," Nausona replied.

"Well, I think I'll just do that. Thank you Nellie Sue," Johnson answered.

Nausona hated being called Nellie Sue, just as much as her sister disliked the name Lou Anne. Even Mrs. Gentry did not call them by those names if she could help it. However, she was painfully cognizant the sheriff and Mrs. Gentry meant no harm. It was their culture. Insulting as it was, it still was their culture. She coped, as did her sister. She politely smiled and went back into the house to help her sister prepare the meal.

"You know Mrs. Gentry, old Abraham Lincoln won the election last month," the sheriff announced as he took his seat in the chair next to her.

Mrs. Gentry looked at him with astonishment. Neither one of them thought it possible, but a man sympathetic to her cause, abolishment of slavery, would be the president of the United States.

"Yeah, he will take over next spring," he continued as he took his hat off. "People around here are very disappointed. I am not sure disappointed is the right word. I dare say they are downright mad." He stopped to take a deep breath. "There is talk of seceding. It sounds like the slave states are going to leave the United States and form their own country," he continued. Sheriff Johnson felt claustrophobic at the thought. The United States was the only country he knew. The only country he could imagine being in. "You know that changes things. My father and I will probably move up north. We heard the counties northwest of us are against seceding. This town is tearing itself apart and we can no longer be part of it," he preached.

Mrs. Gentry looked on in amazement. She could not believe what she was hearing. Her fight, her battle, her struggle to save the slaves, it was going to tear her country apart. The Lord had seen fit to let her live to see the day a kind-hearted president was elected—a president who would end slavery, so she thought. But she never thought the South would react in such a way—to secede from the union was a drastic step she never thought they would take. But here it was. The South had spoken. They would rather form their own country than give up their slaves. She just stared off into the yard. Her eyes watered as her mind raced. She explored all the options. She explored the possibility of a peaceful coexistence between two countries that were once one. However, this option was unacceptable to her. It solved nothing. Slavery would still exist and there would be a government formed just to ensure the continuance of slavery. Other options included keeping the country together. But that would invite violence, even war. She felt helpless—more now than ever. She was sick and she depended on two girls, two pregnant teenage girls, for her survival. She could no longer protect them, nor could she protect their unborn children. The world was closing in on her and she no longer had the strength to challenge it. A tear rolled down her cheek as the truth took root that she was too old to fight the inevitable any longer.

"Don't fret, Mrs. Gentry. I am sure you will be all right. I am sure these fools will soon realize they can't split from the only country they ever knew. It's just the hot heads talking. Calmer minds will prevail," the sheriff stated, wrapping his arm around her shoulder in a futile attempt to comfort her. "Don't worry, my father will make sure, whomever he sells the store to will take care of you, just as he has." The sheriff looked down at his feet and shuffled them. "But Mrs. Gentry, my father can't offer his help to push the runaways up north. Tonight will be the last time. We will leave as soon as he sells the store." He turned to face Mrs. Gentry. "It's over. We cannot do anymore. They are preparing for war and we can't be here when it happens. I suggest you don't be here either."

Mrs. Gentry nodded her head in agreement. She knew it was time. The farm was not producing enough to sustain her and the girls. And without the generosity of the Johnson's, it would be impossible to live. It was time to sell too. It was time to go back to New York. The girls would be safe in New York. It was time to go. She closed her eyes and squeezed the sheriff's hand.

Tears streamed down her cheeks as she nodded her head more emphatically. Yes, it was time to go.

***

Things were disquieting at dinner. The normal conversation did not exist. The smiles and subtle jokes were also missing. The sheriff told the girls the same news over dinner that he told Mrs. Gentry on the porch an hour earlier. They understood, but they did not accept the decision. Nausona thought they would have to leave soon. They had to begin work on the gate portal again and soon. She kept glancing at her sister and saw in her face the same thought. They had over stayed their welcome and it was time for them to go as well. But they wouldn't go to New York. They would go back home.

"Mrs. Gentry, if you sell the farm, we will not be going with you to New York," Laurona blurted. She saw the shock in Mrs. Gentry's eyes.

"Well where do you think you would go?" asked the sheriff.

"Home," replied Nausona.

"Home? Where is home. You cannot go back to Africa. They tried shipping slaves back to Africa years back. It failed. It failed miserably. You are Americans now, you aren't Africans," the sheriff almost yelled. "You don't know the first thing about Africa. You will be alone, all alone. Plus, how would you get there?" he pushed with a hint of satisfaction that he had proven his point.

"Sheriff Johnson, we are not talking about Africa. We have a way back home," Laurona offered. "It will just take us some time to get there," she added.

"What about Mrs. Gentry?"

"She can come with us. The journey is not long and the medical care is much better," Laurona proffered.

The sheriff and Mrs. Gentry searched Laurona's eyes. Her hazel eyes somehow exposed she was telling the truth. He did not know how or why, but he felt comfortable with Laurona's statement.

"You are crazy, but I believe you. Where is home? Is it up north?"

Nausona thought about telling the sheriff the entire truth, but she knew the sheriff would be honor bound to arrest them for murder—for the murder of the slave catchers and Mr. Pathgo. She hesitated at first, then she nodded her head yes.

"Sheriff, if we convince Mrs. Gentry to come with us, would you trust us then?"

"I guess I would have to."

"Good, by next Sunday, then?" Laurona presented.

"Acceptable?" Nausona questioned.

The sheriff thought awhile, and then he shook his head no. Then his head moved from no to a slight yes.

Osguards: Homecoming

"I must be crazy, but...Acceptable." He rose to get his hat and moved to the front door. "Oh, by the way, you will have company tonight." He walked out the door and jumped on his horse. He turned and waved good-bye then rode off.

"That was sudden," Nausona noticed as she closed the door.

"I guess he wanted to get out of here before we said something he did not want to hear."

***

"Looks like another pick-up out there, Laurona," Nausona informed her sister, looking out the kitchen window. "I guess Sheriff Johnson was right. Things are picking up," she added.

He was the son of the local grocer, their contact for the Underground Railroad. With the aid of the sheriff, the girls had ferried almost twenty runaways. It was a surge of runaways. She didn't know if the slaves were getting braver or just more desperate. But for whatever reason, they had their hands full. Mrs. Gentry was still too weak from her battle with pneumonia to take on her former responsibilities with the Underground Railroad. Therefore the responsibility rested on the sisters' shoulders. However, they could not keep up this pace in their conditions. They were due anytime now. With Mrs. Gentry being ill and the girls being pregnant, no one suspected the house of being a safe haven for runaways—at least not anymore. Maybe the traffic shifted to them because of that. Nausona shivered at the thought. Things had to stop soon, but not tonight.

"How is Mrs. Gentry?" she inquired of her sister.

"She is resting. I think she will be fine."

"Let her know we have a pick-up and we will return in an hour or so."

Laurona disappeared from the kitchen and soon returned with two overcoats and their weapons. The chill in the November night was unusually cold. The girls could actually see their own breath in the air. They wrapped their heads with clothes, buttoned their overcoats and began the arduous trek to the creek. Each strenuous step became slower as they moved. Laurona's back began to ache and Nausona's feet started to swell. Their pregnancies caused other assorted pains they never felt before. The additional stress of walking a half a mark to the creek was enormous on their weakening bodies. The walk took them approximately thirty minutes. When they reached the designated spot, they went through the routine of humming the song to make contact, and to take their minds off their pain.

Out of the shadows of the bushes, a family of five stepped out, a father, mother, two children and an old woman they assumed was the grandmother. The twins observed the family as they approached with the father in the lead. Nausona simply gave a slight nod of her head and flashed a

115

halfhearted grin, accepting the family as the intended cargo. Without any words, the sisters turned and motioned for the family to follow. And as they were instructed at the beginning of their journey, the family remained silent and fell in behind their conductors.

They retraced their steps back to the house, while nervously thumbing their pagenays. The family quietly followed them through the fields. Nausona's feet hurt more than they did going to the creek. Laurona was almost doubled over with the pain in her back. Their pains increased with every step. Because of the pain the sisters were experiencing, the walk back took them forty-five minutes. They housed and fed their guests in the cellar. The day was stressful, first dinner with the sheriff and now the pick-up of runaways. The sisters were exhausted. They went to their room and fell asleep almost immediately. They did not even bother to undress for bed; they went to sleep in their dresses.

***

Monday morning came too early for the sisters. Nausona's feet ached with so much pain she could not get out of bed. Neither could her sister. The sun rose and there was no one up to do the morning chores. Mrs. Gentry, still weak from her bout with pneumonia, was also in bed. Their guests stayed quiet in the cellar, afraid to move or make a sound. Their reception last night was not comforting at all. They felt neglected but safe. But now it was morning, they were rested and hungry. No one came to get them.

The morning came and went. Around noon, the crack of thunder awoke the sisters out of their deep slumber as a storm greeted the afternoon. Nausona shot up as her mind fought the haze of rapid eye movement sleep. Grogginess penetrated her conscious mind without remorse. She had to fight to remember who she was, then where she was. The pain of her swollen feet and ankles aided the memory back into her conscious mind. She turned to see her sister in the next bed dazed and confused also. It took more than a few minutes for them to become lucid again.

"What time is it?" Nausona asked her sister.

"Don't know. But it has to be late."

"Jus! We have to get up. People are depending on us," Nausona roared as she pushed herself out of bed. "Only a couple of more weeks, and this baby will be out of me—so I pray."

Laurona gazed at her sister's effort to move in amazement. "Do we have to get up?"

Nausona shot her a strong stare.

"Yeah, yeah, yeah! I know. We have to get up. How did we get ourselves into this mess?" she asked in despair, pushing herself out of her bed.

Osguards: Homecoming

"We go over this every time," Nausona sighed. "Jus must be testing us. He is giving us challenges to make us stronger for when we return," she added, trying to convince herself more than convince her sister.

"We haven't had a chance to work on the gate portal since Mrs. Gentry became ill," she countered. "How are we going to get back home now—especially with the threat of a civil war looming over the land like a vulture?" Laurona stood on her feet and glanced at the bedroom door. "We need help. We cannot do this alone. Not like this, not this way."

"I know that Laurona," she sighed. "I think when Mrs. Gentry is well enough we need to tell her. Maybe she can help. I don't know how, but she may be able to help."

"Great? When do we do this? If you haven't noticed, we are not in the best shape to work on the gate portal. And I don't think Mrs. Gentry has the technological knowledge to fix the gate portal," Laurona interjected.

"I know, but what else can we do? We are running out of options. This country is about to explode and we are stuck in the middle."

"Did you ever stop to think we were not meant to leave? I mean…how can we save our planet, our universe if we cannot stop a Spartan country like this from tearing itself apart? Maybe our destiny is here," Laurona pondered. She moved to open the door.

Nausona stood on her feet. "Maybe, but where do we begin. At least at home, we have a following, a name. We wouldn't be starting from scratch."

"It's been over a universal year. We do not know what is left at home. We may not have an infrastructure to start with. We may have to build one. We may have to build one from here."

"Are you serious? These people can't help us. They are backwards, dangerous and inept. How can they help us begin a fight in our universe?"

But she stopped to think about what her sister said. If they could not get the gate portal working, they would have to make something happen here on ea rth. Maybe she needed to start thinking in those terms. No! She was not ready to give up on the original dream. Home first. She needed to work harder and smarter. She needed to figure out how to get Mrs. Gentry involved.

"Hey, what's that smell?" her sister wondered.

"It smells like breakfast. Do you think the runaways are in the kitchen?"

"Jus, I hope not."

They both found revitalized energy and scurried into the kitchen. Mrs. Gentry was up and preparing breakfast. She had woken up a few minutes earlier and realized no one had fed the guests in the cellar. Someone had to take care of them. They needed to be on the road tonight. The sheriff made that explicitly clear last night. Any delay may hamper the operation, now that the South was talking about war. The South's fervor was high and the slaves were on the receiving end of it. Mrs. Gentry was better. The care the girls had given her had allowed her to make it through a potentially fatal illness. However, she was not fully recovered. At her age, a relapse was entirely possible, especially now that they were moving into the winter season.

"Mrs. Gentry, you should be resting. Let me get that for you," said Laurona

"No my dear, I have rested enough. It is you two who need to rest now. Those youngsters of yours will be here before you know it. You need your strength to bring them into this world." She smiled and turned back to the stove. "Plus, I am interested in you telling me about your home."

"Oh yeah, our home," Nausona murmured.

"I've been waiting almost two years for you to tell me. You promised the sheriff last night that you would try to convince me to come with you. It sounds like I might be interested." She turned and smiled. "There is no time like the present."

"You are right, Mrs. Gentry. But let us take care of our friends in the cellar. Then we can talk," Laurona said.

They fed the runaways and began their lessons on how to conduct themselves for the next station. They went over the path to take and the song to hum at the next stop. This part of the trek was always the most dangerous. Conductors usually led them on the Underground Railroad. But this close to the North, they had to travel on their own. This was in order not to compromise the system. Mrs. Gentry did not fully understand, but she appreciated the secrecy. It just seemed any captured runaway would compromise the system. But she did not know how the system worked outside her little segment either. All she knew was it worked. As far as she knew, no runaways had been captured on her route. This made her proud. A pride she could not share with anyone, not until the sisters came to live with her. Now they spoke openly of the system and her part of it. Now the girls had a part in it as well. Unfortunately, the system was near its end. Her part in all this was about to end. She no longer had the strength or the resources to carry on. The threat of civil war did not make it any easier either.

The Gentry farm sent another set of runaways up North that evening. The wet ground and moonless night made it dangerous and secure at the same time for them to travel. The runaways would leave tracks in the mud. But no one would see them travel tonight. As long as they were up and out of the area by sunrise, no one would find them, even if they followed the tracks. The next station knew how to cover tracks around it. Therefore, if anyone followed the tracks, they would not be able to follow them to the runaways. The system thought of everything—except war.

***

"Now girls, I am ready. Talk!" Mrs. Gentry urged as she sat in the parlor sipping on her tea.

The girls sat on the couch wide-eyed and somewhat nervous. Nausona pulled from her waistband the PARIT. Her sister laid the two pagenays and the two mations on the coffee table. The mations were shining silver five-inch blades with multiple serrated edges. The handles were made of a soft material, but a knuckle guard, similar to brass knuckles, covered the hand. With a push of a button on the handle, the serrated edges danced and pulsated back and forth on the knife. The knife was made to tear up the inside of whatever it was plunged into. It could shred a human's liver, heart or make a lung collapse in an instant. The sight of the PARIT intrigued Mrs. Gentry, but the sight of the weapons frightened her. Nausona told the story, from the beginning on Chaktun until now. Laurona only interjected when she thought her sister missed something important. Mrs. Gentry listened. When Nausona spoke of the killings they were responsible for on Earth, Mrs. Gentry flinched but remained quiet. When they were done, they sat quietly waiting for Mrs. Gentry to respond.

Mrs. Gentry sat with her hands folded on her lap. She was speechless. This story was not what she expected. She thought the girls were from Connecticut or somewhere up north where they were not accustomed to the slave industry. It was an industry. But this wild tale of another planet, machines, which allowed them to travel from planet to planet. It was absurd, wasn't it? She got up and walked to her bedroom. She paused at the door and turned.

"I want to believe you. I mean those gadgets are not from around here." She sighed. "Show me the cave tomorrow, then I will make my decision," she said as she walked into her bedroom and closed the door.

For the first time since they lived with Mrs. Gentry, the girls heard the bolt latch on the inside of Mrs. Gentry's door. With that sound, their hearts dropped. They felt alone.

Chapter 19—Maintenance

The Tuesday morning sun rose as it did every day since the girls arrived on ea rth. But this morning they greeted the day with more than despair. They greeted the sun with uncertainty. Nausona awoke first. She dressed and crept toward the door. She did not want to disturb her sister. However when she shut the door, her sister awoke.

Laurona ascertained it was morning and her sister had already left to start her chores. She rose and dressed, and then went out to milk the cows.

Laurona passed Nausona as usual, as they went about their morning chores. But this morning she did not speak. Laurona felt if they did not speak about talking to Mrs. Gentry last night, the entire episode would fade.

They finished their chores and strolled together to the kitchen. They opened the door and—

"Good morning dears," Mrs. Gentry greeted them.

She had prepared breakfast and had three plates waiting on the kitchen table—just like before she became ill. The smell of bacon and scrambled eggs filled the kitchen. Mrs. Gentry sat at the head of the table and looked at the sisters who stood in the doorway stunned at what they were witnessing.

"Close the door, it is cold out there," Mrs. Gentry continued as she waved them in.

Laurona closed the door, still showing shock on her face. Then she pulled her coat off and laid it on the back of her chair. Her sister followed suit. *What was this?* Laurona thought. *I thought she was scared of us,* her mind pushed. Laurona was confused and definitely off guard. She expected Mrs. Gentry to avoid them at all cost. Avoid them because she didn't believe them and thought them crazy. Or, avoid them because she believed them and thought them dangerous. But how could she not believe them. They had shown her technologically advanced equipment—Technology…a word that had no meaning on this planet. She must have believed them. Mrs. Gentry could not explain the PARIT, or the pagenays or even the mations within the confines of her world, as she knew it. Therefore, she had to believe them and thought them dangerous.

But her actions, this morning, were not consistent with someone who feared for her life. Maybe all she required was a good night's rest. Maybe she had accepted them. Whatever the situation, Laurona was pleased they were sitting down to breakfast this morning. She turned to her sister and witnessed a slight smile on Nausona's face. She instantly knew her sister was thinking the same thing. But, how should they proceed? What was the next step?

"Hurry up ladies, we have much work to do today," Mrs. Gentry offered. She saw the girls were still in a state of shock. "I know I did not dream our conversation last night. Did I?"

"No, Mrs. Gentry. You weren't dreaming," answered Laurona, as she turned to her sister. She snapped her head back to Mrs. Gentry. "But we weren't sure how you took the news last night. I…we thought you were angry or even afraid of us."

Mrs. Gentry looked up from her plate, "No, honey. I was not angry. Maybe stunned. And maybe somewhat scared. No…I think I was more confused. It was so much to take in. One day I am told my country is on the brink of a civil war over slavery. Then the next day, two beautiful girls I thought were runaway slaves, tell me they are princesses from another planet in a civil war. Remember, I am old. I can't take the stress of any of this." She took a sip of her milk, paused for a moment and continued, "I am not just an old lady wondering how I will spend my remaining days, but I am ill. Well, I am recovering from pneumonia—anyway. It took me some time to digest this all. Now, I am ready. I want to visit this cave. I'm not sure I believe your entire story. But I figure the cave will either substantiate your story or discredit it. Either way, I have to see the cave. Plus, those gadgets you produced last night...well they aren't from around her. Then the deaths...the deaths of the slave catchers happened right when you two showed up. And Mr. Pathgo's death, people are saying Mr. Pathgo's death was so unnatural. You two were out that day and those guns of yours; well you said they burn people. That explains a lot of things that have happened around here. So, I want to see the cave."

"Then what?" Nausona asked.

"I don't know," she answered. "But I do know neither one of us can stay here. Things are getting too dangerous—and if your destiny is to get back to this planet...Chakrayou...

"Chaktun, Mrs. Gentry. It is pronounced Chaktun," informed Nausona.

"Please forgive me. Chaktun. Well, if your destiny is to get back to Chaktun, who am I to stop you? In fact, I will help you."

"You can come too, Mrs. Gentry," Laurona offered.

"I don't know. Your world is in a civil war I have nothing to do with. At least this civil war is something I know—besides my family is buried here. I can't leave them. This is my world. Like you love your world, I love mine. It is the only world I know. And I am too old to learn another. But, you must...no I insist, you take me to the cave so I can help you as much as I can. You have to get home."

"We can talk about it later, Mrs. Gentry. If you still feel that way, we will honor it. But the offer is always good. Even after we leave, you will know how to use the gate portal. I will see to that," Laurona promised.

The trio finished breakfast and packed a picnic lunch. Even though the November days were colder and shorter, this day lent itself, weather-wise, for an afternoon picnic. And that was their story if stopped by an inquisitive neighbor. Once the carriage was loaded the women set off to the cave. The sisters carried their pagenays and mations as well as the PARIT. The weapons made Mrs. Gentry nervous, but she did not object. She realized, when the girls did not carry their weapons, they met with tragedy. She thought if she had such misfortune happen to her, she would also carry a weapon. No, she did not blame them, but it still made her uncomfortable.

It took them about thirty-five minutes to reach the cave by carriage. Nausona thought it was such a relief to be riding to the cave instead of walking. Jus knew she would not have made it if she had to walk.

The sisters escorted Mrs. Gentry inside the cave. The three women groped in the dark using the light from the lantern to guide them. They pressed further back into the cave than comfortable for Mrs. Gentry. Mrs. Gentry feared bats, rats or snakes may attack them at any moment. Laurona motioned for Mrs. Gentry to stay. Then the sisters walked up two steps. That was odd for a cave, Mrs. Gentry thought. Then they disappeared into an oval cutout in the back of the cave. Only the light from the lantern kept Mrs. Gentry companied. Several seconds later, a mechanical light shone from the secondary entrance. This time Nausona found the power switch hidden behind a rock below the control panel. They had activated the power switch and the cave came to life. A bright red light illuminated the cave and displayed its cavernous beauty. For the first time the girls noticed material in the cave that would aid them in repairing the gate portal.

Mrs. Gentry followed the light. She entered the room and was enamored by the beauty of the cave and the machines that glowed to life all around her. Her spirit was overwhelmed with the sight of the alien technology. She found a solid rock to rest upon as she studied the cave. She saw the big black metal box in the middle and knew this was the gate portal. Five feet in front of it was what looked like a control panel. It stood waist high on a solid pole about four inches in diameter. An elliptical panel lay on top. Mrs. Gentry watched as Nausona placed what she called a PARIT into a slot on the panel. Then the box jumped to life. Laurona moved to a glass like panel against the far side of the cave. She watched in awe as Laurona pressed her fingers against symbols in the panel and a moving picture appeared in the screen.

The picture moved in and out, displaying different angles and views of planets and stars. It was breathtaking for Mrs. Gentry to watch. Symbols appeared under the picture. It appeared to be writing of some kind. Laurona appeared to be reading the symbols and adjusting her finger pressure to display different views of planets. It must be true, Mrs. Gentry thought. Oh...my...God! The girls were telling the truth. She believed them before, but to be confronted with the truth in such a manner was too much for her to fathom. She housed aliens from another planet in her house for almost two years. Now she felt foolish for feeling protective of two women who obviously did not need her protection—or did they? Without me, they would be dead, or worse. They could be Pathgo slaves. If it weren't for me they would have starved to death. Why did they keep this from me so long? Soon, her resignation turned into indignation.

"Why did you not tell me about this before?" she demanded.

Laurona turned and looked at Mrs. Gentry. Even in the red light, she could see Mrs. Gentry's anger. *How can I calm her down,* she wondered. *What can I say to make her feel better?*

"Mrs. Gentry, it was for your own safety. We could not risk you getting hurt on our account. Besides, we just found out about this cave a few weeks ago. Then you became ill. We have not been back since you took ill. We wanted to make sure you were okay." She paused to see if her words had any effect. Mrs. Gentry's face softened some, but still had the stern look of anger. "Now with the impending civil war, we thought it better to tell you and offer you a chance to come with us. Please Mrs. Gentry, don't be angry."

"I feel you did not trust me," she hammered. "After all I have done for you two. Now to find out you did not trust me, especially with something this important." She paused to take a deep breath. "If you told me earlier who you were and what you were looking for, we could have found this cave sooner. Then you...then you...wouldn't have been..." Her voice trailed off as she looked down at her feet.

"Raped? Is that what you mean?" Nausona questioned, raising her voice as the pain of the event rushed into her conscious mind. "If we had told you earlier who we were and what we were looking for, we wouldn't have been raped and now pregnant with bastard children," she continued with a broken voice quivering from emotion.

Mrs. Gentry raised her head. "Yes, damn it. You wouldn't have been raped," she yelled. Then she looked back down on the ground. "You wouldn't have been raped," she repeated in a slight whisper.

"Mrs. Gentry, if you are blaming yourself—don't." Laurona offered in consolation. "It wasn't your fault. It was no one's fault—except the Pathgo boys," she added. We will be fine. Jus has a way of making us stronger in our time of need," she continued.

Both girls moved to Mrs. Gentry and hugged her. The three women hugged each other tight and tearfully. It was the first real emotion they shared with each other since they met. The hug felt reassuring and family like. It was the right medicine for the emotional illness they had suffered these past twenty months. Mrs. Gentry held each girl tightly in her arms. She did not want to let go. The sisters sensed that and allowed her to hug them. Laurona fought the tears, but soon realized it was a losing battle and allowed them the freedom of bathing her cheeks. Nausona also attempted to fight the tears. She wanted to portray a warrior demeanor—tough and rugged. But she soon surrendered to her passionate side. The side that reminded her she was still a teenager—a teenager pregnant with the baby of her new sworn enemy. How was she going to find the strength to combat that? How was she going to find the emotional, physical and spiritual strength to beat this? She did not know. But for now she found solace in the comforting arms of an old lady—one who was banished to this prison planet by birth. This old lady had the heart and soul of a Toam, the master of the Sixana warrior.

***

Mrs. Gentry watched in amazement as the girls moved with urgent speed throughout the cave. They had been working at a furious pace for about six hours now. They only stopped to eat the lunch they packed—five minutes. However, Mrs. Gentry received some sense of pleasure at seeing the sisters work their problems. She heard earlier the Asher power cells could be energized using one of the pagenays. It did not need both of them. That seemed to place some joy back in their step. Soon after, the girls reverted back to their native language. Mrs. Gentry did not mind. She knew it was a sign the girls were more comfortable in their work, not a sign of distrust. But it was getting late, and also getting dark. It was time to go. The day appeared to be productive. At least, that is what the smiles on the girls' faces were telling her.

"Ladies, you need to finish quickly. We must be on our way," Mrs. Gentry called. She stepped up and pulled the lantern close to her.

Nausona looked over and saw Mrs. Gentry start to leave.

"Laurona, it is getting late. We have minor adjustments to do, but I think we can get this going tomorrow."

"Yes, but what about the coordinates. Remember, we could not set the coordinates on the gate portal on the last planet. What makes you think you can do it now?"

"Well sister, I am glad you asked that question," Nausona countered with a grin. "The last planet did not have a PARIT. With the PARIT, I can write a different code and interject it into the ARIT database. Hopefully, this will adjust the coordinate slide lifts to the coordinates I preset—Chaktun," she added. "It's a risk, I don't know if we can do it. But if I remember my ARIT database class and my Elementary Gate Portal one—oh—one class correctly, it can be done."

"I hope you are right. I hate to think I wasted this entire time getting this old machine to work and then find out it can't send us back home."

"I hate to think we will be stuck on this planet, in the middle of a civil war we have nothing to do with," Nausona added.

"Girls, let's go," urged Mrs. Gentry from the cave entrance.

Chapter 20—The Births

The three women were exhausted. The day's activities were productive. Laurona had patched 'the inner to outer space relay converter' with some spare metal she found in the barn. Nausona had replaced the spring in 'the coordinate slide lifts' with fence wire. Then Laurona had cleaned the 'signal finder and signal booster' cable connections in the creek. Now all that was left was to write a program to replace the corrupt ARIT database and to disassemble one of the pagenays to energize the Asher power cells. That would give them enough power to connect with inner-space one time. If Mrs. Gentry stayed behind, they would have to come back to get her when they knew it was safe. She didn't know how long that would be. Additionally, unless they could hijack a Kulusk planet-to-planet gate portal, coming back would take months if not years with a spaceship. Nausona decided it would be best to wait until it was time to go before telling Mrs. Gentry about this. Maybe the pressure of the news would facilitate her decision to join them. Well she could only hope. Now it was time to relax and....

Pain...sharp and distinct, but pain all the same, shot through Nausona's stomach. She screamed. Then it was gone. What was that, she thought. Then again, the pain shot through her as quick and distinct as before. She screamed again.

Mrs. Gentry and Laurona rushed into the bedroom. Nausona felt the bed wet underneath her. She was confused and embarrassed.

"Mrs. Gentry...I...I...didn't...I..."

"Stop child," Mrs. Gentry ordered. "I do think you just went into labor."

"Went into what?"

"Labor, my child. You are about to deliver a baby."

The pain, the screaming, and the pleading with Jus to relieve her of her suffering continued throughout the night. Mrs. Gentry and Laurona held her hands, and comforted her with cold compresses and wet towels throughout the ordeal. However, nothing seemed to help. The pain became so incredibly unbearable; Nausona thought she would faint from it. Most of the time, she pleaded to be unconscious. It did not work either. Six...seven...eight hours into the night and the baby still had not come. This baby was stubborn, or it was a true Pathgo and wanted to kill Nausona during the birth. Nausona's mind wandered. Would she accept the baby? Would the baby accept her? What would the baby look like? What would it be, a boy or a girl? How could she finish the gate portal now? Why now? What now? Oh! The pain, make it stop—make it stop.

"It's time to push Nausona," Mrs. Gentry urged.

"It's time to what?

"Push honey, push. You must push the baby out, my dear. Push with all your might," she coaxed.

Nausona did as she was told. She pushed, but the pain was too great.

"No. No. I can't do it."

"Yes, you can sweetheart. Women have been doing this for years, even on Chaktun. You can do it," Mrs. Gentry explained.

Nausona pushed again. She yelled with the pain. But she did not stop. She pushed and pushed. She squeezed her abdomen and continued with every ounce of strength she could muster. The pain, why was the pain so great? No one had ever told her delivering a baby would be so painful. What horrible sin did humans do that made women have to suffer through childbirth? Mrs. Gentry tried to explain some time ago that in her religion, the pain of childbirth was given to them by her God because of some sin the first woman committed. She ate an apple or something. How could a God be so vengeful and give this much pain to women for eating an apple? There had to be something else she did to make all women pay for the rest of their lives. Every animal Nausona ever saw give birth did not look like they were in pain, at least not the pain she was going through. Why was woman so cursed?

Her thoughts wandered but her consciousness was on the pain. She continued to push. Now the pain and the sound of her own voice screaming drowned out Mrs. Gentry. She heard nothing, she knew nothing, and the pain was hypnotizing her to where she was no longer aware of her surroundings. *Why are we so cursed?* she wondered. Why? Why? Oh Jus, make it stop. Then the pain was gone. Well not exactly gone, but it was no longer sharp. It was no longer piercing her soul, mind and spirit. It was just throbbing.

"It's a girl," Nausona heard Mrs. Gentry say. Nausona opened her eyes to see Mrs. Gentry holding a baby, somewhat soaked in blood. But it was a baby. Even through the blood stained skin, Nausona thought she was beautiful.

"Is she all right?" she queried Mrs. Gentry. Just as Mrs. Gentry started to say something, the baby let out with a yell.

"Well, if she isn't she could have fooled me," Mrs. Gentry said.

Laurona rushed in and saw her brand new baby niece in Mrs. Gentry's arms. Mrs. Gentry passed the baby to Laurona. "Go and clean your niece."

Laurona did so. Then Mrs. Gentry went back to Nausona and pressed on her abdomen. At the same time, she gently pulled on the part of the umbilical cord still attached to Nausona. The placenta released from Nausona's uterus and came out with ease.

"Judging from the color of your after birth honey, you have a healthy baby girl."

Nausona just watched in amazement as her sister walked in and laid the baby on her chest. The baby searched for his mother's nipple and began to feed. Nausona was humbled by the experience. She had just become a mother. She had not thought much about it while she was pregnant. There were days that she was totally oblivious to the subject. Not until recently did she think more about it—mainly because the pain of carrying was a constant reminder. Now she had another life to think about. A life that was totally dependent on her. She looked down at the nursing baby and smiled.

"Well little sister, you did a wonderful job. She is beautiful," Laurona admired. "What will you call her?"

"I think I will name her Sharyla—Sharyla Osguard" Nausona answered without hesitation.

"Sharyla Osguard. That is so beautiful," complimented Mrs. Gentry. "Does it mean anything in particular?"

"Well Osguard is our family name; you call it the surname I believe. It means *'Guardian of All'* and Sharyla means *'Loving Wisdom,'"* Laurona explained.

"How sweet, and what do your names mean?"

"Nausona means, *'New Beginning'* and my name, Laurona means, *'Blessed Beginning.'* We were in another galactic civil war, as we explained earlier, when we were born. Our parents thought we were somehow the sign of a new and blessed beginning. Right now, we..."

A pain shot through her and she could not complete the sentence.

"What's wrong Laurona?" Mrs. Gentry asked.

"I think it's my turn."

"Okay, just relax and lie in your bed," Mrs. Gentry ordered.

The next ten hours were like the last ten hours. Except this time, it was Laurona doing the screaming. Nausona attempted to help Mrs. Gentry, but she was too weak from her own delivery to be of any substantial aid. Mrs. Gentry was tired and felt faint herself. She had been up for twenty-six hours when Sharyla was born. Now that Laurona was in labor it would be a long time before she could sleep again. Her old frame was working on reserve energy. Reserve energy she really did not have. The pneumonia had taken what spirit she had. Now the entire day in a damp cave coupled with playing midwife to the sisters was wreaking havoc on her body. She attempted to catch catnaps, but they made her more tired. Finally, she made some coffee and drank it. She had a job to do, and she was determined to do it. Her determination pushed her throughout the night. She kept the sisters and Sharyla as comfortable as she could, until Thursday morning when Laurona was enduring the final stages of her delivery.

"It's a girl," she announced. Fatigue was crawling in her voice.

Laurona looked at her sister who now was able to walk. Nausona took the baby and cleaned her just as Laurona had done for her. Mrs. Gentry removed the placenta and examined it as she did for Nausona. Again, the placenta was a reddish color, indicating a healthy baby. Nausona placed the cleaned baby girl onto Laurona's chest and watched as it searched and found one of her mother's nipples. She then began to feed.

"Well sister, it appears you did an outstanding job as well. What are you going to name your daughter?"

"Kashara. Kashara Osguard," she announced with pride.

"Another beautiful name. What does it mean, Laurona?" Mrs. Gentry asked.

"It means *'Free Spirit.'* I want my daughter to know freedom. I want her to be free," she added.

"Well my dear, I want both your children to know freedom. And if it takes sending you through that metal box myself, they will know freedom," Mrs. Gentry stated. "But now girls, I am tired. God did not intend for me to work this hard. I need to go lie down awhile. I think you can handle things for now. Nausona, help your sister clean up and put the bloody clothes out on the porch. I'll get to them later."

Mrs. Gentry turned and walked out the door across the parlor and into her room. She plunged into her seat. It was a harrowing three days. First came the cave and all those gadgets; and then came the twenty plus hours of child labor. It was fantastic and exhilarating, but it also was exhausting. Now it was time to rest. Tomorrow would be another day. But how would they get the gadgets in the cave to work while watching two babies? The dampness in the caves would be harmful to the babies. *I guess fixing the box would be on hold for a while.* Damn those Pathgo brothers—without knowing it, they had interrupted the Osguard sisters' lives again. They must be directly related to those...those Kulusks. That is what the sisters called their enemies— Kulusks. Well those Pathgos must be Kulusks. They must be. Nothing else could explain... Her eyes closed and her mind went blank. She fell asleep at first, but then she stopped breathing and her heart stopped. The last bit of life force faded from her body. The last three days were too much for her body, already weakened from pneumonia, to take. However, the smile on her face told the world her death was pleasant and welcomed. Untimely that it was, it was still a welcomed relief to her spirit to join her husband and children in heaven. She could do no more for the girls. Her spirit knew it, even though her mind did not. Death slipped into the room while she slept and swiped her soul in the morning haze.

***

Nausona knocked on Mrs. Gentry's door that evening, to see if Mrs. Gentry wanted to eat dinner with them. There was no reply. She nudged the door open and saw Mrs. Gentry in her chair with her face slightly down and to the right. The smile on her face was telling.

Nausona instantly knew Mrs. Gentry was gone. She moved quickly to check Mrs. Gentry's pulse. She felt none. Mrs. Gentry's skin was cold and her body somewhat stiff. Rigor mortis had started to set in. Nausona began to cry. Laurona heard her from the parlor and rushed in to see why she was crying. Laurona gazed upon Mrs. Gentry's lifeless body.

"She's dead," Nausona said, looking at her sister with tears in her eyes. "She's dead," she repeated.

Chapter 21—The Funeral

"Ashes to ashes," the preacher read over Mrs. Gentry's wooden casket.

The girls were not allowed to attend the funeral or burial of their friend because they were slaves. Therefore, they could only watch from the back porch of the farmhouse. The burial took place on the hill overlooking the barn. Mrs. Gentry was being buried next to her husband on that hill. A small crowd gathered around the burial plot, Mrs. Pathgo and her boys, the sheriff and his father and an assortment of other neighbors the girls did not know or care to know. The sisters just watched from the porch with awe.

Why? Laurona wondered. Why did her God or Jus decide to take her now—*just when we needed her the most?* She was a true friend, a needed friend and in the end a trusted friend. This was not fair. Mrs. Gentry did nothing but good deeds for people. She did not have to die alone. *Why?* Her holiday season was to begin next week. Last year, she did not understand Thanksgiving, Christmas or New Years. But this year Laurona was ready. She was ready to celebrate Thanksgiving with Mrs. Gentry. If need be, she was ready to celebrate Christmas. She had so much to be thankful for, especially their friendship. And Christmas, the birth of Mrs. Gentry's Jesus, was going to be an exciting time for her. To celebrate a man, the Son of Mrs. Gentry's God, who came to Earth and preached love and forgiveness— similar to the teaching of the Chaktun's Jus?

However, humans had written the Bible. That is why the Bible seemed to contradict everything Jesus taught, Laurona concluded. There were wars in the name of God in the Bible. *Why would an almighty God, worthy of human praise, need humans to fight his battles?* An all-powerful God would say the word and whatever or whoever was in disfavor would certainly perish. Also, there were spiteful disciplinary actions in her Bible, again in direct conflict to the teachings of her Jesus. Again, *why* would an omnipotent God be spiteful? The Pathgos used text from the Bible to justify slavery. Again, why would an all powerful God choose one of his children over the other—*first the Jewish people, now the white people of the United States?* The Bible was so full of contradiction; anyone could take any part of the Bible to justify any actions. Humans had taken their religion and bent it to suit their needs. Chaktun history was full of such stories. However, the movement surrounding Jus had all but stamped out the use of religion to justify personal desires. Just as the Christianity movement should have done around Jesus. Jesus' words were not contradictory. Love thy neighbor was His message. Honor thy God. Live your life, as God would want you to live it. Simple and easy words to live by, just like Jus. Jesus was honorable and worthy of praise in her eyes. She was ready to celebrate Christmas. But as usual, something changed her plans, the death of her earthly friend.

Malcolm Dylan Petteway

Nausona picked up Mrs. Gentry's King James Version of the Bible and read First Peter, chapter three from the New Testament. This was Mrs. Gentry's favorite passage, and it seemed appropriate for her to read in memory of her friend.

The passage identified Godly living. This in her opinion fit Mrs. Gentry. Her eyes watered as she read verses three and four:

"Whose adorning let it not be that outward adorning of plaiting the hair, and of wearing of gold, or putting on of apparel; But let it be the hidden man of the heart, in that which is not corruptible, even the ornament of a meek and quiet spirit, which is in the sight of God of great price."

She stopped and thought a moment.

"She did wear her religion—didn't she?"

Her sister nodded. Then Nausona continued reading aloud. Every verse seemed to fit the life and times of Mrs. Gentry. Her voice quivered with emotion. She finished the passage and closed the Bible. Then she clutched the Bible close to her chest. With a deep sigh she passed the Bible to her sister. Her sister took the Bible and clutched it to her heart.

"Even though we know little of your religion Mrs. Gentry, I am sure your life has afforded you the opportunity for the glory you seek. May you be happier in death than you were in life," Laurona said, quoting a passage from the Lonson, the religious book of Jus.

Nausona nodded in agreement and wiped the tears from her eyes. As she did she looked up and saw Mrs. Pathgo, her sons and the sheriff approach them from the burial area.

"What does she want now?"

Laurona looked up and saw them moving toward them.

"I don't know, but whatever it is, it can't be good."

Laurona decided she should hide Mrs. Gentry's Bible. The old bat may have witnessed her sister reading from it. That would not be good. Slaves weren't supposed to know how to read. Actually a slave reading was punishable by death. She raced through the doorway and stuffed the book under the cushion of the armchair situated just inside the door. When she stepped back out, Mrs. Pathgo and party had just arrived at the bottom stair of the porch.

Mrs. Pathgo stopped and scrutinized the sisters up and down. The sisters did not even attempt civility. They remained silent wondering what the wife of their dead enemy wanted. Mrs. Pathgo closed and lowered her parasol. Laurona wondered what Mrs. Pathgo needed with a parasol in the middle of November. The sun was not that hot. However she was draped in black for the funeral. Maybe the old witch was overheated. Only Jus would know, and she really did not care.

"Pack your things, you are coming with me," Mrs. Pathgo commanded.

130

"What?" Laurona replied in shock.

"Is that how you talk to your new master? Obviously, Mrs. Gentry did not know how to treat her niggas." Her southern drawl was insufferable to the sisters, especially how she dragged out the word niggas.

"Sheriff?" Nausona pleaded.

The sheriff came around to face Mrs. Pathgo.

"You may be buying the Gentry farm from Mr. Gentry in Tennessee, but you don't own it yet, and you definitely don't own these girls." He stopped to catch his breath. "You see Mrs. Pathgo, Mrs. Gentry gave these girls their freedom. I have the signed papers in my safe at the office." He stopped to watch the anger build in Mrs. Pathgo's eyes. He gleaned some satisfaction in telling Mrs. Pathgo the news. "Basically, the papers state that upon her death, Nausona and Laurona are free."

"Who?" Mrs. Pathgo snorted.

"These two sisters," he whispered as he gestured to them on the porch.

Mrs. Pathgo squinted her eyes as if she were going to pounce on the sheriff.

"Very well. Then I want those two niggas off my property now."

"It's not your property yet," the sheriff replied, collecting his thoughts while looking at the sisters. "I believe the sale is not final until the day after tomorrow. Until then, the estate is in probate and these people can and will stay here."

Mrs. Pathgo looked up and heard one of the babies cry inside the house.

"What's that?"

"Madam, I am sure it hasn't been that long since you heard a baby cry," the sheriff mused.

"I know it is a baby, but whose?"

"Don't know. I have to go see. It could be mines or my sister's," Nausona chuckled.

"Oh, I didn't know you bred yet," Mrs. Pathgo pushed, looking for a reaction.

Nausona looked up and realized she gave Mrs. Pathgo just what she wanted—a reaction.

"I wouldn't call it breeding. You might want to ask your sons what they would call it?" she volleyed.

Mrs. Pathgo spied her children as they bowed their heads in shame. At that instant the truth became crystal clear. Her eyes told the story and her sons' silence confirmed it. Slowly, she closed her eyes and shook her head, mortified by the revelation of her children's sins.

"Get you two to the buggy, I will deal with you later!" she ordered.

She watched as her boys ran to their buggy. With her back still turned to the sheriff and the sisters she sighed, "I will comply with your directions Sheriff." She swung around, "But those bastard kids stay. They are part of the estate. And I don't believe you have papers on them. Do you?"

The sheriff's smile dropped and he shook his head no.

"Good, then I expect the children to remain." She turned and opened her parasol and placed it over her head. She strutted to the carriage, imbrued with her moment of victory. When she reached the carriage, she stepped in without the aid of her sons. Once inside, her lady like demeanor evaporated and she slapped both her sons, leaving a red mark on their cheeks. Afterwards, the carriage rode down the road and out the gate.

"What just happened here?" Nausona demanded.

"Mrs. Pathgo has an agreement with Mrs. Gentry's brother-in-law to buy the farm. It appears he agreed. The paperwork and details are being worked out. I expect it to be final the day after tomorrow." The sheriff kicked the dirt underneath his foot. "You need to get going and take the kids. There will be a last cargo pick-up tonight. I suggest you travel with them up north."

"Another pick-up? We can't handle another pick-up tonight," Laurona pointed out.

"It's the last one. My father and I will be leaving for the western part of the state tomorrow. The Underground Railroad is finished after tonight. I strongly urge you leave with them." The sheriff turned and checked his hat on his head and walked toward his horse.

The cry was louder now. Both babies were crying. The sisters rushed in and picked up their children. Laurona picked up her daughter and sat in the armchair near the door. She opened her blouse and allowed the baby to feed.

Nausona had her child and began to change her on the bedroom floor.

"The sheriff is right," she screamed to her sister. "We can't let that woman take our babies!" she continued.

"I know, but I think we should go to the cave and work the gate portal until it is ready."

"Agreed, as soon as we get this last cargo out of the way, we move to the cave. I say we have about twenty hours of work before it becomes operational."

***

The cargo came as the sheriff said. The light shone from the creek in the specified sequence. Nausona packed her weapons and grabbed her overcoat.

"I'll be back in an hour," she told her sister. Then she stepped outside for the last trek to the creek.

Osguards: Homecoming

Laurona stayed with the babies. The night was too chilly for the newborns to travel. She had wanted to accompany her sister, for mutual support. But they both knew only one could go. The other would have to stay and watch the kids. She peered out the window every few seconds to ensure her sister was safe; even though she knew if anything were to happen to her sister, she was too far away to render any assistance. All she could do was watch and listen in horror if this was a trap. She prayed to Jus, "Please let this be a simple pickup." Her hands became wet with sweat as the clock ticked away. After about fifteen minutes, she could no longer see her sister. Her imagination became overactive at that point. She imagined every terrible thing she could think of. What if the Pathgo brothers were at the creek? Could her sister handle it? She just gave birth. Even though she was the stronger of the two, because she was the first to give birth, did not mean she was strong enough to handle any problems if they arose. Why was there a pickup tonight? They had enough to worry about with Mrs. Pathgo hunting for them.

Merely last week, things were good. But with time, things change. They had allowed Mrs. Gentry into their secret. She had helped them in the cave. And now...and now, they were parents of beautiful daughters. But Mrs. Gentry had given her life to ensure these babies were born. She had lived her religion. Now it was her duty, she and her sister's duty, to ensure these babies returned to Chaktun. They had to return to Chaktun to help deliver them from the Kulusks.

One of the babies started to cry. Laurona had to leave her post at the kitchen window to attend to her child or her niece. Her niece, the thought seemed odd. She stopped and listened for a while. Was it her child or her niece? It was Kashara; her cry was distinctive and loud. It was her child. Her child...her daughter, it gave her a strange but warm feeling. She was a mother. The thought made her chuckle as she moved into the bedroom.

Nausona reached the creek and began humming the song, which was the signal for the pickup. A father, mother and their toddler son appeared, silhouetted by the moon. It was around midnight, and the routine began. Nausona marched them back to the farmhouse. Again, the cargo was quiet. Nausona wondered if it was either out of fear of discovery or they did not trust her. She decided it was out of fear of discovery. Nausona knew she had not lived a slave's life. She was pampered under Mrs. Gentry's charge. The people she had helped escape to the North had lived inhuman lives. She had no right to question or intrude on their solitary thoughts as they walked back to the farmhouse. Nausona understood this was a frightening venture in their lives. She was just a small part of it. Therefore, she let them have their solitude. This would be one night she would not impose on the guests for information. Besides, she had all the information she wanted to know. In a short thirty-six hours she and her sister would leave this planet and hopefully never return.

Never return? Was that fair? No, she must return. She must return in triumph. This planet was now in her purview. That meant it was on Chaktun's purview, and maybe on Kulusk's agenda. No. This once prison planet would have to be protected. But, how could she protect it? This barbaric planet was more than four galactic millenniums behind the slowest planet in the republic. They could not survive the technologically advanced intrusion that the Chaktun Republic would do in order to protect it. But she owed it to Mrs. Gentry. Something needed to be done. But again, what? This will require more thought, she decided. She would have to speak with her sister. Besides, she did not know if there was a republic to return to. It had been almost two galactic years. Much could happen in that time—not all of it good.

Laurona was relieved when she saw her sister standing in the kitchen door with the cargo.

"It took you over an hour," she grunted.

"I meant a galactic hour," her sister rejoined. "You know we have to forget the local time measurement and get back to galactic measurement. We will be home in thirty-five hours."

"You mean thirty galactic hours—don't you?"

Her sister just rolled her eyes. "How are the babies?" Nausona pulled off her coat and moved to the bedroom, leaving their guests in the kitchen with three plates of food.

"They are asleep. Hopefully, they will sleep through the night." Laurona turned to their guests. "Eat," she said in English. They looked at the plates and then sat down.

"Where you go?" the father inquired.

"We are checking on our babies. They were just born a couple of days ago," Nausona smiled.

The father nodded, "Good. Good to know you have family. You have husbands?"

"No, their fathers were…well I mean…" Nausona was searching for the right words to explain the babies. "We were…"

"I know," the father interrupted. "The master is…"

He smiled and then began eating his pork and beans. The mother and child soon followed suit.

After the family was fed, Laurona gave them instructions for the next stop on their travel. Once the sisters were satisfied they understood the instructions, the family bedded down for the night in the cellar. The sisters crawled into bed next to their sleeping angels and fell asleep. It was a long day, and they both were exhausted.

***

Laurona awoke to the sound of horses galloping up the front road. It still was dark, but the horse sounds were unmistakable. "Nausona get up," she yelled. Nausona eyes popped open. "Do you hear that?"

"Yes, I hear it. Take the girls and put them in the cellar. I'll get the weapons."

Laurona took the babies, one in each arm, and rushed to the cellar. She laid the babies on the floor as she moved the table and opened the trap door.

"We have riders outside. You stay here. No matter what happens, you stay here. No one knows about this cellar. You are safe." Then she passed the babies down to the father who passed them to the mother. "Please watch our babies." She pointed to the first baby, "That is Kashara, she is my little girl. The other is Sharyla; she is my sister's little girl. Please keep them safe with you until we return." She slammed the door, placed the throw rug over it and the table on top of the throw rug. Her sister tossed her weapons to her. She turned just in time to catch the pagenay in her right hand and the mation in her left hand.

"Ready?" Nausona asked.

"Ready," she answered as she stuck the weapons into the waistband of her skirt.

Nausona opened the front door to see four white men stop about twenty yards from the front porch. Two of the men were Jim and Sam Pathgo. Nausona recognized the other two as the overseers who whipped them almost two years ago.

"What do you want?"

Jim Pathgo shook his head, "I guess you don't know how a nigga is supposed to talk to a white man." He looked at his brother. "You know Sam, mother was right. We have to kill these niggas. They think they are better than us and that is just plain wrong." Then he looked toward the overseers who were riding to his left and pointed to the girls. "Kill them," he ordered.

The overseers raised their rifles. Laurona pulled her pagenay from the waistband of her skirt and aimed at the overseer on the far right. Her draw was slow due to her weakened condition. Before she could push the trigger, a rifle bullet tore through her right side. Her right hand flew up and her thumb pushed the trigger. A blue discharge sailed skyward, nipping a part of the porch overhang. She fell to her hands and knees. Her sister pulled her pagenay and fired at the overseer who had shot Laurona. The blast hit the man in the face and forced him backwards off his horse. The second overseer fired his rifle and hit Nausona. The left side of her upper chest exploded; she spun left and fell face first into the screen door.

Laurona looked up, but the pain blurred her vision. She raised her pagenay and fired at the shadows where she calculated the men were. Her blast hit the last overseer in the stomach. He screamed in blood-curdling pain as he dropped his rifle and reached for his stomach. The blast burned and cauterized the wound and his hands felt a charred mush where his stomach should have been. He looked at Sam with bewilderment then fell off the horse—dead.

"What the hell?" Sam screamed.

Another blast whizzed by his head. Laurona was firing back at the shadows. Her first burst found its mark with the second overseer, but she could not hit any more of the shadows. Sam and Jim jumped off their horses and belly flopped into the dirt. The horses, free from their riders, turned and charged down the road. Laurona's blurred vision told her the riders had turned tail and run. She stopped firing and lowered her head. The pain burned inside of her, worse than the birth of her child. Her concentration on the agonizing pain made her momentarily forget about her sister. *Her sister, what had happened to her sister?*

"Nausona, where are you?" she screamed. "Nausona…Nausona, where are you?" she continued. She attempted to stand. Then she heard footsteps running toward her. She raised her head and aimed the pagenay in front of her. But a hand grabbed her wrist and turned it, forcing her to drop the pagenay.

"I got her," Jim yelled as he pulled Laurona to her feet.

He stepped behind her and clutched her neck with his left arm as he held her wrist with his right hand. He pushed her forward down the two stairs onto the dirt. The pain of the rapid movement almost caused Laurona to lose consciousness. She fought to stay aware. However, she could not speak, as she felt Pathgo's arm collapse her windpipe. She could barely breathe. Blood coming up her throat complicated that as well.

"I got the other one," Sam Pathgo yelled as he dragged Nausona off the porch feet first.

Her stomach, ribs and face pounded the two steps as he dragged her to the dirt patch in front of the porch. He dropped her feet and pulled the pagenay out of her right hand.

"What the hell is this?" he asked his brother.

"I don't know, but I figure whatever it is, these two niggas used it to kill daddy," he replied as he pushed Laurona face first into the dirt. Her outstretched hand touched Nausona's right index finger as they both lay face down on the ground perpendicular to each other. Nausona flicked her finger ever so slightly to let her sister know she was still alive.

"They killed daddy?"

"Yeah, and I bet they killed those slave catchers awhile ago."

"They killed daddy!" Sam said with more anger.

Then he bent down over Nausona and turned her over onto her left side. He drew his pistol and pointed it between Nausona's eyes.

"Die you unholy bitch."

Nausona realized Sam was about to pull the trigger. While feigning unconsciousness, she pulled her mation from her waistband and plunged it into Sam's groin. Sam yelled in immeasurable pain. He slumped and fell to his right. As Sam fell Nausona twisted the mation and pushed the button. The moving serrated edges chopped at his insides. Nausona then ripped the mation from his groin. Blood and parts of his groin stuck to the jagged edges of her mation. She rolled over and got to her knees. She saw the pain in her assailant's face. If she did nothing, he would surely die from the wound she inflicted. But a slow painful death, no matter how justifiable, was not her way. She pulled the mation over her head with her left hand and plunged it into Sam's open mouth.

"No you die, you shredant," she said as she gave the mation one last twist counter clockwise a half a turn. With that, she saw the life leave Sam's eyes. At that moment she fell to the ground, weak and lifeless.

Jim had turned just in time to see his brother fall from the initial mation attack. Before he could move, Laurona had scissor kicked him at the knees. Jim fell backwards and Laurona sprang to her knees as fast as the pain would allow. But Jim was back on his knees. He tackled her and forced her to fall on her back. As she fell, Laurona withdrew her mation but it slipped from her hand when she hit the ground. Jim saw the strange looking knife and tried to reach for it with his outstretched right hand. Laurona kneed him in the groin. He rolled with pain. Laurona, lying on her back, snaked up until she could feel the mation. Jim sucked in the pain and rolled to his knees. He lunged forward for the strange looking knife. Laurona took the mation in her left hand and threw it, like Maji taught her. The mation sunk into Jim's forehead. His forward progress stopped and he slumped, rolled and turned. He fell dead on his back with the mation sticking out of his forehead. Laurona crawled to Jim's lifeless body pushed the button to move the serrated edges and twisted the mation counterclockwise a half a turn—just the way Maji taught them. Jim's body did not move. He was dead. With that thought, Laurona remembered the pain. It was more severe now. It felt like her right side was on fire, and she could not put it out. Her world turned red, white, and then black. She fell next to her slain assailant.

Chapter 22—The Return

The sun rose from the east as it always did. But this time on the Gentry farm, a bloody battlefield greeted the sun. The rooster crowed, but no one could hear him. Six bodies lay lifeless in front of the Gentry porch. Then suddenly a flash of white light appeared from the barn. Two men stepped out of the barn and gazed upon the carnage. The first man stopped for a moment and then ran to the scene. He saw two women and almost froze in his tracks. The other man followed in hot pursuit. The first man bent over Laurona. He checked for a pulse. The second man ran to Nausona and looked at her in horror. He checked for a pulse.

"She's alive," said Maji, holding Laurona's wrist.

"So is she," the staff sergeant said. "Barely," he added.

***

Nausona fought to open her eyes. She felt her surroundings, a soft bed and cool air blowing on her face. However, she could not command her eyes to open or her body to move. Faint sounds penetrated her consciousness; yet, she remained in a fog. *Why can't I move?* she wondered. *Am I dead? What is happening to me?* She fought again to open her eyes. Her right eyelid fluttered open, but shut again. *What is going on? Why can't I move?* Nausona wanted to scream, but she could not control her speech either. She felt her saliva roll down the right side of her mouth. Then she felt someone wipe it off. *No, I am not dead,* she concluded. *Then what am I?* She stopped trying to command her body to move. She reached into her memory. For an instant she could not remember her name. She felt her heart beat faster as she searched her memory. *Who am I?* she wondered. Then in a flash her memory invaded her subconscious like a flood. She remembered who she was. She remembered the death of her parents, her escape from Chaktun, and her life on the prison planet. She remembered it all, the whipping, the rape, her child, Mrs. Gentry and her death. Her death? The thought chilled her, her mind engaged and she sat straight up and screamed. I can scream, she recognized. She heard a door fly open and she opened her eyes. She could not focus at first. She blinked several times, but to no avail.

"Princess, you are awake," a female voice said in a sweet gentle tone.

"Where am I?" asked Nausona.

"You are in your chambers, my princess," was the reply.

Nausona searched the room. Things were still blurry to her, but she could make out the surroundings enough to recognize the voice spoke the truth. She lay back down and the female came to her and wiped the sweat off of her forehead.

"Now, now, my princess. Everything will be just fine."

Nausona kept blinking her eyes, trying to focus on the female who was consoling her. Was it all a dream—a terrible nightmare? Then the pain in her left side assured her it was no dream.

"How did I get here?" she asked.

"Allow me to answer that," boomed a voice from the door. "But first, what do you remember?"

"Maji, is that you?" Nausona answered.

"Yes, your majesty, it is I. The one you know as Maji."

He motioned for the nurse to leave and he sat on the right side of the bed. He lifted her right hand with his hands and held it gently, but firmly enough to reassure her it was Maji.

"However, your majesty, my name is not Maji. It is Chting—Mitiah Chting. And I do apologize for leaving you as I did."

"You did not leave us, we left you. I thought you were dead."

"No Kulusk could ever stop a Sixana warrior."

"I should have known."

"Again, Princess Nausona, what do you remember?"

Nausona blinked once more and focused on the man beside her. It was Maji, or rather Mitiah Chting.

"First you tell me what happened. How did I get here?"

"As you wish." He loosened his grip on Nausona's hand, stood and retrieved a chair.

He pulled the chair close to the bed and looked into Nausona's eyes. There he recognized confusion with a hint of fear.

"First of all, your sister is alive and well. She is resting in her chambers." Chting watched as the fear faded from Nausona's eyes. But the confusion still lingered in her eyes like a rain cloud.

"Thank you," Nausona mustered out.

"Well, where do I begin?" Chting took a deep breath and scanned the room. "After my escape from the planet, I was able to meet up with a large Chaktun Republic resistance cell. We gathered the resources and developed a plan to retake Chaktun. We were successful in driving the Kulusks from Chaktun in four galactic months. After that, I researched the archives for this ea rth. I found reference points for it and well... Sergeant Wtong and I set out for it. It took us fifteen galactic months, but we found it. However, there were no signs of you or your sister. We stayed for a while and continued scanning the planet. On that last day, we registered pagenay fire on the surface. After pinpointing the location Wtong and I stepped there. We found you and your sister wounded in what appeared to be a battle area. You were alive, but barely. We stepped you back to the ship, stabilized you and placed you in suspended stasis. It was the only way we could think to keep you alive until we reached a competent medical facility. The journey back took another fifteen galactic months." He stopped and saw the fear return in Nausona's eyes.

"My baby, Laurona's baby, what about them?"

"What?" Chting said in astonishment.

"Laurona and I...well we..." she stopped and thought it best to tell her story from the beginning.

She took about fifteen minutes to relay her story as best her mind could remember. Chting's facial expression wrenched with emotion as he listened. He felt sorrow, pain and anger mix in his gut at the same time. When she was finished, Chting lowered his head.

"I am so sorry you went through that. I did not know," he murmured as he shook his head in disgust.

"What about our babies?"

"We scanned for life signs in the area. There were none within five marks of the dwelling. And there certainly was none in the dwelling, or underneath it." Chting's color left his face. "Maybe the family you were harboring took the babies with them to freedom?"

"Maybe, but I have to know," she responded.

"I understand. But the republic has been awaiting your triumphant return. We need you and your sister to lead us. The Kulusks are far from being defeated. If they catch wind of this, they will send assassins to kill your children. I believe it is best for us to defeat your enemy, then to retrieve the children."

"I don't like that," Nausona preached.

"You may not like it, but that is what needs to be done. You have a republic begging for you. It has been almost two galactic years since you left ea rth…"

Nausona cut him off, "Two galactic years?"

"Yes, the trip took fifteen galactic months and you and your sister have been recuperating in stasis for the last five galactic months. We just removed you three galactic hours ago, and your sister is being removed as we speak."

Nausona shook her head as her eyes watered. The thought of losing her baby Sharyla shook her to the core. Damn the duty, she wanted her child. But again, an obstacle stopped her—the Kulusks.

"Take me to my sister; I want to be there when she awakens."

"Yes, Princess Nausona. I will do that. But first let the doctor check you out."

"Very well. Send for the doctor."

***

The doctor gave Nausona painkillers and allowed her to be with her sister. Laurona woke up about a half hour after Nausona entered her bedchamber. Chting and Wtong were both with her. Nausona explained what happened and the unbearable situation they must now face. The two sisters cried in each other's arms, as their bodies shook with wrought disgust. Chting and Wtong watched as the sisters' pain manifested itself, framed by the evening sky as they stood on the balcony.

"My princesses, I vow to you this day, that neither I nor my family will rest until your children are safe and sound on Chaktun soil," Chting pledged.

"I too, pledge my dying breath that neither my family nor I will rest until your children are safe and sound on Chaktun soil," Wtong added.

Laurona and Nausona reached out their arms to their saviors and urged them to hug. The four bodies stood at the balcony of the window looking into the night sky holding each other.

"Sharyla and Kashara are on the third planet from the sun in that solar system to the left," Chting pointed out. "We know where they are, and we know how to get them. Trust us. We will get your children."

Chapter 23—The Beginning of the End

The screen faded to black then panned on two elderly women with short gray hair, but sharp hazel eyes that appeared to look through his soul. "I am Laurona Osguard and this is my sister Nausona," the woman on the right announced. "You have just witnessed a holographic creation of our plight on your planet. It is as accurate as our memories would allow."

"We left our seeds on your planet," Nausona said. "This was not a conscious decision, but a happenstance of the situation. We are unable to locate our children on your planet, and we do not know if they are living or dead. We recognize we will probably die before we see our children again."

"Therefore, because our descendants may inhabit your planet, we have no choice but to wrap our arm of protection around you," Laurona continued. "However this protection is limited—limited to protecting you from outside forces or any force of massive destruction. We will not interfere with the natural development of your planet, even at the risk of losing our descendants."

"Our memory of life on your planet is not good. Therefore, our allegiance to Earth is not blind. Take care of our people and we shall take care of you."

The picture froze and a subscript appeared under Laurona, "Died Earth date: January 1939." It faded and a subscript appeared under Nausona, "Died Earth date: March 1939."

The picture screen faded to black as the president of the United States wiped a tear from his left eye. Then Ortho appeared on the screen. Peters jumped, for he had forgotten all the events that led up to him viewing the film. Reality set back in as he stiffened up and looked at the screen.

Ortho began, "The sisters united the resistance movement. However, they did not do it under the banner of the Chaktun Republic. They allowed the republic to dissolve into individual self-governing planet states. Instead the sisters organized the Universal Science, Security and Trade Alliance of Planets—USSTAP, similar to your NATO. USSTAP, under the guidance and supervision of the Osguard sisters, invented intergalactic and intragalactic gate portals. These gate portals allowed space cruisers to step to any part of the galaxy and even from one galaxy to another. With this invention, the organization repelled Kulusk expansion and contained the Kulusk's thirst for galactic domination to a thirty light year radius from their home world. At the conclusion of hostilities, some eighteen galactic years later, Chting and Wtong set out to retrieve Sharyla and Kashara. But by then the trail was cold. Your United States was a changed land. Eventually, the Kulusks found out about their mission and they sent people as well. We have been visitors on your planet for quite some time now, especially in the United States. We search for the descendants of the Osguard sisters. It saddens me to see how the descendants of the most powerful leaders in the known universe are treated as second-class citizens in your country. However, that is not all your doing. The Kulusks have interfered too many times. I am the grandson of the one you know as Maji or Mitiah Chting. I am sworn to find living descendants of our leaders and place them back into our fold as our rightful rulers. I enlisted the aid of your government at first, but I can no longer do this. Just know if you are viewing this tape, we are still among you and we had to stop the devastation you started this day. However, our patience is limited. We may not afford you another opportunity in the future. Rule wisely or perish. It is your decision."

The tape ended and Peters sat in silence for several moments. Then he checked his watch and noticed he had watched the tape for four hours. He was amazed. He gathered the tape and started to put it in the canister when he noticed another letter buried in the seal of the canister. Peters opened it and began to read it. It was from President John F. Kennedy, written on the eve of the end of the Cuban Missile Crisis. The letter contained President Kennedy's account of the Cuban Missile Crisis and how Ortho returned and stopped a nuclear catastrophe. It also described how the film and Ortho's poignant pleas about the condition of the Negro in America moved President Kennedy.

Ortho had appeared to Kennedy—*how convenient*. Ortho did not come and explain what just happened to him. But Ortho should be dead by now. Why didn't another come and sit as his confidant during this time. Did they find the descendants? Were they still lost? What does it mean?

Peters buzzed his secretary.

"Mrs. Charles, get me the Director of the FBI. I have a job for him."

Chapter 24—Meeting the Enemy

"The subject shuttle has dropped out of MOP and is maneuvering on hypersonic power," reported Sheryl's Defensive Systems Officer, Colonel Scott Tyler.

Sheryl nodded as she stepped to the railing and viewed the big screen.

"Slow to hypersonic and stay just out of scanner range of that shuttle."

Her five-foot, five-inch frame turned, walked back to her seat and sat down. Her eyes fixed on the small screen between her navigator and pilot. Space and stars filled the screen. Nothing appeared discerning to help differentiate this part of space from any other part of space—at least to the untrained observer. But Sheryl and her cousins had studied this part of space. They were in Kulusk space. According to the peace treaty, no USSTAP ship should be in this part of space. It was small, about thirty light years in diameter from the Kulusk home world, easily avoidable by any standard of navigation.

"Ma'am we are entering Kulusk space," the navigator informed.

"I know, Captain Kyle. I know. Where else do you expect a Kulusk shuttle to go?" She thought about it awhile. Going into their space would constitute a violation of the treaty. That could give them a political edge during the Osguard Senate. *Can't let that happen*, she concluded.

"Open a vidcon channel to the Kulusk Space Command," she ordered her communications officer.

"Channel opened."

"On mini-screen, please," Sheryl ordered, not knowing exactly what she would say.

The picture on the screen switched from the star field to a man in a blue shroud with gold epaulettes.

"Good day, I am Osguard five–nine," she greeted the man.

"I am Ritchen, Maxum Kie Ritchen. You are in Kulusk space, a clear violation of the peace treaty of twenty-two–forty-five–seventy-eight. What are your intentions?"

Maxum! They even took the honorary title from the Chaktuns, she thought to herself. *How low can a civilization get? And why would the political ruler answer a hail on the military channel? Was he expecting us? Did they think he would frighten me? Well, maybe it is time to use the diplomacy classes Ortho spent on me, and find out.*

"We are in pursuit of a Kulusk explorer shuttle that left Earth just after a failed sabotage attempt to start a nuclear war," she told the Maxum in Kulusk. "We followed it into your space and we know it has landed on your planet. We request your assistance in apprehending the occupants to bring back for trial."

"Your Kulusk is excellent, Osguard Fifty-Nine."

"As is your Chaktun, your eminence," she said.

"I can't help you. I have no knowledge of such an attempt or of any shuttle entering our space," Kie continued.

"Forgive me, Maxum, but I suspect a person of your stature and prominence would not be aware of small details like a shuttle entering your space. May I please speak with your military?"

"I am the military leader as well as the political leader of the Kulusk Empire. I am aware of all. And I take offense at your suggestion it is otherwise."

Kie was now taking the aggressive posture in the conversation. To him, it appeared Sheryl was weak, handed out expressions of respect as if they would change his mind. Everyone knew the Kulusks only respected aggressive and confident behavior, not the sniveling cowardice tone Sheryl portrayed.

"No offense was intended, your eminence."

Sheryl's mind was racing. Diplomacy was a projection of power without the other person knowing you were projecting it, she reminded herself. She had played this game so many times during first contacts in Galaxy Fifty-Nine, the Litaria Galaxy. But those were with people who had something to gain in diplomacy. The Kulusks had nothing to gain. It was like dealing with Hitler. Power was the one thing they understood. And sometimes they did not understand the power until they were hit over the head with it. The Kashara could take out their little empire within three hours. The firepower at her command was too awesome to imagine. But that was not the USSTAP way, and it was not her way. Michael wanted to know where the cowards went. She found out, but she needed confirmation. She typed one word in the keypad attached to her chair—*'Imcams.'* Her fingers were not in the view of the Maxum. She pushed the send sensor. The command went to the Control Bridge scanner crew.

The control bridge scanner crew positioned the imagery cameras toward the planet. They set the cameras for maximum magnification and pushed cycle three. The Imcams focused on Kulusk at the point where they estimated the shuttle had landed. Using the Imcams was a passive way of spying on the planet surface—no residual energy patterns, which other scanners used, could be traced back to them. It was clean, but not perfect. The products of the Imcams were usually flawed, unfocused and misinterpreted. However, it was the best Sheryl could do, without angering the Maxum anymore. She knew something was not right, but she could not quite put her finger on it. Until she knew, she would play this game as cautiously as she could.

Osguards: Homecoming

"Well offense is what I take, Osguard Fifty-Nine," Kie said with indignation. "For this, I have thought to secede from the trade partnership we have with members of the USSTAP. We no longer need the crumbs from your organization, like we never needed the scientific exploration results or security alliances you forced on other planets." His face appeared closer in the screen as he moved forward. "The Osguards are flawed, weak and contemptible creatures who should be crushed and destroyed."

Sheryl received a data link message. The Imcam search was complete. She turned to look into the screen.

"Maxum, you and your people have tried to kill off the Osguard line for years now. You have merely succeeded in making us stronger. I don't know if it is because we are braver and smarter than you, or if it is because you have the intelligence and resolve of a Litheria water beetle. Frankly, I don't think you have the balls to step on my shadow, let alone face an Osguard in combat. Diplomacy will no longer be afforded to you. Thus, you don't have to leave the trade portion of the USSTAP. I will see to it that you are voted out of the USSTAP for good." Sheryl pushed the communication sensor to end the transmission.

***

Kie stood in front of a dead screen, annoyed at the insults he'd just received. That little rox would soon find out the power of the Kulusks. *I will see her head on my wall as a trophy. I will make trophies from all their heads.*

"Did she scan the surface?" Kie asked his men manning the tracking system.

"No sir," someone replied.

"Good, that means she used the Imcams."

"Can you be sure, my eminence?" asked one of the men on the tracking system.

"Yeah, I am sure. Ortho trained them well. But not well enough," Kie said with a gleam.

Kie turned to the trackers. "Keep an eye on them. Let me know when she leaves Kulusk space," he demanded.

Then he walked to the door. The door slid upwards. He stepped through and made his way down the skinny corridor. He did not look at anyone and no one dared to look at him. He kept his gaze caged in front of him, his mind deep in thought. The plan had failed to destroy the Earth. That much the rox had let slip out, he thought. *No matter! I will just have to add the destruction of that prison planet to the third phase of my plan. Its failure was insignificant in the overall scheme.*

He reached his private office inside the Space Command, which also doubled as the Ministry of War. He placed his hand on top of the scanner lock. It jetted a blue light on the panel. The placard read '*Maxum Kie Ritchen. Identity Confirmed.*' The door slid up and he stepped into the office. Prepovnov, Patterson and Larson stood inside his office.

"Welcome home gentlemen," Kie said with an emotionless and flat tone.

"Thanks," replied Prepovnov.

Kie walked to his desk and sat in his brown chair, made from the skin of a Kulusk cow. He gestured for the men to take the seats opposite him. Larson and Patterson obliged. Prepovnov remained standing. Kie shot a glance at him.

"I see that the time on Earth has dulled your sense of protocol," Kie flapped. "My suggestion for you to take a seat was not an offer, but an order. Do not forget you are in the presence of the Maxum."

Prepovnov stood for a moment, taking in the tongue lashing from his ruler. He was not accustomed to such tones. On Earth he was power. On Kulusk, he was just one of the Maxum's minions. He had forgotten, or he chose to ignore it. At the moment, Prepovnov did not know which one. He shot a glance at the open chair then he looked at Kie. He saw the murderous glare in Kie's eyes, and decided that discretion was the better part of valor. This was not the time to challenge the Maxum. He strutted to the chair and flopped into it.

"Better?" he asked not doing a descent job of hiding his sarcasm.

"No, I am afraid not, my friend. Your tone is—how shall I say—not acceptable."

Kie's right hand pulled the top right desk drawer open. He reached in and produced a miniature pagenay. He rested his thumb on the blue trigger. Unlike the USSTAP pagenay, which had two more buttons—red for rendering a victim unconscious and a yellow for stunning a victim, the Kulusks pagenay had one function—to kill.

Prepovnov's eyes widened at the sight of the pagenay. Then he took a deep breath.

"Okay, you've shown us who is boss. I am sorry. Now can we get on with business?"

Kie looked at Prepovnov and a great big grin highlighted his face. He lowered his head, closed his eyes and shook his head. Then as if possessed he snapped his head up and shot an ugly look at Prepovnov.

"No," he said as he clicked the blue button.

The pagenay shot a short blue energy beam that bore a hole in Prepovnov's skull where his nose once was. The force kicked Prepovnov's lifeless body back and over, causing the chair to flip onto its back.

Patterson and Larson looked at their dead partner, lying in the sitting position in the chair flat on its back. Prepovnov had a grotesque burnt, smoldering hole in the middle of his face and his eyes remained open, capturing the grasping shock of his impending death.

"Now, we can talk business," Kie commented as he placed the pagenay back in the desk drawer and closed it. He rested his elbows on the desk and held his face up with the palms of his hands like a schoolboy admiring the teacher he had a crush on. "What happened? How come the first phase didn't work?"

Patterson squirmed in his seat and felt the sweat roll down the middle of his back. Larson looked away, and then realized that was a mistake. He turned to Kie and shrugged his shoulders.

"Sir, we don't know," Larson stated, hoping Kie did not take offense to him looking away. "We launched the missiles and I sabotaged the countermeasures grid as we planned. But the Osguards somehow used their ships to do the job of the countermeasures grid. We registered chromerion particles as we left orbit. My guess is they shielded the planet then destroyed all the missiles with their arsenal."

"How many missiles?" Kie asked.

"We estimate over two thousand," Patterson interjected, trying to be useful to Kie.

"Thus, sixty galaxy protectors were able to destroy over two thousand missiles in a short span of…how long?" Kie queried.

"I say five to ten Earth minutes," Patterson said.

"Five to ten Earth minutes? That is pretty good. I guess we didn't figure on those rox to think so quickly. I underestimated them," preached Kie. "That won't happen again."

Patterson and Larson looked at each other—the fear resounding in their faces. Patterson felt the sweat form on his forehead. He felt his lungs hunt for breath. *I was safer on Earth than I am on my home planet*, he thought. He turned to Kie and saw he reach into the same drawer he'd placed the pagenay. He closed his eyes and tensed his body. He just knew he was going to die. He heard two thuds. He mentally did a body check for pagenay holes. He was alive. He opened his eyes to see two envelopes on the desk. One was in front of him, and one was in front of Larson. He looked at the one in front of him. It had his Kulusk name on it—Tyel Momek. He sighed with relief.

"There is your payment for services to the Empire. Your families have been well taken care of and the land they have worked is legally yours. Go now…and never speak of your mission to anyone, or you will be joining your friend there." Kie pointed to Prepovnov's lifeless body.

"What about his family?" Larson said pointing to Prepovnov.

"Ah, a greedy man. I like that," Kie said. "I will kill his family and split his money and land amongst you two. It is the least I can do to repay you for the services you rendered the Empire."

Larson's eyes widened with surprise. That was not what he was asking, but he dare not object to the ruling. He wanted to see his family and he did need the money.

If Prepovnov, or whoever he really was, hadn't been so arrogant, he would be sharing in the profits instead of being dead. His arrogance had condemned the family he had forsaken for all these years to death as well. Why was he so arrogant? Did life on Earth taint him that much? Larson knew it hadn't tainted him or Patterson. It must have been living in Russia that did it. He forgot who he was and where he came from. He was Kulusk, the fiercest and most dedicated warrior race in the universe. It was a shame he had forgotten.

"You can go now," Kie invited.

Patterson and Larson rose and walked to the door.

"Aren't you forgetting something?" Kie asked.

Patterson and Larson turned and raised their left hand to their forehead in a sad attempt at a Kulusk salute.

"Not that you fools. Your friend, take your friend out and dispose of him. He just doesn't quite fit the décor of my office."

Patterson and Larson raced to Prepovnov. Each took an arm and dragged him out the room. Larson rushed back in and placed the seat upright and looked at Kie. Kie smiled in satisfaction. Larson ran out the door and it closed behind him.

Kie pressed the intercom switch.

"Security, please find the family living on lot twelve, three–one–two and execute them. Their benefactor has shown poor respect to the Maxum and has been summarily executed. They must join him by sundown tonight."

"Soli," the voice pronounced over the intercom—indicating the affirmative.

Chapter 25—Reconnaissance

"The man is a bastard, Michael," Sheryl observed over the vidcon link from her office outside the command bridge. She was pacing in front of the vidcon screen trying to dissipate the nervous energy that had built up since her conversation with Kie.

"I know that. But what is he up to? That is the question," Michael commented.

"I don't know, but it can't be good. We took some Imcam pics and they show an armada on the surface. It appears to be about seventy-five battle cruisers. They look like they are getting ready to do some heavy damage."

"Are you on your way back?"

"Yes."

"Meet us at Capitol Station. We are stepping up things with the political side of USSTAP."

"I understand. But you should know the trade minister for Kulusk will be there. And Kie said he was going to withdraw from the USSTAP trade agreement."

"I know. You told me all this before. I will introduce a bill that the Kulusk Empire be sanctioned for their involvement with the nuclear attack on Earth. We have your tracking tapes and your recording of the vidcon with Kie as evidence."

"What about the armada?" Sheryl asked as she sat down at her desk.

"Something doesn't feel right. I am going to wait until you get here and we will discuss it with the others."

"You know I can get there in..."

"I know, but..."

Sheryl closed her eyes in shame. She had almost given away their secret over vidcon. Even though the vidcon was a secure transmission, they were still too close to Kulusk space to be assured the Kulusks would not intercept it and use Larson, or whoever he was, to decipher it. That is one thing they would have to do when she got back. Assign new secure transmission logic to all ships in the USSTAP fleet. This would be considered a major overhaul. But it had to be done.

But how about what they had been talking about? They could have been intercepted and deciphered as well. But Michael knew that. And he must have wanted it to be. Or the information was not that crucial. Michael was playing some strategic game, and Sheryl realized she let her temper cloud her judgment on the issue. But Michael just smiled and winked at her, just as he did when they were kids. He just told her, all was okay.

Sheryl looked at Michael's image in the vidcon and stared into his eyes. What was her baby cousin up to now? He was always the strategic planner, the thinker in the family. That is why Ortho placed him as the First Osguard, the chairman of the board, the CEO of the corporation. His vision was absolute in building USSTAP and his guidance a must in securing USSTAP. Boy, did Michael have a poker face. She would kill to have that poker face skill. But she had other qualities. Charm and grace were her qualities. So far, they had suited her well. Yes, she had been forced into battle. All the Osguards had battle stories. Yes, she had been forced to kill in hand-to-hand combat. That just went with the territory. But Michael could bluff his way out of more skirmishes than anyone she knew. He was good. And now he was at his best. He was challenged.

Sheryl gazed upon his face in silence as Michael watched her reaction to his wink.

"Sheryl? Sheryl, are you okay?"

Sheryl snapped out of her thoughts.

"Yeah, I'm fine. I think I better get some rest. Besides, I have a lot of explaining to do with the in-laws. I guess my husband has had the third degree for about seven hours now." She paused to push the end transmission sensor. "Michael, you take care. Luv you."

"Luv you too, cuz." The transmission ended.

***

Michael closed the vidcon transmission on his end and sat at his desk, outside the command bridge. Explaining? He had forgotten all about that. After the attack, Michael had showered and changed in his office so he would not miss any of the reports coming through the pipeline. He had totally forgotten about his parents and his wife. He guessed it was about time he paid them some attention.

"ARIT, open vidcon to Osguard zero–three and Osguard two–two," Michael commanded.

"Osguard zero–three here," Shawn's voice boomed, as his picture filled half the screen.

"Osguard two–two here," echoed Patricia's voice, as her picture filled the other half of the screen.

"Hey, it's time to pay the piper. I invite you two to step over and get acquainted with our parents, now that they know—you know."

"Okay, I'll be over in five," Shawn declared, trying to hide the dread in his voice.

"Same here," Patricia added. "I've already indoctrinated my in-laws, guess my parents are next."

"Fine, I will meet you in the command gate portal room in five."

Michael pushed the sensor to end the transmission. He stood to stretch his long legs. He had been sitting for over six hours at his desk wading through a mound of digital reports. His eyes were blurred, but his mind was still racing through the information it had digested. He walked over to the food dispenser.

"Coffee, sweet and black," he commanded.

The dispenser hummed and a white light shone from its port. Several seconds later a cup of coffee, black and sweet, sat in the port. Michael grabbed it in his right hand as he exited his office. The door hummed as it slid to the right and hummed again as it closed behind him. Michael looked right at the stairways leading to the two bridges, and then he looked left. He took a deep breath and turned to his left. He caught the coaster as it opened.

"Command gate portal room," he commanded.

The coaster door hummed shut and he took a seat as the coaster glided through magnetic coils of air in a vacuum tube. Fifty-five seconds later it stopped and the door opened. Michael stepped out and walked the thirty paces to the command gate portal room. There were several gate portal rooms throughout the ship, but the command staff solely used this one. Dependents and other crewmembers used the other gate portals for nonessential business. There was even a gate portal bay used extensively for emergency recall. He thought it would never be used. But it worked properly today.

The command gate portal room door opened as the door slid to the right. Michael walked in just in time to see his brother arrive. Shawn stepped out of the light onto the portal platform. Then his portal closed and he stepped off the platform. Then another white light appeared and his sister arrived.

"Right on time," Michael criticized.

"Yeah, yeah, yeah. Let's get this over with," Shawn jawed back.

The siblings exited the room, each in their private thoughts, each wondering how their parents were taking the news. It was almost the feeling of dread that overcame the three of them. But this was something that had to be done, so they could get on with the business of the USSTAP.

Michael tapped his CC, "Doctor Genesis, this is Osguard zero–one." He waited for the normal transmission protocol to execute. His wife, Michelle Katherine Genesis had earned her USSTAP degree in Bio Molecular Physiology during her time with Michael. She knew she would spend the rest of her life in space with her husband when he proposed and let her into the secret world of USSTAP. She didn't want that time to be spent as just a wife, but as a productive member of USSTAP. She couldn't enter USSTAP in any of the operational corps. That meant going to the Academy on Chaktun and being away from her new husband. So she used the resources available to her on the ship and earned her Doctorate degree. Soon after, she was accepted into the medical corps and assigned to her husband's home station, Capitol Station. She rose to the rank of major in ten years, proud she did it on her own merits and without the aid of her husband. Although, being the wife of an Osguard did have its perks.

"Dr. Genesis here," punched his wife's voice through the subdural receiver in his ear.

"Hey baby, it's me. I have my brother and sister with me. We are on our way to speak with the parents."

"Can you give us another thirty minutes? They are finishing the last holovidpic now. I am sure they will have a lot of questions for you," Michelle pleaded.

"Should we be there as they finish watching the HVP?"

"No, your daughters are doing a good job of explaining the finer details of the situation. They are so happy to finally let their grandparents in on the big secret. Now they can honestly brag about all their accomplishments, instead of making up things to tell them."

Michael felt a pang of guilt hit at his nerves. Had the secret denied them the normal relationship, which all grandparents should share with their grandchildren? He did not know his children were suffering in such a manner.

"You know, it is like a great weight has been lifted off our shoulders," Michelle added. "I don't know why we didn't do this earlier. It took the threat of world destruction to let our parents into our lives. God, it's amazing. But I feel one hundred percent better."

Those words shot into Michael like a spear. His selfishness had literally darkened his family's relationship. He thought he was protecting his parents by shielding the truth from them. Now he realized he was just protecting his own venue. His parents could have died on Earth and it would have been his fault.

Michael sighed, "Okay, you have thirty universal minutes." He pushed the button to terminate the conversation.

"Don't you think that was sort of rude," Patricia noted.

The comment went unheard. Michael's guilt had put him in deep reflection as he continued walking the corridor. Patricia saw the distant look in Michael's eyes and decided to drop the subject.

"Where to?" Shawn asked.

"Officer's Club. I need a drink," Michael answered.

***

Maxum Kie Ritchen closed his eyes as he listened to the recording for the fourth time. His trackers had intercepted Sheryl's message to Michael, and with the help of Glee Joen, formerly known as Commander Larson, he was able to decode their secure transmission. Something he had been doing for years, since Glee infiltrated USSTAP. Those idiots, Kie thought to himself. If they only knew, he was privy to all their secure communications all this time. Kie smiled, congratulating himself for stealth of his operations.

But what is Osguard One up to, he asked himself as he concentrated on the recording once more. He didn't sound convinced about the armada. Maybe he was being extra cautious. I would be in his place. Earth almost destroyed itself and now confronted with the possibility of attack. Kie shook his head. What was there to be cautious about? Hit the enemy when he least expects it. The Osguards had to come and attack the armada while they were in planetary port. It was the most logical thing to do.

Kie thumbed the sensors on his desk. The recording began again. He listened to the interlink communication of Sheryl reporting to Michael. It had gone almost as planned. But there was hesitation. Why convene the Senate? This is the first time in history, sixty galaxy protectors, the most powerful ships known to human, were in the same place to use on an enemy. Kie had drawn them to him. But they still hesitated. Kie could not move on the second part of his plan as long as the Osguards failed to act as anticipated. Did he do something wrong? Did Michael know something he wasn't supposed to know? It had to be the failure of phase one of the operations.

If phase one had been successful, the Osguards' family and friends would have been annihilated. Then the Osguards would have reacted out of sheer emotion and come charging to the Kulusk home world. But that was not so. Earth stood intact, and the Osguards were in full control of their faculties.

Kie shook his head to get the cobwebs out. *Nothing to do, but wait,* he told himself. Their reason will draw the same conclusion. They must attack. When they do, USSTAP will be destroyed, not to mention those rox Osguards. He smiled, but the greed of anticipation would not let him enjoy the moment. He kept thinking, why *won't they come*? He thumbed the sensors once more, and listened to the recording for the sixth time. *I will just have to wait*, Kie thought.

***

Sheryl Tower-Jones had just returned to the bridge. She had just come from visiting with her husband, two sons and her in-laws to see how they were doing. The in-laws were still in shock. The entire story was difficult to believe, let alone comprehend. Sheryl had left them with the three holovidpics she used to indoctrinate her husband several years back. The recordings seemed to explain the situation better than she could ever do. The first HVP told the story of Nausona and Laurona, the mothers of the Osguards. The second HVP told the story of how the two sisters forged USSTAP in the time of galactic war. The third HVP told the story of how Ortho found the surviving lineage, her and her cousins, trained them and sent them into space as leaders of USSTAP. Counting everything, her in-laws should be busy for about six more hours. That was if they watched the holovidpics back-to-back. She knew her sons loved to look at them. They would probably watch them with their grandparents and point out the subtle details that only they would find interesting.

With that out of the way, she had to get back to more pressing issues. The command bridge was the place she needed to be. It was where she could do her most productive thinking. She sat in the command chair with her Centurion of Operations, Jasper North to her right. The Centurion of Engineering, Earnest Sears' chair was empty. He was in his office conducting a ship wide diagnostic test on the new engines. They both knew if this was the flashpoint of another galactic war, her ship needed the engines to be operating at one hundred percent—not a percent less.

Sheryl ran her fingers over the sensors in her command chair's tablet. She wanted to assure herself all was well. It was partly paranoia, but mostly a preparation routine she had a habit of performing before entering any type of known conflict. She had ordered the ship to plot a course for Capitol Station at hyperlight speed. She wanted to chart this area of space, in case they had to return.

"Osguard, the Kulusks are still scanning us," Colonel Scott Tyler reported.

Sheryl nodded to confirm she understood.

"Maintain course and speed," she echoed. Then she looked to her right, "Jasper, how much longer before you have the area charted?"

North thumbed his chair's tablet and read the readouts from the control bridge scanner team. "In another ten universal minutes, we should have all we need."

"Great. As soon as you are finished, go to MOP sixty and get us the hell out of here. I've got an eerie feeling about this whole thing." Then she turned to her communications officer, "Commander Stand, I want you to do a sweep of all channels, record all traffic and send it to the Comm Lab for analysis. Maybe these Kulusks are talking about what they are up to."

"Speaking of comm, don't you think our secure transmissions have been compromised?" asked North.

"Yes, I know they have been. The question is, for how long?" Sheryl pushed.

"How long?"

"Yes, how long," Sheryl repeated. "This Larson character has been with Earth's USSTAP force for almost twenty years. He was personally recruited by Ortho. Now the question is, is this the same Larson? Has Larson been turned? Or is the real Larson dead and the Kulusks replaced him with a double?" He had to have help. I'm sure the nuclear confrontation did not start on its own. I bet the United States and Russia were infiltrated as well," she explained.

"Do you think they were sabotaged as well?"

"Shit, if we were infiltrated what makes you think they weren't?"

"What makes you think Larson was the only one?" North added.

Sheryl stopped at that. What if there were more Kulusk spies in their midst? She tapped her tablet for sickbay. She typed in *'Check crew for Kulusks.'* She knew all humans were biologically the same, no matter what planet or what galaxy they hailed from. But there were always some genetic DNA signature markers that gave a person's origins away. That is how Ortho isolated the Osguards.

The Osguards' Chaktun DNA sequence was tighter than any other human on Earth. Then Ortho ran genetic relativity tests against Nausona's blood and Laurona's blood. A match of ninety-five percent or higher was considered a hit. The sixty Osguards were ninety-nine point nine percent, a definite hit.

She looked at the back of her right hand. She raised it to her face. She began to study it, line by line. The birthmark was so noticeable—a diamond shaped dark mark, the very symbol of USSTAP. It was another commonality among the Osguards. They all had it somewhere on their body. It made Ortho's job a little easier. Once Ortho pinpointed a few of the Osguards with the birthmark and DNA, the rest was easy.

Ortho simply had to track the family line. Well, simple was not the right word for it, she thought. Blacks in America could not follow their genealogy as closely as the other races. Birth certificates and death certificates were a rarity. Luckily, Sharyla and Kashara made it up North where records were kept better than in the South. But still, it was a chore for Ortho and the rest to go through the records. Unfortunately, Ortho could not find two genetic lines of descendants. Both Sharyla and Kashara had at least one daughter who Ortho could not find marriage certificates or death certificates on. Sharyla's first born, Shirley, born in December of 1885 in New Haven, Connecticut and Kashara's first born, Betty, born in May of 1883 in New Haven as well, seemed to disappear after they turned fourteen and sixteen respectively. Ortho knew there were two more lines of Osguards lost in America. He died before he knew the answer to their whereabouts.

Sheryl's tablet beeped. She looked to read it. "No Kulusks onboard." That was a relief. Well it was if she could trust her ship's doctor. Paranoia, it was now making her second-guess her crew. She stood to stretch her legs. She zipped her uniform jacket halfway down and fanned the collar.

"Is it hot in here, or is it just me?" she asked to no one in particular.

"Temperature is two-two chimes," Colonel Tyler reported. Two-two chimes translated to sixty-five degrees Fahrenheit.

She nodded in acknowledgement and zipped her coat back to the collar. Then she remembered hot flashes were a definite side effect of the DNA scan. That was proof the Centurion of Medicine had in fact covertly accomplished the DNA scan. A slight smile crossed her lips. So much for paranoia, she thought.

She raised her arms over her head and strolled to the balcony. She peered down to see the control bridge personnel rushing to complete the charting of this sector of space. Their black uniforms and boots made them look like ants surrounding a piece of food on a kitchen floor. The unique discerning features in their uniforms was the rank on their collar, the USSTAP symbol on their right breast, the corps patch on their left shoulder and the number fifty-nine on their right shoulder signifying they belonged to the fifty-ninth galaxy of USSTAP, the Litaria Galaxy.

All of them wore the corps patch of operations. The other corps patches worn on the ship were security corps, engineering corps, diplomatic corps, economic corps, science corps and the medical corps. Sheryl commanded all the corps because she was the Osguard. Each corps leader wore the rank of Centurion, the highest field officer rank allowed. The ranks above Centurion—Marshal, Commodore, General, and Admiral—were reserved for station officers. They commanded the precincts, the space stations, the world stations and headquarters stations respectively. The sole exception was each galaxy had four more galaxy protectors commanded by admirals assigned to them. Those stations, the galaxy protectors and the assortment of two thousand other ships were all under her command in the Litaria Galaxy—because she was the Osguard.

The responsibility was awesome. She not only had to watch and care for the two thousand and five hundred souls on-board the *Kashara*, but she had to watch and care for the countless number of people who wore the black uniform of USSTAP in her galaxy of responsibility. She had blindly accepted it, like the other Osguards. But for some reason the responsibility weighed heavy on her shoulders this day. Maybe it was because she was the point man in her cousin's galaxy. The one who could start a war, end a war or avoid a war that she may not be responsible for fighting. It was different when her actions led to consequences she either enjoyed or bore in her own galaxy. But her actions today may have lunged Galaxy One of USSTAP into a bitter war. And all she would do was travel back to Galaxy Fifty-Nine like nothing had happened. She took a deep breath and swung back to her seat. *Then I better make sure this ends peacefully*, she told herself.

"Are we ready to get the hell out of here?" she asked North.

"Final marks are in now."

"Great. Pilot, MOP sixty now."

"Tiah," replied the pilot.

The hum of the engines grew as the ship sailed into MOP sixty. The screen went blank. The navigator adjusted the controls and a star field appeared on the screen. It was disconcerting to have a blank screen displayed when traveling at MOP speed. Therefore all ships displayed the star field they had just passed. The ARIT-projected layout remained at the helm between the pilot and the navigator. The command team was afforded both views. It made the time pass easier.

***

"Maxum, the galaxy protector has stepped to MOP speed. They have left our space," the tracker's voice sounded over the intercom in Kie's office.

"Finally," Kie sighed as he laid down a silver ball he was using to play Misuip, a Kulusk game similar to golf. Kie was practicing his close-in shot. He found this relaxing, and it enabled him to think. "Keep scanners on maximum. Let me know when you see any USSTAP ships approach our space," he commanded the tracker.

"Soli."

Kie picked up the silver ball and placed it in a long rod. He stood about ten feet from a makeshift hole, pushed the button on the handle of the rod and swung toward the makeshift hole. The ball rolled down the tube and jetted out the opening at the end. It hit the floor and rolled toward the hole. Inertia slowed the ball to a painful crawl, but it had enough energy to find the hole. It fell with a thud. Kie smiled at his skill. *No, that wasn't luck, that was skill*, he thought to himself. He placed the rod down and sat behind his desk again. He picked up a touch pad labeled *'Operation Osguard.'* He pressed the sensor to open it, and began reading. It was his twelfth time reading the plan. He wanted to know every aspect of it by heart. He wanted to execute any contingency plans without referring to the pad. During the execution of the third phase, he would not have time to refer to the plan. He had to know it. He did know it. But he had to make sure he knew it.

Chapter 26—Reckoning

Michael finished the last swallow of his Jack and Coke. Shawn had finished his Chaktun beer minutes earlier, and Patricia sucked on the ice from her soda. Michael slammed the glass down on the bar and reviewed his watch as he had done a dozen times since they entered the ship's bar.

"It's time to go face the music," he snorted.

"Boy, you sound like you dread this more than I do," Shawn replied.

"Dread it? I absolutely fear it."

"Why? It's me mom could never stand. You were her favorite." Shawn eyes lit up. "That's it. You are afraid that keeping this secret will knock you down a notch or two in mom's eyes. Aren't you?"

"No, that's not it," Michael whispered. "I fear that keeping this secret has caused more damage than good. I was wrong on insisting the entire Osguard body keep the secret."

"It wasn't you. It was Ortho who insisted," interjected Patricia.

"I know it was Ortho's wishes, but the responsibility fell on me when Ortho died."

"Look, Mr. Hotshot. You may be the First Osguard, but you don't command us. We are equal and independent of each other. The one commonality we have in USSTAP is the senate and this political bullshit we are about to do," Shawn bellowed. "We can do whatever we damn well please. Any one of the Osguards could have told the entire planet we existed and you could not do a damn thing about it. So get off your holier than thou horse and come back to reality. We all agreed that keeping the secret was the best thing to do. Besides, you introduced the idea this morning to tell the parents. What more do you want?"

"I want to know I didn't make a mistake."

"First of all, it was not just you. It was all of us. Second, if it was a mistake—so what. Third, we may be Osguards, but we are only human."

"Osguards can't make mistakes. Too many lives depend on us," Michael opined.

"Where is that written," Patricia observed. "We all have lost good people in combat. Shit I lost my best exploration team on a simple scientific recon. The danger signs were there. But I did not catch them. No one caught them." She shook her head. "Listen, anyone can Monday morning quarterback. That takes no brains. But it takes guts to do what we do. Ortho trained us right. We are Osguards. No one else can be us ... but us. So get off your butt and get this shit over with. We have bad guys out there trying to kill us! By default this is your galaxy—this is your problem. You lead and we will follow as long as we can. You better use us while we are here. Remember, we have our own galactic responsibilities to get back to. Mom and dad aren't the problem. It is the Kulusks. You need to be sharper than this if you want to keep this galaxy free."

Michael looked up at his sister, "How did the youngest get so wise?"

"Because I hung out with you two too long."

Michael smiled which spread to his sister and brother.

"Let's go," he offered.

They stood, brushed themselves off and left the bar.

***

The door slid open to the right. Michael, Patricia and Shawn stood in the archway, wearing the black jumpsuit uniform, black thigh high pullover boots, and black suede-like zipper jackets emblazoned with the USSTAP star on the right breast. In front of them sat their parents, Michelle's parents and Michael's daughters on the couch watching the screen. The third HVP had just terminated. The parents turned toward the door as the three walked in and the door whispered closed. Michelle was in the kitchen area. She looked up as well.

"Well, punctual as usual," she chided.

"I try to be," Michael grinned back.

Michelle went to hug and kiss her husband. Then she hugged her brother-in-law and sister-in-law.

"Looks like you guys have saved the day once more," she half joked and half complimented. "Don't you ever get tired of being heroes?"

"No, it comes with the territory," replied Patricia.

Michelle turned to the girls, "It's late. I think you two should go on to bed."

The sisters saw the determination in their mother's eyes and knew pleading would not be in their best interest. They got up, kissed their grandparents and scurried to their rooms.

"Mom, Dad," Michelle addressed her parents. "I have set up quarters for the night next door. If you are ready for bed, we can go there now. Besides, it will give me a chance to speak to you alone."

Like the children, they stood and bade their goodnights. Michelle walked them out the main door.

Michael and his siblings walked into the living room area and sat down. Patricia sat on the couch next to her father, Michael sat down in one easy chair and Shawn took the other easy chair.

"Well. What do you think of all this?" Michael started.

"If I didn't see it with my own eyes, I wouldn't believe it," Parker beamed. "Osguards. You three are Osguards?"

"Yes, daddy," Patricia declared rubbing her father's hand. "Guilty as charged."

"And you just saved the world from blowing itself up?"

"Guilty again," Shawn said.

"I can't believe it," Parker reiterated. "How about you Elizabeth?"

Elizabeth turned to Shawn, "So you don't work in India?"

"No mom. I don't work in India." Shawn explained. "I work in a ship just like this one, a galaxy protector—the *Vedar*. My ship was named after the last Osguard Maxum. Just like Michael's ship was named after the last Osguard Maxim, Neraka."

Elizabeth turned to Michael, "You look like Vedar. Only he was much lighter than you."

"I know. That is why Ortho made me the Osguard for this galaxy. It was psychological, he said. If people saw that I looked like the last Maxum, they would be more loyal. So far, so good! Ortho even said I sound and act like him. He said it was eerie. It was like going back in time."

Then she turned back to Shawn, "You don't work in this galaxy?"

"No mom. I work in the third galaxy, called Minor Man. Earth calls it M-33, the Triangulum Galaxy."

"How can this be? How can you travel so far?" she asked.

"Mom, it's because of the gate portals," Patricia answered. "I can't really explain all the technical details. But the gate portals use inner space, a fourth dimension of some type." She licked her lips as she felt her mouth go dry. "Space is folded upon itself in many layers; we can't see it because we are three dimensional creatures. But anyway, space is folded upon itself and inner space is where different parts of space are connected. Thousands of years ago, humans from other worlds discovered this. Only recently with

Nausona and Laurona's help, were humans able to manipulate the use of inner space to travel to other galaxies. For instance, I am the Osguard for the twenty-second galaxy, Miter Line. It is outside the local group of galaxies, which the Milky Way, Andromeda and Triangulum are a part of. But it is inside the Virgo Star Cluster, the same cluster the local group is connected to." Patricia saw the look of confusion on her mother's face. She knew she was getting too technical for her. "Mom, just think of the gate portals as elevators to different parts of space. Instead of taking the stairs to get where we want to go, we take the elevator. It is quicker and less tiresome to do."

"I guess I understand," she said. "But why? You are my babies."

"Ortho explained it as our destiny," Shawn pushed. "Blame dad. It's his lineage that connects us to all of this."

Parker's eyes lit up with pride. "You mean this could have been me."

"I suppose, if Ortho had completed his search when you were in your twenties. You and your brothers and sisters could have been the Osguards."

Parker smiled a big grin at that thought. Shawn and Michael giggled at their father's pleasure. Elizabeth turned to see Parker smiling and she smacked him on the right leg.

"I would not have gone with you, if you were out here playing space cowboy, Parker."

"Oh, yes you would."

"No, I wouldn't."

"Oh, yes you would. Because you love me." He kissed her on the cheek. She fought the smile, but it soon won the battle. She giggled a little and pushed him away.

"Not in front of the kids."

Michael watched as he thought this was going incredibly well. He winked at Shawn who was smiling at his parents' youthful play.

"Okay, I have one question," Elizabeth said as the smile and giggle left her. "Why the big secret?"

The question Michael was dreading. Well, this called for diplomacy and tact in this instance. He had thought how he would answer this question for the last twelve years. "Because—

"For your protection, mom," Patricia blurted. "As you can see, we have some bad guys, namely the Kulusks, who want to destroy us. We figured the less you knew the better. You had security in the gardens and—"

"How is us not knowing, protecting us?" Elizabeth interrupted.

"Well we didn't want you to worry and—" Shawn was interrupted as well.

"You thought I would blab it all over the place."

"Well...yes," whispered Michael.

"Did the other parents know?"

"No."

"Good, I hate to think I was the only one not trusted. Besides, who would believe me? They would have locked me up for sure," Elizabeth laughed. "Now, the other mothers and I can talk freely about this, I suppose."

"Yes, but be careful—just in the Gardens. We have that pretty much secured," Patricia added.

"Good, then I'm happy."

"You sure mother?" Shawn asked.

"Yes, I am sure. I'm not as terrible as you make me out to be. I was just upset I wasn't part of your lives' anymore. Now, I know why. But now I know I can be part of your lives. I mean I can come to visit you in..." She was searching for the words. "In Minor Man."

"You want to come visit me in Minor Man?" Shawn asked.

"Look. I am not excited about all this space stuff. I don't even understand it. But Shawn and you other two, I love you and I will travel this entire space just to see your smile every so often."

Shawn's eyes watered as he fought back the tears. He stood and hugged his mother.

"I love you too."

She wrapped her arms around him and whispered in his ear, "Just because you are one of these Osguards, don't mean I'm going to stop being your mother." She let go and looked him in the face. "I was born to nag you, and that is what I am going to do—nag you."

Shawn smiled, because he began to understand how his mother really felt about him.

"Mom, if that's how you want to show you care; then, be my guest."

"Boy, that's my job. Now I am tired, where will your father and I bunk for the night?

"It will be my honor if you'd come bunk with me on the *Vedar*," Shawn requested. "You have a grandchild who would love to see you in the morning."

"Fine, how do we get there?"

"Follow me," Shawn said as he led his parents out the front door.

Patricia and Michael stood holding hands.

"What the hell just happened here?" Michael asked.

"I don't know, but I think I like it," she responded. "Listen, I took the liberty to have the Gardens secured by the Earth Security Force."

"Thanks."

"I better get going. It's been a long day. And if I know you, it will be a longer day tomorrow."

"Yeah. Sheryl will be back in a couple of hours. I want to meet in the Senate and talk over a few things," Michael said, turning back into the command figure of the Osguard.

"Okay. What time?"

"0900."

"Okay, I'll get the word to the others. Good night, Michael." She kissed her brother on the cheek and walked out the front door.

Michael sat back down to contemplate what just happened, when he heard the whisper hum of the front door open and close.

"How did it go?" Michelle inquired.

"Better than I expected. And you?"

"A little shaky at first, but they finally understood. In fact once they thought about it they were damn near proud."

"Good. Ready to go to bed?"

"Yeah, I am tired. It's been a long day. And if I know you, it will be a longer day tomorrow."

Michael shook his head, "What is this—a conspiracy?"

"What?"

"Nothing. I'll catch you in the bedroom. I am going to check in on the girls."

***

"Osguard," Commander Oliver Stand, the communications officer called.

"Yes," Sheryl groused.

"I think you might want to see this."

Sheryl stood from her command chair and made her way to the communications station.

"Here and here," Stand pointed to his monitor. "Do you see what I see?"

Sheryl stared at the monitor. She thumbed the controls to focus the picture, and then she scrolled the information. She read the data printout. Her mind was tired, but the information on the screen was like a shot of adrenalin.

"Yes, I see it," Sheryl whispered. "Bring up the Imcam pics from Kulusk," she ordered Stand. She viewed the pics for a few seconds. "Do you see anything odd?" she asked Stand.

Stand was not an imagery expert and was surprised Sheryl was conferring with him over the Imcam pics. Sheryl pointed to a couple of spots on the pics. Stand studied them, and then it was clear as a bell. It was a small detail, but once you saw it, it became the main focus of the pics—no shadows. The ships in the armada weren't casting a shadow. The hills, the trees, and even the docks were casting a shadow. But the ships in the armada were not casting a shadow.

"Decoys?" Stand questioned.

"Decoys," Sheryl agreed. "They wanted me to see those ships. They knew our standard operating procedures. Shit, Larson must have fed them all that."

"Guess it is time for us to act unconventional," Stand observed.

"Yup, and you just fed us the biggest piece of the puzzle. Good work, Commander Stand!"

He just smiled, "Thank you, Ma'am."

Sheryl moved back to her command chair, "How long before we reach Capitol Station?"

"Two point seven universal hours," the navigator answered.

"Okay people; let's get the shift change over with. It has been a long day. And if I know my cousin, it will be a longer day tomorrow," Sheryl suggested. "I'm turning in. I want you to get some rest. I need my best folks totally rested and ready for action." She thumbed her keypad. "ARIT, nightshift call."

Ten minutes later, both bridge crews had been replaced by fresher and more energetic people. Centurion for Security relieved Sheryl. Sheryl left for her quarters.

When she arrived at her quarters, she saw her three boys were asleep. She tiptoed into her bedchamber and saw her husband was asleep as well. She surmised her in-laws were in guest quarters somewhere on the deck. She changed into her nightclothes, crept into bed and snuggled next to her husband. He was still asleep, but he automatically turned to her and gently kissed her on the lips. Then he turned back around and resumed snoring.

Now anyone could have sneaked in bed and this idiot would just kiss them and turn around and go back to sleep, she thought. Then she laughed. *I trained him well,* she added.

The levity of the moment was fleeting. Her mind sped over the events of the day; Earth almost destroyed, secret told to the residents of Osguard Gardens, saboteurs escaped, confrontation with an old enemy, a deception discovered, and an armada of seventy-five battle cruisers parked within striking distance of Capitol Station discovered. What a day. And this morning, her only worry was who was going to win the Osguard Olympics. *What else could happen? Better not ask that,* she thought. *Might find out sooner than I want,* she continued. Then she closed her eyes and said her evening prayers. Five minutes later, she was asleep.

Chapter 27—Nightmares

"We don't have a damn thing," the president's security advisor reported.

Malcolm Dylan Petteway

Peters shot a slight smirk at his security advisor, James Hall. Peters called the special meeting in the Oval Office to discuss the events of the previous day. He wanted to know what ignited the events. He sat at his desk quietly but attentively. James Hall, Vice President George Willis, Secretary of Defense Paul Thompson, and the Chairman of the Joint Chief of Staff, Army General William Oliver were seated across from him. Each man showed signs of fatigue and nervousness. Each had been up all night piecing together what information was available to build a solid picture of what went wrong.

"That's not what I want to hear," Peters challenged.

The men looked around at each other, their faces blanched with gloom. No one wanted to speak. Then all eyes turned to the Chairman. He felt the imaginary searing heat of responsibility burn in his heart. His throat was dry, his pulse raced and he felt tiny beads of sweat coat his neck, and slide down the small of his back. Suddenly, it was hot in the room. He gestured with his eyes for someone to speak, but he only received sharp glares from his companions.

"Well, it seems you have something to tell me General Oliver," Peters prompted.

Oliver swiveled towards Peters with his head lowered. The shame and guilt of his failure of command was evident in his posture. He raised his head, but kept his eyes lowered, focused on the top of the president's desk. Peters sat back in his easy chair, elbows resting on the chair arms, his index fingers and thumbs forming a triangle in front of his face with his knuckles pressing against each other. Oliver noted from previous meetings, this was Peters' posture when he was displeased with the information he was receiving. Who wouldn't be displeased with this news? The world almost annihilated itself and the U.S. nuclear arsenal was the weapon of choice, he thought.

"Well," Oliver's voice cracked. He coughed to clear his throat and then he tried to swallow. His mouth was too dry; it hurt his throat to swallow. He reached for the silver carafe and poured a glass of cool water. He chugged the water down as if it was a shot of whiskey to bolster his courage. Peters looked on somewhat agitated at the delay.

"Well, Mr. President," Oliver continued. "It appears the Vice Chairman is missing." He shot a glance at Peters to see how his opening statement was received. Peters showed no emotion at the news. He remained in his displeased posture.

"We think he penetrated the War Room and activated the launch codes," Thompson blurted.

"What?" Peters said, shifting his posture by placing his arms on the desk and hunching over his desk. Thompson realized they waited too long to tell Peters this bit of information. But they did not know if Patterson was dead, killed by an assassin or if he just could not be reached.

"Mr. President, I am sorry for the delay in telling you this, but we weren't sure of General Patterson's status," Thompson persisted. "We went to his house and all was in order. However, his wife and daughter were gone. It appears from neighbor statements, they have been gone for quite some time…almost six weeks."

"Were they kidnapped?" asked Peters.

"That is our first impression," blurted Oliver. "We think he may have been forced to do this."

"Force or not, he is our man," interceded Hall. Somehow he got a duplicate of the football and used the launch codes to activate the missiles. He killed five good Marines in the process, Marines with families, wives and kids of their own."

"How?" Peters asked as he shook his head in disbelief.

"Don't know how he duplicated the football," Thompson said. "All I know is that he did, and that he shot five good Marines."

"Well shot may be presumptuous," Hall corrected. "The men had dime size holes in their heads, no bullet and no blood, just the holes. He must have used some type of energy gun. Sir, we don't have anything like that on the books. Whatever he used, it isn't one of ours."

"Did it sear the wound?" asked Peters as he thought about the film he'd just seen.

"The preliminary autopsy suggests that. But I really don't know," answered Hall. "Why do you ask?"

Peters started to tell them about the film. He wanted to show them the film. He focused on his right hand bottom desk drawer where he had placed the film. Should he or shouldn't he. His right hand moved to the drawer. He hesitated.

"Never mind," Peters sighed. "I know the weapon isn't ours and it isn't Russian. You won't find Patterson or his family and you won't figure out how he did it."

"What?" Hall asked. "What are you talking about? How do you know?"

"I know. Just say I have been in communications with some other agencies that…" Peters stopped. He dare not tell them yet. "Keep looking." He ordered.

"Sir, one other note," Hall pushed. "The Russians are supposed to be cooperating, but no word on their end."

"Don't worry, I have a call into Sergay right now," Peters mused. "Now go and get me some information."

The gentlemen rose and walked out, more confused by Peters' offhanded remark. *Did the president know more than he was telling his closest advisors?* thought Hall. Whatever Peters knew, he should know. Hall took one last glance at the Commander in Chief. Peters had turned his chair around and was staring out the window of the Oval Office. Hall stood in the doorway for a moment, his mind recounting the short meeting. Was Peters responsible for the situation? And had he cleverly led the investigation to Patterson? Hall thought, he was sounding like one of those conspiracy buffs, who did not trust the government. *Stop being silly,* he thought as he closed the door behind him to leave Peters to his private thoughts.

***

The intercom buzz pulled Peters out of his thoughts. He spun in his chair and punched the intercom reception button on the phone.

"Russian president on line one, Mr. President," announced Mrs. Terri Charles, the president's secretary.

"Thanks," said Peters. He punched the receiver off, picked up the phone and punched line two. "Sergay, how are you doing?

"Frederick, let's not play politics now. I have seen a most disturbing tape, left in our vault by…left by…left by Khrushchev."

"Let me guess, it details the life and times of two sisters named Laurona and Nausona in the United States prior to our civil war."

"It details more than that, my friend. It details—"

"—Sergay," Peters interrupted. "If those tapes are real, then is it safe to talk on this phone?"

"Those tapes?" questioned Sergay, as he concluded there were two tapes. "You have seen what I am talking about?"

"I spent the latter part of yesterday viewing it," admitted Peters. "Tell me something. Did a high ranking official in your military infiltrate your security and launch your missiles?"

"Why yes. It was General Ivan Prepovnov, commander of the Ministry of Defense Twelfth Directorate. How did you know?"

"Our Vice Chairman of the JCS Samuel Patterson was the culprit who penetrated our systems."

"What is going on here?" asked Sergay.

"It appears the Kulusks infiltrated us and tried to start a nuclear war. And I am guessing Ortho or whoever is running this USSTAP stopped it for us. At least that is my guess. What do you think?"

"You may be correct, Frederick. But how can we be sure?"

"We are still here, aren't we? There were more than enough nukes in the sky at the same time to kill this planet three times over. What happened? Nothing. The sky lit up white for about five minutes and the nukes disappeared. Do you have another explanation for it?"

Sergay thought a moment. "No, I have no better explanation. Now what?"

166

Osguards: Homecoming

"Well it looks like we have completed our strategic arms reduction. I fear to say we both have limited nukes left. Therefore, we must come up with a plan." Peters feigned thought, because he knew what he wanted to do. "Let's announce a summit where we come up with this drastic amendment to the Strategic Arms Reduction Treaty. There we can put on the façade of still having our nukes, and that we are willing to give them up for mankind. What do you say?"

"Yes, we shall meet when I come to Washington the day after tomorrow. We will announce this together. I'd like that."

"Good, it's settled. We will come up with an amendment to the START and do whatever it takes to pass it through our respective legislatures."

"Fine Frederick, but what do we tell the people about the white light in the sky. We have several speculations. Plus, many civilian organizations suspected we launched our missiles. It is kind of hard to hide that."

"Well Sergay, we are denying everything. All we will admit to is that it was a scientific test of our defense system."

"Yes, we will do the same. Maybe we can say it was a mutual test in prelude to our summit."

"Sounds strange, but we can work on it when you get here. But for now, deny any launch of nukes. If word got out, panic would rule the streets," warned Peters.

"There are too many people involved to ensure complete compliance with that," Repustinov countered.

"Do your best. The fact there weren't any nuke explosions should validate the statement."

"It's too big, too many people involved. We won't get away with it," Sergay commented.

"We have no other choice. If we tell the truth, the resulting chaos would do more harm than if the missiles did hit. People would panic, the stock market would plummet and people would be seeing aliens everywhere. It turns my stomach to think we are descendants of prisoners. Then to find out there are more advanced races than us who have that much power over us. What do you think the common citizen would do? He would no longer have faith in his country, government or his fellow man. I tell you chaos would rule. And I don't think this USSTAP would step in and save us. Do you?"

"Are you afraid to tell your citizens the descendants of your black population may be the rulers of the galaxy? Is that the chaos you are referring to? Frederick, are you afraid of the truth?"

"Sergay, I am offended at your words. The lineage of the USSTAP is not at question, it is the power of the USSTAP that frightens me. They stopped a nuclear holocaust. How many militaries can do that? They travel to other galaxies. How many militaries can do that? People of Earth aren't ready. They won't handle the news well at all; including your people. How would the Russian society, afraid of outside conquest, react to a force with that much power?"

Sergay paused. His country had always feared outside conquest, the French, the Germans, the Chinese and the Japanese. Fear has dominated their history for as long as he could recall. Frederick was correct. Fear would prevail over common sense. But what he proposed was still too large to conceivably work. However, a lie even this big, would keep the conspiracy experts busy in the wrong direction for decades. By then, maybe the USSTAP would contact them directly and help indoctrinate the population. Was that the right word? Indoctrinate seemed so militaristic. Assimilate the population into the USSTAP? That sounded too ominous as well. Sergay was starting to see what Peters meant. A drastic change, even for the betterment of mankind would meet resistance for the pure fact that it was drastic. Any change must be done insidiously. Similar to the way the communication wave became a part of the human psyche. Just a mere fifteen years ago, the Internet and cell phones were unheard of. Now they are commonplace in every home. But it took years to make the population comfortable with it. Yes, Frederick was correct. Sudden change would be devastating.

"Okay Frederick, I will concede in principle to your plan. But we must hammer out the details together, just you and I. No one else is to be involved. Understood?"

"I understand. I will procure the television time for the announcement in three days. How does that sound?"

"Fair enough," Sergay conceded. "I still don't like it," he added.

"Well, you come up with something else and we will use the airtime I procure to announce that," Peters exclaimed. "Until then, I'll work out some thoughts."

"Fine, I'll see you the day after tomorrow Frederick," Repustinov ended.

Peters slammed the phone on the receiver. He was more furious at Repustinov's reluctance than the situation. But Repustinov was correct. Too many people knew—the airmen who launched the missiles, bystanders who may have witnessed the launch, his cabinet and their staff—they all knew. And how was he to explain the deaths of five marines guarding the War Room? He pulled out his pad and jotted down his thoughts.

***

"Defender two two-zero one flight, this is USSTAP G.P. Nausona. We have you on range."

"Copy that," replied Patricia Genesis.

Osguards: Homecoming

Patricia glanced at her instrument panel and read the distance to go meter. She had been on long-range patrol before, but this one seemed extraordinarily longer than most. The fatigue was about to overtake her.

Twenty more minutes...she reminded herself...twenty more minutes and she would be on the deck of her galaxy protector. She looked at the ship-to-ship readout to check on her wingman. Centurion Adnuk Nospmoht, from Grimn, had served as her Centurion of Operations for a mere two months. They were still trying to feel each other out. Her last Centurion of Operations retired to take a nice little job with a firm on his home planet. He had served with her for four universal years on the Galaxy Cruiser Vision, before he retired. Patricia thought of it as a sign of disloyalty or a sign of disrespect that he didn't follow her when she took command of the Galaxy Protector Nausona. She could not figure out which yet. Nor did she dwell on it as much...except for these long-range patrols.

Now she had another Centurion of Operations, a watchdog from the Miter Line Galaxy, to ensure she had the Galaxy's best interest at heart. Oh how she envied her brother, Michael. At least he was an Osguard of his indigenous galaxy. It was tougher for the other fifty-nine Osguards to hammer control and demand respect from a galaxy with a population different from them. But somehow she managed...

A loud thump followed by the sharp tilt to the starboard side erased her concentration. She thumbed the controls with her right hand to stop the tilt, thanking God for the tubular binds keeping her arms in place and her hands in the ready position on the controls.

"Defender lead, this is two. What is your situation?" demanded Adnuk.

"Defender two, this is lead," Patricia responded studying her controls. "It looks like I lost my starboard engine...repeat...it appears I lost my starboard engine."

"Standby lead, I am coming in for a better look."

Adnuk, who was twenty-two marks away and two-thirds a galactic plane below, adjusted his speed to full hypersonic to catch his lead defender. Thirty seconds later, he thumbed his left horizontal control thrusters to match galactic plane settings. As he approached, he slowed to one-third hypersonic speed to match lead's speed. He looked up to surmise his lead's damage.

Patricia's defender's starboard engine was missing from the half spar. A slight fire had occurred but was snuffed out by the oxygen absent space. That was the good thing about space—explosions seldom left fires. And that is what Adnuk saw, an engine that had exploded.

"Lead this is two. Your starboard engine has exploded and is no longer operating. Have you applied engine shutdown procedures?"

"Tiah!"

"How is your energy?" asked Adnuk.

"I'm pissing away my energy at two lengths per universal minute,"
she responded.

*"Yeah, I was afraid of that. It looks like dialairtic gas is venting from
the starboard engine. Can you close the energy vent to the engine?"*

"Tried that...no luck."

*"Defender two two-zero one, we have you on scanners, we are
moving to your position...repeat we are moving to your position. Shut down
and wait for us...repeat shut down and wait for us. We will be there in ten
minutes," came the voice from the G.P. Nausona.*

*Another thump and a hard pull to the left started Patricia's defender
into a spin. Then the ship shot at hypersonic speed toward the uninhabited
planet fifty marks away from them. It was like the engines slung her in that
direction.*

*"G.P. Nausona, this is Defender two two-zero one. I have lost port
engine. I am in a cylinder spin. No thrusters, no energy...repeat...no
thrusters and no energy. I see a category 'C' planet, trying to adjust pitch
control to miss the planet, but I am being pulled by its gravitational force...I
am being pulled—"*

*Patricia's voice dropped off as the gravitational pull of the planet
and the cylindrical spin of her defender applied forces on her body with such
magnitude it caused her to black out. Her body remained strapped in
position and her helmet and clear chromerion mask automatically applied
oxygen. But the forces draining the blood from her brain overcame any
recuperative actions the flow of oxygen could effect. Her mind drifted into a
cloud of darkness, she lost all feeling and her body unconsciously fought the
weight of the gravitational forces pushing against it. As she approached the
planet's atmosphere the defender's chromerion shields deployed offering her
some protection.*

*Yet the cockpit became hotter and hotter as the ship entered the
planet's atmosphere. Adnuk could see the ship begin to burn. He knew the
angle was too steep for safe entry.*

*He had to do something, but what? Then without thinking, Adnuk
sailed his defender at hypersonic speed toward Patricia. He inched his way
through the hot atmosphere and deployed his grappling hook. He timed the
spin of Patricia's defender so the hook would catch her defender at what was
left of the port engine. It grabbed the port engine spar. The torque of
Patricia's defender bent the line and began to spin Adnuk's ship.*

*Adnuk applied reverse engine power and opposite roll control. The
hook pulled and tugged at Patricia's defender, stopping the spin, but the two
defenders were locked in a wobbly descent toward the planet's surface.
Adnuk pushed the engines to their limit, but he could not get reverse pull.
The gravitational forces, along with the lifeless weight of Patricia's*

defender, were too much for his engines. His cockpit began to burn as he saw his chromerion field deteriorate from the heat of the atmosphere.

"ARIT calculate and execute entry trajectory for us," Adnuk yelled.

The ARIT thrusters ripped and roared as his reverse engines slammed to idle. The ships sliced through the atmosphere at one-half hypersonic speed, more than ten times the cautionary speed for planetary atmospheric entry. Adnuk recognized this and applied reverse thrusters after clearing the upper atmosphere. The gravitational weight along with the G-force of falling at one-half hypersonic speed was too much pressure for the grappling hook. Adnuk's ship jerked away with such a force that he slammed against the cockpit canopy.

The grappling arm ripped from its grip about five marks from the surface. As it ripped, it shredded what was left of the port engine, sending a spark through the venting lines to the cockpit. The spark ignited the energy and colored a path of fire to the control panel in the cockpit. Many flashes and explosions, like firecrackers, danced in the cockpit as the spark found new life with every hot wire and button it came into contact with.

The life support sensors indicated an impending fire in the cockpit and executed an immediate ejection for the unconscious Patricia. The canopy blew and the seat fired its occupant out into the cold air of this strange planet. As the seat fired, the oxygen feeding Patricia's mask fueled the last spark and exploded what was left of the defender into a million pieces. Patricia barely cleared the explosion as her body tumbled the remaining two marks before her parachute opened.

Her right arm felt like it was on fire when Patricia awoke. Her head hurt like hell and the pain in her left leg was excruciating. She had landed in a field of tall grass. She was on her back looking at the night sky of...of what... Where the hell was she? Last she could remember, she was in a crippled defender, spinning off into...into a planet. Oh God, was this the planet? Had the defender ejected her? What a ride! What a rush! And she was unconscious for most of it. What had happened to her, she wondered.

She tried to move, she tried to bring her right arm up—nothing. In her mind, she could feel her arm moving, but she didn't see her hand where her mind told her it should be. Again, she moved her arm—at least, so she thought. She turned to her right side.

She screamed. All she could do was, scream. Her arm was gone. Nothing left of it but blood and mangled seared flesh. Her leg...her left leg...it was gone too. Again, nothing remained but burned seared flesh and blood. She screamed...she screamed... The scream rang in the night air like a church bell. All she could do was, scream.

***

"Honey, wake-up…wake-up!" demanded Joseph Archer.

His wife Patricia was having another nightmare. From her blood-curdling scream, he knew it must be of the accident again.

"Wake-up, Patricia!" Joe ordered as he shook his wife.

The sweat streamed from her pores and her body stiffened with fright, but she failed to wake up. She kept screaming and screaming.

"Patricia…Patricia, wake-up!" Joe yelled again.

This time, Joe patted Patricia's face. Patricia shook her head with each pat as if she was now fighting the sleeping gods to wake up. Her screams slowed to a whimper as Joe buried her face into his chest and wrapped his arms around her.

Patricia awoke, with her body drenched in sweat and her heart racing, she grabbed onto Joe as tight as she could.

"Okay, baby…it's okay," Joe said as comforting as he could. "You're safe now."

"Joe…Oh Joe, it was terrible," she murmured in a broken voice.

"I know baby…I know," but it's all over now. You are safe and sound, back on the *G.P. Nausona.*

"Yeah, safe and sound," she repeated hugging Joe tighter.

"You know baby, the doctor says you need to talk about this," Joe urged. "Keeping it locked up like this isn't good for you. You know I am here. I will always be here. You can talk to me."

"I know honey, but I am not ready yet. I am simply not ready to talk to anyone about it—not even you."

"Okay, Patricia. But you need to talk to someone. It doesn't have to be me, but you need to talk to someone soon."

Chapter 28—Capitol Station

"Capitol Station dead ahead Osguard," the navigator reported to Shawn.

"Thank you Lieutenant Murms," replied Shawn. "Proceed with standard docking procedures." Shawn turned to see his parents enter the top level of the Command Bridge. He rose from his seat and stepped up to them.

"Isn't she beautiful?" he asked as he gestured to the main screen.

Parker and Elizabeth remained silent as they took in the view from the screen. They had never seen anything like this; they never imagined anything like this. The scenery froze them in a hypnotic trance.

G.P. Vedar slowed to subsonic speed as it entered the approach to Capitol Station. The station was an amalgamation of seventy self-contained gray stations. They littered the space line like drifting snowflakes. Each station was diamond shaped. They were of different sizes and placements inside the area. The bigger stations had rings around them. A five-story ring, horizontally attached at the base, encased the biggest station. Around the ring several galaxy protectors had docked looking like bees in a honeycomb. The *Vedar* maneuvered through the corridor of stations toward this station. The biggest station was eight miles wide at the base and two hundred decks long from point to point. Soon it filled the entire view screen. The nearby sun of the Chaktun solar system framed the beauty of the station. The station had several window ports of different sizes and shapes. Some ports were oval, some square, some rectangular and some shapes only Picasso could describe.

"See those stations over there," Shawn pointed to several of the smaller stations they passed to the right with rings encasing them, left to right, diagonally. Several ships, similar in design but smaller in stature were docked on those rings. "Those are precinct stations. Different corps operate those stations. That one in the middle is the science corps precinct. The others are operations, economics and security. Some of those without docking rings are warehouses. We store goods retrieved throughout the universe. There are no docking rings on those because we use micro-portals to transfer the goods." Shawn saw the look of confusion on his parents' faces. "Think of the transporters on that science fiction show you like to watch dad."

"Then how come we use that stepping box?" his father asked.

"It's called a gate portal, dad. Micro-portals don't work on live tissue. Whatever it transports cannot be alive or it will kill it. We don't know how to transport the soul, the energy, which makes us alive. The micro-portal disassembles you at a micro-cellular level and it reconstructs you at the other end; but it doesn't pass on the pulse that tells your heart to beat and your lungs to breathe. Therefore, we just use it to transport solid goods, nothing living."

His father nodded that he understood.

"There, further back are our lab stations. That's where we conduct our research. Whatever we discover, we share with the entire alliance," Shawn said, pointing to the smaller stations to the left. They were similar, but the ships surrounding them did not bear the USSTAP signature design or markings.

"Those stations are the billeting stations. The fifty thousand representatives and their staff reside over there."

Shawn paused to let his parents take it all in. Then he pointed to the ships moving across the screen. "Those are different ships from all over the universe coming here for the Osguard Senate."

"The what?" Elizabeth asked.

"The Osguard Senate. It's when all the Osguards come together and review the pacts, treaties and regulations passed by the Universal Parliament. You will learn more about it later."

"Lord, I don't know if I want to learn about all this," Elizabeth squawked.

Shawn lifted his head and looked at the view screen. He saw the ship approach the biggest station.

"Mom, Dad; welcome to Millmum Main Capitol Station," gleamed Shawn. "Here is the Capitol and the Headquarters for the Universal Science Security and Trade Alliance of Planets—pronounced eu-stap for short. We're on a tracker vector to port."

"It's so beautiful," whispered Elizabeth. "In all my life I never thought I would see something so beautiful. I never figured I'd be riding in a space ship either," she joked.

"Son, why are we here?" Parker said never taking his eyes off the screen.

"Well, we have not quite solved what happened on Earth, and we figure the safest place for you and the others is here at Capitol Station."

"You think we are in danger?" asked Elizabeth.

"Don't know, but we don't want to take any chances. The entire mess with the Kulusks is still murky and we don't know how far they will go. Remember they attempted to blow up Earth."

"Shawn, you are scaring me," Elizabeth shrieked.

"Mom, this is the safest place in the universe. Nothing can happen to you here. Plus you'll get a chance to see the senate; you'll see some of the stuff we do as Osguards. You wanted to know. Now here is your chance."

"It's all too much to take in at one time," Elizabeth said placing her hands on her face as to shield herself from learning any more information.

"Imagine how we felt when we learned about all this. At least you don't have to worry about being the Osguard," Shawn offered.

The ship used manual thrusters as it maneuvered into position. The docking ring soon took up the entire screen. The *Vedar* floated into place and the docking clamps locked with a loud thump, which vibrated throughout the entire ship.

"It's time to go," Shawn told his parents. He ushered them off the bridge, through the port and down the two steps toward the coaster entrance. Several minutes later they stepped onto the reception port ring of USSTAP headquarters.

"Good morning Osguard zero–three, Mr. and Mrs. Genesis," A young ensign greeted.

"Good morning ensign," Shawn greeted back. "Mom and Dad, this is…" Shawn turned to read the ensign's gold plated nametag on the left breast of his jacket. "…Ensign Green. He will take you to your quarters and show you around as necessary. After you are settled, he will take you to the community hall where you and the others from the Gardens can meet and talk. I know you have much to talk about since the evacuation. After that, I am told the Combined Galactic Symphony will perform. That's our version of the New York Symphony; the difference is our symphony plays the classical songs from all over. The music is not R & B, but it is good. Michael, Patricia and I will pick you up. The ensign will procure the appropriate clothing for the event."

"Okay, son," Parker said as he shook his son's hand.

Elizabeth gave Shawn a kiss on the cheek, "Bye, son."

Shawn turned and walked back through the docking bay and disappeared into the *Vedar*.

Elizabeth and Parker turned to the ensign. Elizabeth nodded they were ready to proceed.

"This way," Ensign Green said, gesturing with his hands to follow him. He took a couple of steps backwards, facing them. When he was satisfied they were following him, he turned and positioned himself a half a step in front of them.

Elizabeth took in the surroundings. The corridors were similar to those on the galaxy protectors. A thin brown colored carpet blanketed the floors and ran waist level onto the walls. However, unlike the galaxy protectors, the walls were not made of a reflective polished and shined brown glass. These walls contained murals. Continuous paintings and pictures ran the entire length of the walls. They were so beautiful; she had to stop to admire them.

"Beautiful, aren't they?" Green said, stopping to give Elizabeth time to appreciate the detail.

"Yes, they are," she added. "What are they?"

"They are murals and pictures of different points in history throughout the universe. As I am sure the Osguard told you, this is the Capitol Station for the fifty thousand representatives throughout the universe. Each planet is represented through these images. They tell a story. Some tell a story of that planet's beginning. Some tell of that planet's religion, politics, and great leaders. There is no restriction on what is depicted on these walls. It kind of helps us understand each other. For instance, the one you are looking at tells the story of Telpa Nori from Timiea in the fifteenth Galaxy known as Miopsolan.

Telpa Nori was the first leader to unite the planet under one government. In this image, Telpa Nori is fighting the last of the Crese with his bare hands. In this battle, it is written he mortally wounded twenty Crese while defending the women and children of his home village. Word of his heroism spread and he soon became a living legend. You will see other images throughout the station detailing his life and times. It is sort of a game to find the images in order to complete the story. I personally have not found all the images to complete this story. As you saw from *G.P. Vedar*, this is a big station. And all the walls are covered."

"I see," said Elizabeth, not taking her eyes off the image of Telpa Nori raising one Crese off his feet with his left hand, back handing another with his right and stepping on the throat of another with his right foot. Something about this muscular man performing super human feats hypnotized her.

"It's quite impressive, but there are others," Green insisted.

"Are they all so violent?" asked Parker.

"No, some are just images of natural spots on the planets, like waterfalls, gardens, plains. You know…that kind of stuff."

Parker moved to the opposite side of the corridor to examine a different image. "What is this one?"

Green shifted his body to see the image Parker referred to. "Yes, this one is very interesting. It is the sunset on Zelehand, a planet in the thirty-sixth galaxy, known as Mishlyte. You see—Zelehand orbits three suns and only parts of the planet experience night. In this particular image the sun on the right is setting, while the sun on the left is dawning. You see how the image captures the suns' reflection in the water—"

"How can you tell which sun is setting and which is dawning?" Parker interrupted.

"I can't. That is what the artist said in his notes. I guess he just knew." Green turned to Elizabeth who was still studying the picture of the shirtless Telpa Nori in battle. "Shall we continue?"

Elizabeth snapped out of her trance and walked over to the men. "Yes, I am ready"

***

The buzz of the alarm pierced her mind like an ice pick. Sheryl Tower-Jones sat straight up in bed fighting the dizzy cloud of sleep. She groped at the alarm button. She missed it the first and second time, but she hit the button on her third swipe. She wiped the sleep from her eyes.

"ARIT, what time is it?" she demanded.

"0700 Universal Standard Time," the ARIT replied.

"Great. ARIT, ship's location?"

"Capitol Station Headquarters, dock twenty-three."

"Great." Sheryl slid out of bed and dragged herself to the bathroom. She heard her husband and children in the dining area. She showered and dressed to join them. Her husband, Gregory Jones, had fixed scrambled eggs and bacon this morning, or he had ordered it through the food processor. Sheryl kissed her sons on the cheek as she greeted them good morning. Then she squeezed her husband and gave him a passionate wet kiss, which lasted several seconds.

"Missed you yesterday," she said as she looked at him with loving eyes.

Osguards: Homecoming

"I missed you too," he said beaming pure love. "You know any other husband would be jealous or insecure at your position. I mean you are never around..."

He stopped for fear of opening old emotional wounds. It was hard for him to accept his secondary role as husband to an Osguard. He had to leave his home, forgo his degree and trek behind his wife in some far off galaxy. The price was enormous, more than he had bargained. But he looked at his kids, and the legacy his wife was leaving for them and it cut the edge off the hurt a little. He loved his wife, but it ate at his manhood to let her go off and constantly risk her life for USSTAP. They had gone through counseling several times. With the same result, he stayed because it would hurt too much to leave. It was not easy but with time, it became manageable.

Gregory had taken the lead of the other husbands and wives; and furthered his education. He had studied the USSTAP economic model and now was a colonel in the economic corps. His department was responsible for overseeing the intergalactic trade treaties with Galaxy Fifty-Nine, the Litaria Galaxy. It actually had become fun and he enjoyed his work. The position allowed him to travel on the Kashara with his wife. This made it easier on the kids, who traveled with them. Since their marriage, they had not seen combat or military action, until now. This was the first real combat situation he saw his wife engage in.

He had read the reports of the earlier years when she commanded the *Galaxy Cruiser Spar*. They seemed to be the dark years of the USSTAP. Mosleck pirates, the Kulusk Empire, the Grudgea Federation and the Toniea Republic were bitter enemies. Since then, the space pirates were eliminated through attrition and war. The Grudgea Federation and the Toniea Republic dissolved from within, which made their fragmented planet states more than willing to join USSTAP. It was in everyone's best interest. All the planets keep their sovereignty, and USSTAP provided the muscle and the brain for intergalactic cooperation. He remembered how proud he was of her as he read the report detailing how she made contact in the Litaria Galaxy and incorporated those planet states into USSTAP in five short years. That galaxy was not as developed as USSTAP, which made the negotiations smoother.

He knew his wife was an Osguard. He couldn't change that. He didn't want to change that. Now that his parents knew the secret of the USSTAP, it made things somewhat easier to handle. Having to bear his pain alone without being able to confide in his parents made things worse. The talk he had with them last night was like lifting a great weight off of his chest. They understood and supported his decision to stay with USSTAP. They were proud of him and Sheryl. Things were going to be better; he knew it now.

"I'm sorry Sheryl," he apologized. "I love you and I don't mean to add to your problems. Everything is fine. The kids are fine, my folks are fine and we are fine. You do what you have to. I know if the Kulusks keep messing up, things could be worse. It is your destiny to be an Osguard and I accept it as my destiny to be your husband." He leaned over and kissed her again.

Sheryl smiled, "I know it's tough on you, but thank you."

"You're welcome." He stepped to the sink and retrieved a plate. "Here, I ordered you some breakfast." He placed the plate in front of Sheryl.

She sat down, "Thanks honey."

"I'm going to drop the kids off with the grandparents. They should be on station by now."

"What?"

"Yes, all the Osguard residents are being billeted on station and they are going to meet in the community hall at twelve hundred hours. Your agenda is on the table. You have a meeting with the other Osguards at zero nine hundred hours. Right now, I have to go by the office and run some simulations on how this event may affect trade in Galaxy Fifty-Nine." He gave his wife and kids another kiss. "Chuck, I'll be back to pick up you and your brother at zero eight thirty hours. You be good until then," he commanded his oldest son. Then he disappeared out the door.

"Well fellows, it's just you and me for a couple of minutes," Sheryl addressed her sons. "Any questions?"

She received blank stares.

"Are you excited about seeing your grandparents on the station today?" The children giggled and nodded.

"Great, then you go and wash up now and I will get your clothes ready. Okay?" The kids scampered off to their room and she heard the shower head turn on. She finished her breakfast and went over the night shift reports. Nothing strange, docking procedures were normal and the crew started their port call privileges. Business as usual, except for the pesky Kulusks.

***

The room reminded Michael of his science lecture hall in college. It was set in a deep well type room. With seats and rows of tables situated every two steps. However the Osguard Senate room was circular and at the bottom of the well sat a holographic projection stage to display briefings, diagrams and schematics. Unlike a lecture hall, this room had balconies shielded by glass for observers. The positions at the tables were numbered. The first row nearest the stage was numbered one through ten. The second row was numbered eleven through twenty-five. The third row was numbered twenty-six through forty-five. The last row was numbered forty-six through sixty. Each number designated where the corresponding Osguard sat.

Osguards: Homecoming

Michael was the first to arrive. He had to set up his presentation for this emergency meeting. It was 8:50 when the other Osguards started trickling in. Michael knew he had to live or die by what was decided in the meeting today. Technically, he did not have to call the meeting. He had the authority to pursue what he deemed the proper course of action. However, his plan needed the cooperation of the other Osguards and their ships. This was one of the few times this awesome amount of firepower would be in the same place at the same time in the universe. He had to make use of the situation. He also knew for this very same reason, the Kulusks decided to raise their ugly heads. Michael understood the Kulusks wanted to destroy the Osguards in one victorious blow. He also knew the others were painfully aware of this. That is why no one had objected to the way Michael had handled the situation thus far.

Michael tried to apply what he learned at Rutgers University as an International Relations student when dealing with different races in the galaxy. For the most part, it worked. Many military strategists throughout the universe, including Sun Tsu of Earth, Tomaji Luna of Tasier and Simon Dej of Memsme stated, one needed to know the enemy in order to defeat the enemy. Therefore Michael was aware he had to understand the Kulusks in order to defeat them. Michael had studied the Kulusks for years. Understanding them was difficult. Most galactic confrontations were due to frustration that turned aggressive, a simple shifting of power or simple racism. Michael tried to think like a Kulusk. But he could not quite put his finger on what motivated the Kulusks into action.

Whether it was pure frustration, a shift in power or simple racism, Michael's job was clear. He must stop the aggression in one fell swoop. Even if it was deeper and more convoluted than that, Michael did not have the time or energy to correct it. Therefore, if it was misdirected aggression for some perceived transgression, he could not do anything about it. Michael convinced himself it was one of the latter two reasons. He rationalized the Kulusks' actions this way to ease his conscience. His plan would cost lives—innocent lives of those who may not believe in the Kulusks' act of aggression. He could not afford to dwell on that. If he concentrated on the innocent people who could die, he would lose. And failure was not an option.

Michael looked around and saw the other Osguards were in place. As the room clock struck 0900, a hush fell in the room. All eyes seemed to be on Michael. He took that as his cue to start the meeting. He rose and moved to the center of the stage. His eyes swept the room in long glances. He took several breaths as he thumbed his room control PARIT to secure the room. A low hum and a change in light color washed the room as the ARIT searched for listening devices and unauthorized personnel in the room. His PARIT blinked the words *'ROOM IS SECURE'* on the screen. Michael placed the device down in his chair and moved back to the center of the stage. Again he

179

looked around in long drawn out glances. He felt his mouth dry and the butterflies flutter in his stomach. It was time. He knew it, but still wanted to delay the inevitable. He couldn't.

"Osguards, I hope you have read the report by Osguard Sheryl Tower-Jones. In it you will notice the Kulusks are harboring the fugitives who infiltrated the United States and Russian nuclear command centers and launched the ICBMs. I am getting reports from General Lo as we speak. His investigations show three men, General Ivan Prepovnov, the Russian Commander of the Ministry of Defense Twelfth Directorate, General Samuel Patterson, U.S. Vice Chairman of the Joint Chiefs of Staff and USSTAP Earth Force Commander Rick Larson, executed this operation. We fear these men were Kulusk plants sent to Earth years ago to work their way through the military structures in order to execute this attack. It seems elaborate and far-fetched. But it is true. Sheryl followed their shuttle to the Kulusk home world after we stopped the attack.

I feel the attack was not meant to kill us; but it was meant to enrage us. Whether it succeeded or not, I believe the Kulusk plan was for us to send our galaxy protectors to Kulusk in a retaliation move; thus, leaving Capitol Station undefended and prime for an attack. Sheryl found evidence of an attack force on Kulusk. However, through further investigation, we believe that evidence to be a decoy. Sheryl has also discovered message traffic in the tenth sector. The message traffic is consistent with a large armada. We cannot tell how many ships, or even the size or type of ships, or if they are even in the tenth sector anymore. It could be another decoy. We can send scouts to the tenth sector, but that would take time." Michael stopped and took a deep breath. The words forming in his mind plagued his soul like cancer.

"We can do one of three things," he continued. "We can do nothing and let the Kulusks hide forever. We can open up diplomatic channels and tell the Kulusks we are aware of their plan. Or we can do as the Kulusks want and send the galaxy protectors to Kulusk."

The hum of whispers hovered in the room at Michael's last statement. The shock of the options generated disdain in their voices. Michael knew this and allowed the discourse to continue a few seconds longer.

"Now before you think me crazy." Michael picked up the PARIT room controller and pushed a button. This is what I propose." The holographic image of the planet Kulusk appeared on the stage. The image of sixty galaxy protectors surrounded the planet. "I propose we give them what they want. Because they won't enjoy it long enough to celebrate," Michael continued.

***

Osguards: Homecoming

"Father, there still is no action from USSTAP," Kie's son Xer stated over interspace communications link from the armada in the fifteenth sector. "I am afraid the plan has failed."

"Son, do you doubt me," Kie reflected. "They will come. And when they do, you will destroy all that is USSTAP. I want everything destroyed at their precious Capitol Station. And while you are at it, destroy Ea rth."

"When Father?" Xer asked.

"Soon, my son. Soon you will lead the Kulusks to victory over our ancient enemy. The prophecy will be fulfilled tomorrow. This I promise you," Kie responded with a blood curdling tone.

Xer felt the force in his father's words. They inspired him and deleted any doubt he would have his day. Xer was ready. He had been training for this day all of his life. His father had breathed every detail into the fiber of his being. The USSTAP would be crushed and the Osguards would be eliminated. This he was sure.

"Soli," Xer responded as he cut transmission off.

Xer looked around his battle bridge. He saw the members of his crew working out last minute details. He knew they were skeptical and also disappointed the battle had not occurred yet. He sat back in his command chair and surveyed the viewing screen. He commanded eighty battle cruisers; the most the Kulusk Republic ever put to space at one time. In his mind, the USSTAP was no match for his armada. The Kulusks produced each battle cruiser with one purpose in mind—combat. The Kulusk ships waddled through space like porcupines. The new shockdel guns strategically placed in several spots throughout the hull replaced the antiquated pagenay guns. The shockdel guns had ten times the accuracy and range as the pagenay guns, and they shot pure melenai pulses. Pulses designed to rip through chromerion fields like a hot knife through butter. The Kulusks had been working on the gun since the last galactic war with Chaktun. Now they had perfected it and were ready to test it in battle. A slight smile crossed Xer's lips as he dreamt about the destruction of USSTAP. *What a sweet victory,* he reflected.

"Communications," Xer snapped.

"Soli," replied his communications officer from behind him.

"Tell the armada to run battle drill delta," Xer ordered.

"Soli," the communications officer responded.

Xer knew the armada was restless and needed something to keep their minds busy. Besides he wanted to ensure their readiness. What better way than running another battle drill. Xer smiled again as he saw the armada come to life and maneuver as one entity vanquishing an invisible enemy.

***

Kie watched the blank screen he just used to talk to his son. His mind drifted to the plan. He did not know why the Osguards had not appeared in

181

Kulusk space yet. His son was correct. Without the Osguards coming to him, his plan was surely doomed. In the simulations, the plan went seemingly well. What factor did they not foresee? What detail did they not account for? He picked up his touch pad labeled *'Operation Osguard'* and began reading. He stopped and thumbed his communication panel again.

"Send coded message on channel dark three red two," he commanded. "Message follows. Begin back up plan bravo two one." He tapped the communications to end transmission.

"That should bring the rox Osguards to us," he smiled as he put the touch pad back down.

Chapter 29—Assassin

Parker sat with his wife by his side and his grandchildren in front of him in the midst of the entire Osguard Gardens community. He observed and studied every detail presented to them. His feelings had experienced the emotional roller coaster of the century. They ran the gamut from betrayal to pride. Now, with every word of the presentation, Parker Genesis' heart filled with honor. He felt the betrayal of his children not telling him sooner. Then it faded to pride as he witnessed the holovidpics of their most triumphant adventures. However, fear overshadowed the exhilaration as he watched. His only solace was he knew his children were safe now, and they had survived whatever he witnessed in the holovidpics.

He felt shame and embarrassment when he witnessed Patricia's accident on some planet he could not remember or hardly pronounce. For that was the time he was so angry at her for missing Thanksgiving dinner with them. Now to find out she was fighting for her life in a USSTAP medical facility in a galaxy millions of light years away. He and Elizabeth thought she didn't want to come, or that she placed business above the family. Tears rolled down his face as he saw the image of his daughter and the extent of her injuries. God, he almost lost her and he did not realize it.

The same feeling of guilt arose when they showed a holovidpic of Shawn in combat. He missed Christmas with the family that year. Again, Parker and Elizabeth were disappointed. Now the holovidpic showed Shawn was somewhere in space—Parker could not remember where. But Shawn was somewhere in space fighting to keep the peace treaty alive between two warring factions. Shawn's efforts and sacrifice almost cost him his life and the foundation of the USSTAP. Obviously, Shawn was successful, because the two factions were now part of USSTAP.

Then there was Michael. He had missed so many promised visits. His life was just as convoluted. He was the first of the Osguards to taste battle. He was the first of the Osguards to kill in combat. And he was the first of the Osguards to broker a new alliance. He seemed to have been Ortho's favorite. However, this favoritism did not keep him in the nest of safety. In fact it continuously put him in danger. Ortho, and now the USSTAP community, almost expected Michael to be damn near omnipotent. That was a hell of an expectation for anyone to live up to, let alone Michael who was sensitive and too caring at times. But on the holovidpics, Parker and Elizabeth witnessed Michael's dark side; a side Michael must have shielded from his parents all of his life. Parker almost did not recognize the image of his son, or any of his children when they dealt out cold and calculating orders that resulted in someone's death. Parker thought of the toll it must have taken on his children to know their decisions made in combat resulted in mass deaths. One consolation was the deaths were that of the adversary—but, how about the deaths of those under their command? The toll of command was heart wrenching as well.

Parker understood it from his brief tour in Korea. Death and combat were bitter pills to swallow for the price of peace. But those brave men and women who answered the call and fought bravely and with honor would never be forgotten. He smiled at the thought of the honor his children bestowed on him and all of mankind. They were willing to sacrifice all, because it was their destiny to ensure peace.

Parker turned to his right to nod at his brother Armstrong. He saw the same collage of bittersweet pain and pride swell in his eyes. It must have been harder for Armstrong to watch his two sons during the holovidpics. Armstrong was a retired Methodist minister, who thought his sons would follow him into the ministry. When they didn't, it broke his heart. Armstrong hid the pain of his disappointment behind his work. He thanked God every day his sons weren't on the streets, selling drugs or worse. However, he still harbored a disappointment God had not touched them to do His will. Now he knew God had destined his children to save the soul of the universe. That was a supercilious way of thinking about it. *But it was true*, he told himself. His prayers were answered, he just had not known about it. His children had answered a higher calling with self-sacrifice and integrity.

Armstrong and his wife, Brenda, both felt the gamut of emotions as well. They observed their children, Roger and Clyde, through the holovidpics. They too were not spared from their share of physical escapades. They cheated death several times and somehow—with the grace of God, Armstrong thought—they made it through. However the sorrow of the lives damaged by his children's actions suddenly weighed heavily on Armstrong's heart. In his profession, he was trained to resolve confrontations without violence. He thought he taught his children to do the same. Mixed emotions continued to surge inside of him. Pride, anger and shame rained on his passions like a summer thunderstorm.

"Thank you for your patience and welcome to the USSTAP family," the speaker, USSTAP protocol officer Major Cheribat, a Chaktun native, started his closing remarks.

Thus far the presentation had taken three hours, but to Parker and his brother it seemed like just a few minutes. Parker quickly stood and stretched. He turned again to Armstrong. He saw his younger brother Coltrane and his sister Holiday—Holly to her friends—scurry to him. Elizabeth tapped Parker and motioned she wanted to usher the grandchildren to the snack table. He nodded in agreement and watched as his family moved through the crowd of their neighbors, many still in shock with silent gestures of delight painted on their faces.

"I can't believe this!" blasted Coltrane shaking Parker out of his train of thought.

Parker turned to see his two brothers and sister standing next to him.

"I know. It is all kind of hard to imagine, but here we are—light years away from Earth."

"I don't know whether to be furious or happy at Sandy," Holly gleamed. "My daughter—an Osguard—I'm not quite sure I understand what an Osguard is. But all I know is our children have lived through some rough times these past years and we had no idea." She paused to wipe a tear forming in her right eye. "If only Frank was alive today, he would be so proud of her. It's not fair he had to die and not know what Sandy has become. If only Ortho had found us sooner, he may have done something to keep Frank from dying from lung cancer. Sandy told me last night that USSTAP has a cure for cancer and Frank could be alive today if..." Holly's emotions caught in her throat as she raised her hand to cover her mouth.

Parker hugged her, and felt her tremble within his arms. He didn't know what to say. He felt as lost as his wife did. They enjoyed the benefits of USSTAP's medical treatments for the last twelve years without knowing it. For all he knew, he could have had cancer, diabetes or some other debilitating disease USSTAP had cured without his knowledge. Life was unfair. His brother-in-law Frank Bass could be here sharing in this moment if he had not died so early in Sandy's life. *Life was not fair, not fair at all*, he thought.

Elizabeth and the grandchildren joined them from the snack table. She witnessed the scene and allowed the siblings to bond in this special moment. She patted Holly on the back, while she regained her composure. Holly straightened and wiped her eyes. Armstrong offered her his handkerchief. She smiled, took it and sat down. Coltrane sat next to her as he watched his baby sister dealt with her pain.

"Parker, I haven't seen Shawn's in-laws, Debrlina's parents," Elizabeth said. "I know they live in Kansas City. Do you think they are alright?"

"Aunt Debrlina is Chaktun, Mama," Kashara said. "They live on Chaktun. I am sure they are alright."

"What?" Elizabeth asked.

"Yeah, Aunt Debrlina is Chaktun," Sharyla explained. "Uncle Shawn met her on Chaktun while he was in training. In fact, many of the Osguards married Chaktuns," she continued.

"How about…" Elizabeth's throat cracked.

"No, mommy is from Earth," Sharyla smiled. "In fact, we need to go see our other grandparents and say hi to them."

Sharyla and Kashara searched the crowd until they saw them and scampered away without saying good-bye.

"Well, what did you expect," Parker confessed. "You saw the life they live. I hardly think many of Earth's women would fit into this category. Shit, we're lucky! Michael and Patricia found them somebody who will put up with this crap. I know you would have dropped me like a hot potato."

"Well, that's different," remarked Elizabeth. "You ain't no Osguard."

"Hell, I could have been one," Parker replied. "We all could have been one," he bellowed as he wrapped his arm around Armstrong.

Armstrong smiled. "I think God had this all planned out from the beginning. We could have been, but God chose our children. I for one will not question His wisdom." Armstrong widened his grin. "Besides I am hungry. Let's see what kind of food that snack table has. I see my wife is already over there." He kicked Coltrane's foot. "Coltrane, your wife and my wife are about to eat that entire snack table. I suggest we go get some grub before it is all gone."

"You go on ahead," said Coltrane. "I want to make sure Holly is alright."

"Fine, suit yourself," Armstrong answered back.

"I am fine. I think I want to get some food anyway," Holly said, rising with the help of Coltrane. "Besides, I got a feeling there is much more we have to learn before the day is out. I need my strength to keep up with all this," she continued.

"Yeah, they have some fancy concert tonight, Shawn told us," Parker grinned. "Can't wait to hear what kind of music these folks like. I bet it's boring like the opera."

"Opera is class," Coltrane butted. "But I guess you wouldn't understand class, you uncouth Billy goat."

"Billy goat…Why you ungrateful, K-Mart wearing—"

"Stop you two," Elizabeth pleaded. "You are the parents of the most prestigious people in the universe and you're acting like fools."

"We're just playing, honey," Parker responded. "We always do this. That's what brothers do."

"Fine, but I suggest you start doing what Osguards do," she argued. "You are the parents of the Osguards, a birthright—a birthright that came from you. So I guess that makes you some type of important too."

Parker, Coltrane, Armstrong and Holiday stopped to reflect on that. They had joked about it, but until Elizabeth said it aloud, the thought had not taken serious root in their conscious minds. Now it did, and it was scary. Could they have done what their children had done?

***

The auditorium was huge. It reminded Parker of the Superdome. However, it was shaped like the theaters he'd seen on television. The usher directed him and his wife to a box seat, situated two stories above the main floor. On the main floor, several thousand people, representatives from the congress the usher told him, were bustling to their seats. The representatives were dressed in the richest looking clothing, cloaks and smocks, their version of a tuxedo he imagined. Yet, Parker was surprised to see the representatives looking...well looking human. The science fiction films he had watched in the movies had tainted him to believe aliens from space would look like fishes, dinosaurs or have pointed ears. Not so. To his surprise, everyone he had met was quite human. Some features were noticeably different, but would blend easily on Earth. They came in different shapes, sizes and colors. Some appeared to be a mixture of races and some appeared to have stepped from Earth. Italian features, German features, African features, Oriental features, Hispanic features, they were all present—a myriad of races he could find in any major city in the United States. But they represented planets throughout the universe. Armstrong was right, God made man in his image. Not just man of Earth, but man of the universe. Parker's head ached trying to discern the possibilities.

He and his wife sat in their assigned seats. Again, he was overwhelmed at the scene. Just a few short days ago, he was worried about cutting his grass. Now he was light years away from home being entertained by the USSTAP Universal Symphony. He pinched himself to see if he was dreaming. So much, so fast, he could not digest all the information at one time. What the hell was he doing? He turned to his wife and saw the radiance of her beauty electrify the box. Whatever was happening, Elizabeth was in her element—or so it appeared. Why was he so nervous?

The door to the balcony box seats swished open as he saw his sons and daughter standing in the archway wearing red tunics over their black jumpsuit uniform. The red tunic had the USSTAP elongated diamond encased in two orbits centered in large print. A belt that made the torso flare a little tightened the tunics. His children reminded him of the three musketeers; they simply needed a feather hat to complete the ensemble.

"Don't you dare laugh dad," Patricia ordered. "This is our dress uniform. We trade the coat for the tunic and—Voila. You have a dress uniform." Patricia raised her arms as if she were a model and spun around twice to allow her parents to get the full affect.

Parker gagged trying not to laugh. Elizabeth nudged him with her elbow to drive home the point.

"Very sharp. You guys look very sharp."

Shawn grunted in disbelief and leaned over to kiss his mother. Michael copied his older brother, as did Patricia. All three feigned the cold shoulder toward their father.

"Oh, this is the way you treat your father?" Parker grunted.

"You laughed at us," Patricia replied.

"I'm sorry, but you look like the three... "

"Don't say it," interrupted Michael.

"—The three musketeers," finished Parker. "There, I said it. Now I feel better."

"Dad, this is the traditional garb of the Osguards," Michael explained. "Well at least it was when they were the Maxus of the Chaktun Republic. We continue to wear this as a tribute to our forefathers. Your forefathers," Michael added.

A touch of guilt pained Parker when he heard those words—forefathers.

"Okay, I'm sorry. I should have known it was important for you to wear those things. I'm sorry."

***

On the slight raised main theater floor the delegates continued to mingle. The cacophony of their conversation rang in the hall, amplified by the acoustic powers of the theater. In the midst of the hodgepodge of representatives, the Kulusk trade ambassador, Manidul, and his aide, Junitel, advanced to their seats. Junitel snuck a peek upwards to the Osguard balcony seats. They circled the theater in rows of two. He took mental notes on each box and the number of people sitting in the boxes. While he walked next to his ambassador, he placed his right hand in his pocket to check it once more. It was in his pocket and ready. Junitel felt warmer. His nervousness had generated sweat under his armpits. He felt each drop of the wet sticky liquid form and then drip from his body. He imagined he could count each drip. His mind was working overtime, sizing up his targets and his escape route. Escape route? Why should he bother? He was in the middle of the heaviest secured complex in the entire galaxy. Why deceive himself? There would be no escape. However, for his own mental health he needed to devise one. So he looked, calculated and formed a strategy.

Malcolm Dylan Petteway

Their seats were in the fifth row and to the left, seats eleven–E and twelve-E. He peered upwards again and fixed his gaze on the lower box to his right. He recognized the people in it. Great, so far the intelligence reports were correct. He was at the correct spot. Junitel squinted as he noticed the right energy border that framed the box. A chromerion field, he thought. The Osguards were no fools. They surrounded themselves with protection. Chromerion fields protected their boxes and there were security guards armed with delta belts stationed at every door and exit.

The delta belts contained an impressive array of weaponry. The belt held a quick release holstered coronet side arm strapped low on the side of the thigh at hand level. The gun was a sleek sexy looking eight inch barrel black weapon with a curved handgrip conformed to fit in the owner's hand. The gun shot rapid coronet energy pellets at the speed of light. The impact of anything traveling at the speed of light, especially a coronet energy pellet, not only put a hole in its target, it ripped through its target cutting clean seared grapefruit size holes. Also the belt contained a palm-size three-button pagenay strapped to the right hindquarter of the belt. The blue button zapped the blue beam that burned its target with high unbearable heat. The red button corresponded to a red beam of energy, which overloaded the human axons and dendrites in the nerve cells with heat, rendering its victim unconscious. Lastly, the yellow button corresponded with a yellow beam briefly disconnected its victim's axons and dendrites causing momentary sensory deprivation and momentarily disorienting its victims. Then finally, the belt housed another remote control weapon called a mation II. Upon the call of the owner, this weapon shape shifted a metal liquid polymer into any type blade. The operator had to push the black button and audibly state the blade desired and the weapon would conform into that blade. It could change from a knife to a saber to a sword or even to a machete.

The delta belt was the epitome of personal defensive weaponry for USSTAP. It was the top level of defensive equipment right below full combat gear. Due to DNA locking, each weapon on a belt could only be operated by its owner. This precluded an adversary from using a USSTAP weapon against its owner. A flaw in combat thinking, Junitel thought. This also precluded a buddy from using your weapon as well. However, as he searched the theater with his eyes, he noticed there were more than enough guards available to handle any situation without borrowing a weapon from another guard.

Junitel took a deep breath as he again checked his right pocket. It was still there. It was still prime, and he was still ready to use it, even though the odds were against him. He had promised his Maxum he would carry out the orders without any regard for his own safety. He pulled the shockdel gun out and aimed.

***

The back door swished open. Michael turned to see Debrlina and her parents enter the balcony. Major Cheribat was a stickler for protocol, Michael thought. Major Cheribat ensured his parents were seated first before he gathered the in-laws. Now he was bringing the in-laws to the balcony in order of the oldest to the youngest sibling. His brother's wife and family, then his and then Patricia's would enter the balcony—in that order. He waved, smiled then turned back around. As he did, his program slipped from his lap. He bent down to pick it up—

The round from the shockdel gun's melenai pulse sliced through the chromerion field, and whizzed by Michael's head. He heard the sound of the back of his chair splitting open like it was hit by lightening. He looked up just in time to see the slitanium polymer shield slammed down in front of him. The interruption in the chromerion field triggered the shield to close shut. Michael twisted to see his chair cracked where his head was just a split second ago. Then he heard the blood-curdling scream. His mother's scream rang in his ear as he hopped to his feet to see his father lying in his overturned chair with blood strewing from his left hip.

The round had ripped the back of Michael's chair and hit his father. The shock stunned Michael for a half a second. He tried to scream for his father, but his shock kept the sound stuck in his throat. Only a low moan fueled by rage came from his lungs. The two door guards rushed in with coronet guns at the ready position. Debrlina Genesis, a nurse, raced into action.

She tapped her CC, "Medical emergency; main theater; balcony one. Osguard zero-three's father is down. Repeat Osguard zero-three's father is down." She rushed to Parker and surveyed his injuries. "We got to get him to Med Deck now."

The two door guards hovered over the family as Debrlina worked to control the bleeding. She ripped a part of her tunic and made a makeshift bandage over Parker's wound. She pressed down trying to stop the bleeding. When she looked up into Parker's face she could see his life force hovering in his opened eyes trying to make a decision whether to leave or stay and fight.

Debrlina screamed, "Stay with us Dad. Stay with us." She pulled her PGP and reset the numbers then pushed the activate button. "Guards, pick up Mr. Genesis and step him through," she ordered. The guards did as they were told, moving Elizabeth out of the way in order to pick up Parker. One guard, carrying Parker, and Debrlina stepped into the light and it closed behind them.

Michael, Shawn and Patricia remained silent as they stared at the space in which their father disappeared. No words were spoken, just shared pain as they held on to each other's arms. The guard looked on in amazement. His leaders were in shock. Something he thought he would never see, nor did he ever want to see.

"Osguard," he whispered.

That word—Osguard, and the power it carried with it, the power in which they had lived their entire adult lives, woke them out of their trance. Michael stood and looked at the guard. "Report," he ordered.

***

All the shields on all balconies slammed down with a powerful thud. The sound cracked the theater like thunder. Junitel fired a second shot, but it hit the shield and exploded with the force of a small firecracker. He did not know if he had hit his target or not. Everything went so fast. But now there was no target to shoot. The shields had activated. He did not count on that. He did not even know about the shields. His intelligence department had let him down. He swung to the exit he had planned to use. He pushed his ambassador down as he rushed to the exit. The room was in chaos. The other representatives were running as if they were in danger. No one knew where the shot had originated. No one but...

The pain lasted an instant, but he knew right away what it was. A coronet pellet struck his chest and burned a giant hole through his body. The thought took a split second, but it was there. Junitel knew he was dead. The pellet had disintegrated his heart and left lung, more like vaporized it. The guards didn't want him alive. If they did they would have used the pagenays. No, the insult of an assassin in the Capitol Station was too much for them. Death was his only reward, and the guard who shot him ensured he got his just reward. Didn't they want to interrogate me, he thought? Those fools, they could have captured me and ... Junitel's brain activity ceased as he fell to his knees then flat on his face with his hands still clutching the shockdel gun.

Death was quick, neat and relatively painless. The USSTAP built their weapons to deliver death in this manner. There was no honor in allowing an adversary to suffer as he traveled toward death. No there was no honor in that. And it was all about honor. At least that was the Sixana creed. It was all about honor. And after all, every member of the USSTAP was a Sixana Warrior. And the guard, who shot the would-be assassin, felt the juices of his warrior spirit flow through him as he came upon his kill. He kicked Junitel's lifeless body.

When Sentinel Talion Shilego from the planet of Grujin was satisfied his target was dead he holstered his coronet gun, tapped his CC and reported.

"This is Shilego...Assassin is down. Scan theater for unidentified weapons."

Chapter 30—Alert

FBI Special Agent Tony Musoto pulled his four-year old Ford sedan toward the gate. He read the sign embroidering the top of the metal gate— OSGUARD GARDENS. He was assigned to the Richmond, Virginia field office three weeks before his boss handed him this assignment. At first he thought it a joke, an initiation prank. His boss handed him the names of several people, several people who lived somewhere in Virginia over a hundred years ago. His job was to find their descendants. He laughed at the thought of the assignment until his boss closed the office door and told him to sit down. *This assignment was hush-hush. It came straight from the top, maybe even the president.* Yeah, Musoto thought. Those were the words to entice a gullible young agent into the prank. Musoto took the assignment with reservation. If they wanted to pay me for running around on a wild goose chase—let them, he thought.

However, he soon found out it was not a wild goose chase. With today's computers and the Internet, most of the information the boss sought was at his fingertips. He traced the Pathgo family. They once lived near the town down the street. But like all post-civil war historic episodes, their land was sold and the family moved away. Now a state prison sits on the land the proud Pathgos once owned. It was poetic justice, Musoto thought. Coming from a poor Italian family he could not relate to the historic proud traditions of the glorious South. He enjoyed the fast life the big urban city offered. That is one reason why he hated his reassignment from Los Angeles to Richmond.

It had to be punishment for his mistakes during the Vega investigation. But it wasn't his fault. He was new to the Bureau and he just followed his partner's lead. Yet, the judge didn't see it that way. So the evidence was booted for an improper search warrant and the wiretaps deemed illegal—they called it fruit from a poison tree. Dominic Vega walked out of that court a free man because Musoto was not specific enough in obtaining the warrant. Where was the justice? Dominic Vega ordered the murder of several small businessmen, because they wouldn't sell him their business. Tony's investigation was pristine; his drunken partner ruined it with…

Tony shook his head. That was old news. Now he was in Virginia tracking down a list of names from a century ago. If this wasn't a gag, then it was busy work to keep him from the real investigations. Fine, he thought. If that's the way they want to play, so be it.

His train of thought was interrupted by a knock on his window. Musoto looked up and saw a black clad security guard at his window. "Shit. I didn't even see him," he chastised himself. "I've got to get a hold of my senses. That could have been a perp with a gun. Shit, shit, shit!" Musoto rolled down his window and smiled.

"Can I help you," the guard said.

"Yes, I am Special Agent Musoto with the FBI. I would like to take a look inside," he said displaying his badge.

"Well, I am sorry Agent Musoto. But this is private property and I can't let you inside," the guard said looking toward the closed gates. "Is there something I can help you with?"

"What do you mean private property?" Musoto squawked. "I just want to take a look around. These are public streets, aren't they?"

"No sir," the guard put forth. "This is a private retirement community."

"What do you mean private? Who owns it?" Musoto said holding his temper in check.

"Sir, this is private property and I can't let you in unless you have a warrant."

Musoto turned to look at the community behind the bars. There was that word—warrant, again. Musoto and warrants did not work well together and the very mention of the word made his blood boil. But Musoto understood a warrant was necessary to protect the citizens from unlawful search and seizure. It was just a shame the same laws protected the criminals. Then Musoto looked on his list. This was a gag; these names are from a century ago. Why get upset at this. Osguard Gardens may not have any connection to his assignment. He turned to the guard and smiled.

"You're right," he offered in a peaceful tone. "It's just I have been given a crazy assignment to track some people down. And a couple of those people were—are named Osguard. I just thought there was a connection."

"Sorry, can't help you," the guard replied as he rose and started to walk back to the guard booth.

"Can't or won't?" shouted Musoto.

The guard turned around and stared at Musoto for a second and then he smiled, "Either way sir, the results are the same. Have a good day."

Musoto watched the guard return to his booth. Now he thought there may be something to this case. The guard was more than uncooperative. He was almost antagonistic. Musoto didn't like that. There was something wrong here and he wanted to find out what it was. Curiosity had replaced his nonchalant attitude about this assignment. Musoto waved to the guard, rolled up his window and backed the car from the gate driveway. He wanted to get to his motel room, jump on his laptop computer, and research the land records on Osguard Gardens. If nothing else he wanted to prove to the guard he had not thwarted this investigation.

***

"General Lo, this is Sentinel Watlins at OG post one," the guard said into his CC. Several seconds passed as the protocol for the communications went through its cycle.

"General Lo here," the voice came from his CC subdural receiver.

"Yes sir, we just had a visit from an FBI agent who wanted to look around."

"Okay, what happened?"

"Nothing, I turned him away. I thought you would want to know about it."

"Roger, copy. Keep an eye out. He may return. We will get our legal department on it and see if they can run interference. Lo out."

***

Elizabeth, Michael, Shawn and Patricia raced through Millmum Main Capitol Station corridors. They hopped a coaster to the Med Deck. Security personnel wearing delta belts stood guard throughout the corridors. Someone had attempted to assassinate an Osguard and they were there to make sure no one else tried. Every thirty seconds a bio-metal sweep canvassed the entire station, checking for unauthorized weapons. The security guard who shot Junitel had retrieved the weapon and scanned it into the ARIT computer bank. It was a special gun that shot energy pellets the ARIT did not recognize. That is why it was not caught in the theater sweep.

Now the ARIT knew the characteristics to search for. With every sweep, the rooms and corridors of the station would turn yellow for a fraction of a second. It appeared no one objected to this invasion of privacy, because they knew what had happened tonight was a prelude to a USSTAP state of emergency. The corridors were bustling with people of all manners racing toward the safety of their quarters. Planet representatives, their aides and their families rushed under the protective eye of the security forces to barricade themselves in their quarters. Panic had not set in yet, but it was rising to that level.

When Elizabeth, Michael, Shawn and Patricia reached the Med Deck, a nurse pointed them to the area where Parker was being treated. As they made their way toward the area they heard Admiral Toneilk, the commander also known as the sire of the station, speak over the station's intercom system. He spoke in his native tongue of Chaktun, which was also accepted as the universal language of USSTAP. Elizabeth could not understand him. She recognized it as Chaktun, even though she had barely been exposed to the language for two days.

"People, this is the sire speaking. Please return to your quarters in an orderly fashion. We have had an incident in the theater, which involved unauthorized weapons fire. Until we clear this incident, we require your cooperation in staying calm and moving as quickly as possible to your quarters. We will let you know when you can leave again. I repeat, please stay calm and move to your quarters for the night. USSTAP personnel are to assume Alert One."

With the end of the transmission, the alert board, which was on every deck and section, switched to the number—one. This put the station's personnel in a state of immediate readiness for confrontation. It was one short of battle stations. In the one hundred years the station existed, it had never used the alert system other than for practice. This was the first time it had illuminated due to a real contingency. However, the years of practice had bred into the USSTAP personnel the correct sense of urgency.

All station personnel including the members of the economic corps, medical corps and science corps activated their personal armory, retrieved, and placed on their delta belts. Michael, Shawn and Patricia witnessed the transformation, from a peaceful organization to one poised for battle, executed before their eyes in a matter of seconds. Only those medical personnel directly involved in patient care did not wear their delta belts. But they were in arms reach.

Michael tapped his CC as he watched in amazement the transformation, "*G.P. Neraka*, this is Osguard zero–one." He waited for the usual delay.

"*G.P. Neraka*, go Osguard zero–one," rendered a female voice over his CC subdural receiver.

"Place the ship in Alert One. Deport and assume guard position for the area in sector two–G," Michael ordered.

"Do you need some help, brother?" Patricia said as the female voice replied "Tiah."

Michael tapped his CC to end the transmission. "What do you have in mind?"

"Let's get all our ships out there, just in case this was the first strike of an attack. We need to scan a three hundred and sixty degree perimeter," Patricia replied.

"Fine, good thinking sis," Michael managed a smile. "I knew you weren't all looks. You have some brains."

"Thanks," she said trying to manage a smile, but the pain of her father's situation halted the attempt. "ARIT, this is Osguard two–two. Open a channel to all Osguards," she ordered.

"Channel opened," came the female voice over the room's intercom system.

"Osguards, this is Patricia Genesis. I need you to take your ships outside the station's boundaries and assume a guard position. We need to scan for enemy ships in the sector. This may be a prelude to an attack. I suggest we all go to Alert One."

"All replies are positive," said the ARIT voice over the communications system.

***

"This is Millmum Main Capitol Station Control," advised the space traffic controller, Commander Terilela, from the observation deck. "*G.P. Loclam* on port one you are cleared to deport and take heading two–two decimal three–four, mark zero–five."

"This is the *G.P. Loclam*. Copy, two–two decimal three–four, mark zero–five. Tiah," came the voice over the intercom.

"This is Millmum Main Capitol Station Control. *G.P. Nitram* on port six zero, you are cleared to deport and take heading one–two–two decimal one–three–four, mark zero–eight."

"This is *G.P. Nitram*. Copy, one–two–two decimal one–three–four, mark zero–eight. Tiah."

"This is Millmum Main Capitol Station Control. *G.P. Sregaem* on port three-zero, you are cleared to deport and take heading two–two–two decimal two–three–four, mark one–zero."

"This is *G.P. Sregaem*. Copy, two–two–two decimal two–three–four, mark one–zero. Tiah."

"This is Millmum Main Capitol Station Control. *G.P. Sucram* on port one five, you are cleared to deport and take heading zero–zero–two decimal zero–three–four, mark zero–one."

"This is *G.P. Sucram*. Copy, zero–zero–two decimal zero–three–four, mark zero–one. Tiah."

Terilela repeated the command for each galaxy protector, strategically placing the fleet around the Capitol Station arena as dictated by Toneilk. Toneilk walked the plank behind his lead controller watching every move she made. He was nervous about an attack. He had never tasted combat, not like his counterparts in the other galaxies. He had been an economic corps desk jockey most of his career. Now he was on the front line of what could be the start of another galactic war with the Kulusks. He had studied them and learned their tactics. But somehow this did not fit their normal modus operandi. It was only by the grace of Jus, he had sixty of the most powerful ships ever made by man at his disposal. If there was a confrontation this day, he felt sorry for the Kulusks.

***

Outside the stations the galaxy protectors disconnected from their ports and plodded on towards their departure routes as set up by Toneilk and his staff. The ships set up in a three hundred and sixty-degree circle at various points on the galactic plane. Multiple scans at different energies and various times began as soon as the ships departed. The ships took five minutes to get into place and then they assumed stealth mode seven.

Stealth mode seven energized the special energy absorbing slitanium metal in the hull of the ship. However the energy expended cost them. There was not enough power to fully energize their chromerion fields and weapons at the same time. Each stealth mode prioritized which systems would receive power. Stealth mode seven powered the chromerion fields at half strength, their weapons at full ready, and extinguished all external lights, including the power lights that traced the outside of the engines from bow to stern. In this mode, nothing but the hypersonic drive and thrusters were available for maneuvering. In this situation, conventional wisdom noted that maneuvering was the essential characteristic for combat, and MOP engines or the hyperlight drive could be forgone, because they were only good for getting to and getting away from a fight. So the galaxy protectors sat poised and ready for battle, searching the heavens for an unseen enemy, whom they knew would come.

***

In a small motel directly off the main highway, the pizza was cold. But that was how he liked it. He devoured the seventh slice of his delivered pizza as he tapped on his laptop. It was amazing how the Americans took a simple Italian delicacy, like a pizza pie, and drastically changed it so no native Italian would recognize it. This particular pizza was a prime example, Musoto thought. It had pineapples, anchovies, sausage, green peppers and jalapenos. He imagined his grandmother turning in her grave every time he ordered pizza. She was such a prude when it came to Italian cooking. She also was the best Italian cook he ever knew. No one, not even those fancy Italian restaurants he visited in New York, could have held a candle to his grandmother's cooking. Oh how he missed her. He was her pride and joy and he deeply loved her.

Musoto took out the last slice of pizza and shoved half of it in his mouth. He tapped his keyboard once more. The screen switched to city records. He clicked on property titles. The computer requested an address.

Musoto typed in *'Osguard Gardens'* and then clicked *'OK.'*

The computer went blank as it searched the web. Several seconds later the screen blinked *'Not Found.'*

Musoto groaned. Then he switched back to city records and clicked on city map. He found the area labeled *'Osguard Gardens'* and clicked on it.

The picture magnified large enough for Musoto to decipher street names and landmarks. The subdivision was constructed in a circular pattern with off streets turning into cul-de-sacs. It contained about one hundred and fifty houses on two hundred and fifty acres of land. Directly in the middle was a park.

Osguards: Homecoming

He clicked onto the park and read the name—*'Elizabeth Louise Gentry Memorial Park.'*

He stopped chewing on his cold pizza and searched the top of his bed for the list of names his boss assigned him to track. He found it under a stack of other papers. He scanned the list. Halfway down the list, he found the name Elizabeth Louise Gentry. Bingo, he thought. There is a connection.

He had not done a computer search on her yet. Maybe now was the time he thought. He clicked the backwards arrow to get back to the city records.

He put into the search window, *'Elizabeth Louise Gentry.'*

The window closed and returned with a short biography on Gentry. Next he conducted a by-name cross-reference with Gentry, Pathgo and the Gardens. He found Gentry and Pathgo. They lived in the area at the same time. Great, he thought. He was on to something. But the name Osguard still did not hit a cord. Then he cross-referenced land records. Bingo, the Pathgo's had purchased the Gentry land from her brother-in-law after her death. He plotted the land as described in the deed transfer. Shit, Osguard Gardens sits directly on the Pathgo-Gentry land. How come he did not pick this up the first time he ran the Pathgo name? Then he saw the land was in Mrs. Jessica Pathgo's name, not that of her husband, Phillip Pathgo. Well he made a mental note to check all possible family connections when checking for property.

Musoto then clicked his computer several times, until he found *'land deeds.'*

He searched the database for the land deed for Osguard Gardens. Another hit. A company called Unlimited Associations owned Osguard Gardens. The paperwork called it a retirement community for the families of the board members. Then Musoto tried a global search of Unlimited Associations. The computer printed out a brief synopsis of an import/export business with its headquarters in Richmond, Virginia. Finally, he thought he was getting somewhere. He jotted down the address. He would pay the company a little visit tomorrow.

Not bad for a couple of hours of searching on a computer. He got more information this way than wearing out his shoes knocking on doors and interviewing people. The way of the old gumshoe days were gone. The computer was the easy, efficient and effective way to conduct an investigation. It was amazing what people put on the web, including things they wouldn't tell their best friends. But somehow the anonymity of the web or the seductive power of the web made people place all sorts of information on it. Secrecy in the information age was unattainable. The new age was for the technological people. Those who did not get on board would perish like the dinosaur. He would not perish. In fact, his plan was to flourish in the age and soar to the top. Maybe even become the Director of the FBI one day.

Then his bubble burst. He was on the blackball list after Los Angeles and he knew it. He would be lucky if he made it to ten years as a field agent. There was no future in this job.

He slammed the laptop closed as he sunk into the bed and rested his eyes. The strain of staring at the small screen had given him a headache. He pushed the papers aside, crawled into the fetal position, and fell asleep.

***

The Genesis family, including Michael's uncles and aunt, sat in the waiting area, worried about Parker. Parker had been in surgery for over three hours now. That was supposedly too long with the technology USSTAP possessed. Michael played the scene over and over in his head. If he had not moved to pick up the program, the shot would have torn his head clear off his neck. *What the hell was it?* he thought as he massaged the back of his neck.

Toneilk stood six feet tall with silver hair streaked with his original black hair on the sides. He walked up to Michael unnoticed by the family.

"Excuse me, First Osguard," he said in Chaktun. "Can I speak with you?"

Michael lifted his head and stood to meet Toneilk.

"What is it?"

"Sir, the person who shot your father is dead. It was Junitel, the Kulusk ambassador's aide."

"I know, the guard told me earlier," Michael lamented. "What else do you have?"

"Well sir, we have interrogated Manidul...well I mean we have questioned him," Toneilk corrected himself. "He appears to know nothing of his aide's actions. In fact, his aide almost killed him trying to escape."

Michael took a deep breath and raised his head skywards. Looking at the ceiling, he stretched his arms.

"It figures. Kie never trusted his politicians. He thinks they are too weak. I am sure he knows nothing." Michael finished stretching and beckoned at his sister and brother to join them. They rose from their seats and walked over.

"It's time to give them what they want," Michael told his siblings.

"What? Not now. Dad is—"

Michael interrupted Patricia. "—I know, they know, we all know. But it is what they expect and it is what they get."

Before Patricia could rebut her brother the doctor walked through the med deck doors to the waiting room. They turned to him as he reached Elizabeth. Michael grabbed his sister's outstretched arm and they walked to the doctor. Michael's heart was in his throat as he saw the doctor's eyes.

"Mrs. Genesis, we had to operate on your husband for quite awhile. But—"

Elizabeth feared the word but. Her knees buckled underneath her as she started to faint. Armstrong and Coltrane grabbed her, one on each side. They lowered her to her seat.

She looked up, "But what? Is he dead?"

The doctor turned to see Michael, Shawn and Patricia behind him and realized he had chosen the wrong English words to brief Elizabeth. The doctor was from Uranthea and only knew English somewhat.

He turned to the Osguards and spoke Chaktun, "Your father is still in a coma. He lost a lot of blood and the weapon damaged his nerve cells. We had to amputate both his legs from the hip down. It was quite a shock to his system. It overloaded his senses. We will have to wait and see if he will snap out of it."

"But he is alive, right?" Michael asked.

"Yes, he is alive for now," the doctor cautioned. "But if he stays much longer in this coma, I can't assure you if he will stay alive."

"What is it, Michael," his mother pleaded.

Michael turned to his mother and uncles.

"Dad is in a coma, mom. The weapon really hurt him bad. They had to amputate his legs in order to save him. But he ain't out of the woods yet."

Elizabeth closed her eyes in a deep prayer.

"He is alive. That's all that matters. He is alive." She turned to the doctor, "Can I see him?"

"Yes, but only for a moment," he said in Chaktun.

Patricia nodded. "Only for a moment, Mom…Dad needs his rest." Patricia looked at her uncle, "Uncle Armstrong, can you and Uncle Coltrane take Mom to see Dad? When you are finished, we will go in."

Armstrong nodded. He and his brother helped Elizabeth to her feet as Holly grabbed her bag and Debrlina, who helped in the operation, escorted them through the doors.

"What are his chances doctor?" asked Shawn.

"Actually, real good. Your father is in excellent shape and as soon as he wakes we can neutralize the damage caused by this weapon."

"Do you have the specs on it?" asked Toneilk, who slipped into the conversation, unnoticed.

"Not quite," answered the doctor. "But it is real nasty. If he had taken a direct hit, he would be dead. The metal from the chair seamed to absorb most of the energy. All I can tell you is the energy pellet had a melenai ore at the point. It took a long time for us to dig it out of your father."

"What is a melenai ore?" asked Shawn.

"According to ARIT, it is metal denser than anything we have in the USSTAP inventory. It is very rare and hard to find anywhere."

"How did it penetrate the chromerion field?" asked Patricia.

Malcolm Dylan Petteway

Toneilk reached into the thigh pocket of his black jumpsuit and pulled out the shockdel gun retrieved from Junitel's dead body.

"Our lab can't really tell, but it appears this little hummer makes the melenai ore, like a pagenay makes its pellets. Unfortunately, the ore can penetrate the chromerion field like a hot knife through butter. It has the explosive power of four coronet gun pellets when it hits. Your father was lucky; somehow the chair absorbed the energy before it hit him. If it had hit you straight, your entire body would have exploded, melted or just disappeared in a puff of smoke. This is a nasty bugger."

Michael picked up the shockdel gun and inspected it. He had in his hands the instrument that may be the cause his father's death…if he doesn't survive the coma.

"Shit, if the Kulusks have ship size weapons like this, we are in deep trouble."

"Do you still want to go?" Patricia asked.

"Yes, but I want this gun to go through the full gamut. I want to know its weakness. And I want to know yesterday," Michael ordered Toneilk as he placed the gun back in his hands.

Just then the doors whispered open and Elizabeth, Armstrong, Coltrane and Holly walked through. Elizabeth was bawling as was Holly. Armstrong and Coltrane were visibly fighting back tears of their own. Debrlina walked over to Shawn and hugged him.

"Do you want to see your father now?" she asked.

They all nodded, yes. Debrlina hooked Shawn's arm and walked him through the doors. Michael and Patricia followed. The walk seemed long, but it was just a few steps. Debrlina and Shawn turned into the second room on the right.

Parker was lying in a med bed covered by a medical aurora field to monitor his life signs. Two brain stimuli Medical ARITs or MARITs were attached to his temples on both sides. An optical MARIT kept his eyes wide open and a breathing MARIT that reached into his lungs was inserted in his mouth. On Earth he would be considered a vegetable, kept alive artificially by machines. On Earth the discussion would be, do we pull the plug? But in USSTAP no such discussion would ever enter a doctor's mind. As long as the patient had a spark of life, no matter how small, MARITs would be used to continue life.

This is what Elizabeth was unprepared for. She was shocked to see her husband strapped to the MARITS with no sign of life—at least none that she could see. But the USSTAP technology could see the minute spark of life. It recognized Parker was fighting for it. And the MARITS were a slight compensation so Parker could conserve his energy for that fight. Michael, Shawn and Patricia knew this all too well. Patricia was in this exact state four years ago, after her defender accident. She fought for her life and won. Now it was her father's turn.

Michael and Patricia went to the right side of the med bed and Debrlina and Shawn went to the other. They looked into their father's eyes and saw his life force hovering inside. His eyes were much better than they were on the balcony. There, Debrlina knew his life force wanted to escape the pain and search out the eternal light of Jus. She fought long and hard to keep his life force in place. So far, she was effective. But now it was up to Parker.

Michael touched his father's hand and caressed it with his index finger. "Dad, I am so sorry." Michael choked on the words. "I should have never brought you here. I should have known it was too dangerous."

"Michael, it is safer here than on Earth," Patricia tried to comfort her brother. "On Earth, anyone could have hurt him."

"Yes, but they weren't aiming for him. They were aiming for me. Now look at him."

"Look brother, no one could have predicted this. It isn't your fault. So stop with the self pity."

"But..."

Michael couldn't finish. Something grabbed his finger. He looked down, saw his father's hand had reached for his, and had a good hold on it. Michael's eyes welled up as he began to cry.

"Look, he has my hand."

Shawn and Patricia looked and their eyes watered.

"He's coming back," Debrlina said. She shot to the foot of the bed to read his life signs. "He is getting stronger." Then she moved to the head of the bed and removed the optical MARITS. Parker's eyes remained opened. "He's out of the coma." She ran to the foot of the bed and pushed the blue button. A slight humming alarm echoed in the room. "Look you three, you need to get, so we can revive him properly," she ordered.

Michael, Shawn and Patricia took a step back and watched as the med team poked, pried and pushed their father back into the land of the living. *He's going to make it*, Michael thought. He wiped a tear from his eyes as he reached for his siblings to hug them.

"He's going to make it," he shouted.

Chapter 31—Unlimited Associations Inc.

Musoto stood in front of the Cochran Business Building in downtown Richmond, Virginia. He looked up to catch the thirty-two-story building. It was magnificent in design with dark shining glass and luminescent brown steel spars. Its unique concave feature made it stand out as a tourist attraction in the city. Recently built, it housed many of the major corporations that called Richmond their home. The tenants of the building included a national car rental company on one floor and a major insurance company, which occupied seven floors. These companies were seduced by the governor's rhetoric of tax cuts and labor negotiations. Several organizations set up temporary satellites in the building on a trial basis. The first to sign on was Unlimited Associations.

Unlimited Associations occupied the seventh and eighth floors. His research indicated it was a private company, not found in any of the stock market literature. The research did not shed much light on what Unlimited Associations was. It just indicated it was an import and export business. In his field of work, this usually meant smuggling. Could he have discovered a drug smuggling operation, or something more sophisticated. He could be on to something big. This could make his career. Boy, wouldn't that be justice? They sent him on a nowhere case to get him away from the real meat and he could end up busting some international smuggling ring.

Musoto just smiled as he pushed the thought to the back of his mind. No sense in getting excited now. So far, it was just routine follow-up on a list of names from the past. But somehow, the assignment was getting exciting. Musoto did not know if it this was because there was something there, or if it was because he had an overactive imagination. Whatever the reason, he felt alive on this case. He was ready for something to happen.

He strolled into the foyer and searched the directory board. He saw Unlimited Associations on the seventh and eighth floors, just as the computer information told him. He turned to catch the elevator, jumped in and pressed the number seven. The elevator doors slid close and he politely glanced around the elevator to see who was on board with him. It was Quantico training to always survey the surroundings; especially in closed in areas. The guard who surprised him yesterday still weighed heavily on his mind.

Inside the elevator were seven professional-looking people, four men and three women. They all appeared to be employees in the building. The lady to the right of him was wearing a smart looking blue business jacket with a matching skirt that appeared to just cover her rear end. Her legs were muscular and toned, and definitely highlighted by the high-heeled shoes she was wearing. He caught a whiff of her perfume, which actually drew him to stare at her more than a glance. She was quite attractive with brown hair pinned in a bun behind her head. He imagined what she would look like with her hair free flowing and her glasses off. He knew she dressed like this to get the attention of her employers. It was a game played in the work force all over America. *Why didn't she wear a pants suit, or a skirt that approached her knees? Because she would not get the attention she wanted wearing that. Well, if she was dressing for attention, then I hope she gets it. I just hope some poor slob with raging hormones doesn't assume the attention she wants is sexual*, he thought.

Then their eyes met, he felt embarrassed because he knew she caught him checking her out. She beamed a warm smile and he darted his glance to the floor readout above the elevator door. It was approaching five. *Thank God*, he thought. He could feel the blush appear on his face. He snuck another glance in her direction and saw she was still smiling in his direction.

"Are you new in the building?" she asked with a hint of sexiness in her voice.

Musoto looked stunned at her question. He pointed to himself, "Who me?"

She nodded, yes—still sporting the sexy school girl smile.

"No, I am just visiting a business—Unlimited Associations. Do you know anything about them?"

"No I don't," she said in a slight sexy whisper. "I really don't know what they do. I work for Blue Armor Insurance upstairs. You sure you don't want to come visit with us?"

"Maybe some other time. Right now, I have business with Unlimited Associations."

"How can you have business with a company and you don't even know what kind of business they are in?" she asked with a confused look on her face.

"It's my job," he declared. The elevator halted and the doors opened. "This is my floor. Nice meeting you…"

"Mona," she offered. "I am on the twentieth floor, if you want to stop by and check out our business. Just ask for Mona Richards, okay."

"Okay, I just might do that," he smiled and walked off the elevator. "By the way, I am Tony Musoto…"

The doors closed as he said his name. The last image he saw was of Mona winking her eye as the doors shut. Tony stood in front of the elevator door for a quick second, reviewing in his mind what just transpired. She hit on him. She actually hit on him. This was a first. It was quite flattering. He would have to visit the twentieth floor before he left the building, just to see whether she was playing or really interested in what she saw. Either way, his morning had started off pleasantly.

Tony turned around and saw a large circular desk with a sign that read *'RECEPTIONIST'* on it. He approached the desk to see another beautiful woman behind it. This one was a dark skinned black woman. She had a hands-free phone clipped to her ear. She was jotting down a message from the call. She looked up and raised her trigger finger to gesture she would be with him in a minute. Tony smiled and placed his arm on the desk as he took a seat in front of her. He watched as she finished the message. She appeared to be in her early twenties. The mahogany color of her skin uniquely highlighted her light brown eyes. Her dark black shoulder length hair framed the smooth round features of her face. Then when she looked up, she flashed a wide, bright smile that enhanced the softness of her voice.

"Can I help you?" she offered.

Tony took out his badge and flashed it to her, "I'm Special Agent Tony Musoto of the FBI. I wonder if I could talk to someone about Osguard Gardens."

"Hold on, I'll see if there is anyone around who knows what you are referring to." The receptionist pulled out a directory and thumbed through the pages. Her finger stopped halfway down the third page of the directory. She clicked the mouse of her computer several times, and then she spoke into her microphone.

"Mr. Daley, there is a Special Agent Tony Musoto from the FBI wishing to speak to someone about an Osguard Gardens." She listened for a moment. "Yes sir, I will do that." Then she clicked the mouse one more time. She looked at Musoto, "Please have a seat. Mr. Daley will be here to speak with you in a moment. He is finishing up a phone call to Washington D.C. right now."

Tony turned to his right and saw a small waiting area. He went into the area, found a seat and picked up the USA Today paper off the coffee table. He glanced at the front page. The headline particularly got his attention. "**U.S. AND RUSSIAN PRESIDENTS WILL ANNOUNCE NEW ICBM ARMS REDUCTION TONIGHT**," was the main headline. Then the secondary headline in smaller print said "**FRIDAY'S WHITE LIGHT TO BE EXPLAINED**." A picture of the U.S. president and his Russian counterpart graced the story. Musoto scanned the story for important facts. He read that the presidents began a secret summit meeting yesterday and now were ready to announce an amendment to the START treaty. They called it the Chaktun amendment. What a funny name, thought Musoto. Also, the article referenced the white light in the sky last Friday afternoon was a joint defensive exercise connected with tonight's announcement. Musoto ran his fingers through his straight and stringy jet-black hair. World politics was getting stranger by the day he noted. After he read the article he summarily dismissed it as a political trick and searched for the sports page. He found an article on the Dallas Cowboys and began to read about their relentless off-season woes.

***

In the military command center of the Kulusk capital of Renard, Kie paced back and forth. His agitation was apparent and frightening to the command center personnel. They had witnessed Kie kill because someone bore bad news. Now, Kie was searching for some news no one in the center had.

"Check your scans again," Kie barked.

"Nothing, Maxum. The space is quiet," stammered the operator.

"It has been thirty universal hours since I sent the message. Something should have happened by now, and our sky should be littered with those rox Osguard black ships. Why aren't they here?" questioned Kie. The entire political process was to begin in six universal hours. The Osguard Senate, the Special Session of the Congressional Representatives and Parliament were all to begin soon. Was his plan falling apart? Were the Osguards in that much control of their human feelings that they didn't want revenge? Had he underestimated them?

He turned to the operator once more, "You keep an eye out. I want to know the moment anything unusual appears on your screen."

"Soli," the operator replied, trying to muster a tone of professionalism to hide his fear.

***

"Special Agent Musoto?" chirped a voice from the receptionist desk.

Musoto looked up from his paper and saw a white balding man in his fifties looking his way.

"Yes, I am Special Agent Musoto."

"Good, I am Mr. Robert Daley, Vice President of Domestic Affairs. How can I help you?" he said walking and offering his handshake.

Musoto shook his hand and noticed Daley had a much firmer grip than he expected.

"Well, I have some questions about Osguard Gardens and my research tells me your business owns that particular community."

"You're pretty good, Special Agent Musoto," Daley chimed. "It is not a matter of public record we own it."

"Well sir, it is a matter of public record. It took awhile, but you were listed on the Internet as the owners," teased Musoto.

The smile wiped off Daley's face as if he just heard someone in his family had died. Musoto took mental note at the shock on Daley's face and knew he had hit a nerve.

"That's too bad. My company prides itself in its security. I will have to correct this," Daley countered.

"Why? Does your company have something to hide?" continued Musoto.

"No, we don't," Daley disputed. "Let's continue this in my office."

Daley stepped from the waiting room into a narrow corridor. Musoto followed him. Musoto noticed paintings of people on the walls. However they had no names associated with them. He thought it somewhat strange.

"Who are these people on your wall?" he asked.

"Don't know. They have something to do with the owners of the company. We just grin and bear it when we look at them. Some of them are quite beautiful. Take this one for instance." Daley pointed to a picture of two light skinned black women with auburn hair, dressed in vibrant colors. They had a slight pleasant smile similar to Leonardo De Vinci's Mona Lisa, not sad but not quite happy either.

"All we can see is they are related. They look like sisters. But we don't know who they are, or if they are still alive." Neither Daley, nor Musoto had any idea they were looking at a painting of Nausona and Laurona Osguard.

Musoto studied the picture for a second. They were quite beautiful. Something about their eyes demonstrated strength and power. But something about their smile showed a great sadness. It was amazing how painters could capture the human emotions of their subject and bring them to life in a still painting. Whoever painted this was a true artist. Musoto searched for a signature on the painting.

"You won't find any," said Daley.

"Find what?"

"You won't find a signature or a date. These paintings are truly mysteries to us."

Musoto straightened up and reflected a moment on that statement. Why should something be a mystery to a vice president? Something was not right.

"So what kind of business is Unlimited Associations?" asked Musoto.

"You mean you didn't learn that from your Internet research?" Daley remarked with a even voice as he turned into his office and motioned for Musoto to take a seat on the couch.

Daley sat in the easy chair next to the couch. He sat somewhat higher than Musoto. This gave Daley the psychological edge of power. It was an old but effective business trick.

"Well, my investigation reveals you are in the export and import business."

Daley noted Musoto used the word investigation and not research. His defenses went into super hyper drive now.

"Investigation? What are you investigating?"

"I am not at liberty to say at this point."

"Well, I am not sure I am at liberty to be answering your questions without a lawyer."

"No sir, this is not a criminal investigation. You can call it an official inquiry. No crime has been committed, at least to my knowledge," Musoto said in hopes of easing the tension he inadvertently raised. "In fact, I am trying to track down some people for questioning and I believe I can find some answers at the Gardens."

"I am sure you are wrong. The Gardens is our retirement community. It is a specific area set aside by our founders for their families upon retirement. You won't find anybody essential to your investigation there, I assure you."

"Well sir, please let me worry about that?

"Okay then, who are you looking for? I will have them meet you here, with a lawyer of course."

Musoto was stuck. He couldn't give any names on the list. They were all dead. But maybe…

"I am looking for a family named Osguard, a family named Pathgo and a family named Gentry. Can you help me?"

Daley smiled. His defenses eased somewhat.

"We may own the community called Osguard Gardens, but as God as my witness, no one by those names reside at the Gardens.

"Are you sure?"

"Yes, I am sure."

"Then can you tell me the names of the people who reside at the Gardens?"

"Look, Special Agent Musoto. I know you have the resources to find out the information. However, I am not at liberty to tell you the residents of our private estates. I'm sorry I can't help you."

"Why not?"

"Like I said earlier, our founders pride themselves on security. I don't know you are really FBI. You could be someone fishing for information to kidnap or hurt our family. I'd rather you go through official channels to get that information."

"That is somewhat paranoid, don't you think?" Musoto responded.

"Let me tell you this. We are in the import and export business. We deal with many rare and exquisite diamonds, gems and stones. We are above board and very legitimate. We have a very exclusive clientele list, including many politicians in Washington. Our transactions are private and final. We handle more money than the national debt. So yes, the founders are paranoid. Wouldn't you be?"

Musoto thought about what he just heard. Somewhere in that barrage of statements hid a veiled threat—an exclusive clientele list, including politicians in Washington. Daley said that to let him know they had some powerful juice behind them. Wait a minute, could this case really be for real? Could it have come from Washington itself? It was a slim possible connection. But it was a connection.

"Yes, I suppose I would be a bit paranoid," Musoto answered.

Musoto knew he did not have enough for a search warrant and he had hit several dead ends on the Internet while researching Unlimited Associations. He thought discretion would be the better part of valor.

"Well, can you tell me this much? What do you do for Osguard Gardens?"

"Come on, Special Agent Musoto. That should be obvious. We manage the property. We provide security and we pay the taxes on it. What else do you expect us to do? The family members retire there and live off a nice pension from the company. We ensure they receive their pension and anything else they need."

"Okay, can you tell me more about your business?"

"Not really, Special Agent Musoto. We are legitimate. You can check the custom ports throughout the world. We have crossed every 'T' and dotted every 'I'. You will not find anything inappropriate or improper in our business dealings. Now, if you would excuse me. I have work to do." Daley rose and gestured for Musoto to leave through the door. "I will have security escort you out."

As if by magic two black clad security guards appeared at the door. They were dressed like the one he had encountered at Osguard Gardens.

Musoto peered around at Daley, who was edging himself around the back of his desk.

"Thanks for your time."

"Don't mention it. And I really mean that. Don't mention it," reiterated Daly as he sat down and pushed some papers around.

The security guards escorted Musoto past the pretty receptionist who flashed that same smile at him, and onto the elevator. Once inside the elevator Musoto pushed the button for the twentieth floor. *Might as well get some joy out of the day since that was a bust,* he reflected.

Chapter 32—Evacuation

Parker Genesis lay in his med bed totally aware of his surroundings, but unable to move or speak. He had a new doctor, Captain Susan Tillman. He had recognized her as one of Michael's friends from college. She and Michael had become quite close and now she was a doctor in USSTAP. That was the only connection he could think of.

Susan connected a brainwave MARIT to Parker's forehead. Then she reached over and turned on a monitor of some type.

Parker thought, *"What are you doing?"*

Susan looked at the monitor.

"Good, it's working fine. Mr. Parker, I've just connected a brainwave MARIT to you. It will display whatever you want to say, but can't. Now be careful this thing may register something you may not want others to see. You have control of it by pressing this button.

The words, *"What are you talking about?"* displayed on the monitor. Susan tilted the monitor for Parker to see.

Parker's thoughts, *"What the hell? What's this bullshit?"* displayed on the monitor. He depressed the button and the screen went blank.

"Now, I know this seems a little intrusive, but only you control what will be seen on that monitor. So if you have any nasty thoughts, I suggest you keep it off," joked Susan.

The door swished open and Elizabeth walked in. She was smiling to see her husband alive and without those damned MARITS all over him. But he had a new MARIT sitting right in the middle of his forehead.

"Susan, what's this?" she pointed to the MARIT.

"I'll let Mr. Genesis explain it to you," replied Susan.

"Is he speaking now?" queried Elizabeth.

"In a way. Move over here and I will demonstrate." She motioned for Elizabeth to take the seat next to the bed where she could view the monitor and her husband at the same time. "Say hello to Mr. Genesis," she said.

"Hey honey. How are you feeling today?"

Parker tapped the button connected to his right hand. The screen lit up with the words,

"Better than yesterday."

Elizabeth read the words.

"Is that Parker?"

"Yes, it is," the monitor printed. *"Susan put this gadget on my head that allows you to see what I am thinking. It's kind of cool. You always wanted to read my mind."*

"Is this permanent?" Elizabeth asked Susan.

"No. Mr. Parker will regain his strength in a couple of days. Then we will give him a set of ARIT legs and he will be good as new."

"MARIT legs?" thought Parker.

"Yes, they are MARIT manipulated, but human controlled. They will look and feel like your original legs. In fact your daughter-in-law is making them up as we speak. She is the best in her field you know."

"The best in her field? What field?" Elizabeth asked.

"Michelle is the station's top Bio Molecular Physiologist. She has gained universal recognition in creating her MARIT prosthetics. In fact the doctor who saved your husband's life had a MARIT prosthetic hand. He lost his in a boating accident on his home planet. Michelle operated on him personally."

"Will Michelle do Parker?"

"I don't know. You will have to talk to her about that when you see her."

"Lord, I didn't know she was a doctor. She never told us," cried Elizabeth. "All the grief I gave that poor child and she is about to give my husband his legs back."

"Don't you feel like a fool," Parker thought. Then he tapped the button to turn the monitor off before Elizabeth saw it. When it went blank, he turned it back on. *"Need to be careful,"* he thought.

"Careful about what?" asked Elizabeth.

"Nothing," he thought and then he depressed the monitor off again. He saw Susan hold back her laughter in the background, because she had read the original thought prior to Parker turning it off. She winked and left the room.

***

The Osguard Senate room was alive with the buzz of all the Osguards offering their opinions on the situation. After a while, Michael stood up from talking to several of his cousins.

"Please take your seats. I have an announcement." Michael waited for the clamor to die down as he watched the Osguards take their seats. "It's time to put the plan we all agreed on into action. But first, we need to usher our families to safety. I have arranged with the Chaktun Maxum to house our families and the other civilian populace until this matter is clear. Several Chaktun transport ships plus our own startrams will transport the families to Chaktun. I had thought of bringing our parents back to Earth. But if we fail, Earth will be defenseless against the Kulusk invasion. Chaktun offers the best chance of survival. Do you agree?"

Michael waited for someone to speak. No one did, they just nodded in agreement. Then Shawn stood from his seat.

"Michael, what about Dad? He can't be moved in his condition right now."

"Well, we might have to leave him on the station. I thought about delaying this until he was ready to move. But if we wait any longer, the Kulusks will do something more drastic to get our attention. I am afraid something might be in the works now. That is why I want to make this contact now."

Shawn sat back down. Michael was right. Besides, moving the parents to Chaktun was just a precaution. The plan was foolproof. Nothing could go wrong. Every Osguard ran separate simulations and with minor differences the outcome was the same. The analysis of the Kulusk weapon was not encouraging. USSTAP would take a lot of damage. But if everyone stuck to the plan, the damage would not be insurmountable. However, every simulation displayed casualties. None of the Osguards were comfortable with casualties, especially casualties from an offensive action they started. In the years they had commanded the USSTAP, this would be the first time they conducted an offensive action, which might start a war. But in their eyes, this action was to stop a war.

"Then we are all in agreement," offered Michael for the last time. "All political forums will be suspended until this action is complete. The representatives of the Congress and the Parliament will travel to Chaktun for political asylum as necessary. We will meet here in three universal hours and proceed with the agreed upon action. Until then we must supervise the evacuation of Main Capitol Station."

With the chime of the bell, all the Osguards retreated from their seats and through the exits.

***

"I'm not leaving your father," screamed Elizabeth. "The rest of the family can go, but I am not leaving your father."

"Mother, we need you to watch the kids," pleaded Patricia. "They will be going to Chaktun as well. We have duties to perform during this crisis. Besides, Michelle and Debrlina will be here with Father." Patricia hugged her mother. "Do you think we like the idea of leaving him like this? We don't want to. But he is too weak to move." She pulled away to look into her mother's eyes. "Moreover, the station will be fine. It's just a precautionary move. Everything will be fine."

"But, Parker needs me," Elizabeth pleaded.

"Your grandchildren need you more. Furthermore, I spoke to Dad just a few minutes ago, and he agrees. He wants you safe and he wants you with the grandchildren."

"Their other grandparents can watch them," she demanded. "No, I am staying here and that's final."

Patricia turned away in exasperation, "Michael, see if you can talk some sense into her."

"I would, but it won't do any good."

Patricia turned to Shawn.

"Don't look at me. Mom never did a damn thing I asked her to."

Elizabeth looked at Shawn with that *'Don't sass me boy,'* look. Shawn stepped back shaking his hands in front of him and his head—*'NO'*. Elizabeth turned back to Patricia.

"It's settled," she said. "I'm staying."

"Mom, you are impossible," said Patricia. "Fine, but you do everything Michelle and Debrlina tell you—you hear me!"

"Yes, I hear you."

"Fine, let's go see how the rest of the world is doing," Patricia quipped as she turned toward the door.

Shawn and Michael gave their mother a hug and started to follow their sister out of the room.

"Shawn," Elizabeth called.

Shawn turned in quiet anticipation.

"Shawn, you are my oldest, and I may have treated you differently than your sister and brother. But that doesn't mean I love you any less. It was…I mean you were my first-born. Babies don't come with instructions. What I am trying to say is…I'm sorry for any pain I may have caused you."

"That's okay, Mom. I guess I am going through the same thing with my son—I understand."

"Well understand this young man," Elizabeth pushed in a command demeanor. "I want you to kill as many of those Kulusk bastards as you can— kill them for what they did to your father. And I want you to look out for your brother and sister. You are the oldest, and I am counting on you…I've always counted on you."

"Right, Mom. I'll do just that," Shawn said as he left the room.

***

The convoy was to rendezvous in sectors two through five–G. Eduardo Sanchez, the Centurion of Operations aboard *G.P. Neraka* stood beside the hatch of his defender. He was to be the commander of the convoy, leading the evacuees to Chaktun. Then Michael wanted him to return to the station and set up a protective orbit using the defenders from the other galaxy protectors. Sanchez was not fully versed on Michael's plan, but he had known him long enough to know he had thought it through to the smallest detail. And if he were needed to protect the station, then he would protect the station in his defender. The only comfort to Sanchez was he would command the defenders of all the galaxy protectors. Each galaxy protector contained five squadrons of ten defenders. Therefore he would sire the largest fleet of defenders to gather in USSTAP history—three thousand. It was definitely an honor. One he did not expect, but happily accepted.

He stepped onto the ladder leading to the cockpit of his defender. The four metal steps clanged when his black booted feet stepped up. He hopped into the seat and pushed the glass-plated control to slide the canopy forward and shut. He checked his readings on the control panel. Power distribution read normal. His balance read normal. The cabin pressurized normally. He turned for his helmet and slipped it over his head. The helmet surrounded his head with a clear round composite glass, as was the canopy and the control panel. It was strong enough to take a direct hit from weapons fire and not shatter.

He switched on his radio.

"Convoy lead to all squadrons, report when ready."

Sanchez sat and listened for the five squadrons of defenders from *G.P. Neraka* to report. When he was satisfied he flipped the radio again.

"*Neraka* control, this is Defender zero–one, zero–two. Fleet ready for departure."

"Copy, Defender zero–one, zero–two. Hold for departure instructions."

Sanchez expected the delay. It was a difficult thing to launch the fleet all at once. He did not envy the controllers in the Control Bridge. They had their hands full today.

"*Neraka* Fleet, this is Control Bridge. You are cleared for departure in sequential order. Heading is zero–eight–five decimal zero–three–four, mark zero–zero."

"Tiah, Defender zero–one, zero–two fleet," Sanchez replied.

Sanchez fingered the control panel and energized his thrusters. Then he slipped his right hand into a tubular bind and grasped the controls for pitch and roll thrusters. He slipped his left hand through a similar tube and grasped the acceleration and horizontal thrusters. His engines that ran along the side remained off as his thrusters fired to life. The bay doors glided open in front of him as he listened for the roaring sound of the fleet igniting their thrusters. Once the doors opened he moved his controls to lift the defender straight up about ten feet and crept forward. He paused at the doors to allow the fleet to fall in order. The bay shook with the power of the thrusters lifting fifty defenders off the deck at one time. The sound reverberated throughout the bays. It was deafening. Sanchez watched his rear monitor as the last ship lifted into place.

When Sanchez was satisfied, he moved forward, penetrating the chromerion field protecting the bays from the cold vacuum of space. Once in space, Sanchez moved his defender to his designated position. Again, he watched his rear monitor as he looked for the fleet to fall into order. He was satisfied all were in proper order after three minutes.

"*Neraka* fleet, hypersonic now," he commanded as he fingered the controls to change from thruster to engines.

His engines that ran the entire length on both sides of the defender, similar to the galaxy protectors, hummed to life. A thin red light glowed along the outside of the engines, signifying they were in hypersonic speed.

Like Christmas tree lights, all fifty defenders' engine lights illuminated red and for a quick moment, space looked like a disco club. Then the lights moved, dancing and darting their way to Sector two–G through five–G.

"*Neraka* fleet, this is *Neraka* Control Bridge, you are self-nav. Repeat, you are self-nav. *Neraka* Control Bridge relinquishes navigation. Have a safe journey. *Neraka* Control Bridge out."

"Tiah," Sanchez replied for the fleet as they roared to their appointed destination.

***

Outside the station in the cold recesses of the outer space that blanketed the area, the hustle of multiple startrams and transport ships entered and exited the station region every fifteen universal minutes. The evacuation was going smoothly. The transport ships and startrams grouped in sector five–G, closest to the Chaktun solar system. There, a squadron of defenders from the *G.P. Neraka* flew cover for the convoy.

The startrams looked like a bigger cousin to the defenders. The middle segment of the startrams was hollow and could connect to a passenger cabin that accommodated twenty-five passengers or a freight cabin. These startrams were equipped with the passenger cabin.

Terilela and her staff of space controllers were busy ensuring proper spacing as they cleared each approach and departure. Their earphones were buzzing with radio chatter and their scanner scopes were filled with hits from all the ships in the area. Never in her life did she imagine so much space traffic in such a small area. The sweat beaded around her brow as her fiery red eyes watched the entire operation on the main scanner. Controllers were solely responsible for their own sector of space, but she was responsible for the entire space surrounding the Capitol Station region.

She concentrated on every word said. Several times she had to interject to deconflict ships from hitting one another. It was a hurried experience that seemed to last forever. However, Terilela managed to get five hundred ships in, docked, loaded and out within the prescribed fifteen minutes per ship. At first, she thought it an impossible mission, but when her team had successfully cleared one hundred ships, they felt like experienced professionals who had done this all their lives.

Galaxy protectors and galaxy cruisers in the area loaned their startrams for the evacuation. The ships, coupled with the long-range gate portals, allowed the evacuation of over one hundred thousand people in three universal hours. Toneilk's evacuation plan worked to perfection. Again, Toneilk was cognizant of the fact he had the additional startrams from the galaxy protectors. He was well aware the plan had flaws that appeared transparent with the current situation. He made a note to revise the plan for future use.

At the top of the third hour, the last transport ship was loaded and given departure instructions. Once it departed, Toneilk sent a signal to the Osguard Senate room that the evacuation was complete. Michael received the signal and transmitted it to the other Osguards at their seats.

"Well family, it's time," Michael sighed. "ARIT to the Kulusk High Command, attention Maxum Kie Ritchen."

Michael waited for the protocol to clear and the connection to reach over nine hundred light years away. The connection actually traveled through gate portal technology in order to cover such a long distance. Michael heard several tones, and then Maxum Kie Ritchen's face appeared. Sheryl Tower-Jones watched as Kie stared into the monitor. Her gut filled with anger at the man who wanted to start another galactic war.

"Maxum Kie Ritchen, I am the First Osguard of USSTAP, Michael Genesis."

"Yes, what do you want?" spurted Kie, who was surprised to see Michael alive.

"You are harboring several fugitives who have attacked my mother world, Earth. I want to discuss a trade. It appears your ambassador's aide attempted to assassinate me two days ago. As you see he did not succeed. And tragically, he was killed in the process. However, we have your ambassador, Manidul in protective custody. I propose a trade. We give you Manidul and you give us the three traitors you are harboring."

"Can't do that," Kie sassed.

"Why?"

"I killed them." Kie bluffed. "See, they failed me. Earth is not destroyed."

"You admit complicity in their actions?" Michael asked, surprised at Kie's revelation.

"Admit it? I claim it, as well as the assassination attempt on you. I am glad you killed the rox, because he failed me too. Do whatever you want with Manidul; he is of no use to me now."

The transmission ended. Cut from Kie's side. The Osguards looked at each other in astonishment. Michael was right. This fool wants a war.

Michael transmitted the recorded transmission to Chaktun with instructions to show it to members of the Parliament and the Congress.

"Well family, it is a go," Michael asserted. "Time to step," he ordered.

Chapter 33—Preparation

The alarm peeled Musoto from his deep peaceful slumber. He tried to reach it, but something was different. This wasn't his bedroom. Then a smooth silky arm reached across Musoto's chest, rubbing his chest hairs and surprising him a little. The hand switched off the alarm and came to rest on his chest. Mona Richards' fingers teasingly pulled on his chest hairs. The pull stung a little, which somehow aroused him as he fought the sleep. Mona pulled closer to him under the covers and let her bare breast massage his back. Musoto imagined he could feel her nipples stiffen with excitement.

His mind flashed to last night. He smiled as he remembered the bliss he felt in her arms when he sunk his manhood into her. Musoto had made love to several women before, but last night he had sex—no consideration for feelings, no consideration if his partner was enjoying it, just pure lust released with reckless abandonment. Mona knew what she wanted and did not hesitate to take it. She did not play shy or cute, she was pure ecstasy wrapped up in human form.

Musoto was drenched in sweat, his and hers. He moved like a lion going for the kill. Their bodies were timed perfectly like a Swiss watch, moving in unison to bring the explosive power of nature to its climax. After that, Musoto was spent, too tired to talk, and too tired to move. He fell to the side, trying to catch his breath, but only caught the wonderful unconscious state, which usually comes after sexual gratification. Obviously, Mona fell asleep too, or she did not mind that he did. She probably took satisfaction knowing she was responsible for his feeble state. Musoto took no shame in it. He was glad for the experience. And if he gave her pleasure at the same time, it would be gravy. But he had to know. His pride did depend on knowing. He remembered her screaming at the top of her lungs, and the mouth on her—.

At first her cursing made Musoto blush. But after awhile, it excited him more than he ever had been before. With every curse word he pushed harder, deeper and wilder. Her vocal response told him he did exactly what she wanted. That pumped him up more and more. No, she couldn't have faked last night. It was too perfect. But he wasn't sure. He had to be sure. Why did he have to be sure? He had the best time of his sexual life with her last night. That was all that mattered. No, it wasn't. A man wants to know he's a man, especially with a woman, particularly when he has sex with a woman. He needed to know. It was an unwritten law, all men had to know.

"Well, how was it?" The words escaped his mouth before he had time to formulate the thought. How teenager like, he reprimanded himself. This woman must think him a total dork.

"What do you mean how was it? Didn't I tell you last night," Mona teased.

"I know. That was last night, this is now," said Musoto as he laid his hand on top of hers resting on his chest.

He was actually trying to feel for a pulse when she responded. This was a crude, but effective imitation of a lie detector test. Not many people could perfect this technique, but Musoto believed that he had.

"Well, let me show you," she responded pulling the covers from her body, exposing the pleasure palace he had visited last night. She pounced and straddled his waist guiding his pleasure to her rapture.

Osguards: Homecoming

"I liked it so much, I want more. And I want it now," she smiled as she intimately introduced him to elation again.

Musoto's eyes rolled back into his head as he allowed Mona to have her way with him. He had his answer. He was the man. He had satisfied the most sexual, sensual being he had ever met. He smiled then joined Mona in a curse fest as their bodies melded into one.

***

The news hit Colonel Gregory Jones like a ton of bricks. *G.P. Kashara* was preparing for combat. He never thought he would see the day the *Kashara* would be led into battle. He took a deep breath as he polished the last of his Nerian coffee. Somehow the Nerian coffee always settled his nerves. It had no caffeine in it. In fact it had the opposite effect of Earth's coffee. Nerian Coffee soothed the spirit, calmed the mind and relaxed the muscles. Gregory always thought the litmone bean in it would be considered a narcotic in Philadelphia, where he was born and raised.

Gregory poured a second cup from the carafe. He sat alone at the kitchen table staring at the report he'd just spent two days working on. It was real, he thought. USSTAP couldn't avoid it. War was inevitable, and he had the proof in his hand. Why now? The Kulusks had been quiet and non-threatening. Then he reflected back to his Sixana training. The victor always lulls his opponent into a false sense of security. It was part of the misdirection of the art. On the basketball court, he would call it a head fake. The USSTAP had been duped. And he had proof the charade was much more sinister than any of the Osguards could have imagined.

The door hummed open and Sheryl walked through. Gregory looked up and barely acknowledged her presence. Sheryl caught the momentary eye contact and realized Greg was in a foul mood.

"Now, what's wrong with you?" asked Sheryl. Then she raised her right hand signaling him not to answer. "Look Greg, I don't have time for your pity party. There's some real shit going on out there and I have a job to do."

Greg didn't look up.

Sheryl walked past him at the kitchen table into the office. She flopped into her chair and fingered the crystal ARIT screen. She began reading the ships status reports.

"You know, we have to shove off in two universal hours," she added without lifting her eyes from the screen. "If you are going to act like this, you can stay on Capitol Station."

Greg's eyes burned with ire as the words echoed in his ear.

"Why did you say that," he managed to say without raising his voice. "Are you embarrassed of me? Or do you think I am too weak? I am not man enough to ride this ship into battle?" He paused to elicit a response. None came. "So which is it?" he said somewhat louder.

Sheryl sat quiet, pretending to read the ships status reports. But the conversation had stolen her attention from ship's business. After several seconds of feeling Gregory's glare, she looked up.

"What the hell do you want from me? You knew who I was before we married—"

"—Right, only after I popped the question," he interrupted. "Up until then, you led me on. You had me thinking you were some big time corporate executive or something."

"Look I never planned on falling in love with you. Shit, I was hardly ever on Earth. I only saw you three weeks a year. How could I have known you were serious?"

"You mean you weren't," Greg asked in surprise.

He stood and moved closer to her desk, hovering over her like a predator with his arms stretched out at the sides.

Sheryl looked up at the sudden movement and realized she had pushed the wrong buttons.

"Calm down Gregory," she said trying to settle him down. "I loved you and I still love you. I just don't want to see you get hurt."

"What the hell do you think I've been trying to do," Greg said throwing his hands up in desperation. He spun around and sat back down at the kitchen table. "It's not that my manhood is hurt," he claimed. "I just don't want anything to happen to you. I don't like seeing you taking risks with your life. We have children who depend on you."

"They depend on you as well. They depend on both of us, honey," she said, calculating the terms of endearment would hasten the open dialogue. "But I am an Osguard. It is my destiny to protect the USSTAP. I can't shirk my responsibility."

"You can't or you won't?" questioned Gregory.

Sheryl stood up and sauntered over to Gregory. She sat down in his lap and wrapped her arms around his neck. Greg darted his stare downwards toward the floor, avoiding eye contact with his wife.

"You are right; I won't shirk my responsibilities as Osguard. It's who I am. It's what I have been trained to do all my adult life. I can't change it, just like the dove can't change the fact he can fly or a leopard can't change his spots. It is what God has made me. I can't turn back this gift from God. Think of what you said when I told you about this ten years ago. Do you remember?"

Gregory moved his head a little, but dared not look up.

"Yeah, I remember."

"What did you say?"

"I said going to the ends of the universe with you is how I want to spend my life."

"Did you mean it?"

"Yeah, I meant it"

"Then what's the problem?"

"I can't stand the thought of losing you. I have to live with that every time you do something dangerous. Now you are about to lead this crew into battle against the Kulusks. You don't know what weapons they have. That gun that shot Mr. Genesis is a nasty weapon. I just know this ship isn't coming back. Or worse, it comes back with you dead."

"Again, I ask you, do you want to stay on the station?" She lifted his chin so their eyes would meet. "If you feel that this battle is my last, it may be for the best you stay on the station for the kids."

Gregory looked into her hazel eyes and reflected on her words for a moment.

"Shit, I don't want my kids thinking I'm a coward. Besides, if this is your last battle, I want to be there with you." He forced a nervous laugh to ease the tension of his words. "Besides, the kids are with our parents on Chaktun." Then the finality of the situation struck him in the heart. "Hell, you keep telling me, it is their destiny to be Osguards as well. I can't stop this train. I might as well ride it for all it's worth."

"Why?"

Gregory handed her the report from the table.

"This is why."

Sheryl hopped off Gregory's lap and moved back to her desk. She keyed the ARIT tablet and scanned the report. She rushed to the conclusion her husband had written. The shock in her eyes told the story. For the first time she was frightened.

"Are you sure about this Greg?"

Greg nodded once.

"How could we be so blind? ARIT contact all the Osguards and push this report to them." Sheryl connected the ARIT tablet output connector to her terminal and stroked several keys on the black terminal.

"Complete," sounded the voice over the room intercom after several seconds.

Sheryl then turned to her husband who was now standing next to her. She stood up and gave him the biggest kiss and hug.

"You may have just saved the USSTAP. All USSTAP planets, ships and stations will be on full alert. If your data is correct, we can flush them out when the time is right."

"You didn't even check the data. You didn't question it."

"Why should I? I trust you."

"Because I'm your husband?"

"No, because, you are the best, damn colonel in the economic corps. No one else had even thought to check this information. The other economic corps members sat back and shoved this all onto the operations corps. You didn't."

"I might have, if I wasn't married to the Osguard who would be risking her life to stop this ludicrous war before it gets started." He reached for his wife and embraced her as hard as he could. "Besides, my Toam said we were all Sixana warriors before we were members of any corps or members of USSTAP. Honor, Power and Grace, forever," he yelled as he remembered the Sixana creed.

"Fine. I am proud of you, baby," she said pulling away from him. "But now, I have new business to attend to because of your report." She tapped her terminal once more. "ARIT, send the following message to all USSTAP planets, ships and stations in Galaxy Fifty-Nine, the Litaria Galaxy. Use priority Brown seven, blue two frequency."

She tapped some more onto the keys. When she was finished she read what she had typed. Then she attached her husband's report and hit the send key.

After several seconds, ARIT reported, "Message transfer complete."

Greg smiled at his wife, for he knew she was in her element. He couldn't change it, even if he tried. Now he understood what his mother went through, worrying every day about his father, a cop in Philadelphia. How she wanted to leave so she would not have to worry. But if you love someone, leaving won't stop the worry—it will only intensify it. Those cops' wives who left their husbands because they couldn't take the pressure anymore seemed remote and removed to him now. He realized taking the pressure with Sheryl was much better than taking it without her.

Greg slipped back to his desk and called up his data. He reviewed it several more times. The entire USSTAP was about to act on his conclusion of this data and he wanted to make sure it was correct.

***

Michael nodded once in agreement. He hated the thought, but it was the best solution. He turned to Shawn who also nodded in agreement.

"Okay, you two will stay here and watch Mom and Dad for us," Michael told his wife and sister-in-law, Debrlina.

"It is for the best Michael," Michelle said. By the time you sort this crap out, your father will have his new legs."

"That soon?" asked Shawn.

"Yeah, that soon," she replied. "I have his old ones in the lab and I am masking the MARIT prosthetic limbs as we speak. I plan to assist Susan in the operation tomorrow morning."

"Is he stable enough to do this," Patricia asked.

"Yes, he is," Michelle said. "Besides, every day he goes without his legs, the more time he has to fall into self-pity. Right now, he is happy to be alive. But that will wear off soon. He will soon step into depression. We need to stop that. Once he sees his legs…and he will see his legs, every scar and hair follicle he can remember…it will help the healing process—mentally as well as physically."

Patricia rubbed her right arm and shifted her weight to her left leg. She felt her fingers caress her arm and the pressure of her weight on her leg. She shot a small smile.

"I can attest to all of that," Patricia said. "After my defender was sabotaged and I woke up in that medical ward, I was so happy to be alive. But depression started to creep into my soul as I realized my arm and leg were gone. I started to think I was less than human—not a woman. I was to marry Joe that summer. I remember lying there, looking at where my right arm should be and telling myself that Joe wouldn't want me now. I couldn't feel the warmth of his touch anymore. I couldn't hold hands with him, at least not with my right hand. I couldn't touch him like I use to. I was no longer whole. I was a freak, a monster. I had no faith the MARITS could replace what I lost. I would be Frankenstein's monster of some sort. I started to wish that I was killed in that accident." Patricia lowered her head at the admission.

Then she snapped her head up and looked right at Shawn and Michael.

"I swear if the medical team had waited one more day before they gave me my MARITS, I would have gone crazy. I might have killed myself."

Michael and Shawn looked at each other. This was the first they had ever heard of their sister talking about suicide. Michael had no idea his sister's ordeal was that rough on her psyche. All he knew was that it was rough for him being several galaxies away and praying for her recovery. She was in that coma for so long. When he heard she woke, he had jumped for joy. As he was sure Shawn did. That entire episode in their lives was traumatic. But it never occurred to Michael that Patricia almost gave up. He just imagined her as a fighter with more than the will to live, but the will to pursue life to its fullest. This revelation came as a shock to Michael. And by the look in Shawn's face, it was a shock to him. Michael reached out to touch Patricia on the arm. He hesitated. He did not know which one was the MARIT arm anymore.

"Yeah, I have forgotten which one was real too," Patricia said placing her arms out for comparison.

Michael gave in to his confusion and pulled Patricia toward him. Shawn covered both of them with a bear hug. Patricia fought back the tears. Her revelation was part of her therapy, which was long overdue. Her soul felt better, but still not complete.

"They are my arm and leg," she whispered. "They look and feel real and I went through therapy thinking they were real and all I had to do was to get them to work again. Michelle is right. We need to get those MARITS on dad as soon as possible."

"How soon will he be able to walk?" asked Michael turning to Michelle and showing the first signs of enthusiasm since the incident.

"It's up to him. But the MARIT will pick up his brain waves to command the use of his legs. However, it will take some doing for him to control his new MARIT legs with accuracy. He may be in therapy for a while. But I will be with him every step of the way."

Michelle looked at Michael and saw the guilt riding his face like a bronco-busting cowboy. The more he tried to shake it, the harder it hung on. But like the bronco-busting cowboy, the guilt would either eventually fall off or break Michael. She knew it, so she did not placate Michael anymore than necessary. However, she knew his guilt would only fall off in the heat of battle. Strange therapy, but work always took Michael's mind away from whatever was troubling him. Michelle lowered her head in thought. It was too bad the heat of battle in this situation was not a metaphor, but the actual thing. Michael might get hurt or even killed, trying to expunge himself of the guilt.

"What's the matter, baby?" asked Michael.

"It's been a long time since I had to watch you go off into a fight. I got used to the peace around here. And now, it starts over again. I am having some difficulty accepting the situation."

Michael embraced his wife. "Look baby, we got this all under control. Everything will be okay. I promise you."

He held her tight as she laid her head on his shoulder.

Debrlina looked at Shawn with her sad puppy dog look. Shawn realized Michelle said exactly what Debrlina was feeling. He reached out to her and squeezed her as tight as he could. The two couples, each in a passionate hug, remained quiet for several long seconds, sharing unspoken love.

"Well, I guess you guys want to be alone," Patricia finally said. "I didn't know it was a couple's party, I would have brought a man," she joked.

But no one laughed. The seriousness of the moment had penetrated the room like a cool breeze from the ocean.

"I'll just go find my man," Patricia said, back stepping toward the door and waving her hands as if in search of something.

Patricia left the room unnoticed by the two couples embraced in the moment, which was mixed with passion and fear.

All of a sudden Patricia was overcome by an urge to hug her husband Joe. Like her brothers, the thought of what they were about to embark on did not hit her until now. This was battle. It had been so long since she had tasted battle, that the euphoria of the event had clouded her family obligations. She was a mother and a wife. She needed to comfort them as well. It was too late to comfort Mitiah. He was on his way to the mother world with Joe's parents. But Joe was on the ship and he too was unusually quiet. Now she realized why. She needed to comfort him somewhat before they left for battle. Or was it she who needed comfort?

The thought quickened her pace as she made her way to the gate portal room to step to her ship. Unlike her brothers, her mate would be on the ship with her in combat. This fact had blinded her to the fear that must have surrounded Joe throughout the ordeal. Fear—what an ugly word for a Sixana warrior. But, it was still a part of her humanity and apparently her marriage. She needed to address that fear prior to leaving. She knew that now, and that is what fueled her pace as she began to race to the gate portal room.

The halls were quiet due to the departure of the delegates and other family members. However she hardly noticed. She charged into the gate portal room and demanded immediate connection to her ship, *G.P. Nausona.* She stepped into the light and disappeared.

She reemerged on the *G.P. Nausona,* and skipped off the platform without acknowledging her gatekeeper. She rushed through the hallway at a good sprint. She reached her quarters and burst into the room, hardly giving the doors a chance to open. She saw Joe standing in the middle of the living room area, perplexed as if he was searching for something. She rushed to him and gave him a long passionate kiss. Joe was surprised at first, but soon relented to the emotion and kissed her back with just as much passion.

The intercom erupted in the room.

"Osguard, this is the bridge," a female voice boomed.

"Not now, later," ordered Patricia barely breaking her lips from Joe.

"But, Osguard—," the voice insisted.

"Can't it wait? I am busy," Patricia blasted.

"I suppose it can," rendered the voice as the intercom link ended.

"Now where was I?" Patricia asked, planting her lips on Joe's and slipping her tongue into his mouth.

Joe did not know what got into Patricia, but he liked it. He leaned over, picked Patricia up without breaking the kiss, and carried her into the bedroom area. The lights dimmed in the bedroom as Joe snapped his finger. Patricia was on her way to beginning the last part of her therapy.

Chapter 34—The Groundwork

It was a long night, and she spent most of it in the car watching for any movement in the house. She had followed Musoto and some woman here from the Cochran Building. She thought this FBI agent was about to stumble onto something. But all he had managed to do in the past eighteen hours was shack up with some bimbo from the twentieth floor of her building. Now Stelana Rican, or as the members of Unlimited Associations knew her, Stephanie Rikes, felt somewhat foolish raising the alarm to General Lo about Musoto's visit to the office.

When Musoto stopped by yesterday and spoke to Mr. Daley, Stelana placed a phone call through the private switchboard to Earth Precinct Headquarters and spoke to General Lo. General Lo was already aware of Musoto's investigation and asked for Stelana to follow him and report as necessary on his movements. So far, Musoto had not done anything worthy to report, except the usual male conquest of a wild and promiscuous female. This was something Rican could not get accustomed to—the sexual irresponsibility of her adopted planet.

On her home planet of Chaktun, sex was a blessed thing held in high esteem between two people, not as a sporting event as she had noticed the people of Earth treated it. On Chaktun the act of making love was taught since birth as a sacred, deep emotionally binding occasion shared amongst those who had united under the blessing of Jus. Any form of sex before this event was strictly forbidden and occasionally punishable by law. Even though such punishment had not happened for over one hundred galactic years, it was still on the books. The fear of judicial punishment paled in comparison to the embarrassment one could bring upon a family if caught.

And the term unwed mother was an unheard of subject. The stigma of such a thing had led families to bankruptcy. This was a harsh and inhuman punishment for doing something that came as natural to man as breathing. But responsibility and restraint were the byproducts of this code. This ultimately brought order and discipline, which allowed Chaktun to escape some of the social ills that Earth faced today, single parents; overcrowding; homelessness, especially amongst children; poor healthcare; famine; death; sexually transmitted disease and the worse social disease of them all—class struggle. In her limited opinion, all of Earth's social ills were due to the blurring of the lines between human rights and self-indulgence.

Stelana learned of her adopted planet in the USSTAP Academy on Chaktun. She had joined the alliance as a promise to her grandfather before his death. Her grandfather Stelanar Rican, whom she was named after, was a proud Sixana Warrior who had fought side by side with Laurona. He was so enamored with Laurona and her vision of what human rights in the universe should be that he practically ate and breathed everything USSTAP.

His stalwart stance for USSTAP was what influenced her father and mother to join USSTAP. They were both presently colonels aboard the *Galaxy Cruiser Scriptanal*, Osguard Thirty-Five's old ship. Her father was part of the engineering corps and her mother was part of the diplomatic corps. She had learned much from traveling with them. Her father taught her how gate portals transported people through inner space and how the gravogenic engines on USSTAP ships moved them up to sixty light years per hour. Her mother taught her how to peacefully brandish your will onto others. Her mother called it diplomacy. Stelana called in brainwashing.

But, for all their teachings and manipulations, Stelana went outside those corps and settled for the economic corps. The economic corps was truly her calling. She wanted to see how the flow of worthless material in some parts of the universe came to be of intrinsic value in another part of the universe. What made commodities so valuable or not so valuable? Why did humans place value at all on natural goods? It was a mystery that delighted her to decipher.

Unfortunately, her first assignment was to spy on Unlimited Associations' management of USSTAP's interest on Earth. The members of Unlimited Associations had no idea of USSTAP's existence. They were truly in the dark about the alliance. Unlimited Associations' sole function was to receive and distribute the economic bounty from the material garnered from USSTAP. General Lo planted her in the corporation as a receptionist because he knew eventually she would have access to all transactions and no one would be suspicious of her in that position. It sure was handy today, to call in sick and have no one question her motives. This allowed Stelana the ability to follow Musoto as directed by General Lo.

Stelana's deep reflection popped as she saw Musoto emerge from the house. She checked the computer printout in her hand and rechecked the address. No, this was not Musoto's address. It must be the bimbo's address, she noted for the hundredth time. Maybe this was not a lover's tryst, she continued. With that thought, she made another mental note to advise General Lo to have someone follow the woman. She might be his partner and her first impression could be wrong. Then she watched as Musoto gave the woman a passionate kiss on the front steps. The kiss took almost thirty seconds. And while he was kissing her, Stelana watched Musoto move his hands up her dress and massaged her buttocks. Stelana figured her first impression was right. This was a booty call, nothing more, nothing less. However, Musoto could still have told her something that may be of interest to USSTAP.

Stelana watched Musoto get his last lustful feel as she tapped the address in her recording PARIT. When she finished, she watched Musoto hop into his government vehicle and drive off. Stelana took one more look at the bimbo. *What a whore*, she thought as Mona Richards blew a kiss at the vanishing Musoto. Stelana started her car and drove in slow pursuit of Musoto.

Musoto drove through the neighborhood until he reached the on ramp to the highway. He slipped into the southbound lane for I-95. Stelana made a mental note that he was not heading toward Richmond, but heading toward Osguard Gardens. At least that is what she surmised. He would have to take several back roads, and travel almost one hundred and twenty miles prior to getting to Osguard Gardens. For all she knew, Musoto was about to embark on another sexual conquest. She took a deep breath and blew it out hard. It was going to be a long day and she was already feeling the hunger pains of morning cramp her stomach. Why didn't she put a homing device on the car? she wondered. Now would have been a perfect time to stop and get something to eat, and then pick him back up on an ARIT. But no, she wanted to do it the old fashioned way. How stupid, she chastised herself as she hooked right onto South I-95.

***

The night was particularly rough on him. Several images kept creeping into his dreams. The blood seemed to be the constant in all the images. Blood was on his legs, his stomach and on the floor where he lay. He woke up several times in a cold sweat, unable to scream or let the nurse know he needed help. But somehow the machine they had Parker connected to, always summoned the nurse as he woke. She would sprint into the room and do what she could to comfort him. One time she used a cold compress to wipe the sweat from his forehead. One other time she read for an hour from a book of Chaktun poetry translated to English. The last time she just held his hand until he fell back asleep. When he woke for the day, Captain Katlin Price, of the medical corps was still holding his hand. He managed a smile as she massaged the back of his hand with her gentle touch.

Parker clicked the conscious reading MARIT button on his right hand.

"Thank you."

"No problem, Mr. Genesis," Katlin replied. "It's my job." Katlin lowered Parker's left hand and smiled at him. She massaged his forehead, "You need to get some rest. I know your daughter in-law and Doctor Tillman will be in here soon to run some preliminary test for your new legs."

"New legs?" the monitor printed.

"Yes, I hear they will connect them very soon," answered Katlin. "After a while, you won't be able to tell they aren't real."

Parker's face turned red.

"Aren't real?" the monitor printed.

"Yes, MARIT technology has come a long way," she said trying to calm Parker's agitation. "Look at your daughter. Bet you didn't know her leg and arm are MARITs."

Parker looked around in disbelief.

"Patricia's leg and arm aren't real?"

"No sir. The defender accident took them. She has been without her real arm and leg for quite some time now," she added. "Look, I have to go now. I am sure the doctor will explain everything to you when she visits." Katlin patted Parker's shoulder and then backed out the door, showing a gracious and pleasing smile until the door hummed closed.

Parker turned his head in self-pity, but forgot to turn off the monitor.

"No legs," the monitor displayed. *"Now they want to put some bionic crap on me. I'm not sure I want this. Shit, I'm not sure I want to go on with no legs either. God, how come you didn't take me when you had the chance? Life like this is no life. Elizabeth deserves better than half a man. She should have all of me or none of me. God, why didn't you let me die? This isn't right. I can't ask the family to take care of a cripple. Lord, why? Why am I still breathing? I should be dead. I don't want those machines attached to me. I want my legs back. Lord, give me my legs back or let me die. I've lived a long life, and I am ready to come home. Please, Lord. Do you hear me? Let me come home. It is better than living like this. I can't let Elizabeth be burdened with me. It is just not..."*

A sound from the door startled Parker. He turned to see Elizabeth standing there. She had walked in as the nurse left and read the monitor as Parker was thinking. She grabbed his hands and clicked off the monitor at the same time. Parker did not realize his thoughts were on the monitor or that she had read them. She wanted to make sure it remained that way.

"How are you feeling today, Parker?" Elizabeth managed to ask.

Parker swung his head toward the monitor and saw it was off. He did not remember if he had turned it off before he went into his self-pity dialogue. He started to click the monitor on when Elizabeth's hand, still on the button, stopped him. She reached up with her left hand and clicked the MARIT off his forehead. It pulled off with a slight sting and a snap.

"Why don't you try telling me how you are feeling," she ordered. "Susan told me you don't need this anymore. She showed me how to disconnect it. So there, it is disconnected."

Parker tried to force the air through his throat, but only managed a cough as the dryness of his throat pulled on his vocal chords.

"Here, try some water," Elizabeth suggested as she handed him a drink of water from the bedside table.

Parker pulled his head up, accepted the water with his left hand, and sipped from the cup. He opened his mouth to give it another try.

"Fine," he vocalized in a harsh voice. Then he coughed to clear his throat, "I am doing fine," he pronounced more clearly.

"Good," Elizabeth said as she planted a kiss on his lips. "I love you," she whispered as she looked into his eyes."

"I love you too," Parker coughed.

"Then that's settled," she said as she pulled away. "Here, Patricia left you something. It's a holovidpic. She wants you to see it before your surgery this afternoon."

"What surgery?"

"You are getting your legs this afternoon," she announced.

"No one bothered to ask me anything about this," he grumbled.

"They asked me and I said yes for you."

"You didn't have the right to say…"

"Parker, I have been married to you for over forty three years now. I've nursed you when you were sick. I washed your butt when you had that heart attack and couldn't move. I think that gives me the right to make decisions about this. Because I will be damned before I become your legs. You are just going to have to be a man, get those legs and start walking. Do you hear me?"

"Maybe I don't want to. Maybe I want to go on like this. And if you don't want to be my legs…that's just fine with me."

Elizabeth fought back the tears forming in her eyes.

"Ah, you are going to throw away forty three years of marriage just like that. Well Parker, you are a bigger fool than I thought. I am not going to throw away anything, especially our marriage that easily."

"See, you are the one who is throwing away our marriage, because you don't think I am a man anymore now that I don't have any legs."

"You better go look in the mirror…because it isn't me who doesn't think of you as a man. It's you."

A tear rolled from her left eye as she spun around so Parker could not see it run down her cheek. She wiped it and turned back to Parker, staring at the floor to avoid eye contact.

"I think you better see Patricia's holovidpic before you call this surgery off." Elizabeth tossed the ARIT player and the holovidpic on top of his chest, turned and stormed out of the room in a huff.

Parker watched in anguish as he saw the agony on her face when she turned and left the room. He gave a heavy sigh and placed his right arm on top of his forehead. *Hell*, he thought. *I could have handled that better.* He dropped his arm down to his side. The force of his arm hitting the bed made the ARIT and the holovidpic bounce on his chest. He looked at it for a long moment, wondering what Patricia had to say in a holovidpic she couldn't say to him in person. Well, what the hell. Parker took the HVP and placed it into the ARIT player, like his granddaughter showed him several days earlier.

Patricia appeared in the screen. She explained her accident, an act of sabotage, which took her leg and arm. She explained the feelings and emotions she went through in preparation for the surgery. Parker's eyes welled with water as he watched his daughter describe the exact pain he was experiencing, but could not put in words. Then the dramatic shock of seeing his daughter's body, torn and mangled from the wreck, took him to another feeling—a feeling of rage. Patricia had included holovidpics of her rescue, operation and recovery. Parker cried as he touched the screen in a veiled attempt to offer comfort to his daughter. The accident happened some years ago, but he did not know. There was some reflection of the accident and the seriousness of the accident during the family indoctrination. But he did not know how mentally, physically, emotionally and spiritually wrenching the entire ordeal was.

Then the player showed the MARIT prosthetic mating operation and her recovery. The MARITs looked like her God-given limbs. Lord knows he never knew the difference. How many times had he held her hand or massaged her feet, not knowing what he was touching were MARITs. And Patricia responded to every touch, no matter how slight, as if she felt it. She did feel it. The MARITs were real. They weren't God-given, but they were still real.

Patricia had an ordinary life after the accident. She married and had a child. The MARITS did not stop her from living her life to its fullest. Why the hell was he afraid, he wondered? He should be anxious to get this operation and start the recovery to a normal life. But still he was afraid. He was afraid of the unknown, and fear held him like a dog on a steak bone. He felt trapped by it. Why? He did not know.

The HVP ended with Patricia explaining the present situation, and that they would not be there for the operation. The mission they were about to embark on was dangerous and it needed their full and undivided attention. Therefore, he was to do as Elizabeth and Debrlina said. And he'd better be ready for a five-mile run when she returned. Parker turned the HVP player off and said a silent prayer.

He prayed for the success of the mission and the safe return of all of them. Then he prayed for strength to make the right decision. He understood the consequences and did not relish the thought of being an invalid the rest of his life. He closed his eyes and held on tight to the holovidpic in his right hand.

"Come back to me and I will walk for you," he whispered.

Two hours later, Susan, Debrlina, and Michelle entered Parker's room, pushing a cart. A white sheet covered the top of the cart. Parker wiped his eyes to focus on them.

"Mr. Genesis, I have something to show you," Susan announced.

She pulled the sheet back to reveal two human-like legs…Parker's legs.

"These are the prosthetic MARITS I made for you, Papa," Michelle disclosed. "I used your original legs to map every detail. Once you have them, you won't be able to tell them apart from your original legs."

Parker keyed in on Michelle's use of the word original. She did not say real...she said original. What he was staring at was an abomination to God. God gave him his legs; these were cheap imitations of the Creator's work. But Parker realized his legs were gone—shot off by some alien thug he never knew. And this was the only course of action in restoring his life to some sense of normalcy. He touched them and studied them like a kid in a science lab. Every scar, pimple and hair he could remember was there.

"I assure you, Mr. Genesis...you'll come to see them as your original legs," Susan told him. "Once they are attached you will not be able to tell the difference. Even your own blood will circulate through the legs. So if you cut yourself, you will bleed. The one precaution is you can't have a civilian doctor X-ray these legs. The X-ray would show the difference, as well as any intrusive medical procedure. You must always see an USSTAP doctor. But you were unknowingly doing that anyway."

"The residents of the Gardens were all seeing USSTAP doctors," Michelle corrected. "The USSTAP doctors have cured many residents from cancer, diabetes and other disorders. In fact, Papa, USSTAP doctors have already repaired your heart, and that is why you have not had a recurrence or residual effects from your heart attack from fifteen years ago."

This put Parker's mind at ease.

"Okay, I will concede to this procedure on one condition," Parker barked.

"What is that?" asked Debrlina.

"That you and Michelle are in the operating room, making sure this thing is done right."

"You have my word. We will be there."

Chapter 35—Arrival

"Two universal hours until we reach Kulusk, sire," announced Lieutenant Shondel Jamar, *G.P. Neraka*'s navigator.

"Continue on course on speed," Michael replied as he gazed at the star field on the main viewing screen. He adjusted his gaze to study the screen between the pilot and the navigator with the ARIT projected path. His mental calculations confirmed the navigator's statement, two universal hours until battle. Not much time to ensure everything was ready, but he still had to go over the plan once more.

Thanks to Sheryl's husband, all USSTAP were aware and poised for action. If he was correct, the Kulusk threat had expanded beyond this little confrontation. It had expanded to areas where they had traded and maybe even further. If Gregory's facts were correct, and he had no reason to think otherwise, this was the Kulusks' attempt to take over USSTAP throughout the universe, and not just this small part of the galaxy. That is why all Osguards used secure channels to send and receive the information so far gathered—including information on the Kulusk gun. If that hummer were ship mounted, it would give the attackers the advantage. The chromerion field could not stop it; only the slitanium metal used for stealth mode could dissipate the energy from the Kulusk gun. That would mean energizing the slitanium to stealth seven or higher. The trade off was dangerous. It took a lot of energy to move to stealth seven or higher. The energy needed to activate the chromerion field would be sacrificed and the galaxy protector weapon arrays would not be as accurate. This would mean battle at a closer range. It was a big sacrifice. Even if the slitanium worked, the ship's vital portions would be exposed. However there were no other options. The biggest and the most lethal ships in the universe would go into combat naked, or at least half naked. They had agreed to go stealth factor seven. All USSTAP ships were ordered to go stealth factor seven when engaged by Kulusks or Kulusk allies carrying the Kulusk gun.

Michael went over the strategy again and again. He had every ship's position, maneuver and alignment memorized—as he was sure the others had done as well. But it was hard to play the battle out in his head. He lacked important intelligence. He did not know the strength, size or number of the enemy. Would he be engaging their main force or did they split their forces throughout the universe? He didn't see how they could have split their forces throughout the universe, since USSTAP had control of the intergalactic and intragalactic gate portals. All that could have been shipped outside the area was information. And Gregory had done a great job pinpointing that through economic trade logs. That was a good man Sheryl married. *I am glad he is on our side*, Michael thought as he cracked his first smile in four hours.

Michael again looked at the ARIT-projected layout at the helm. He saw sixty galaxy protectors in a three-layer arrow formation, traveling from negative five to positive five on the galactic plane. That was a tight formation and they were doing it at MOP sixty—sixty light years per hour. He stopped to think about the magnitude of this feat. Lord knows when he was growing up he never imagined leading such a group of people in such a manner. Sixty galaxy protectors traveling MOP sixty, with no more than twenty-five mark separation between ships, stacked in a ten unit galactic plane. No one blinked twice about this. No one thought this was dangerous. It was readily accepted as if we were taking a trip to the local market. *This is one for the record books,* he noted. Michael chuckled at the thought as he looked at the majestic beauty of the galaxy protectors displayed on the helm's screen.

Mass firepower, surprise and economy of forces were the staples of the USSTAP battle plan. Michael convinced everyone that security in this matter must be sacrificed for victory. However, that sacrifice will mean lives.

Hopefully, the strategic prowess of the Osguards as an eclectic entity would constitute the difference.

***

The ride was long and her stomach began to ache with hunger pains. However Stelana watched her prey with eagle like intent. Musoto had done exactly as she feared and traveled back to Osguard Gardens. She had followed him on several trips as he surveyed the landscape from outside the fenced area. Every so often, Musoto would stop, exit his car and walk up to the fence as if to study it. Then he would take out a pocket instamatic camera; snap a few pictures and write something in his black pocket flip notepad so common among police investigators.

Stelana did not understand exactly what Musoto was up to, but she understood enough to put the Garden's security on alert. As soon as they arrived in the area, she had contacted security with her CC and informed them of the situation. Occasionally, she would notice a black clad security officer on the other side of the fence taking equal interest in Musoto. She wondered why they did not stay hidden and watch Musoto from a secure area. Then she realized their job was to secure the area from intruders and not to conduct intelligence. Thus, they best served their objective by a show of force. In the long run, this may be all that was needed. At least that is what Stelana hoped.

However, Musoto appeared not to be frightened or worried about the security on the opposite side of the fence. In fact this appeared to heighten his curiosity. Why not? He was a cop after all. Any form of security in this fashion for a place that was simply described as a retirement community would pique any investigator's attention. Stelana weighed the option of calling the security shack and telling them to back off. But it was too late. The damage was done. However, she did decide to let them know their strategy backfired. Stelana tapped her CC.

"Sentinel Rican to Osguard Gardens' Security Force." She waited for the normal protocol to attach the communiqué.

"Lieutenant Sparks of the Osguard Gardens, Security Force, can I help you?" the voice chimed over her CC subdural receiver.

"Yes, I am the operative watching the FBI agent who is surveying the Gardens. I suggest you pull your security forces back out of sight. They are attracting undue attention from this guy. We want him to go away satisfied there is nothing to see here. Your security forces make the Gardens look like Camp David. This guy isn't going anywhere as long as he sees your forces."

"No can do, Sentinel Rican...Our charter is to protect the area from all intruders. If a show of force deters the intruders, then our job is done."

"Lieutenant, this is not an intruder. This is a suspicious FBI agent who will not stop at your display of force. In fact your display of force may encourage him to get a warrant and legally intrude onto the Gardens. I urge you to pull your troops back."

"No, Sentinel Rican...I can not and will not do that. We have the situation under control. Why don't you let us handle it? You can babysit the man after he leaves here. But as long as he is snooping around here, I will handle the situation like I deem necessary—Sparks out."

The transmission abruptly ended and Stelana tapped her CC to ensure the connection was terminated. She pulled out her PARIT and made a note in her log of the conversation for future action if it came to that. She shook her head and whispered to herself, "I hope the idiot knows what he is doing."

***

Musoto peered through the chain-link fence as close as he could. He made out the houses in the distance. There was about a half a mile of ground between the fences and the nearest house. He had to use binoculars to see the houses with any clarity. They seemed normal and recently built. They could not be older than five or six years old. They had a strange quality about them. Most looked as if they were constructed of various color brick with high, wide and peculiar designed white poles balancing second floor porches and banisters. None were shaped the same, but you could tell the same company designed them. The roofs weren't exactly flat, but they slanted at a low angle. They were much different than the roofs normally found in these parts. Even though the architecture was odd, it was quite pleasing to see. Musoto did not know if he was more attracted by the mystery of the Gardens or the houses. Whichever attracted him the most, he knew he had to get inside for a better look.

Yet, he knew that would be difficult. The area was surrounded by a ten-foot chain-link fence topped with concertina wires. The perimeter reminded Musoto of the outside of the federal prison. Besides, there were cameras posted every fifteen yards on the fence. Then there was the black clad security force—which reminded him of a special operations force like a police SWAT unit. Musoto wondered if they were hot wearing all black clothing in this heat.

Yes, this place was hiding something. There were more security measures here than at a military installation—all that was missing were the signs stating the guards could use deadly force. But watching them walk around with their side arms in full view conveyed the message. The intent was clear...*stay out*. However, Musoto was not easily persuaded to not do something. Therefore the security force's message was lost on him. *Too bad they didn't realize that*, he thought as he smiled.

Just then he came into eye contact with one of the black clad security guards on the other side of the fence. Neither man attempted to avert their gaze. They stared at each other like boxers in the ring about to battle in front of a sold out crowd. Each squinted with intensity to see which one would blink first. With each passing second the tension steadily built around them. Musoto kept his eyes locked on the security guard staring with caution as he began to step back to his car. The guard stepped toward Musoto matching his pace. Finally, they stood across from each other, with the fence between them. Both hesitated in their pace long enough to stop at this point and mentally sum each other up.

Musoto could not identify the weapon in the guard's holster through his peripheral vision. He dared not look directly at it, because he felt for some reason that may be construed as a threatening gesture or at least one that would give some insight of his intentions. But Musoto did notice for the first time the barrel had to be at least eight inches long and the handle was cut to conform to a man's grip unlike any weapon he had ever seen. *The firepower of that weapon must be amazing*, he thought. *So why does a rent-a-cop need such a powerful weapon.* Then he noticed other devices on his belt. Devices he did not recognize. Now Musoto's heart skipped a beat. *What the hell is this place?*

With that, he began his slow pace back to his car turning his head to never let the guard out of his sight—to the point he began to walk backwards. The guard did the same, as he watched Musoto with noticeable distain. Musoto stopped at the driver's door of his vehicle and watched the guard turn and continue to walk the perimeter.

"What the hell was all that?" Musoto wondered aloud. Then he noticed for the first time his hands shaking at his side. '*Shit*,' he chastised himself. "What kind of agent are you…letting a rent-a-cop scare you into the shakes. But damn, what kind of weapons was he carrying?" Musoto jumped into the car and began going through his pictures to see if he had snapped any of the guards with those strange weapons.

***

"Why do your guards have on delta belts?" Stelana asked Sparks through the CC.

She had noticed the close encounter Musoto had with the guard and realized the guard was wearing a delta belt. This was a definite security violation, especially to a trained weapons expert. She knew the sight of the belt would confuse him to a point of more suspicion. She almost screamed at the guard to move away from him when she saw the episode. But that would have blown her cover, and if Musoto had recognized her as the receptionist from the Cochran building, the gig would be up.

Osguards: Homecoming

"Sentinel Rican, we are at Alert One. Enemy agents have infiltrated USSTAP and have even attempted to assassinate the First Osguard. They missed, but seriously injured his father instead. For all we know, this Musoto could be a Kulusk infiltrator. We are proceeding as protocol dictates. If he isn't a Kulusk plant and he is who he really says he is; we will handle that later. But for now, we have our fleet poised for war and entering Kulusk territory and we on the home front are ordered to be in Alert One." Starks paused to let the words sink into Stelana's consciousness. "But, I am sure you are aware of that," he added with sting.

Stelana was not aware of it. She had ignored her daily status update for the last week, because it usually was full of information not pertinent to her or her position. She felt so stupid for playing an operative without the latest information that was certainly available to her. The entire USSTAP was in Alert One. This was unprecedented and showed the urgency of the situation did indeed outweigh any nuisance Musoto could cause. No wonder General Lo had entrusted her with the assignment instead of one of his top security corps members. They must be all out checking identifications and running other types of security checks.

Stelana hit her dashboard with her right fist, slamming it down so hard that a crack began to run from the edge.

"You do have your delta belt?" asked Sparks.

"Well sir..." she swung around to the back seat to check to see if she did bring her equipment bag. It lay in the back seat. She formulated her delta belt would be in her equipment bag, but she really did not do an inventory. When General Lo gave her the assignment last night, she dragged the equipment bag from its hiding place in her apartment and threw it in the back seat. She couldn't remember the last time she checked it. It was something she considered unnecessary for her present assignment...well not necessary until now.

"Yes sir, I have it," she forced herself to say.

"Good, it may be necessary," offered Sparks. "According to our briefing, it should get pretty hot around here any minute now. This man you are watching, he could be just the first wave. Keep an eye on him."

"Tiah—Rican out."

* * *

Maxum Kie Ritchen paced behind the console operator in the military command center of the Kulusk capital of Renard. His thoughts were shaken by the delay of what he had considered to be the inevitable. He had planned each move like a chess match. He looked for every move and countermove his opponent would make. He just did not consider the patience of his quarry. This oversight had cost him valuable time—time he could ill afford. His plan depended on the coordinated effort of cells throughout the known universe. He had set up revolutionary cells in every galaxy through his trade partnership with USSTAP. They all stood ready to attack.

Unfortunately, he could not send arms and ships to assist his newfound allies in the other galaxies; therefore, the mass of the attacking force was with his son. That is why he had to annihilate the galaxy protectors while they were all in one area. His allies did not have the forces to contend with the galaxy protectors. Yet, there were still galaxy protectors in the galaxies sired by the trusted admirals of the region. His plan called for the quick destruction of the USSTAP forces in this galaxy, the capture of the intergalactic and intragalactic gate portals and then the transfer of his fleet to each galaxy, taking them one by one.

Kie Ritchen's timetable saw the completion of his war in a short ten universal years. He envisioned the destruction of USSTAP would leave easy plundering of the member planets, because their military had been reduced to a perimeter guard and not a galactic force. The poor fools relied on USSTAP for that. How unfortunate for them and fortunate for him to have the vision of conquest so close at hand.

Yet, if the Osguards don't attack, Kie Ritchen knew he would be forced to confront their full force directly. Even though his ARIT simulations calculated victory, it also calculated his forces would be so depleted the second phase of his plan would not be attainable. He would not be able to send his forces through the portals and plunder the other galaxies at will. He would have to rebuild his forces then send them through the gate portals. By that time, the remaining USSTAP forces in the other galaxies could recoup and unseat his victory.

Still, the destruction of the Osguard lineage would be worth it. Therefore, if the Osguards' patience or their cowardice did not allow them to attack, Kie Ritchen had no qualms on attacking first. His one reservation was he would put his son, who was leading his forces, in mortal danger if he did so. Nonetheless, he would have it no other way. The Ritchen line must avenge its honor by personally spilling the lifeblood of the Osguard lineage.

Oh how he envied his grandfather for sneaking onto the prison planet and personally lynching two Osguard descendents. The thrill he must have felt scorching through his blood to see those two rox females hang from their necks, choking and crying, gasping for their last breath. Kie Ritchen watched the holovidpic of that moment almost weekly. For some reason, it gave him solace in his moments of despair. Shirley and Betty were their names as he recalled. It was regrettable his grandfather did not stay and examine the area for other descendants. He could have ended the lineage right then and there—almost one hundred universal years ago. But then Kie Ritchen would not have the satisfaction of killing over a hundred descendants of the Osguard lineage this day—well at least his son would have the pleasure. Kie

Ritchen slowed his pace as he thought of his options. No matter what happened this day, he knew he wanted his revenge.

He stopped and studied the overhead screen as he leaned against the railing to support his weight. He squinted as he attempted to read the mathematical equations streaming awkwardly up and down and across the screen. Then he reached over the shoulder of the counsel operator and pushed a button to change the screen menu to a video display of space. This display was less accurate than the scanner display showing the mathematical equations representing moving bodies in space. When the moving bodies were new or no longer constant this alerted the ARIT to scan that section for ships. In the present display, the ARIT scanners had to perform double duty and it took a fraction of a second longer to detect irregular movement caused by ships. But this was an acceptable delay to Ritchen. Watching numbers and equations fill the screen gave him a headache. At least the peacefulness of the star field on the present display eased his tension somewhat.

The signal chirped and the circled-pix displayed on the screen.

"Magnify," ordered Ritchen.

The console operator touched some buttons and the screen magnified to the pix. The screen filled with sixty streaks and tracks moving at MOP sixty. Since they were traveling faster than the speed of light, no visual could capture their image. However, interpretive data identified them as galaxy protectors.

"There they are," Ritchen sighed. "Signal all forces to proceed with the attack."

Chapter 36—The Report

Peters' report was dismal. The number of retained nuclear weapons was a small fraction of what was once an impressive arsenal. Senator John W. Bass, the Senate Majority Leader from the state of Washington, shook his head in disbelief as he read each line of the report. In the Oval Office with him was his counterpart for the Democratic Party, the Senate Minority Leader Thomas C. Payne from New York, as well as the Speaker of the House, Republican Representative Joyce T. Eldridge from Texas and House Minority Leader, Democratic Representative Warren S. Leaks from North Dakota.

Peters watched the foursome read the reports, hoping he had put enough truths in it to be credible. Peters did not reveal the existence of outside forces that may have ended a nuclear holocaust before it began. He credited the destruction of the errant missiles to a secret Joint Anti Ballistic Missile Defense initiative started by President Ronald Reagan and President

Malcolm Dylan Petteway

Gorbachev of Russia some years ago. His report stated military funds under four presidential administrations, both Democratic and Republican, were diverted to fund the project. He had his auditors work all weekend to doctor the General Accounting Office accounts to add credibility to the story. However, he felt a tinge of regret lying to the leaders of the legislative branch of the government.

But what else could he do? The truth in the hands of professional politicians like these would not stay a secret long. In fact, Peters felt he was taking a risk by allowing them access to the information of the events leading up to the destruction of the majority of the United States' and Russia's ICBMs. But, he needed their support in passing the new treaty he had signed with Repustinov last evening. Things had to move quickly and he could ill afford the normal political wrangling of Congress in this matter. He needed this treaty fast tracked.

Bass examined Peters as he closed his folder. He leaned back in his chair and waited for his companions to finish their review of the report. His gaze settled on Eldridge who sat across from him with her legs crossed as his were. He noticed she kept backtracking herself in an attempt to fully understand the one hundred page report. At one point she marked lines of text with a highlighter she always carried inside her coat pocket. The intensity of her study reminded Bass of a college student cramming for final exams. However, Eldridge's dark hair highlighted with streaks of gray and her bi-focal glasses precariously hanging at the tip of her nose contradicted Bass' first opinion. She must have been fifty-five or so he guessed. However, her slim athletic cut body as evident by her muscular legs, displayed by a business suit skirt that stopped above her knees, suggested to Bass that Eldridge was not all business.

Bass peered over to Peters as the last thought of Eldridge sailed from his head. Peters had observed Bass' little mental diversion. Bass blushed with slight embarrassment and then shrugged his shoulders as if to say, 'I am only human.' Peters' lips curled up in a smile as if to say, 'I know, we all are.' Then Bass scanned the other gentlemen in the room. They weren't quite finished either. The foursome had been in the room digesting the report at Peters' request for almost two hours now.

Bass' eyes were strained and his head hurt from reading and rereading the events that allegedly happened this past Friday. He did not know what to make of it. But he had written several questions he was more than eager to ask Peters. Right now, this entire report was more than unbelievable; it was unconscionable. *How dare the president defy Congress' wishes about the Anti Ballistic Missile Defense or Star Wars Defense initiative?* Congress, over the years, had been more than adamant about this subject. It was not to happen. But it did. And it worked to save the world from self-destruction at the hands of two lunatics, who somehow infiltrated both the United States and the Russian military at its highest levels.

The sound of the other members clearing their throats broke Bass' concentration. He snapped his head up and saw the other three members had finished and appeared as eager as he was to ask questions. However, protocol dictated since he was the ranking member of Congress in the room, he would start the session with comments. Bass took his cue, as Peters knew he would.

"Mr. President, this is a very interesting report. It is somewhat hard to believe, but it is interesting." He paused to let the political meaning of his words sink into Peters' consciousness. "You mean to tell me that we almost came to nuclear war with Russia last Friday and now over two thirds of our nuclear capability is destroyed?"

"Listen Senator," Peters sighed aloud. "I have neither the time nor the inclination to play politics with you today. I have no energy to search for meaning between, among, on top or in the words that you say. I am as straightforward as I can be. The report says it all. Our security was lax. General Samuel Patterson, my Vice Chairman of the Joint Chiefs of Staff, either deliberately or under duress obtained the security codes to enter the command center and launch our ICBM fleet. At the same time in Russia, General Ivan Prepovnov, Commander of the Ministry of Defense Twelfth Directorate, did the same exact thing. We don't know how and we don't know why. As the report states, we are sparing no expense to investigate the matter. Unfortunately, both suspects have vanished from the face of the Earth without a trace. The only good thing about this mess is the new Anti Ballistic Missile Defense system was in place on both sides and we were able to stop it." Peters knew he lied with the last statement, but his fervor from telling the truth at the beginning carried over and pushed the last statement with the same zeal as he started with.

"So you mean that the threat of nuclear war was never real?" Eldridge asked with a hint of flippantness.

Peters was prepared for this question and had briefed Repustinov to answer the question in the same manner. "No, the threat was real. Neither system could be activated without the other president's consent. It was a fail safe for exactly this type of scenario. Therefore, if we truly wanted to attack Russia with nuclear weapons or them us, the attacking president would not have given consent to initiate the missile defense system."

Leaks shook his head in disbelief, "You mean to tell me the Russian president had the key to our nuclear defense?"

"Yes, as we have the key to his nuclear defense."

"That's preposterous," bellowed Payne. "That's like giving the key to the jewelry store to the thief."

"Look, neither side wanted to totally delete the prestige and power of nuclear weapons, but we did not want the possibility of accidental launches either. It was very fortuitous of President Reagan and President Gorbachev to plant the seed or we all would be dead right now. So you can sit there and judge like you are God or something. But it worked and it worked as advertised." Again Peters' fervor gave credibility to the lie. "Besides, I did not ask you here to discuss why things happened, I asked you here to help your country, to help your planet." He paused here to let the plea appeal to their humanity. Even though he said he wasn't playing politics, Peters was playing politics. He just hoped their guards were lowered enough not to recognize it.

"Just a minute, Mr. President...I think we still have to discuss what happened last week," Bass insisted.

"I don't give a damn what you think Bass. You're nothing but a blow hard idiotic politician that probably sees an opportunity to get a Republican president in office over this." Peters stood and walked from behind his desk and stood over Bass pointing his finger right in his face. "I don't have time for your bullshit. Now listen and listen well. Those idiotic third world piss ant dictators and terrorists we have been doing battle with for over two decades will see this as an opportunity to bleed us dry. We no longer are the most powerful nation in the world. We shot our wad last Friday and it will take us years, if not decades, to get back to that level again. Need I remind you of New York or the Pentagon? What I proposed in the treaty signed last night will allow us to move from nuclear dependency and to a strong conventional force. But if you attempt to broadcast this administration's or any other administration's dirty laundry in this matter, you will doom this country to constant and bitter fighting with those bastard dictators and terrorists. For once man, look past your political agenda and think of this nation." Peters lowered his hand, but kept his glare on Bass.

"Sir, I take offense at your suggestion that I have ulterior motives other than my country's well being," Bass said hoping Peters would back down to civility once more.

"You know Bass; I don't care what you take offense to. If you aren't going to help me get this treaty through, then get out of my office. And if I hear any leaks to the media or to the floor about what is in this report I will have you arrested for treason. You see Bass; I don't have shit to lose on this one. For thirty long minutes last Friday, I saw this country, I dare say this planet, almost explode. I swear that won't ever happen again. Now if you want you can leave, I have business to attend to." Peters went back to his seat and sat down. When he looked up, Bass was still in his chair. "I said you can leave now," he reiterated.

"No sir, I'd rather stay," Bass said.

"Fine then," Peters continued. "You know what is at stake. We need to push this treaty for reduced nuclear arms. Then I need people in place who will confirm the destruction of the nonexistent weapons."

"Mr. President," Payne interrupted. "I will do as you ask, but I need proof these weapons are destroyed."

Peters was taken aback from his own party leader questioning his word. But he thought about it and realized it was a fair question. One that he was prepared to deal with, but hoped he did not have to.

"Fine Senator Payne," Peters said. "I will arrange for you four to tour our nuclear weapons bases with free access to everything. You can count the number of weapons personally if you like. I say the tour will take you about a month to do. If you want, we can set up everything by next Monday. But on one condition." Peters paused for any objections, but received none. "Once you are satisfied about the legitimacy of our weapons inventory, you will support this treaty and get it through as fast as you can when it hits the floor next month."

"If I am satisfied, you have my word I will support it," Bass piped up. "But if I am not we will talk about this illegal missile defense system."

"Fair enough Mr. Bass," Peters said, ensuring he did not use the term senator as a direct affront to Bass' challenge. "Whether you are satisfied or not, I will be willing to talk to you about our alleged illegal missile defense system, which just happened to save our lives last Friday."

The dig hit hard as Bass blinked his eyes several times. He knew whether the system was illegal or not, the surprising nature of its existence saved the planet, if everything Peters said was true. But that was the differentiator. Was everything he said true? Bass did not believe so, but wanted in the game long enough to decide for himself.

"Then I will do as you ask," Bass stated. "But Mr. President, if I find you're hiding something I will not honor your request."

"Bass you are a bastard," Peters said shaking his head. "But I am not hiding anything so I know you will honor my request. It's a deal."

***

Toneilk trained his scanners in a three hundred and sixty-degree arc throughout the galactic plane on a steadfast long-range setting. He wanted to detect any enemy ships approaching at the earliest moment. His surveillance crews had been on prime alert since the departure of the Osguardian Galaxy Protectors—almost fifteen hours now. Three hours ago, two of the four Millmum galaxy protectors, *G.P. Ainibyl* and *G.P. Bessian*, traveled through the Intragalactic gate portal and began a protective orbit around Capitol Station. Two hours ago, ten galaxy cruisers poured through the intragalactic gate portal and joined the *Ainibyl* and the *Bessian* in their protective orbits. Any other time, Toneilk would consider this an overwhelming show of force, but not today. The power of the melenai ore gun frightened him. The chromerion field would be of no use to the station or the ships. Basically, he felt like the station and anything and anyone around it would be sitting ducks to the Kulusks. Now the shame of never tasting battle was bearable. He wished he could still say that when all was complete. But deep inside his spirit, he knew his time had come.

"Any signs yet," said Sanchez who had accompanied Toneilk on the command deck.

Sanchez and his complement of defenders returned from escorting the evacuees almost thirty minutes ago. His defenders were prepped and ready for duty within fifteen minutes of landing in alpha bay. The other defenders from the Osguardian Galaxy Protectors stood ready for immediate launch in alpha, beta, charlie and delta bays. Their assignment was to fly close support for Capitol Station. The galaxy protectors and cruisers would handle the brunt of the fight. The defenders' role was to counter any enemy vessel that penetrated the protective orbit.

"No, nothing yet," Toneilk replied. "Is it always like this?" he asked a moment later to break the silence.

"Like what?" Sanchez replied.

"You know…like this—quiet and tense at the same time."

"Oh you mean before a battle," Sanchez quipped. He tilted his head to the right to think. He paused for a long moment and then looked into Toneilk's eyes.

"Your first battle I presume?"

"Yes, it is. I always thought I was missing something, by not having combat time. But now I am standing here poised for combat and I am praying it never happens."

"Yes, it is," replied Sanchez.

"You're sure it is coming?"

"No, I mean it is always like this prior to combat—quiet and tense at the same time."

"Oh, I see," Toneilk nodded. "Then it is not just I?"

"No sir, it's not just you," Sanchez assured. "But let me tell you. If you weren't a bit fearful, something would be wrong with you. No one enjoys combat. We just do it."

"How do you know you are ready?"

"You don't," Sanchez said putting his hand upon Toneilk's shoulder. "You don't. You just train for it to come, and pray it doesn't. You have a fifty-fifty chance one of the two will occur. I always bet on prayer. So far prayer has worked about seventy-five percent of the time. I hope it works this time."

"We all do," Toneilk deadpanned. "But I think prayer isn't going to work this time," he added as he turned to face one of the multiple monitors scanning the heavens for the invasion force. "I don't think prayer will work at all this time," he repeated under his breath.

Sanchez leaned over and peered over Toneilk's shoulder at the monitor.

"Sir, you and your people will do fine. Remember you are Sixana warriors first, sworn to protect the interest of the USSTAP and your home planet. Remember…Honor, Power and Grace, forever."

Toneilk cocked his head toward Sanchez and nodded in agreement. Sanchez stood straight and moved toward the next station on the right. He peered over the operator's left shoulder and scanned the monitor. He saw nothing unusual, but his gut told him it was time. It was a warrior's feeling that the fight was about to begin and he should prepare now.

"Admiral," Sanchez called from the station. "I think I best get to my ship. I have a gut feeling an immediate launch will be necessary when the Kulusks come a knocking."

Toneilk nodded and dismissed Sanchez from the bridge. Sanchez stood tall and straight like a performer on stage and made his way through the door. He disappeared in the shadows of the corridor he traveled.

Toneilk took a deep breath and said a silent prayer for Sanchez and the other warriors who would fly their single seat defenders against the Kulusk's main attack, if need be, to protect his station. The thought of the fear raging in Sanchez's mind shamed him. Even in battle he knew he would be secure in the station. All Sanchez had for security was a defender…a ship made for space battles against other single seat ships—not an armada of Kulusk battleships.

"Sire, I have eighty contacts in sector Two–G, heading three–three-zero decimal two–nine–eight mark negative seven through seven. Range …fifteen light years. Speed … MOP fifty-five," chimed Terilela breaking Toneilk's concentration. "Sir they are Kulusk battle cruisers."

"Well they are coming. How long until they arrive?" he inquired.

"Seventeen universal minutes."

"Sound the alarm USSTAP wide, alert the fleet and send the coded messages to the Osguards. The fight is on."

Chapter 37—Press the Attack

His heart quickened with anticipation, as the target area grew larger on the screen. His mouth became dry as he felt the blood coursing through his veins. The moment was at hand. The moment he had dreamt about all of his life. His father Kie Ritchen had promised him this moment for years, and now it was about to happen. Xer was about to eliminate the enemy of the Kulusks. He was about to annihilate the USSTAP's Capitol Station; secure the main intragalactic and intergalactic gate portals and finally kill all the Osguards in one victorious day. He knew it would be a long and tumultuous day that needed his full concentration. One step at a time was all he needed to concentrate on. The first task at hand was to destroy Capitol Station.

He checked the time to target clock. He was within ten minutes of starting the most glorious day in his life. They would write songs of this day on his home world. He would be immortalized in folklore and in books as the man who brought honor back to his world. Yes, to Xer this was a great day indeed—one he needed to savor.

"Signal the armada to drop from MOP on my mark," he commanded his helm officer.

"Soli," the helm officer complied.

A few seconds later the helm officer signaled Xer the armada was ready for his orders.

"Drop to entry hypersonic speed...ready...ready...now," Xer commanded.

The Kulusk armada slowed through the MOP speed range at the same time. The helm officer called out the speed as they ticked by on his ARIT, "—MOP fifty—MOP forty—MOP thirty—MOP twenty—MOP ten—hyperlight—entry hypersonic speed."

As the armada entered hypersonic speed, the laws of normal light reflection and refraction took hold and their image emerged from the dark cover of space. The Kulusk ships had flat white bottoms covered with dark gray tortoise like shells. Each crevice on the ship's upper hull contained a shockdel gun port, protected by a second chromerion field generator. The engines, like their USSTAP counterpart, ran the length of the ship on both the port and starboard sides. The engines were attached where the curved hull met the flat bottom hull and curved upwards similar to a lip. The size and shape of the ship, plus the placement of the engines restricted the maximum speed of the Kulusk battle cruiser to MOP fifty-five. This was an effective trade-off to the Kulusks, for the ship's design made it almost indestructible in combat.

***

"Sir, we have a visual on the Kulusk armada," Terilela reported to Toneilk.

Toneilk did not have to be told. He saw the ships as they entered the visible spectrum when they slowed to hypersonic speed. So did the sires of the *G.P. Ainibyl* and the *G.P. Bessian*. The ships moved toward sector two–G on an intercept course. Toneilk did not envy them at all, two galaxy protectors against an eighty-ship Kulusk battle cruiser armada. It was suicide. Even with ten smaller galaxy cruisers at their side, the likelihood of victory was slim.

Osguards: Homecoming

"Prepare defenders for launch, ready battle stations on all stations, chromerion fields up and repeat battle alarm on all USSTAP frequencies," Toneilk ordered, letting the numerous drills kick in. He had trained for such an eventuality, in hopes his training was a deterrent. Now he realized his training was not a deterrent, but a preparation. His subconscious was amazed at how calm he was in barking the orders and how professional he was in just what to do. Although Toneilk was congratulating himself for not faltering in his orders, he also was praying for guidance when the crap hit the fan. He wondered if he could make the right decisions in the heat of battle. Or would his inexperience cause unnecessary death and destruction? He was untested and untried in combat. Now his first test was a final exam. He tried not to let his concern show on his face as he studied the personnel on the combat bridge.

Each person there depended on his leadership and ability to make things happen and save their lives. He knew that, he respected that, but he also resented that. Why should he have to hide his fear to make everything work? He was just as scared as they were, but because of his position he could not show it. At least they had the luxury of showing it, if they wanted to. But as he looked around, none of his troops showed any fear on their faces. In fact their faces contained the same stoic and professional demeanor they always had. Somehow, he drew his strength from them and suppressed his fear. He then climbed into his command chair and thumbed the screen to get an overall picture of the battle situation. He saw the track of the Kulusk ships and the track of the USSTAP ships—estimated time for combat was seven minutes.

***

The room crashed into darkness and the red light illuminated. She lifted her head off the bed as the irritating siren, which sounded like an overgrown electric alarm clock, kept buzzing in her ear. She turned to Parker to see if the noise disturbed him. He had just come through his operation and was still sedated. Elizabeth had now been awake for twenty-four hours straight. Or had she dozed off several times since she started her watch? In her fog and haze she no longer could remember. All she knew was her husband had his legs back. They looked and felt like the legs she remembered. She just prayed when Parker woke up, he would feel the same. But he was not awake yet and something was happening. Her stomach turned with fear, as her mind fought to grasp onto reality once more. She was in space, light years away from Earth, praying for the full recovery of her husband who was shot by some enemy she had never heard of using some sort of ray gun she never dreamt of. The events happened so quickly, it made her head spin.

Malcolm Dylan Petteway

The door whisked open, Debrlina and Michelle scurried in wearing their delta belts, wearing full black body armor and helmets with chromerion face covers, carrying rifles of some sort in their hands.

"It's started," Debrlina reported as she sat in the chair closest to the door.

Michelle pulled the other chair out of the corner, sat in it with her legs folded underneath her.

"What's started?" asked Elizabeth.

"The war," Michelle whispered as she pulled out her tactical ARIT. "The Kulusks have sent an armada and they are about seven minutes away. Hopefully, Michael's plan will work and this thing will be over in an hour or so."

"What plan?" asked Elizabeth dryly.

"I don't know what plan, but he would not have left us like this unless he had a plan," Michelle responded. Then she looked at her PARIT that surveyed this sector of the station, to ensure she knew who was in the area. Then she looked to the corner of the room and whispered to herself, "Michael, you better damn well have a plan."

"Don't worry, Momma. We will make sure nothing happens to you or Papa," Debrlina assured her. "We are loaded down with full combat gear. No one will bother us without a fight."

Elizabeth grabbed and squeezed her husband's free hand. How she wished she were back home. If they were home, Parker would not be like this and they would not be praying for their lives. How a few short days changed their world! Just last Thursday, she was happily preparing dinner for her family in their own kitchen and her only worry was if she would have enough food to feed them before the picnic. Oh, the picnic was a thing of the past now in her mind. She wanted to know what her children did, but not like this. This was insane. Why did this have to happen to them? Why did God put them in this predicament? Tears formed in her eyes as she began to weep.

Debrlina rose, stepped over to her mother-in-law, and wrapped her right arm around her in an effort to console her. It seemed to make her sob even worse. Debrlina looked over at Michelle as they both shrugged. Neither daughter-in-law knew what to say in this instance and neither one attempted to say anything. Sometimes letting emotions run their course was the best way to handle them—especially emotions of sadness. They both learned that once they joined the USSTAP. It was drilled into their head almost every day. Emotions could run or ruin your day. It was up to them to decide which. And if you couldn't decide which, then you must wait until you could. In this case they knew not which, so they would wait.

***

Osguards: Homecoming

It has been over thirty minutes since the Osguards had dropped out of MOP. The repeated attempts to contact the Maxum have gone unheeded. Michael was now getting nervous. No word from either Capitol Station or from the Maxum. Could he have been wrong about this, or had something gone wrong with his calculations? He knew neither and the uncertainty plagued doubts on his confidence.

He turned to his communications officer, Major Best.

"Anything yet?"

"No sir, I am…Hold on sir, I have a communiqué from the Maxum," Major Best reported.

"On my board," Michael ordered.

"Tiah."

Michael sat in his command chair and pushed several keys on his console. The picture of Maxum Kie Ritchen appeared. "Maxum Kie Ritchen, I am Osguard One."

"I know who you are. What are you doing in my space?"

"I am returning your ambassador and request an audience with you about the recent events in USSTAP territory."

"I care not about my ambassador or the events that happened to you."

"Well, I thought—"

"Osguard, recall message from Capitol Station," Major Best interrupted.

"Ah, that would be my son, taking revenge on your Capitol Station. I gather it would be too late for you to stop him and you…"

Michael terminated the transmission in the middle of Maxum Ritchen's diatribe.

"Signal all ships to engage Intragalactic portal engines on my mark," Michael ordered

The Intragalactic portal engines were a new addition to the galaxy protector class ships. It allowed the transformation of the ships through inner-space without the use of the mechanical and bulky gate portals that populated strategic areas of space. It was the most guarded secret in USSTAP, which Sheryl almost leaked in her earlier conversation to him when she was returning from chasing Larson and crew to Kulusk. However Sheryl had done an excellent job in mapping this area during her return so they would have the coordinates to use in this event. Once engaged, the ships could return to Capitol Station within seconds. Michael counted on Kie Ritchen not knowing of this advancement. He knew Kie Ritchen wanted to draw the massive firepower away from the USSTAP territory so he could target something and then come after them. However, he was not entirely sure on what Ritchen wanted to target. Was it Chaktun, Earth or Millmum Station? He took an educated guess and calculated it would be the station, because it was the heart of the USSTAP. From the recall message, he deemed he was correct. He smiled and clicked the intercom.

"Osguards this is it. We are about to return to the Capitol Station using our new IPEs. Once we get there remember the plan. Don't leave your wingman." Michael paused because he knew everyone was more than aware of the plan. "Engage engines…ready…ready…now."

The engine nacelles strips turned a sparkling white light and then shot a white beam in front of each galaxy protector. The beam turned into a white oval opening into inner-space in front of each ship. Sixty white inner-space openings darted the space realm like a checkerboard. The ships used thruster power to maneuver into their individual openings. They pushed forward into the white light, entering on the front side of the oval. Each ship disappeared bit by bit, until it vanished, swallowed by the consuming radiance of inner-space. In seventy seconds the lights closed, leaving no trace of the mighty Osguard fleet.

***

"Maxum, the Osguard ships are gone," reported the console operator to Ritchen.

"What do you mean, they are gone?" he queried.

"Multiple massive energy surges occurred…similar to what we experience in gate portal travel, but at a more massive scale. Then the ships vanished. Nothing, no trace, I have nothing on scanner."

Kie Ritchen looked at the scanner, and then he looked at the sensors. He did not recognize any readout as that of the Osguard ships. He played the last two minutes of read out over again and watched with maximum intensity. He witnessed what the console operator reported. He recognized the signature. It was gate portal travel signatures he was reading.

"No, they didn't," said Kie, realizing the ships must have stepped. "No they didn't," he screamed as he hit the console operator on the shoulder. "Quick get me my son, I need to warn him."

***

Xer took pleasure in firing the first blow in what he knew would be the destruction of his enemies. He ordered the first shot onto *G.P. Bessian*. The shockdel gun fired a wave through the space. It's red bulge sailed toward *G.P. Bessian*. The *Bessian* did not detour from its attendant course. It sailed at hypersonic speed with *G.P. Ainibyl* in close trail about ten marks behind it. The red bulge penetrated the chromerion field with a slight sparkle, but its path was not altered or slowed. The bulge sailed undisturbed and punctured the starboard engine nacelle. The resulting explosion ripped the engine from its spar and forced *G.P. Bessian* into a sharp turn to its right, spinning the large ship almost one hundred and eighty degrees. The resulting fire on the right spar glowed like the sun as the energy tanks ruptured and ignited in many balls of fire.

Both ships held their position as the *Bessian* executed its fire suppression process. Xer saw the resulting damage and ordered another shockdel hit. The melenai charges rocked the ship with a thunderous burst and sailed towards the *G.P. Bessian*. Five seconds before the hit, *G.P. Bessian* went pitch black and reverted to stealth mode ten. The melenai charge lost its lock. *G.P. Bessian* used its thrusters to move, but it could not escape. The melenai charge hit on the port engine, but the blast just dissipated into sparkles.

***

"The *Bessian* is hit," Terilela reported to Toneilk aboard the command bridge. "She has lost her starboard engine. It was completely sheared off. She is reporting multiple fires, hull breach on decks four through eight. She only has thrusters." With each detail, the urgency in Terilela's voice became apparent. "She is energizing her slitanium cover. She is going to stealth mode ten—.

—Lead Kulusk ship is firing her guns. The *Bessian* is trying to maneuver. Sir, she can't move fast enough. She will be hit in two—one—."

Silence hovered over the bridge as all the participants expected to see the *Bessian* explode with the latest barrage of weapon's fire. But to everyone's surprise, the red bulge of melenai energy spattered off the skin of the *Bessian* with sparkles.

***

"Direct hit...no damage. I repeat...no damage," Terilela reported with glee.

"Direct all the fleet to implement alpha plan alpha at once," Toneilk ordered.

"Tiah," said Terilela as she executed his instructions.

***

"General Xer, direct hit...no effect," reported his helm officer.

"What do you mean no effect?" Xer demanded. Xer turned to his weapons officer seated behind him up one level, "Weapons officer check your instruments again."

"They all check grade - A," he reported.

"No they could not have known about the shockdel gun...could they?" Xer whispered to no one in particular. "That idiot Junitel must have used his shockdel gun when he tried to assassinate one of the Osguards. Of course, they must have it. They had time to analyze it." Xer walked over to his weapons officer. "Try to compensate, they did not have time to alter their

249

chromerion fields to defeat the melenai pulse of the shockdel gun. Alter the frequency until we can hurt them even when they go stealth," he commanded.

***

The *Ainibyl* went to stealth mode eight with her chromerion field down and her weapons fully charged. She sailed behind the *Bessian* and used her for cover. When she was in striking distance, she popped up one half mark on the galactic plane and fired a barrage with her weapons array. Several bursts of her pagenay guns sailed toward the lead Kulusk ship while her coronet guns targeted the ships on the flank and her Asher torpedoes locked onto the ships above and below the lead ship. The *Ainibyl* did not remain in view to watch the effects of her weapons. She dove back behind the *Bessian* using her stealth mode ten frame as cover.

The lead ship, commanded by Xer took several pagenay bursts with minimal damage. The bursts succeeded in weakening its chromerion field by ten percent, which Xer's crew easily compensated by diverting additional energy to the field. Ships two and three on her flank took direct hits from the coronet gun pulses. They too sustained minimal damage to their fields, but were able to compensate by diverting energy as well. Kulusk ships four and six took direct hits by the Asher torpedo. The Asher torpedo exploded upon hitting the ships protective fields, but the kinetic energy from the explosion caused a wave that jolted the ships and caused slight hull fractures. These two ships slowed in the formation and affected stopgap measures to prevent hull breaches.

Xer ordered all ships to concentrate their guns onto the two galaxy protectors. While the Kulusk armada was calculating their firing solution, five galaxy cruisers at stealth mode eight popped up from behind the other five galaxy cruisers that were at stealth mode ten and let loose with multiple weapons fire.

The Kulusk armada had forgotten about the cruisers during their initial engagement. The pagenay beams, coronet pulses and the Asher torpedoes, sailed through the dark cold space and engaged on seventeen of the leading attack vessels. The seventeen Kulusk ships disengaged their firing solution on the two galaxy protectors and retargeted on the five galaxy cruisers. They calculated the solution and fired at will upon the cruisers.

The cruisers descended down in front of the other five cruisers and went to stealth mode ten. The red pulses of the Kulusk guns found their targets, but by the time they reached the cruisers their slitanium hulls were energized, absorbing the destructive pulse of the shockdel guns. The other five cruisers sprang to life, changed to stealth mode eight, energized their weapons and sailed from behind the first wave of cruisers and let loose with their own barrage of weapons fire. Once they discharged their weapons, they sailed in front of the other cruisers and changed to stealth mode ten just before the shockdel guns could complete their intercept.

This leapfrog maneuver did not allow the cruisers to lock onto their target, so every weapons release was done manually and without ARIT control. Even though the USSTAP were surviving their attack their weapons fire had little effect in curtailing the attack. The Kulusk armada moved without hesitation toward Capitol Station. Soon the cruisers began a backward leapfrog maneuver to stay in front of the armada in the hopes their weapons fire could eventually alter the armada's course.

***

"Sir, the armada is still advancing," reported Terilela. "Our weapons have no effect."

This news came as a big surprise to Toneilk. No one in the history of the USSTAP could ever sustain such an onset of weapons fire and not be affected. But the Kulusks were.

"Launch the defenders to set a protective orbit around Capitol Station," he ordered.

He understood the likelihood of such a feat was impossible, but he had to do something. He watched the defenders launch from the bays and sail through the opening ports like a swarm of bees to a kill. He closed his eyes and gave a silent prayer of protection. As he watched the men he had just sent to their deaths fly into the mouth of hell with courage, he wondered where the Osguards were.

Chapter 38—The Cavalry Arrives

Twenty marks above the galactic plane and above Capitol Station, large white ovals dotted the skyline like solar flares. One—two—twenty—twenty-five—forty—fifty—sixty ovals, four miles in diameter, opened with the brilliant white light of inner-space.

"Sir, I have multiple gate portal openings, twenty marks above," Terilela reported to Toneilk. "It's them…it's the Osguards!" she stated with the enthusiasm of a sportscaster watching a team score.

The Osguardian Galaxy Protectors lumbered through the oval openings, using thrusters, since the gate portal engines were eating most of their power.

"The *Neraka*—the *Gamian*—the *Vedar*—the *Kashara*—the *Loclam*—the *Sucram*—the *Sharyla*—the *Sregaem*—the *Nitram*—the *Laurona*—the *Nausona*—the *Uluz*…"

251

Terilela named each ship as they passed back into normal space. With each name called, the smile on Toneilk's face grew wider and wider. When she was finished, she had counted all sixty ships and a feeling of relief passed upon the entire bridge crew.

"Pass all tactical information on all USSTAP frequencies now," Toneilk ordered, hoping to let the Osguards know of the dire need for action.

The galaxy protectors energized their engines for hypersonic travel and darted to sector Two–G to enter the fray of battle.

***

"Xer, this is Maxum Kie Ritchen," came the voice over tactical.

Xer was surprised to hear his father's voice in the middle of his victory. He felt he had no time for conversation and muted the channel, as he pushed the strategy to deal with the pesky cruisers that annoyed him like ants.

"General Xer, I think you should see this," interrupted his helm officer.

"See what?" Xer asked, irritated at the interruption.

"See this," the helm officer said as he pointed to the main viewer.

In the main screen, the sight of the sixty Osguardian Galaxy Protectors sailing toward them crowded the field of view. Xer swallowed hard at the sight.

"This can't be," Xer wailed. "No...no, where the jorum did they come from? They were supposed to be over three hundred light years away—not here."

He clicked on the frequency containing his father's transmission and listened.

"Repeat...Osguards have somehow stepped through inner-space. I suspect they are stepping back toward Capitol Station...acknowledge. Repeat...Osguards have somehow stepped through inner-space. I suspect they are stepping back toward Capitol Station...acknowledge."

"This is Xer, I acknowledge your transmission. Repeat...I acknowledge your transmission. Osguardian ships in view. Repeat Osguardian ships in view...Xer out."

Confusion gave way to anger in Xer's mind. He tapped the console again, "Kulusk ships sixty one to eighty, proceed with attack onto Capitol Station. All others break off the attack and follow me. We are about to go Osguard hunting."

The armada split its forces with the front sixty ships that were sustaining the attack from the ten cruisers ascending to twenty marks above the galactic plane and the rear guard pushing forward through the attack.

"Osguard fleet, sixty butches heading zero–nine–eight decimal zero–zero–nine, mark one–zero and climbing," reported Terilela over tactical frequency. Butch was the combat term used for an enemy vessel with hostile intent.

The *Galaxy Cruiser Mitiah* heard the transmission as it popped up for its attack during the leapfrog maneuver. The Offensive Weapons Officer, Major John Wrightson, adjusted his weapons calculations to search for the climbing ships. At the crest of the pop up maneuver, Wrightson manually targeted the middle of the cluster and let loose on the weapons' fire. The pagenay beams pierced the vacuum of space to hit the middle of the cluster as the Asher missiles and the coronet guns spread wide to flanking ships.

The pagenay beams struck the bottom of Kulusk ship thirty-two with such an impact it cut through the hull and emptied out the top. The coronet guns hit Kulusk ship thirty-five and forty-five, also on the white bottom. The resulting damage from the explosion tore through the port engine on ship thirty-five and the starboard engine on ship forty-five. The hull crumbled around the engine connections as fire engulfed the area on both ships. The Asher missiles found their target on ships fifty and fifty-one. The Asher missile ripped through the bottom of the hull through the ship and tore through the bridge, killing the command crew on ship fifty. The other Asher missile caught the tail end of ship fifty-one and demolished the alpha-landing bay. The hit flipped the ship twenty degrees nose down and forced it to collide on top of ship fifty-two. The resulting explosion engulfed both ships into total annihilation. Orange fire sparks along with black debris particles and yellow glowing metal fluttered through space as the oxygen rich atmosphere of the ship melded with the igniting properties of fuel and gases.

"Sire, two butches destroyed and four butches badly damaged...one of those butches is disabled," Terilela reported to Toneilk.

"What happened?"

"The Mitiah took a belly shot on the ascending attackers. Their belly is the soft spot...it's unprotected," she shouted.

"Push that to all the fleet," he commanded.

***

"Osguard zero–one, acknowledged," Michael noted at the revelation. He touched his screen to open up a frequency to all Osguardian ships. "All even Osguards, descend and change course to heading two–five–nine decimal three–one–two, mark negative one–zero. Proceed toward Capitol Station and defend against enemy ships. All odd Osguards follow me in formation, maintain heading, but descend to mark one–zero. We need to get below them now. Reverse alpha plan alpha. Need you to leapfrog under your wingman when you take those shots."

Like a flock of birds changing direction in mid flight, the lower echelon to the 'V' formation veered right and started a descent staying in formation. The top echelon, led by Michael, descended ten marks as soon as the lower formation was clear.

Commander John White, the *Neraka* Defensive Officer picked up the ascending attackers on his screen. He touched his screen to get a proper readout, and then he passed the information to the offense officer, Commander Wang Li. Li nodded he had received the information.

"Sire, enemy ships up and locked into weapons array," Li reported.

"Fine," he acknowledged. Michael opened the interlink frequency to all ships in his formation. "Fleet, slow to thrusters and convert to stealth mode ten."

The fleet slowed together and vanished by letting the pitch-blackness of space envelope them, hiding any visual cues of their existence.

***

"General Xer, we lost them visual—switching to scanner," reported Xer's tactical officer from behind his left shoulder.

"Fine," he acknowledged. "Maintain course and heading." Xer sat in his chair as he kept going over the events of the last few minutes. He had lost five ships in a matter of a heartbeat and he did not know why. The news came as a shock to him, but he could not deter from his intended course of action. He wanted to meet the Osguard fleet head-on and engage them in battle. But as long as they continued the leapfrog maneuver, he would not be able to inflict any real damage onto the fleet. But, they could not inflict any damage onto him either. And the sole difference was he could maneuver his armada at hypersonic speed while firing and defending his armada. The USSTAP ships were using a leapfrog tactic to counteract the blast of the shockdel guns. This was a slight advantage, but it still was an advantage he could use to push his way toward Capitol Station.

***

Michael's fleet came to a halt once they reached ten marks directly in line to Xer's passing armada; therefore, Xer's tactical officer had a difficult time processing the scanner's mathematical calculations.

"General Xer, they must have stopped. I have no contact on scanner either," Xer's tactical officer reported.

"Fine, keep an eye open," he commented. "We know their technique. This time when they come out of stealth mode, fire in their direction. Forgo waiting on a firing solution. I want you to pass that to all ships, even the second armada heading toward Capitol Station.

***

"Osguard zero–one, we plotted the Kulusks' position to be directly over us in twenty-five seconds…" reported White.

"Good, report to all ships in this formation to convert to stealth mode zero, lock on all weapons and fire at will in fifteen seconds."

White thumbed his control tablet to execute Michael's command, "All ships acknowledged."

"Four—three—two—one—now, stealth mode zero, weapons lock and fire at will," ordered Michael as he clinched both fists in front of his face.

Michael's fleet de-energized their slitanium hull and applied full power to the weapons arsenal. Li took half a second to re-engage his firing solutions, and then he strummed the console like a concert piano player as he fired a barrage of weapons on the last four ships in trail. The ripple effect resonated throughout the fleet as the last weapons fire sailed upwards to its target from Sheryl's ship, *G.P. Kashara*. The *Kashara*'s pagenay blast ripped the front part of Xer's ship, collapsing several decks and tearing a hole behind the bridge.

The dark vacuum patch of space between sector two–G and one–G lit up with silent explosions, as several of the Kulusk ships blew up in tiny particles of raining metal, blood and body parts. Other ships had parts of their hull fly off as holes ripped through them from bottom through the top, cutting critical ship components and killing personnel as they were sucked into space. The barrage fire took ten seconds to release, but the resulting carnage caused time to slow to almost a halt as the laws of space and physics worked together, lighting the area like fireflies in the night.

Michael's fleet sprang into stealth mode ten as they ascertained the damage their first barrage of weapons fire had caused. Weapons were not optimum in this mode, but they were on ready in preparation for returning weapons fire.

"Osguard zero–one, this is Capitol Station command bridge," Terilela echoed over secure interlink frequency. "Twenty butches destroyed, fourteen disabled and twenty one damaged, but still combat capable. Take heading zero–nine–five decimal zero–one–zero, mark zero–zero."

"Osguard zero–one fleet acknowledge," Michael reported. "Set the coordinates navigator and push the fleet."

Again with the elegance of birds in flight, the fleet changed direction and moved toward the limping twenty-one Kulusk battle cruisers.

***

Xer's Kulusk armada traveled at half hypersonic speed because of the massive damage they sustained. Several ships were in the process of fire suppression and other ships had lost their navigation control. However, they all had one thing in common, they had full weapons capability and they intended to use it.

Xer saw the victory of the day slipping from his grasp. With his head cut and bleeding from the unforeseen weapons barrage, he looked around his battle bridge and counted the dead. He only had his helm and weapons officer functioning at full capacity. His communications officer and tactical officer lay dead in a pool of their own blood—probably sustained when they hit their head when the ship was rocked from whatever hit them. Xer did not even try to figure out how it happened; he just knew that somehow the Osguards had penetrated his fortified chromerion field. The battle cruiser should have withstood any direct attack.

Close in, direct attack? That was the key. They weren't engaged in close combat. Those rox had fired from underneath—where there was just one chromerion field generator. A second field generator did not fortify the ships' underbelly, because no ship should have ever come that close in combat. There weren't any combat critical components exposed at the bottom of the ship, no strategic value to hit in the bottom of the ship. At least that is what he thought until now.

"Descend...descend...tell the armada to descend! They are hitting us from beneath," he ordered his helm officer. "Tell the others to divert secondary chromerion field power to protect the underbelly!"

The rapid descent of Xer's armada was erratic and caused several near misses among his ships. Michael's fleet saw the descent and realized the armada was descending right into them.

Michael called, "Evasive maneuvers now!" over the interlink.

The fleet dispersed in several directions, running from the descending armada and concentrating on avoiding a collision with each other. The *Sucram* came within point five marks of the *Gamian* as it veered ninety degrees port and descended. The *Sharyla* cut in front of her sister ship the *Kashara*, nearly missing her bow by one mark. The *Sharyla's* stern filled the view screen of the *Kashara* to the point the crash alarm sounded and the crew prepared to abandon ship. However the *Sharyla* passed to the starboard side as it ascended between two Kulusk battleships.

As the *Sharyla* ascended, she fired her pagenay weapons onto the two Kulusk ships. The *Sharyla* did not target its weapons on the bottom of the ship but on the port and starboard sides. Fortunately, the ships were damaged enough that the chromerion fields were not at full strength. The ship to the right of the *Sharyla*, hull split where the pagenay beams struck, breaking one of its spars and causing several internal explosions. The ship to the port side of the *Sharyla* took the hit and started to list toward its starboard side as internal explosions ripped inside her hull. The *Sharyla* cleared the Kulusk armada by swinging ninety degrees to her starboard and continuing the ascent to mark twenty-five.

The *Kashara* braced for an impact that never came. She pulled a ninety-degree turn while descending to her port side. Then on the outside of the turn, she began a rapid ascent to mark twenty. She saw her sister ship take her shots at the two Kulusk battle cruisers and added her coronet guns to the ship on her starboard side and the *Sharyla's* port side. The ship had already begun its list when the *Kashara's* guns ripped through her bridge and opened it up to the black abyss of space. Several Kulusk crewmembers died as the vacuum of space sucked their bodies into eternal oblivion.

"Disengage...disengage!" Michael ordered over the interlink frequency as he saw the resulting destruction of the two Kulusk battle cruisers. "Reform...inverted 'V' at decimal zero–zero–five, mark two–zero," he commanded once he saw the formation had escaped the collision.

It took two minutes, but Osguard zero–one fleet reformed as directed. When Michael was satisfied he strummed his control tablet.

"Kulusk leader, this is Osguard zero–one, call off your attack and surrender now..."

"Osguard zero–one," Xer responded. "I am Xer Ritchen, son of Maxum Kie Ritchen of the Kulusk Empire. I do not recognize your authority to make such a demand. It is you who should surrender. We will make this as peaceful on you as we can. You have thirty seconds to comply."

Michael cut the transmission.

"Is this guy crazy?" He turned to his communications officer, Major Best, "Report on Osguard zero–two fleet."

Chapter 39—The Heat of Battle

The tactical officer in the lead ship in the second Kulusk armada had had enough of the leapfrog maneuver. Even though the weapons coming from the USSTAP galaxy cruisers were not affecting their advance, it was irritating to move around power distribution to cover gaps in the chromerion field that their weapons were leaving. It took the field almost a full ten universal minutes to regenerate at the weak points. If the Osguards had figured that out, they would have continued hitting the same spot. But they weren't—this made the tactical officer surmise the Osguard ships were manually operating their weapons. He further concluded the Osguard ships couldn't get a proper firing solution, which meant they couldn't use the full potential of their weapons. That is why the field was holding up so well. But it still was a bother to continue to compensate the field at every weapons volley.

Then the tactical officer had a stroke of genius hit him. He watched the cruisers perform their leapfrog maneuver several more times to confirm his theory. He did not return fire at the dissatisfaction of the ship's commander. But he put his finger up and told him he had a plan. He calculated the leapfrog maneuver's timing. They were predictable. Well they had to be predictable in order to keep pace with the Kulusks moving at hypersonic speed. The cruisers were in and out of hypersonic speed during their tactical maneuver. This was a definite drain on their engines and a definite advantage to the Kulusk tactical officer.

The tactical officer studied the ships as they moved in and out of stealth mode ten. He took control of the weapons array, picked a point in space, and fired. As he fired, the *Galaxy Cruiser Sletimion* moved to stealth mode eight and started its pop up maneuver. The red bulge of melenai energy scorched across the heavens on an intercept course. The *Sletimion*, because of its stealth mode, had just engaged its scanners to get information for a manual firing solution.

The melenai ball hit the cruiser on its port side directly below deck two. The hull cracked as the half energized slitanium covering tried to absorb and dissipate the energy from the blast. The ship lurched backwards from the blast as the ARIT systems shorted out on the bridge. The ships movement flung crewmembers throughout the main cabin. Some flew as far as ten feet. Heads cracked against bulkheads and instrument panels buckled. The ship stopped its movement like a car hitting a brick wall at sixty miles an hour.

Two other Kulusk ships saw the stranded USSTAP cruiser in their ARIT targeting solutions and opened fire with a barrage of melenai pulses. The *Sletimion's* defensive officer lying flat on his back saw the impending barrage of melenai pulses from his position in the view screen. He hopped to his knees, reached for his console, ejected some ARIT decoys and pushed for stealth mode ten.

The decoys caught the attention of the first five pulses and veered them off to the right. They exploded within point two marks of the starboard engine, sending compression waves toward the engine. The engine covering bent and cracked at the fuel lead in. Orange dialairtic gas that fueled the engines began venting. The last five pulses found their mark on the bow of the *Sletimion*, but not before the slitanium had energized. The slitanium covering absorbed the hits, but not fully. The skin had been ruptured by the first blast and compromised by the crack in the hull at the starboard engines. Melenai pulses traveled throughout the hull in red-like electrical static arcs and fried what was left of the ARIT systems. Life support, communications, weapons and even the slitanium covering had all lost power. The ship was floating dark and lifeless, ready to take another hit from the Kulusk guns.

Now two more Kulusk ships trained their weapons onto the *Sletimion*—making it a total of five Kulusk battle cruisers aiming at her. The other USSTAP cruisers looked on with horror. They felt helpless, paralyzed at seeing the destruction of the *Sletimion* before their eyes.

"Fire at their bottom hull... it's unprotected!" Terilela's voice shrieked over the interlink frequency. "Fire at the butches bottom hull; it is unprotected. Go full combat mode. Repeat…Go full combat and fire at the bottom of their hull."

Major John Wrightson, the offensive systems officer on the *Galaxy Cruiser Mitiah*, the *Sletimion* wingman, had thought he just had a lucky shot earlier, but now he knew it wasn't just luck. Before he knew what he was doing, he took over piloting control, went full combat mode and descended to mark 00. The *Galaxy Cruiser Quegod* and the *Galaxy Cruiser Ebuhs* followed. As soon as Wrightson saw white from the five leading ships he locked on target using ARIT firing solution and fired. The *Quegod* and the *Ebuhs* again followed suit.

Aboard the five lead ships that had a lock onto the doomed *Sletimion*, the alarm buzzed. It shook each weapon officers' attention from the firing solution. They simultaneously checked the readout and saw it was nothing but a fresh attack by the other cruisers. So far their attacks had been like throwing spitballs at them. The lead ship's weapons officer placed his finger on the firing panel and began to press it…

The jolt was violent and crushing. A pagenay blast ripped through the lead Kulusk ship and out the bridge top. The weapons officer caught the searing heat of the pagenay as it burned through his body taking the embers from his burnt flesh out into space as the bridge opened up to the cold recess of the dark mass. The other four ships received similar damage as several hull breaches caused the nature of space to enter and take life one by one. Bulkheads failed, walls crumbled and crushed as Kulusk crewmembers were thrashed from side to side with each jeering bump and explosion.

The commander of the second ship flew up to the ceiling and cracked his head open, splattering part of his brain matter out onto the ceiling. He fell and broke both his legs as the G-force caused three times his body weight to crash to the floor. However, he did not feel it, because he was already dead from the massive head trauma.

The first five of the trailing fifteen Kulusk battle cruisers saw the horror in their view screen and automatically targeted the three vessels underneath their partners. Fifteen red bulges of red melenai pulses sailed toward the *Mitiah, Quegod* and the *Ebuhs*. The USSTAP ships alarms buzzed and they deployed full ARIT decoys and pushed to stealth mode ten as they engaged thrusters to descend even lower on the galactic plane. The pulses went ballistic once the ships went into stealth mode and dissipated behind them.

The *Sletimion* managed to get her thrusters working and steered in the middle of the Kulusk carnage to hide from the oncoming Kulusk battle cruisers. She powered down her thrusters and was able to stop the venting fuel leak into space. She clung to the lifeless underbelly of the lead Kulusk battle cruiser while she watched the parade of butches pass. The ships did not stop to help their fallen comrades, they continued on their course toward

Capitol Station. This was a fortunate happenstance for the crew of the *Sletimion*.

Once they passed the *Mitiah, Quegod* and the *Ebuhs* began rescue operations for the *Sletimion*. They were now out of the fight along with the *Bessian* and the *Ainibyl*. There were only six galaxy cruisers and a myriad of defenders to stop them from reaching Capitol Station now.

***

"Tiah" reported Osguard Two, Roger Genesis, the son of Armstrong and Brenda Genesis. He took command of the second fleet and directed them on an intercept heading with the twenty butches enroute to Capitol Station. Roger Genesis, the sire of the *Galaxy Protector Llamdion*, understood his cousin's directions, and he thought he knew how to execute them. This was not his primary galaxy of responsibility, but this was Capitol Station, the capital of all of USSTAP. This was his home galaxy, the place of his birth. All the Osguards had the right and the duty to protect it from their archenemy—the Kulusks.

Besides, he knew if Sheryl Tower-Jones' husband was correct, this battle was being played out in all the galaxies in the USSTAP sphere of influence. Thus it had to stop here, where the Kulusks were forging the main brunt of the attack.

"Osguard zero–two fleet, butches heading zero–eight–zero decimal zero–zero–seven at mark zero–five," Terilela reported to the fleet.

"Osguard zero–two fleet, acknowledged," Roger responded. "Osguard zero–two fleet, ascend to mark negative fifteen, slow to thrusters and hold at decimal zero–zero–three," he ordered copying the same tactic he heard Michael's fleet was executing some fifteen marks above him. "Switch to interlink frequency beta brown two," he added to allow free flow of information amongst his fleet not to interrupt Michael's fleet.

"Galaxy cruisers, this is Osguard zero–two," Roger crackled on the interlink frequency. "Fall back to the outer perimeter of Capitol Station. You can't do anymore here. Let us take it from here. One of you circle around and go and check on the *Ainibyl* and the *Bessian* ...lend assistance if possible."

Roger waited for the acknowledgement. When he received it, he studied the tactical screen and saw the *Galaxy Cruiser Mitiah* begin its evasive maneuvers to circle around and check on the two galaxy protectors. The *Ainibyl* stayed with the damaged *Bessian* to ensure no Kulusk battle cruiser came back to finish the job. But the Kulusks had one thing on their mind—the destruction of Capitol Station and the capture of the GGPs on the aft side of Capitol Station. Either way, destroying targets of opportunity was not in their charter. Or worse, their commanders weren't allowed to think outside the order of battle.

Osguards: Homecoming

If the latter were the case, it would make Roger's job somewhat easier—unless, his destruction was included in the Kulusk order of battle. Ten will get you twenty his destruction was in the order of battle, so he thought.

Osguard zero-two fleet halted their movement as Roger directed and slipped into stealth mode ten. The defense officer aboard the *Llamdion* calculated the approximate position of the approaching Kulusk butches by using their last known heading and speed.

"Sire, we plotted the Kulusk position to be directly over us in ninety seconds," the defense officer reported.

"Good, let's do it by the numbers…signal the rest of the fleet to stand ready," Roger commanded.

Ninety seconds later, as the Kulusk armada sailed over them unaware, Roger's fleet de-energized from stealth mode ten and powered up their weapons arsenal. The switch in mode to power application took one point three tenths of a second. Weapons lock took another point five seconds. The fifteen ships left in the Kulusk armada failed to notice the transformation. The underbellies to their hulls were blind spots, which lacked sensor and scanner ability. The single notification of the impending doom was the buzz on the tactical officer's console as the ship registered the lock on from the USSTAP vessels. But by then it was too late.

The pagenay blast, coronet guns and Asher missiles pulverized their targets. Ship debris and human body parts exploded from the Kulusk ships like geysers. The trailing five ships went first, followed by the middle ships then the lead five ships. The pagenay beams seared through the hull like a drill through mud, meeting no resistance as it pierced the top of the ships. The coronet guns sliced enormous cuts along the hull, ripping it open and allowing the inside to succumb to the vastness of a dark frigid grave. The Asher missiles took no mercy as they embedded into the middle deck through the bottom hull and exploded with the force of a sixty-five kiloton nuclear warhead. The resulting spray of destruction from the Asher missiles demolished the ships it hit.

***

"Osguard zero–two fleet has engaged the advancing force," reported Terilela. "Ten butches destroyed…five disabled. They are stopped. The Osguards stopped them," she added with a sigh of relief.

"Don't celebrate yet," Toneilk warned. The enemy isn't through until we have them in custody. Keep an eye out for more," he ordered as he massaged his face with his right hand.

He thought it was too simple. Twenty minutes ago they were staring at the face of death and now they are looking at victory. Something was amiss. But he could not put his finger on it.

Malcolm Dylan Petteway

***

Sentinel Talion Shilego checked his watch for the third time. He had received the coded message a short while ago, but it seemed like a century had passed. He wondered how he had become so entangled in the entire situation. He wanted to run, hide and somehow assuage the responsibility of his actions from his soul. But he knew that was impossible. He was in too deep to stop now.

Shilego stood his post at the front entrance of the medical ward wondering how he'd lost his youthful exuberance. He remembered when he turned nineteen on his home planet of Grujin how he fell in love with the idea of space travel, seeing mysterious places, experiencing different cultures and learning various languages. He saw the USSTAP as the perfect vehicle to accomplish all his wants and wishes.

He remembered telling his parents he wanted to join the USSTAP. They were somewhat disappointed. They wanted him to stay near and help raise his five younger siblings. But Shilego saw that as a prison sentence. It was neither his fault nor his responsibility to take care of his younger siblings. His parents chose to have six children, even though they had no means to support them.

He grew up poor, dreaming of better times, and USSTAP appeared to offer him that opportunity. The USSTAP didn't care about his social status or his education. They cared about his heart and his courage. As for Shilego, he had plenty of both. He demonstrated this well to the USSTAP recruiter in Grujin. In fact the recruiter commented on how impressed he was about Shilego's spirit and attitude on the application visa. At first, Shilego thought this was normal wording for an applicant, but he soon found out different.

During Shilego's examination cycle, five hundred applicants applied. Most were educated professionals with money and influence. Shilego remembered being dejected on that first day as he listened to his competition boast about their accomplishments and credentials. Shilego knew he had neither and felt he was wasting his time, until his interview with Marshall Raelc Latsyrc, the Sire of Grujin USSTAP Precinct Headquarters.

Marshall Latsyrc saw something in Shilego, and was not afraid to tell him that. It was a great experience. Shilego had never been treated so equally or fairly by anyone, not even his own parents. At that moment he knew he wanted to join USSTAP more than ever. Marshall Latsyrc made his wish come true.

Shilego was one of fifteen chosen from that cycle to attend the USSTAP Academy on Chaktun. In three years, Shilego graduated in basic studies and became a fourth level Sixana Warrior. Because of his credentials awarded at the academy, USSTAP selected him for the security corps. At first, Shilego was enthused at his newfound selection. However, he soon became disillusioned with the career choice.

Since his graduation two years ago, he had been with the security corps on Millmum Main Capitol Station. His dream of travel and adventure was stunted by the mundane assignment of babysitting the representatives of the different planets. The one real adventure he had accomplished so far was to kill the Kulusk assassin. However, that was not really an adventure. Kie Ritchen had paid him to do that.

Well, at least Kie Ritchen paid his parents. It was dirty money, but his parents needed it. Shilego's parents contacted him and told him they would lose the farm to the government because of back taxes. They asked for his help, but the debt was too large for Shilego to make a dent in. Then Junitel approached him with an offer.

Look the other way. That was all he had to do. Look the other way. Shilego stomped his foot at the thought. Why did he agree to look the other way? At first, it was simple. He was not doing anything illegal or dishonest, he thought. All he was doing was a favor for a political dignitary. This was the acceptable rule of politics—wasn't it? His little favor paid his parents very handsomely. They kept the farm, and were able to save enough money to send his brothers and sister to professional school. He was doing what his parents always wanted—he was taking care of them.

But things turned ugly. Two months ago Junitel asked for more favors—favors like acquiring USSTAP travel documents, security channel encryptions and USSTAP log books. And of course Shilego refused. But he was in too deep. He thought about turning himself in. But Kie Ritchen had other things in mind.

Two weeks ago, Shilego received a human finger in the mail. It had dried blood on it, but it also had a ring on it. It was the ring he gave his sister before he left for the academy. Shilego contacted home, and found out his sister had been missing for a month. Armed rebels had kidnapped her from her study room at the professional college. The rebels contacted his parents and warned them not to cooperate with authorities or they would never see their daughter alive.

The message with the finger said the same thing, except it had an added message, *'Don't turn on your friends, or you will receive a collection of your family's fingers torn from their dead bodies.'* The message was even signed, *'Maxum Kie Ritchen.'*

Ritchen had trapped Shilego and there was not a thing he could do about it. The venal stench he had ignored earlier now choked his honor into nonexistence. Now he was Kie Ritchen's dog. And doing the master's bidding left a foul taste in his mouth. He had dishonored USSTAP and the Sixana Warrior creed. He had to, or his family would die. The one pleasure in this entire situation Shilego allowed himself to feel was the killing of Junitel.

When Shilego received the coded message to kill Junitel he almost jumped for joy. However, he did not know Junitel would attempt to assassinate Michael. He just knew the message stated, *'He will know when.'* And when that moment came, Shilego took aim and fired without remorse. He thought his servitude to the Maxum was over and he could sleep easy. But that was not to be so. That became obvious when Shilego received his last coded message a few hours ago, *'Kill Osguard One's parents.'*

Chapter 40—Face-To-Face

Several white lights formed on the lawns outside the houses. Musoto watched the light show through his binoculars. Something was happening. Green clad individuals with weapons drawn stepped out of the light. Then the sirens went off like a four alarm blaze. Something was not right and Musoto had to get a closer look. Ten…fifteen…no twenty-five oval lights appeared. Musoto wondered where they came from, but most of all where did the green clad men come from. They were not there prior to the light appearing. Now they were there—looking mean and ready to do battle. The ominous posture of these men with their guns drawn could not be good. Some of them had odd-looking bulky rifles. Again, he could not identify them. In his mind, Musoto had all the probable cause he needed to enter the property. There were armed men invading the homes of innocent citizens.

Musoto hopped from his car and ran toward the front gates. The guard was not in position, but the gate was still bolted shut. Musoto ran up to the gate, grabbed it with both hands and began shaking it like a prisoner in a cell calling for the guard. After several seconds, Musoto came to his senses and realized he could not shake the gate open. He stepped back and looked up. He saw the gate was approximately ten feet in height. Yeah, he could reach the top, and then shimmy over the top and voila—he would be in. He just needed to get a running start so he could grab the top with his hands when he jumped. Musoto stepped backwards three more steps, clapped and rubbed his hands together, as if to warm them for the task he was about to ask them to perform. He counted in his head, "One—two—."

—A cold metal object pressed against the back of his neck stopped his mental count. Musoto recognized the feeling. He had felt metal, like this, pressed up against his neck one other time in his life. That was when he failed to check behind him during a raid of an apartment, searching for a bank robbery suspect in Los Angeles. The suspect got the drop on him.

Musoto remembered he didn't wait for backup. He thought he had the element of surprise. He had followed the suspect from a bank robbery for over four blocks to a small one-room apartment on the second floor of a dilapidated building. He had called in his position on his radio, but he felt he did not need any city police blowing the collar for him. So he crept up the stairs, trying not to make a sound. But the condition of the building did not allow him to be quiet. However, he thought he was silent enough for the neighborhood and for the suspect not to hear him. He later found out he was wrong in his thinking—almost dead wrong.

He found the apartment door and crouched outside for several minutes. Then he heard what he didn't want to hear. The Los Angeles police were responding with full sirens. He knew the sirens would scare the suspect off. He couldn't let that happen. So in a split second, he decided to take the suspect down by himself. He pulled his service pistol and kicked in the door prior to visualizing a clear plan. He stepped in the doorway in a crouched position; gun raised, heart racing and palms sweating. He scanned the room from left to right, just as his instructors taught him at Quantico.

Nothing—he saw nothing. He saw no one. His adrenalin slowed as he surmised the suspect was gone. He must have left through the window. Then he felt it. The cold hard metal of a pistol pressed against his neck. Then a fraction of a second later, he heard the pistol cock. Yeah, he entered the room just like his instructors taught him at Quantico, except for one small important detail. He didn't have a partner checking his six. Those entry techniques, he learned at Quantico, were only foolproof with a partner. He had just made another mistake on his way up the ladder to bureau chief. Well, at the time, he realized this mistake would cost him more than bureau chief—it would cost him his life.

He closed his eyes in anticipation of the inevitable—his death. He heard the shot. It rang in his ears for what appeared to be minutes. Actually, it was a split second. He did a mental scan of his body. He felt no pain, felt no blood dripping. He didn't even fall from the force. *'Am I dead?'* he remembered asking himself. Was this how it felt to be murdered? It was almost peaceful.

As he finished that thought, he heard a thump behind him. He opened his eyes and turned toward the thump. On the floor lay the suspect with a gunshot wound that ripped from the back of his head through the front. At this time Musoto noticed he was covered with the suspect's blood and white brain matter. He turned to the door and eyed a young uniformed police officer holding a smoking service revolver. The young officer was frozen as if time stopped for him. His still eyes and the painful grimace on his face told the story.

Musoto later learned this was the officer's first day on the job and his first shooting in the line of duty. Musoto owed that officer his life, but never got the chance to thank him personally for his act of selflessness. Back then; Musoto was too proud or ashamed to face the officer. Several months later, when Musoto swallowed his pride and wanted to thank the officer it was too late. Officer Timothy Chiles had been gunned down in the line of duty, stopping a bank robbery. The official report said Officer Chiles hesitated when he had the suspect cornered. That hesitation cost him his life. Musoto always wondered if he had waited for backup that day and the suspect was taken alive, would Officer Timothy Chiles be alive today. He wondered if the horrific scene Officer Chiles had to face that day, weighed on his conscience so much, plagued at his guilt so much that it caused him to hesitate that fraction of a moment when he needed to react the most. Musoto blamed his machismo. It had killed Officer Timothy Chiles, just as sure as if he'd pulled the trigger that day Chiles died.

Now his machismo had done it again. However, there was no Officer Timothy Chiles of the Los Angeles Police Department to save him now. Musoto cursed at his ineptness in dealing with the situation. Again, he was waiting for the fatal blow—the blow that would drill a bullet into his head and take his life from this Earth. He resolved he had deserved it for his incompetence. He had failed Officer Chiles in Los Angeles, he had failed the dead businessmen by not bringing Dominic Vega to justice and now he had failed the bureau chief by not completing a simple information gathering assignment. The doom and despair he felt seconds ago when he first felt the gun press up against his head was switching to acceptance—acceptance of his fate.

"Go ahead and shoot." Musoto challenged his assailant.

"Turn around, Agent Musoto," rang Stelana's sweet but stern voice.

She had witnessed the invasion of the Kulusks inside the Gardens as well. She alerted the security forces and General Lo of the event. However, when she finished alerting her companions, Musoto was gone—his car was empty. She did not know if he was part of the invasion force or not. So she had to find him. She pulled out her PARIT and scanned the area. The scan was intermittent because of the several inner-space portals opening and closing inside the Gardens. It caused the PARIT to jump and give erroneous pictures. However, the scan was constant about one individual. The individual was moving up the road, running she dared interpret. The individual was heading toward the main gate. Now why this individual did not take his vehicle, she did not know. But it gave her an opportunity to catch up with him. She drove to the main gate just in time to see Musoto adjust his stance as if he were going to jump the gate. Well, that proved he wasn't in league with the Kulusks. No Kulusk would jump the gate. They would have used a portable gate portal device.

"I said turn around Musoto," she repeated.

Musoto turned around and saw the barrel of Stelana's coronet gun. His eyes widened as his mind raced to place her. Then after several seconds, his face grimaced with recognition.

"You're the receptionist from..."

"That's right Mr. Musoto," she agreed. "I am the receptionist from Unlimited Associations."

"What are you—?"

"Never mind that," she said as she picked up a stick. "Look you fool..."

She threw the stick to the top of the gate. Musoto watched the stick sail to the top of the gate and hit at one of its points. A great flash of white light arced at the stick, it flashed then disappeared.

"You were about to commit suicide," she continued.

Musoto swallowed hard as he turned back to Stelana. In his mind, he saw his body being zapped by the white light and being sent into oblivion.

"What the hell is that?" he asked pointing to the gate.

"Never mind that," she said as she holstered her gun in her delta belt. "You go home, and let me handle this. You are way out of your league."

Musoto went for his gun when he saw he was no longer a prisoner.

"I wouldn't do that if I were you," she warned looking at his hand slipping under his suit jacket. "Not unless you want to end up like that stick."

She pointed her left hand out revealing a remote control device she had hidden in it. She stroked the blue button and a flash of blue light sailed from the pagenay and hit the gate. The gate glowed red hot, liquefied and then disappeared within two seconds.

Musoto pulled his hand out in plain sight to show Stelana, he was no longer going for his gun. In the distance, Musoto heard strange popping noises. He couldn't quite make out what the noises were.

"What's that?" he asked.

"What's what?"

"That noise...what is that noise?"

"Trust me, you don't want to know," she said. She took two steps toward the entrance and then turned to Musoto, "Go home, Mr. Musoto. There is nothing of interest to you here. Consider this top-secret...national security...or something like that. We have it under control."

She turned and sprinted past the gate opening and down the road toward what Musoto assumed was a firefight of some type. However, he did not know the weapons used in this firefight, but he knew he had to be in the thick of it. Maybe it was that machismo factor again, but he could not let a pretty young girl—especially one who saved his life—run into a firefight unescorted. He watched as Stelana flashed down the street in Olympic fashion. He was impressed with her physical strength as he watched her cover almost the entire street in several seconds.

Malcolm Dylan Petteway

Once he was sure she was not aware of him anymore, he barreled his way past the gate and sprinted down the same street as Stelana. His breath was labored as he ran, but the thought of what was happening powered his legs to keep going. He had not run this hard since he quit the football team in college. Even the training at Quantico didn't push him as hard as he was pushing now. As he got closer and closer to the park, the sound of what he thought was weapons fire, rang louder in the air. In fact the air tasted stale and the heat stung his skin as he approached the firefight. He dove behind a car and peered over the hood at the scene.

Inside the park area, several black clad men from the security detail were firing the same kind of weapon Stelana held on him. Every so often he noticed blue, yellow and red streaks of light whooshing through the air. The security force was entangled in the firefight against the green clad men he saw appear out of nowhere. Musoto watched as he withdrew his weapon.

The green clad men must be the attackers, but were they the bad guys? Musoto had no way of telling. Until a few minutes ago, he was acting as if the security force and everyone in the Gardens were the bad guys. If he interfered, how would he know he was playing on the right side? All of a sudden, charging in here like a bull in a china shop seemed to be a bad idea. However, the lady who saved his life, she was part of the security forces. It was a stretch, but she worked at Unlimited Associations. But, what if she was a plant for the attacking force—the green dudes? Oh, his head hurt with the possibilities. Why didn't he call for backup? Didn't he make this mistake before, and didn't it cost lives. Backup, why didn't he call for backup? Backup…backup! Then the thought struck him. His cellphone…he had his cell phone. He rummaged inside his coat pocket, pulled his cell phone and dialed 9-1-1. He started to push the send button when he felt this searing pain of heat attack his body and the lights went out.

Stelana stood over Musoto's motionless body. She had seen him dive behind the car and try to calling on his cell phone for help. She realized she should have known better. Even if he had left, he would have been back with help. When she saw him sneaking around in here, she knew it was her problem to correct.

So she hid behind him and pointed her pagenay at him. When she saw he was using his cell phone, she knew she had to act. She thumbed the blue button for a split second. She thought she wanted to kill Musoto. He could have still been in league with the Kulusks. Even if he wasn't, there was much explaining to do to satisfy his curiosity. Killing him would alleviate any cause for explanation. However, that would be murder, it would go against everything the Osguards stood for, and it would go against the book of Lonson—the book of Jus. She was very passionate about her religion; and the lone thing rivaling her religious passion was USSTAP. Killing Musoto would be a betrayal of both her oaths.

She moved her thumb to the red button and depressed it—slinging a short blast of red light into Musoto's back. As advertised the energy overloaded Musoto's axons and dendrites causing unconsciousness. The blast should keep him in this state for at least an hour, at least she hoped. The look on his face told her Musoto never knew what hit him. She reached down and retrieved the cell phone. She pocketed the cell phone in her jacket.

"Sorry, I had to do that," she whispered. "Life is a bitch sometimes," she added as she rolled him underneath the car. "At least here you will be safe."

***

The sound at the door was faint but still noticeable. Someone was on the other side, but they had not activated the entry code or pushed the buzzer for entry. Debrlina rose from her seat, half asleep. She strolled to the door with her coronet pistol raised halfway up, but still pointing toward the ground. Michelle shifted in her seat as Debrlina passed. Elizabeth had fallen asleep lying across Parker's chest.

Debrlina approached the door and stopped. She listened for the noise once more—she heard nothing. She scanned the door system and read it was still locked from the inside. She shrugged her shoulders, thinking she must have been asleep and imagined the sound. She was secure in the knowledge no one could get in as long as they kept it locked from the inside. Well no one could get in without blasting the door, and if that happened, the person would be met with coronet fire from their long guns and pistols. She shook her head in rebuke for her silliness and then turned back to her seat.

Before she could take a step forward, the door hummed open. She turned to see a USSTAP guard standing in the doorway. The uniform relaxed her fear for an instant before she realized the guard should not have been able to open the door. In a matter of a few split seconds, Debrlina's face went from shock to bewilderment then to fear.

Shilego recognized the fear and reached out to grab Debrlina. She tried to step back and bring her pistol up. But Shilego grabbed the pistol shaft with his right hand and Debrlina's throat with his left hand. With his right hand he twisted the shaft counterclockwise, which broke Debrlina's hold on the gunstock. With his left hand, he squeezed Debrlina's throat, collapsing her windpipe and keeping her from making a sound.

Debrlina grabbed hold of Shilego's left wrist and tried to turn it counterclockwise to break his hold, but he was too strong. She raised her left leg and shot her knee into his groin. The pain shot through Shilego like a hot poker, but he did not relinquish his grasp. However the pain caused Shilego to forget he had Debrlina's coronet gun in his right hand and he hesitated as he waited for it to subside. During this hesitation Debrlina raised both her hands above her head and came down with two pounding blows to the sides of Shilego's neck. Under the thrust of the blow, a slight cracking noise told Debrlina she had damaged his collarbone.

Shilego loosened his grasp a bit. Debrlina sensed this, clubbed her hands and shot a force upward at Shilego's stiff elbow. Again, a slight cracking noise told Debrlina she had done some damage. But the lack of oxygen was making her lose consciousness now. Her vision narrowed and blurred as she fought to breathe. She had used precious oxygen in her attempt to get free. She raised her hands one more time and came down on the sides of his neck.

The bone cracked again and Shilego dropped the coronet pistol out of his right hand. The gun made a slight thud on the rubber like floor, then bounced up once and made another thud. Michelle shifted in her chair; still asleep after the gun came to a rest.

Shilego grabbed his coronet gun from his right holster and raised it to Debrlina's forehead. Debrlina's eyes widened as she recognized the gun through her foggy vision. With her last mantle of strength she swiped at the gun with her hands. Shilego pulled the trigger just as Debrlina hit the shaft with her right hand. The blast passed her left shoulder, grazing her hair and landed in the wall above Parker and Elizabeth. The sound echoed like a cherry bomb in a barrel. The sound was unmistakably a coronet round.

The blast woke Michelle and Elizabeth from their peaceful slumber. Elizabeth screamed as she saw what was happening. Shilego's attention drifted to Elizabeth and Parker as he aimed his coronet pistol over Debrlina's left shoulder. He stared for a few seconds at the couple. Deep down inside he did not want to fire his pistol, but he had to think of his sister. He loosened his grip on Debrlina enough to allow her to fall unconscious at his feet. He held the pistol on Elizabeth as she continued to scream.

Michelle drew her pistol and pointed at Shilego. She was about to fire but her instinct told her not to fire. Shilego stood there with his pistol pointed at the Genesis's, not moving, not budging, but still like a mannequin. Tears streamed from his eyes as he stood there.

"I am sorry," he muttered. "I don't want to do this. They are making me do this. They have my sister."

Elizabeth's screams turned into a whimper at seeing the human side of her attacker. She didn't understand him for he was speaking in Chaktun. But something about his demeanor calmed her. Although she felt the fear of death sting her heart and cover her soul, she was no longer hysterical.

"Who has your sister?" screamed Michelle.

"The Kulusks. They have my sister. And they are going to kill her unless I kill them," he said shaking his pistol at them.

"Put the gun down," Michelle urged. "We can work this out. It isn't too late."

"Yes it is," he yelled. "I am a traitor. I gave the Kulusks everything they asked for. Now they are here, attacking and I am to blame. Good people are going to die today, and I am the blame." He fought to hold back the emotion as he felt the water build in his eyes. "Tell the Osguard I tried. I gave the Kulusks false interlink frequencies and I told them the residents of Osguard Gardens were back on Earth. But somehow they knew they were here and Kie Ritchen told me I had to kill them or I would never see my sister alive again."

"It's not too late," said Michelle, keeping her pistol trained at his chest. "We can correct the mistakes. We can help get your sister back. But if you do this...there is no turning back. It will truly be too late."

"I am sorry," he said again. "Please tell my folks I tried. Tell my sister I am sorry. Tell the Osguard I am sorry. I really wanted to be a Sixana Warrior, but I have betrayed my oath and I have betrayed my Osguard. All I have left is my family. Try to understand...I am doing this for my family."

"No, you don't have to do this," Michelle preached. "We can help. We can get your sister back...I promise."

"No, it's too late," reiterated Shilego as he stiffened his arm to take the shot.

Michelle saw he was going to shoot and she had no choice now. It was him or her in-laws.

"No...No...No..." her voice echoed in the room as she pulled the trigger. The blast ripped into his chest and flung him back through the door and onto his back. His coronet pistol flew into the air, slammed onto the ground behind him, slid two feet, and came to rest at Commodore Tion Leitl's feet.

Commodore Leitl, the commander of the Millmum Security Corps, had rushed to the area with several guards once his scanners registered the first coronet blast. He had just arrived to see the last seconds of the drama. He picked up the gun and walked over to Shilego's body. He knew he was dead. A direct hit by a coronet pistol rarely left anyone alive. But he bent down and checked for a pulse anyway.

He looked up at Michelle who had rushed to revive the unconscious Debrlina.

"He's dead," he pronounced. "How's she?" he asked, nodding his head toward Debrlina.

"I think she will be alright," she said moving toward Elizabeth who had fainted without her noticing. "Mrs. Genesis will be fine also," she said checking her pulse.

"What happened?" Leitl asked.

"Obviously, the Kulusks have his sister and ordered him to kill the First Osguard's family," she synopsized.

"I don't think anybody has his sister," he remarked.

"What? What do you mean?"

"I just got a report about a universal hour ago. It appears his family, including his sister died in a fire. The farm burned to the ground on Grujin two universal days ago. I was going to tell him after all this crap was over. I needed him to be straight during the crisis."

"Well Commodore, he wasn't straight. If you had told him earlier we may have avoided all this," she said as she holstered her gun."

***

She had just walked two paces from the car when her body was rocked from the explosion. The gray light of confusion enveloped her consciousness as her body flew ten feet in the air and slammed to the street pavement face first. Stelana's pagenay flew from her hand when her body hit the ground. The fury of the blast produced heat with such intensity the paint of the car that shielded Musoto and her from the initial blast, bubbled and ran like raindrops. The shockwave turned the car over on its side, exposing the unconscious Musoto to the violent blast. His body rolled and hit the underside of the car. The force pinned him against the undercarriage with such magnitude he broke a rib.

Small burning pieces of Parker and Elizabeth Genesis' house poured onto Stelana like snowflakes in a blizzard. Her mind fought her subconscious for control of her body. Blood trickled from the right side of her forehead where she made contact with the pavement after being blown fifteen feet across the street. She rolled to her side in an effort to get her bearings. In her blurred vision she barely made out the form of a green clad man running out of the house next door to the one that had just exploded. She tightened her abdominal muscles to force the blood back into her brain as she continued to fight for control. She did not want to black out now.

After several seconds, her conscious mind stirred to life and she pulled herself to her knees. She looked up at the house she saw the Kulusk soldier run from. Then her brain connected…Torko bombs. They are bombing the Gardens. She stumbled to her feet, picked up and holstered her pagenay. She turned to the car she had placed Musoto under. Musoto, she thought. She had to get Musoto.

She ran as fast as her hurt body would allow her, to the other side of the toppled over car. She saw Musoto face down on the pavement. He was still breathing, but the heat from the blast had singed his clothing and hair.

"Jus, give me strength," she prayed as she cradled Musoto in her arms.

She picked him up and carried him to the street corner. She set him down, retrieved her PGP and activated the invisible door. She shoved Musoto into the white light and activated her PGP to close the invisible door. Then she tapped her CC.

"Osguard Gardens medical...this is Sentinel Rican." She waited a few seconds for the protocol link to take effect.

"OG medical...go Rican."

"I'm sending you a civilian. He was hurt in the explosion out here. I don't know the extent of his injury, but practice maximum security protocol on him," she ordered.

"Copy...maximum security protocol. We have him now. OG medical out."

"Break...Break...Sentinel Rican to Lieutenant Sparks," she continued.

"Sparks here...go Rican," the voice boomed over her CC subdural receiver.

"Be informed...the Kulusks are using Torko bombs to destroy the houses. I have—"

Just then the house next to the Genesis' exploded carrying extensive heat and a powerful shockwave knocking Stelana off her feet. She rolled to her stomach and covered her head with her arms and hands. She listened as the red embers from the blast hit the pavement. As they dwindled in intensity she rolled and sat up. She witnessed green clad Kulusk soldier moving toward another house.

She popped up on one knee, pulled her pagenay and aimed a red beam of light that sailed above her intended target's head. The Kulusk soldier turned in distress and responded with a coronet rifle blast that exploded on the ground in front of her. She rolled away from the explosion and found cover behind another automobile. She looked over the hood and shot another blast. She again missed her target, but in his maneuver to evade the blast he had tripped on the sidewalk and dropped his coronet rifle. Stelana shot a barrage of blasts driving her assailant away from his dropped weapon. The Kulusk darted between two houses and disappeared.

Stelana crept from behind the car and then jogged the fifty yards up the street, where the Kulusk soldier dropped his weapon. She picked it up and looked in the direction he had run. She saw him moving across the empty field behind the houses. She dropped the rifle, broke into a sprint and ran between the houses to the back. She jumped the six-foot chain fence without breaking her stride. The Kulusk turned and saw Stelana was in pursuit and increased his pace across the field.

Stelana was in a full sprint, arms swaying, feet kicking high and taking deep breaths with every stride like an Olympic runner. The Kulusk, weighted down by his full combat gear was losing ground to the athletic Stelana. Realizing this, the Kulusk withdrew his shockdel sidearm and began firing behind him as he ran. The shots were wild and errant, exploding above, behind and to the sides of her. She did not even maneuver to evade the shots. She continued in a straight line attacking her pursuit with lion-like tenacity.

The Kulusk reached the edge of a ravine to a valley with trees and darted down the hill toward a dam that controlled the water from a nearby creek. He scurried behind a tree halfway down the hill and used it for camouflage. Stelana reached the top of the ravine and held her position as she scanned the area for her prey. The Kulusk fired a melenai blast that exploded two feet in front and below her. The blast flung her up in the air several feet. Stelana tucked and rolled as her body hit and tumbled down the hill. As she tumbled down the hill, her body hit several rocks and tree limbs, and gravity combined with the laws of physics showed her no mercy. She rolled past the Kulusk, who laughed with glee as he saw her tumble the remaining fifteen yards.

Stelana's body came to a stop at the foot of the ravine spread eagle and face down in the creek. The Kulusk rushed to his victim in order to finish the kill. His eyes grew with hunger as he came upon Stelana's motionless body. He walked to her feet with his shockdel sidearm in the ready position. He raised the gun and pointed it at the back of her head.

Stelana felt his presence as she fought once again to stay conscious. She swept her feet in a scissor like motion, catching the Kulusk's leg. She rolled over on her left side and sat up, causing the Kulusk to fall to the ground and drop his weapon. Then she raised her left leg and smacked him across the face with her left foot. She withdrew her mation II.

"Blade!" she screamed.

The mation II spit out a gray crystal like liquid, which instantly melded into a seven-inch long, two-inch wide silver knife. She grasped the mation II with both hands and plunged it deep into the Kulusk's chest. The Kulusk soldier's eyes widened with surprise as the specter of death moved into his corrupt soul.

"Serrated blade!" she commanded

The blade morphed into a serrated blade inside the Kulusk's chest. The edges formed several points protruding backwards. The sound of the muscle and bone cracking inside his chest excited and sickened Stelana at the same time. She wanted to take him alive as a prisoner, but circumstances dictated otherwise. She knew she had to kill or be killed. For a fleeting moment, she thought she could have rendered him unconscious with a pagenay blast, but a blast used this close in combat could also affect her. Her Sixana training kicked in and told her the weapons of choice, in a fight like this, were her own body and a mation II. She used both.

She then twisted and pulled the blade from her victim's chest. Blood, muscle, bone and part of his lung stuck inside the serrated part of the blade. In horror, she watched as the life force of her enemy slipped from his body. His eyes rolled back in his head as he released the last gasp of air his body would ever know, into the day. She savored her first kill as a Sixana warrior. At first it was frightening, but then it was exhilarating, then it turned morbid.

She sat looking in his dead eyes for several moments as her mind retraced what she had done. She had taken another's life. Even though it was in combat, it still was nothing to be proud of.

She rose to her feet and said a silent prayer to Jus for his soul.

"Retract," she ordered.

The mation II blade liquefied and dropped onto the Kulusk's body, along with the bone, blood, muscle and lung particles, which had adhered to the serrated blade.

Stelana returned her weapon to her delta belt and turned toward the top of the ravine. Her body racked with pain told her she was not going to make it back up. She balanced her weight against a nearby tree. She realized the blood on her arms and pelvis was not the Kulusk's but hers. She was hurt and hurt bad.

She pulled her PGP from her belt and activated it for Osguard Gardens' medical. She stepped inside the white light and disappeared leaving a bloody but dead Kulusk by the creek side, across from a cave. The same cave Laurona and Nausona had planned to use to escape Earth—the cave that housed the old, antiquated Kulusk gate portal machine.

Chapter 41—Death or Surrender

Terilela cross-referenced her data that now was coming at an excessively high rate of speed. The information flow was saturating her controllers. But inside her spirit, she knew her controllers were handling the situation as best they could. Right now, her hands were just as full trying to distinguish the important messages from the chaff. If she made the wrong decision and did not process the correct data, it could mean disaster for the USSTAP forces in battle. She had gathered reports of butches attacking USSTAP assets throughout the sixty galaxies. She even received reports of several skirmishes on Earth, including the sanctuary known as Osguard Gardens.

She didn't understand why Osguard Gardens was a target of attack. It held no strategic value. The single valued assets of the Gardens were the occupants, and they were safe on Chaktun. Besides, if the Kulusk plan had worked, Earth would be a nuclear wasteland. In order for the Kulusks to stage any attack on Earth meant the Kulusks had to use long-range gate portals—a practice banned years ago. This was unfathomable. No, that would entail a level of deception even inconceivable for the Kulusks. Yet, they were here and they were there. Hell—they were everywhere. There was no form of evil too vile for the Kulusks—was there?

Terilela snapped out of her trance as the light on her monitor illuminated. It was Major Best of the *Neraka*. She flipped the switch and captured the transmission from Osguard zero–one fleet.

"Admiral Toneilk, Osguard zero–one fleet is requesting status of Osguard zero-two fleet on secure interlink delta red one," she informed.

"Tell Osguard zero–one fleet that Osguard zero–two fleet has stopped the advancement of the attacking Kulusks and are now awaiting further instructions," Toneilk ordered. "Push all combat ships in our area to secure interlink beta–blue–three.

"Tiah."

Terilela forwarded the status report to Osguard zero-one fleet then thumbed her control panel informing her controllers to switch all USSTAP ships in the area to secure interlink beta blue three. When her board flashed green, she knew all ships had reported up on secure interlink beta blue three.

"Complete, all ships on beta blue three, sire," she reported without turning from her monitor.

"Good," Toneilk responded. "Open a channel to all the ships on that interlink."

Toneilk waited for Terilela to comply with his instructions. He heard the familiar tone indicating an open channel. Terilela turned, looked at him and nodded.

"This is Admiral Toneilk from Millmum Main Capitol Station Control. We have scattered reports of conflicts throughout the USSTAP sphere of influence. So far, the butches are being repelled. However, we are sustaining a considerable amount of damage and some casualties." He took a deep breath and paused a second before continuing. "Osguards, butches have stepped into Osguard Gardens on Earth and our security forces are warding them off as we speak."

Michael's heart leaped into his throat at the last statement. He had done the right thing, by moving the occupants from the Gardens. Even though the decision may have cost his father's legs, the other occupants were safe. If he had not done this, something terrible could have been happening to them right now. The thought of an attacking force landing in the middle of the Gardens and butchering his parents, their parents—he slammed his fist on the arm of the chair. His anger exploded inside like a volcano erupting. His eyes narrowed and the vein in his neck projected.

"This ends now," he uttered with force. "This shit ends now," he repeated. Then he turned to Major Best, "Send the acknowledgement."

"Tiah," Major Best replied as he fingered the key for acknowledgement.

"Open a secondary channel to the Kulusk lead ship and play it on interlink for all ships to hear," Michael ordered.

Osguards: Homecoming

"Xer Ritchen," Michael called. "This is Osguard zero–one. Your forces are defeated. Surrender now or be destroyed. This is your one and only warning."

Michael waved his hand at throat level indicating to Major Best to terminate the transmission. Michael wasn't sure if he was bluffing or not. His anger coaxed him to destroy all enemy ships, but his oath to the USSTAP and the other Osguards forbade such a violent act. He knew if he stepped over that imaginary line, he could not return. He searched the faces of his bridge crew. Their demeanor did not alter one bit. In their minds, he guessed, they knew he was bluffing. Most of them had traveled with him before, and knew Michael loved to bluff his way out of danger. Many times it worked, and on those few occasions it didn't work, the enemy wished he were bluffing. Michael didn't really bluff; he just forced his opponents to make a move he would counter, either lightly or severely.

But below him lay several thousand men, whose sole sin was they were born Kulusk. It seemed a pity to condemn them to death for the act of their immoral and insane leader. Yet, they chose to follow him. Therefore, they might have to pay the ultimate price—death. But why should it be at his hands. Michael really didn't know what he would do next. Should he fire weapons at them? Should he fire weapons around them? Michael found his anger easing as he tried to make the final decision. He just hoped they would surrender peacefully.

"Sire, they are charging weapons," Li said.

"All ships, stealth mode ten now," Michael ordered.

Both fleets went to stealth mode ten as the remaining combat ready Kulusk ships charged their weapons. Soon the dark liner of space illuminated with multiple red balls of energy as the melenai pulses pressed toward the Osguardian fleets. The fleets energized their slitanium hulls, darkened their windows and faded into the tapestry of space. The slitanium hulls absorbed the red melenai pulses like sponges and dissipated their energy like static arcs away from the ships. The display was similar to a neon light show. As the pulses hit the ships, a red glow illuminated the entire ship then faded out in pitch-blackness.

"Sire, they are launching their fighters," Li reported.

On the ARIT view screen an electronic display showed several hundred small ships launched from the Kulusk ships' bays. Even the ships rendered useless in the battle several thousand marks behind them launched their fighters. Soon the screen became so littered with the smaller crafts, they masked their mother ships. Li read the count from the left side of his monitor. One hundred—two hundred fifty—nine hundred—two thousand—three thousand, he read. The final count on his monitor reached three thousand and fifty.

"Sire, they are splitting," Li reported. "Two thousand fighters are moving toward Capitol Station, the others are running attacks against us." He paused to monitor the screen. "The lead wave is firing on us. Two—one."

The next second the *Neraka* was rocked by direct pagenay fire. The ship shook and personnel lost their balance—some fell onto the floor, others grabbed hold of something to steady their balance while others just let the laws of gravity work their bodies.

"Fifteen direct hits. Hull breached on decks seven and eight. Starboard engines damaged, life support dropping," yelled the officer from the engineering monitor.

Michael recognized the countermove. Xer knew his new weapon was useless against him when he was in stealth mode, so he upped the ante by using his fighters and their conventional pagenay weapons. Michael had to either come out of stealth mode to deal with the pagenay fire or remain in stealth mode and let the pagenay fire rip him apart. If he came out of stealth mode, those new guns on the Kulusk battle ship would have him for lunch.

"Well warriors, it looks like we have a fight on our hands," Michael sighed. "Open a channel to both fleets."

Michael dispatched his instructions to both fleets. He received acknowledgements from all ships. He smiled and switched to the channel connecting him to Xer.

"Ritchen, this is your last warning. Surrender now or die." Again, Michael gave the signal to end the transmission.

"Second wave of ships attacking," Li pursed.

"Stealth mode seven, divert weapons power to the chromerion field. It's time for us to play a little rope-a-dope," Michael added.

The *Neraka* and fourteen other ships illuminated into stealth mode seven. The second wave of weapons fire struck their targets. The *Neraka* starboard engine failed and her hull cracked open more on deck seven. The crew applied emergency corrective actions without hesitation. The other fourteen ships took on less damage. They received cracks in their hulls and several hits to their pagenay ports. But just as Michael suspected, as soon as the fighters cleared from them, the battleships targeted their shockdel guns on them. The resulting hits from the shockdel guns not only caused hull breaches on the *Neraka* and her sister ships, but parts of each gigantic galaxy protector's skin ripped off exposing her insides to space.

Luckily, the inside chromerion field stopped the leakage of personnel and material into space. But for those fifty or so personnel on those damaged ships, whom the hull protected from the coldness of space a second ago, now were staring into space without anything to protect them but a shaky chromerion field. It now was a horrid experience. They rushed to escape into the bowels of the ship, to place more metal between them and space.

Osguards: Homecoming

However, while the fifteen Osguardian ships took wave after wave of pounding punishment from the fighters and the shockdel guns, the other fifteen ships remained in stealth ten and used their thrusters to maneuver under the remaining Kulusk ships. The maneuver took almost fifteen minutes, but they managed to place themselves undetected.

"Shields down, energy dissipated, we can't go stealth mode anymore. We are full view and without a field sire," reported Li.

"Status on others?" asked Michael.

"Osguard zero–five, zero–seven, one–one, one–three and one–five are reporting the same. Osguard zero–three, zero–nine, one–seven, one–nine, two–one, two–three, and two–five are partially capable. But one more hit by those guns would change that. I've lost link with Osguard two–seven and two–nine." Major Best's face drew pale as a ghost as the words rolled off his lips.

"How about Osguard zero–two fleet?"

"No contact sire."

The words hit Michael like a ton of bricks. No contact…what did that mean? Were they still operational? Or did the Kulusks finish them off. The thought sank into his heart as he plopped into his chair. He looked at his control panel for a split second then engaged the interlink frequency.

"Any time now…we can't take another hit," he pleaded into the interlink frequency.

***

"Centurion Sanchez, they are flying right to you," Terilela informed.

The wave of Kulusk fighters, which had split off from the battle, was now in visual range. They appeared like a swarm of bees making their way to a target. Sanchez swallowed hard as he veered his defender into the path of the onslaught. Two thousand, nine hundred and ninety-nine other defenders followed him in a box formation. He engaged his hypersonic engines and pressed the attack.

The butches lined up in his targeting scope like clay pigeons. Briefly, he was reminded of when he was a small child playing the video game called Space Invaders. The difference was he was not alone, and his fleet outnumbered the attacking fleet. Would that make them the sitting ducks? He analyzed the situation, tapped his interlink radio and delivered new orders.

"Osguard groups twenty-one through forty—split right into a lateral V formation. Osguard groups forty-one through sixty split left into a lateral inverted V formation. Osguard groups one through twenty, you're with me. We are going straight down the middle, inverted T formation. Everyone watch the crossfire…don't want to be downed by friendly fire," he warned. He searched his scanners. The butches were within firing range. "On my mark …split."

He locked on his coronet guns and pagenay pods. "Three—two—one—mark..." he ordered pressing his firing buttons, throwing a wave of silent destruction through space. He hit his intended target, which made the other butches scatter from formation like debris in a tornado. As the USSTAP formation split, covering the flanks, they let loose their lethal barrage of weapons into the fray of Kulusk fighters—adding more to their confusion. Then it happened.

A second wave of Kulusk fighters descended from several marks high on the galactic plane. Somehow the clutter of the first wave masked them. They fired upon Sanchez and the other defenders flying down the middle of the fray.

"Osguard groups one through twenty, evasive maneuver black four. Repeat—groups one through twenty, evasive maneuver black four," ordered Sanchez.

Sanchez put his defender in a steep twenty-degree nosedive and employed his port thruster to maneuver his ship to the right during the descent. He watched his galactic plane elevation meter click down as he passed each mark on the galactic plane. The readout ran through negative one hundred and thirty—negative one hundred and forty—negative one hundred and fifty. He knew if he got below negative five hundred on the galactic plane he would lose the ARIT beacon lock with the station. In fact at this level he knew the lock was intermittent at best. He looked at the meter once more. He was passing negative three hundred. He compensated the controls to move to level flight. Once he regained level flight, the meter read negative four hundred on the galactic plane.

He scanned the space above him. He saw several pagenay blasts from all different directions at his nine o'clock. He did a quick survey around him. He could make out several figures in the distance. He hoped they were the groups he ordered to execute evasive maneuvers. He fingered his ARIT to locate the ships in his section. Amazingly, all ships reported within negative four hundred and fifty and negative two hundred and fifty on the galactic plane. He reestablished ARIT lock with Millmum Capitol Station.

"Osguard groups one through twenty, rejoin on these coordinates," he said into the interlink as he electronically sent the coordinates to each ship.

On the interlink, Sanchez could tell the Kulusks split second victory on him ended when the flanking defenders in groups twenty-one through forty pounced on the Kulusk fighters. He thanked God he had split up his forces, because if he hadn't, that last Kulusk maneuver would have taken a lot of good warriors out.

It took several minutes and much interlink communications to rejoin groups one through twenty—one thousand defenders. Then Sanchez heard

Osguards: Homecoming

it—Michael's plans. They were under attack by more of those pesky fighters as well as by the battle cruisers.

"Osguard groups twenty-one through sixty, you have to deal with those fighters, the Galaxy protectors are in trouble," Sanchez voiced over the interlink. "Millmum Control, vector Osguard Groups one through ten to the high fight and vector Osguard Groups eleven through twenty to the low fight," he requested.

As if by magic, trajectory and coordinates flashed on each fighter's control monitor. Terilela had commanded her controllers to take over navigation for the fighters. The controllers of the galaxy protectors usually did this job, and her people had not had much training in it. But they had to deal with it for now. The defenders engaged their hypersonic engines and rushed through space to meet the enemy.

**

Osguard Thirty-One was not in place yet; it would take another two minutes to get in place for a proper firing solution using thrusters. He heard the plea from Michael and was about to order full combat mode and take his chances. But even if he destroyed the battle cruisers, the fighters still would destroy the other Osguards. Somehow, this plan sounded better in theory than in execution. He could not wait the extra two minutes. Perfection was not a luxury he could afford in this battle. Close enough would have to do.

Osguard Thirty-One, Clay Trent fingered his interlink, "Osguard zero–one beta fleet—full combat mode, fire at will, full spread."

Fifteen galaxy protectors illuminated just off the port bow of the Kulusk lead ship. Xer had hardly noticed their illumination when he saw the incoming array of weapons. Xer's eyes widened as he started to scream. But his scream did not come. An Asher missile tore through the bridge and exploded with the nuclear ferocity of a Thirty-five-kiloton weapon. The resulting fire, damage and debris happened in a split second.

Clay's brother, Osguard Thirty, Mark Trent, heard his brother's plight in the upper battle. He too was in the same predicament. Osguard two fleet had split and he was leading the beta portion, in stealth ten, behind the attacking Kulusk fighters to a more optimum firing range. But he would take too long to reach optimum firing solution. He felt the pressure of the decision ease as his brother had made his. It was easier to do the same thing. He too could not wait the extra time it would take to get optimum firing solution. He too knew as his brother thought; perfection was not a luxury he could afford in this battle. Close enough would have to do.

Mark fingered his interlink, "Osguard zero–two beta fleet—full combat mode, fire at will, full spread."

A mirror image of the upper battle occurred in the lower battlefield just mere seconds apart. Fifteen galaxy protectors illuminated in full combat mode, just below the starboard bow of the lead Kulusk ship, and ripped their weapons into the five remaining butches. The resulting explosions from both battles glowed like a supernova. Multiple hits seared the blackness of outer space and acted as a beacon to the approaching defenders.

The brightness disoriented the Kulusk fighters and they broke off their attack on the undefended Osguard ships. They veered upward at hypersonic speed trying to read their instruments but couldn't. The vastness of the consecutive explosions blinded them. They put on their autopilots, which gave them crash avoidance vectors away from the undefended Osguard ships and each other. However, the multitude of ships in one place at one time trying to avoid each other was too astronomical for the computer to compensate in time. Several collisions occurred within the disintegrating Kulusk formations; resulting in many explosions and fireballs being swallowed by the vacuum of space.

Pockets of the Kulusk fighters tried to regroup in the far edge of the upper and lower battlefields. Confusion and fear dogged their heels as they saw the last of their ships, or at least the debris from their ships, float in space like a junkyard field.

In the upper battle, Centurion of Operations for the *Galaxy Protector Neraka*, Eduardo Jamie Sanchez led his defenders toward the edge of the battlefield. His monitor lit up with coordinates sent by his controller on Millmum Main Station of the butches. They were flying toward them from the explosive arena of the last battle. This way, they could hide from their scanners in the midst of the debris and visual identification would be difficult considering the explosive light show behind them.

Sanchez opened fire with both his coronet guns and his pagenay pods. The other five hundred ships in his detail mimicked his actions, and another laser show could be seen in the darkness. Massive blue lights dotted the area, and at the end of the light trail was an explosion. Sanchez looked upon this as shooting ducks in a barrel. The enemy had corralled their forces in an obscure and dimly lit part of the sector, but failed to cover their six while they tried to regroup. Under the laws of the USSTAP, until someone gave the sign of surrender, Sanchez was still legal to execute the battle. Even though part of him wanted the Kulusks to surrender, he did not give them the opportunity to think it over. Michael gave them a chance and they answered with firepower. One chance was all they got, and Sanchez was there to make sure.

After the first volley, Sanchez swept his defender to the right and raised his nose several degrees and let loose with another volley. The maneuver was simple but effective. He turned to see his wingman follow him in trail and hit the targets two marks beyond the targets he aimed for. Definite kills on both counts. The two defenders rolled right another twenty degrees and swept the Kulusk formation during the turn. Several other defenders began mixing it up with individual Kulusk fighters—in, what would be called on Earth, a dogfight.

Individual Kulusk fighters turned toward Capitol Station as others turned toward the undefended galaxy protectors in what Sanchez guessed were suicide runs. Sanchez chose a pair of butches heading toward the undefended galaxy protectors and raced after them with his wingman, Colonel Tyler Spurl in trail. Sanchez spun to check his six and saw his wingman was still tied to him at his five o'clock. Then he faced forward to target the butches he was chasing. They were gone.

Sanchez checked up, down, left then right. No sign of the two he was chasing. Then he checked his monitor for controller input. There they were. Somehow they had circled underneath him and now were about to engage his six o'clock. He keyed the interlink to warn Colonel Spurl, but as he keyed it a bright flash caught his peripheral vision. He turned toward the flash and saw what was left of his wingman floating in a hodgepodge of debris.

Sanchez executed a one hundred and eighty-degree turn at hypersonic speed. This caused him to lose sight of his assailants. When he regained visual picture again, his assailants were gone. He checked the monitor again, and saw the two were two marks above him and diving. He pushed his engines to go backward but it was too late. A pagenay blast cut through the bow of his ship, exposing critical life support equipment to the vacuum of space. Sanchez felt the air in his cockpit rush out and the coldness of space rush in. Before, he could activate his space suit, a spark ignited his oxygen supply and his cockpit exploded from within.

***

"Centurion Sanchez's and Colonel Spurl's ships have stopped transmitting," Terilela reported. "I believe they have been hit sire," she added.

"How many so far?" Toneilk asked.

"We've lost contact with one hundred and fifty defenders sire. We have established contact with all galaxy cruisers and protectors in the region. They are reporting moderate casualties."

He closed his eyes bracing for the news. "How many?"

"Initial reports indicate we have several hundred injured and two hundred dead sire."

"That's light, but it is still around three-hundred and fifty people who were walking and breathing less than an hour ago, who are no longer with us now," he commented. "How do the earthlings say it? This shit stinks…"

"Yes sire, it does. But the Kulusk losses are in the thousands if not the tens of thousands," she added.

"Yes, we know that," he said. "But do the USSTAP personnel who gave their lives know that? Or did they die wondering what the hell they were out here for? I can't help but wonder why man has to fight to the death for material things? Life is too short."

Toneilk realized this was not the time to be philosophical, but the time to act, because if things weren't done right, he and plenty of others would be joining the dead today.

"Query the butches for their surrender again," he ordered.

Terilela played the surrender request on all known frequencies in their native tongue of Kulusk.

"Kulusk invaders, your leader has been killed and all your battleships are destroyed or heavily damaged. You have nowhere to go. Surrender now or be destroyed."

Several seconds went by before Terilela received any reply.

"Sire, I have a surrender message from one of the damaged ships," Terilela reported. "He is telling all Kulusks to stop hostilities and return to the nearest Kulusk ship. He says once his fighters are aboard he will surrender all the forces to us."

"Do you believe him?"

"He sounds legitimate sire."

"Replay message on secure interlink for the Osguards."

"Tiah."

Terilela replayed the message on the secure interlink as requested. Michael heard the message and replied with a cease-fire command. Within ten minutes, the battle stopped as quickly as it started. USSTAP defenders escorted Kulusk fighters to the nearest Kulusk battle cruiser. The combat ready galaxy protectors then cordoned off an area around the damaged vessels awaiting their final response. Osguard zero–one beta fleet and Osguard zero–two beta fleet, a total of thirty galaxy protectors surrounded the five remaining Kulusk battle cruisers.

Twenty minutes later, the ships gave the signal for their surrender. Boarding parties shuttled to the ships and secured them for USSTAP personnel. The war was over within two hours of the first shot.

Epilogue—Homecoming

"Well Mr. Musoto," Stelana began. "You have been with us for over a week. We told you everything you wanted to know. We showed you our holovidpics, we showed you documentation and you even heard the playback of the little war that just happened. We have been completely honest with you. Now we are about to let you go, and I want you to be honest with us. What are you going to do with all this information?"

Musoto eased off his bed and walked up to Stelana's face. He stood four inches taller than she as he looked down into her eyes. He was so close Stelana could feel his breath on her face. She started to step back, but thought that a sign of weakness. So she lifted her head and stared into his eyes with the same intensity.

"What can I do with the information?" Musoto asked.

Stelana never flinched from her position.

"You can write the truth in your report and expose our entire operation."

"Yeah that will make me a hit at the bureau," he said as he stepped back. He turned to face the wall of his nicely decorated room. "I would be branded as a nut case for sure."

"I don't think so," she said as she walked behind him and put her hand on his shoulder in a demonstration of support. "I believe the president actually sent you. You see—we sent him a note after we stopped the nuclear missiles. He must have gotten curious and sent the FBI to go investigate. I believe he is the one waiting on your report."

"So what if he is?" he said turning to look over his shoulder at her. "The report still has to go through the chain. And I am sure they don't know a damn thing."

"Here is what I suggest," she said spinning him around so they could see each other's faces. "You go back and demand to see the president to give him a confidential verbal report. If he really sent you, they will make it happen. If he didn't well...I don't know what to tell you."

"And if I see the president?"

"Tell him the truth...well at least the partial truth. Tell him that Earth has enjoyed the protection of the USSTAP for over a century. If he wishes to keep that protection he will cease his curiosity, or we will forgo our charter to his planet and allow people like the Kulusks to invade without any remorse."

"You wouldn't?" he asked with surprise.

"Look the Osguard family is on Chaktun now. There is no reason for us to waste resources protecting this barbaric planet anymore—other than sympathy."

Musoto broke away from Stelana's grasp and sat in the chair next to the bed. He crossed his legs and folded his hands on his lap.

"That is blackmail."

Stelana walked up to his seat, "No, that isn't blackmail. That is politics."

"Same difference."

"Maybe, but I believe you are better off telling him this anyway."

Musoto massaged his face as he thought about it.

"I tell you what," he began. "I will do as you request, if you let me in."

"In what?"

"In this. I want to join your organization."

"For what? As what?"

"Security," he shouted. "Shit woman, I almost broke you wide open. If I can do it, some other guy can do it just as easy."

"Dah," she feigned. "We weren't exactly hiding from you. We just figured the president would be smart enough to leave it be."

"Well you figured wrong. Let me work your company security and I will cover the tracks for you."

"I think we can do that by ourselves."

"Yeah, I guess you can. But I can no longer be an FBI agent after knowing this. I need some place to go." His eyes made a puppy dog expression when he looked up at her.

"Look, I am not promising anything, but I will check with my supervisors and see what they think."

Musoto stood up and grabbed her by the shoulders this time.

"I will relay your message no matter the outcome with your supervisors. There is no way I will let this president mess up this operation."

***

Eight hundred light years away, above the atmosphere of Chaktun, two large black figures floated in the dark mist of space. As the sun reflected energy over the upper hull of the ships, the Chaktun letters and numbers illuminated. The lead ship read, *'USSTAP 5501 GALAXY PROTECTOR SHARYLA.'* The second ship read, *'USSTAP 5901 GALAXY PROTECTOR KASHARA.'* Osguard Fifty-Five, Juanita Genesis-Clark commanded the *Sharyla*. Her cousin Sheryl Tower-Jones, Osguard Fifty-Nine, commanded the *Kashara*.

The ships journeyed from Earth, their adoptive mother world, carrying precious cargo to their natural mother world. The trip was solemn and reflective for the Osguards. During the entire trek, Juanita sat in the cargo bay guarding the cargo like a mother bear guarding her cubs.

She stared at the long cylindrical bronze box thinking of her destiny and what her family had endured for her to get here—for her to be an Osguard in the largest fleet...no...the largest organization known to humankind. The beginning of her fate was in that box. She did not understand it, but she accepted it.

She accepted it for all those family members who came before her, who endured Kulusk instigated beatings, lynchings and segregation laws in the United States. She knew the history of the United States was not favorable for the black human. But she also realized most of the hatred her family, as well as other black families, had endured was instigated, if not started by the Kulusks in an effort to eradicate the black human and thus eliminate the Osguard line. However, she also understood white humans of the United States did not need much prodding to husband the hatred.

It was there all along…hatred…prejudice…racism. Whatever the politically correct term for it was, it remained the same—the exploitation and defamation of the black human for the betterment of the white human. The United States, after the Civil War, was fertile ground to raise the ugly specter of racism—a specter that wouldn't ever die…a specter that always changed faces throughout time. One day it could be a white face against a black face, then another day it could be a black face against a white face, then again it could be a black face against a black face, or even a white face against a white face. The ugliness morphed as needed, feeding on the chaos it created and the killing it performed.

The cargo was the beginning of that. Unaware of its reality and of its station in the universe, the cargo had existed from day to day—praying each day for a better life that never came. And for each successive generation thereafter, the prayer remained the same…with the same results—nothing. That is nothing, until sixteen years ago, when Ortho found the Osguards and told them of their destiny, which they claimed after Ortho's death twelve years ago.

Juanita stood over the coffin and rubbed her hand over the top as if she could gain some energy…some insight…some wisdom from the occupant. She closed her eyes and imagined she could see the occupant of the coffin standing in front of her.

She fought her mind to focus on the dream. The haze of unconsciousness formed a picturesque scene in her psyche. She was beautiful…dressed in a long white flowing gown. Her auburn hair was pinned back and her hazel eyes sparkled with life. She appeared to be twenty-five and happy.

The figure she imagined smiled at her and held out her hand. Juanita pushed her hands forward as if she could take the lady's hand in hers. But the lady's hands were just out of reach. The more she strained to touch them, the further they were out of reach. Juanita imagined she was looking into the lady's face. Then she heard it. She heard what made her life as a space nomad worthwhile. She heard the peace her heart had been aching for all these years. Juanita imagined the lady spoke to her in the most beautiful and angelic voice.

"Thank you my daughter," she imagined the voice saying. "You and the rest of my children have made my life meaningful. You have made my suffering bearable. You have made my world complete. I am proud of you."

The image faded away as Juanita fought her mind to keep the image alive. Then Juanita opened her eyes to reality. The cold, dark and stark reality of truth slammed into her consciousness. There was no lady in the cargo bay with her. It was just she and the coffin. Her ancestor, Sharyla did not speak to her. She was dead. She had been dead for over one hundred years. And the one thing left of her meager existence was in that coffin.

***

Michael sat in the first row overlooking the audience. He was wearing his red dress tunic, as were the other fifty-seven Osguards. The courtyard of the old Maxum palace, the Steeple, on Chaktun was large. It was too large for Michael. But the ceremony must continue, no matter how ostentatious Michael believed it was. The good thing about the ceremony was the parents were here. All of the parents and in-laws of Osguard Gardens were in the courtyard.

It had been almost an entire week since the First Universal War, as it was now being called. Michael didn't like that. Even though battles raged throughout the sixty known galaxies, the term 'First' suggested there were more Universal Wars to come. Besides the so-called war lasted two hours, and that was counting every battle in every galaxy. In reality, Michael wanted to de-glorify it, but there were many in the political arena who wanted to keep the flames of the fight alive and well. Michael and the other Osguards gave in to the pressure for the sake of those personnel who gave their lives to protect the USSTAP. Anything less would be a dishonor to their memory.

Despite this, the families spent a quiet and peaceful time on the mother world during this week. They learned about their history. Some of them acted like school children listening to their favorite teacher and drank all the information offered to them.

Michael saw his mother and father sitting in their spot. He smiled at his father as he saw Parker adjust the pads in his ARIT chair. The doctor said he would start therapy next week and would be walking by the end of the month. That was good news, but somehow Michael still felt responsible for his father losing his legs. But he was alive. And Michael didn't know if he would have been able to say that if he had kept the parents on Earth. The attack on Earth was vicious. The Kulusk attackers destroyed several of the houses prior to succumbing to USSTAP security forces. Deep down inside, Michael realized he had made the right decision, but it still pained him to see his father have to struggle to learn how to walk again.

Then he turned his attention to his mother. She stared at him, devoid of emotion. It was obvious to Michael: his mother had experienced more than she bargained for. She complained about being kept in the dark last week, and now the light she so fervently demanded, illuminated the truth, it baked her very spirit into a deep forlorn state of depression. In a few short days, his mother had experienced two assassination attempts, the crippling of her husband and survived a universal war. Sometimes ignorance was bliss and Michael prayed he could give that bliss back to his mother. But Pandora's Box was opened and there was no way to erase the past.

Michael then glanced over to the courtyard wall. He studied the length of names inscribed on the wall. The wall contained the names of all the USSTAP personnel who had died in combat. Today they were about to add one thousand five hundred and sixty-eight more names to the wall, including his friend and second in command, Centurion Eduardo Sanchez. Michael still could not believe he was gone. Again, Michael felt a pang of guilt.

Michael had personally recruited Sanchez almost a decade ago. Sanchez was the Air Force ROTC commander at Rutgers University. Even though Michael was not interested in AFROTC, he saw something in Colonel Sanchez he admired. Later Sanchez told him it was leadership that Michael saw in him. At first Michael thought it was a recruiting pitch, and it probably was, but it did not make the statement less true. Michael learned that after Ortho trained him.

Leadership was intoxicating, like a fine wine or a beautiful woman. It was pleasing to all the human senses. A glimpse of it would awaken your soul. A taste of it would tantalize your thirst. Truly, the more you saw of it, the more you hungered for it. And those who had the ability to produce it were revered as gods in Michael's book. Therefore, Sanchez was always godlike to Michael; thus, he never thought Sanchez would die.

When Toneilk told Michael of Sanchez's death, it hurt like hell. Michael couldn't breathe and couldn't move. The news froze him in time. It seemed like hours before he regained his mental capacity back, but it was really a few seconds. Yet, in that few seconds, Michael ran the gamut of emotions he never thought he had. Now he was about to honor his friend and all the others who fought so gallantly in the First Universal War. A universal war he planned and executed.

This thought almost choked him as he gasped for air. He was ultimately responsible for the deaths of one thousand five hundred and sixty eight USSTAP personnel and a countless number of Kulusks—estimated to be in the hundreds of thousands. Was there another way he could have handled the situation? Should he have ignored the Kulusks? Was his move brash and unwarranted?

Sometimes, Michael thought so. But the Universal Parliament, all the sixty Galactic Congresses and the other Osguards of the Osguard Senate praised Michael for his leadership, courage and strategic thinking in the crisis. Even the nagging voice in the back of his mind was silent. It was even silent throughout the final moments of this harried episode. However, Michael knew the families of one thousand five hundred and sixty-eight personnel must feel otherwise.

All Michael could do was to set them up and make sure they had neither want nor need for any life sustaining resources, including education for the kids, housing, food and travel. The USSTAP pension was very fair for those killed in combat and Michael made sure the families did not run into any bureaucratic nightmares attaining their benefits.

In the far right corner of the courtyard, two gate portal doors opened. Juanita and Sheryl stepped through wearing their dress red tunics, marched to their seats and sat down. Now all sixty Osguards were present. Michael stood and gave the command of attention to the USSTAP personnel. Those in the audience who were able stood. Michael went to the podium and began barking orders.

Two more gate portals opened and six pall bearers each carried the caskets of Kashara and Sharyla through. The procession stopped at two open graves. The officials lowered the caskets onto the platform covering the graves.

"Ladies and gentlemen welcome to our homecoming," Michael began. "We have carried our ancestors back here to the mother world, from Earth, to be buried in the Osguard family plot next to their mothers, Nausona and Laurona. We now commit Sharyla and Kashara to Jus, the father of all and the keeper of eternal life. Welcome home, our ancestors, and may you forever rest in peace."

Osguards: Homecoming

ABOUT THE AUTHOR

Malcolm Dylan Petteway is a military analyst and a twenty-year veteran of the United States Air Force. He flew B-52's as an Electronic Warfare Officer and has 3,000 flight hours and 300 combat hours. In his distinguished career, Malcolm has used his knowledge in the art of war, military weapons and combat defenses in planning over 400 combat sorties. Besides his Meritorious Service Medal with three oak leaf clusters and numerous other awards, Malcolm is the recipient of the U.S. Air Force Air Medal and the U.S. Air Force Air Achievement Medal for his actions during Operation Enduring Freedom. Malcolm Petteway is a graduate of the U.S. Air Force Academy and California State University.

ISBN: 978-0-9843645-0-3

www.ingramcontent.com/pod-product-compliance
Lightning Source LLC
Chambersburg PA
CBHW071256170626
46809CB00001B/245